T0121714

DALLAS

Also by CHRIS ADAMS:

Non-fiction:
INSIDE THE COLD WAR: A Cold Warrior's Reflections—1999
IDEOLOGIES IN CONFLICT: A Cold War Docu-Story—2001
DETERRANCE: An Enduring Strategy—2009

Fiction:
RED EAGLE: A Story of Cold War Espionage—2000
PROFILES IN BETRAYAL: The Enemy Within—2002
THE BETRAYAL MOSAIC: A Cold War Spy Story—2004
OUT OF DARKNESS: The Last Russian Revolution—2006
REQUIEM OF A SPY—2010
TEXAS: A Free Nation Under God—2011

DALLAS

NOVEMBER 22, 1963

Lone Assassin or Pawn

CHRIS ADAMS, WITH MARY WARD

iUniverse, Inc.
Bloomington

Dallas
Lone Assassin or Pawn

iUniverse books may be ordered through booksellers or by contacting:

iUniverse
1663 Liberty Drive
Bloomington, IN 47403
www.iuniverse.com
1-800-Authors (1-800-288-4677)

ISBN: 978-1-4759-8040-0 (sc)
ISBN: 978-1-4759-8042-4 (hc)
ISBN: 978-1-4759-8041-7 (ebk)

Library of Congress Control Number: 2013904683

Printed in the United States of America

iUniverse rev. date: 03/18/2013

CONTENTS

"Forgive your enemies, but never forget their names."

President John F. Kennedy

DALLAS

November 22, 1963

The deadly bullets that sprayed the President's black limousine convertible at 12:30 noon as it moved slowly westward past Dealey Plaza on Elm Street in Dallas, Texas, on that sunny fall day, quickly riveted the airways with the news. The fatal shots plunged the nation into shock.

No matter where you're from, mention 'Dallas' and it conjures up a range of images. For many it's Texas—The Dallas Cowboys, J.R. and Southfork, Nieman Marcus; each with considerable pride. But none of our memories or feelings are as serious, indelible or grim, as the reminiscence of the assassination of President John F. Kennedy on that fateful November day. Each of us who are old enough to remember the tragic event also recall exactly where we were—fifty years ago—at the moment we heard the shocking news.

When we began to discuss this work and reflected on our memories of the tragic event, my co-author offered, "I was in bookkeeping class when it came over the PA system and we were sent home from school immediately. We were all confused and frightened!" Another friend had told me, "I was in my college history class and someone jerked the door open and shouted that President Kennedy had just been shot in Dallas! I will never forget the chill of that moment."

This author's vivid recall of that day was driving back to Ellsworth Air Force base following a tour of duty at a Minuteman ICBM launch control center in the far reaches of South Dakota.

The music on the radio was suddenly interrupted with the news of the assassination. The conversation between my missile deputy crew commander, Bill Cisney, and me promptly froze; we rode on in silence, trying to absorb the shocking news. After a while, I shared my thoughts with Bill which reeled back to thirteen months prior to that day. I was a young B-52 pilot during the Cuban Crisis and President Kennedy had ordered Strategic Air Command bombers to assume an airborne alert posture. The president's decision and directive to fly our nuclear loaded bombers up to the closest edge of the Soviet territories challenged and thwarted their overt military intentions in Cuba. Soviet Supreme Leader, Nikita Khrushchev, backed down in the face of potential U.S. horrific retaliation—to the relief of the world—and was as well in large part, to his own humiliation.

Many of you will also remember that critical phase in history and even more so, the assassination of the President of the United States just a year later. As I reflected on both of these historical events with military friends, there was a natural migration of thought toward a conspiracy theory—revenge by Soviet zealots for their embarrassment suffered at the hands of a bold and determined President Kennedy.

Fifty years later there remain more questions than answers, more conjecture than responses and more assertions than defense. The story herein, albeit a fictional tale, delves into some of the lingering mysteries and intrigue. Within hours of the tragedy and his arrest, it was discovered that the accused assassin, Lee Harvey Oswald, was a former U.S. Marine electronics specialist who had previously defected to the Soviet Union and lived there with apparent immunity for almost three years prior to returning and allegedly committing the treacherous deed. The disclosures plunged the United States and parts of the world into a tumultuous period of suspicion and discovery. A '*conspiracy theory*' began to emerge naturally from various sectors, pointing in as many directions, even though there was no specific evidence to support such unfounded speculation.

In the Soviet Union, traditional paranoia almost always loomed over suspicions of any sort. During the Cold War, the *triumvirate* of power that ruled the Soviet Union included the Communist Party, the KGB and the Red Army. The Party leadership depended upon the KGB for domestic control and repression of Soviet citizens. The KGB also assisted in fanning the flames of communism and fanaticism to vulnerable nations around the world. The Army maintained the military force to keep allies in line and to challenge enemies. Absolute power amongst any one of the three forces was tenuous, and trust was non-existent. Paranoia amongst the three equaled the lack of trust.

The Chairman or Supreme Leader of the Party was permitted to serve as the head of the triumvirate, but only at the pleasure of the other two, as history often proved. The GRU might have been considered the *brain* of the Army General Staff and was created by Lenin after the Revolution as an act of self-preservation from the ravages of the KGB.

The KGB and GRU intelligence and spy agencies had become legendary for their corrupt deeds. Their respective massive and complex network of skilled operatives and capabilities in surveillance, intelligence collection and processing rivaled all other such organizations around the world, including the U.S. Both spy agencies frequently resorted to any and all, including lethal, means to achieve their objectives.

Weeks prior to the assassination, Lee Harvey Oswald——who had returned from the Soviet Union a little over a year before——had received provisional approval for a visa from the Soviet Embassy to travel to Cuba. Immediately following the murder, Soviet and Cuban secret police and intelligence agencies were directed to seal any files relating to Oswald. Mild panic and their traditional paranoia settled on the Soviet leadership. Neither the Chairman, the Politburo, the KGB, GRU or the Army General Staff, possessed full cognizance over their massive and broadly spread spy agency activities.

The central story developed herein is a tale threaded around and through actual historical events. As such, it addresses documented, thought to be factual information and situations, including prominent personalities of the time whose presence and influence also made history. The blend of facts and fiction, or *faction,* is woven around the assassination of an American president during a critical period of the Cold War era.

Within this narrative, you will meet our principal character, Aleksandrovich (*Sasha*) Katsanov, a skilled Soviet GRU operative spy whom you will remember from the preceding works. Sasha had spent several years working undercover with an assumed name in the United States prior to the Kennedy assassination. Numerous *backstory* situations, episodes, previous and new characters are brought forth as the story evolves in order to fill in previous circumstances which have a bearing on the characters and the present chronicle of people and events.

While many of the referenced activities actually happened, this remains a *manufactured* story drawn from comprehensive research coupled with the authors' experience, imagination and creativity. A few historical personalities are portrayed as it is perceived they actually were. The names of numerous others who were in fact involved at the time have been changed to protect their association and innocence. The fictitious characters integrated into the tale are solely of authors' own creation.

In developing this novel, the authors benefited substantially from many sources, including numerous visits to the Soviet Union: Moscow, in particular, as well as the former Soviet cities of Minsk, Kiev and St. Petersburg, as well as Helsinki, where Lee Harvey Oswald stayed while awaiting his Soviet visitor's visa. Other background sources include the Warren Commission Report, various independent documentaries and the open source files of newspapers from around the country. Several extraordinary and comprehensive research and documented efforts include: *"Legend: The Secret World of Lee Harvey Oswald"* by Edward Jay Epstein, *"The Sword And The Shield, The Secret History of the KGB"* by Christopher Andrew with Vasili Mitrokhin along with *"Requiem of a Spy" and "Profiles In Betrayal"* by Chris Adams. Each of the latter works provided elements of the back story and starting point for this narrative.

Lastly, in bringing the reader into the life and times of the former closed and mysterious Soviet Empire, we have inserted a few Cyrillic words and Russian proverbs in phonetic form throughout the text in hopes that this style will make for interesting reading and understanding. English transliterations of these are found in the Glossary. Enjoy.

ACKNOWLEDGEMENTS

I want to first recognize my good friend and *co-conspirator*, Mary Ward, who joined me in this project; bringing her exceptional professional background skills and diligence in meticulous information research, manuscript development and literary guidance. In appreciation for her contributions, it is my pleasure to add her name as supporting author of this work. I also want to especially acknowledge and praise, Paulette Chapman, for her exceptional skill in reviewing and meticulous editing of the manuscript; I take full credit for any errors or omissions detected beyond her work. Of course, it takes the abiding counsel of family, friends and the knowledge and intellect provided by the many colleagues whose paths have been crossed over the years, coupled with the blessings of extraordinary first-hand experiences and travels to create such a story as this venture reveals. Accordingly, we have drawn from all of those resource treasures and wish to thank each and everyone who willingly and graciously participated in this writing adventure, always providing quality suggestions and advice. I want to particularly recognize the many friends and acquaintances developed throughout my travels in the former Soviet Union States. Their real names are not revealed herein, but their personalities and valued contributions are an integral part of the story. I also want to pay special tribute to the professional intelligence, investigation and law enforcement agencies within our government, many whom I have had the privilege of knowing and working with, and who continues to keep our great nation secure. One of the joys of creating a narrative is the opportunity to introduce the names of family and friends into characters roles. Accordingly, I have again done so herein; grandkids and friends will be surprised to discover who and where they are. Last and critically important to any book publication, of course, is its cover design; we want to give very special recognition and appreciation to Craig Holloway for his professional and exceptional artistic skills in creating this cover. Our personal thanks to each and all!

CSA

PROLOGUE

"You needn't be afraid of a barking dog,
but you should avoid a silent one."

A Russian Proverb

The news of the tragedy spread simultaneously around the world.

Washington

Intelligence and police agencies in the United States quickly began to assess any possible shortcomings which might have occurred during the planning of the president's trip and his personal protection. It soon became known that the United States Department of State, the CIA, FBI, and Office of Naval Intelligence (ONI), as well as the Soviet secret police agencies, the KGB, and its counterpart intelligence bureau, the GRU, each had had dealings with, and or some knowledge of Lee Harvey Oswald, prior to the murder of the President.

The principal question and concern within U.S. security and law enforcement organizations was "how" could they have overlooked the simplest ploy for an individual with a weapon to position himself so as to look directly down on the president's motorcade?

Conflict quickly evolved between the CIA, FBI, and the ONI regarding background information on the suspected assassin that might be within their respective files. The series of *"dots"* of relative background information and intelligence were too broadly scattered, filed away and protected to be coherently *connected.* Sparsely released factual information, resulting rumors and zealous news reporting served further to fuel the flames erupting from the tragedy. When it was revealed that Lee Harvey Oswald was the suspected assassin of the President, virtually every agency, U.S., Soviet and others, quickly distanced themselves from any previous association with the accused. This was understandable due to numerous instances of oversight and intelligence lapses, resulting in inevitable embarrassment.

Moscow

The senior officer in the Kremlin Command Center, with nervous apprehension, reached for the hand piece of the red telephone on the console before him and initiated a call.

"Dah, dah . . . What do you want?" came the gruff and gravelly-voiced response.

"Tavah'reeshch Premier, this is General Butakov in the Command Center. Sir, forgive me for disturbing your evening, but the President of the United States . . . er' . . . *Kennedy* has been assassinated!"

"What? What are you saying? How do you know this? Is this some trick? Who are you again?"

"Sir, I am General Butakov, in the Command Center. I am telling you that President Kennedy, of the United States, was assassinated approximately two hours ago . . . in the State of Texas . . . in the city of Dallas, Texas. That is all we know at this time, Sir."

"How do you know this, General? How did you receive the message?" the leader of the Soviet Empire was obviously vexed as he screeched back at the equally perplexed general calling from the Kremlin Command Center.

"Sir, I was notified by the KGB watch officer at Lubiyanka. He was alerted by our embassy in Washington. Sir, it is the truth! The American president is dead! We are now receiving broadcast information from western radio stations throughout Europe. There are few details except that he was assassinated in the city of *Dallas*, in, uh, the state of *Texas*, in the United States. There is no indication on the broadcasts regarding who killed him."

"I will advise you as soon as more information is available. Do you have any instructions for me at this time, Sir?"

Absorbing the enormity of the news, the Soviet leader finally responded. "Dah! Dah! You idiot! Notify the general staff. I wish to meet with them in the Command Center in one hour. Also have the KGB and GRU chiefs report to the meeting. Keep me fully informed of any additional facts as you receive them."

"Yes, Tavah'reeshch Premier, I will notify the senior staff and gather as much information as I can." General Butakov was happy to terminate the conversation and with a visibly shaking hand, placed the telephone hand piece back in its cradle. It was not unusual for Soviet leaders to *kill the messenger* for delivering bad news.

Colonel Alexandr Katsanov was working late in his office at Khodinka Center on Golgol Boulevard, the headquarters of the GRU, when his special phone to the Director General rang. "Yes, General?"

"Sasha, I have just been informed that the American President, uh, . . . *Kennedy*, has been killed, assassinated, in the United States. There are no details other than we now hear that he was shot by an unknown person while riding in a motorcade in the city of Dallas, Texas. I have been summoned to the Kremlin Command Center, to meet with the Chairman. Would you like to accompany me?"

"Comrade General . . . Sir, I am shocked! What could have happened? Yes, General, I would be honored to accompany you. I will await you at the VIP Portal," replied *Sasha*, the nickname Viktor Alexandrovich Katsanov had been called since birth.

General Dimitriy Tushenskiy, Chief of the Intelligence Directorate of the General Staff, more commonly known as the GRU, had been Sasha's mentor since he was first recruited out of Aviation College and into the GRU to become an agent. The young officer was now in his early thirties with the experience of an agent twice that of his age. Intelligent, personable and physically fit, he had been the ideal agent to insert into the United States. He was tall for a Russian, over six feet, with darkish blond hair and fair skin. He had also developed his western social skills and English language with perfection.

While the KGB was by far the most well-known, mysterious and powerful secret police organization in the world, most analysts agreed that the *second* most powerful secret police and intelligence organization was also within the Soviet Union—— the *GRU.* The KGB had many predecessor identifications dating back to the Revolution of 1917. However, through all the cosmetic name changes thereafter, the agency sustained a treacherous reputation of imposing fear and terror wherever its brutal operatives roamed. The GRU was not as well-known throughout the world, but it was equally powerful, secret and subversive.

Under Stalin, the GRU mission was focused more toward the collection and exploitation of foreign technology. Throughout the history of the two secret intelligence agencies, *turf battles* frequently erupted. Consequently, it was not unusual for serious clashes to occur. Even though they frequently worked in mutual support of one another, competition at all levels from the generals to the agents in the field was persistent, often counter productive and even led to occasional bloodshed.

Dimitriy Tushenskiy, Director General of the GRU, was not of the traditional Soviet senior officer mold. Well-educated and exceptionally intelligent, he reflected a more relaxed and considerably polished demeanor than was the norm for his peers. He stood tall and erect; the array of medals on his uniform earned him respect for his record as a hero in the Great Patriotic War. He was a protégé of Marshall Zhukov, the *'Russian Bonaparte.'* A devout and loyal communist and Soviet senior officer, Tushenskiy, much like Zhukov, considered the United States an archenemy of the Soviet Union, but he also believed that somehow a peaceful solution to their differences could be reached. He had witnessed the respected relationship between Zhukov and Eisenhower in the closing days of *The Great Patriotic War,* as the Soviets referred to World War II. And, he like many in the Soviet Army, looked forward to a cordial union with the United States following the victory. Stalin, before his death, of course, saw it much differently.

Following the recruitment of Sasha ten years before, General Tushenskiy had monitored the bright young agent candidate's training and closely followed his progress during one of the most bizarre and unique undercover espionage activities ever undertaken by the Soviet Government.

Sasha Katsanov, the son of a Soviet Air Force general and a schoolteacher mother, had been an excellent candidate for the assignment he would ultimately undertake. He had been meticulously trained, skillfully *Americanized*, and slipped into the United States. His mother had taught him to read and speak English exceptionally well and tutored him in the arts. Having a father who was a Soviet officer enabled him to develop self-confidence, easily blending into the military culture and role.

The handsome young Russian assumed a GRU/KGB *created* American identity and through an ingenious scheme was inducted into the U.S. Air Force where he became an officer and a proficient pilot. After several years of patiently waiting and becoming well established as an Air Force bomber pilot, pursuant to a GRU plan, Sasha hatched an extraordinary scheme to *actually steal a B-52 bomber*! The opportunity presented itself during the Cuban Crises when Strategic Air Command bombers were placed on airborne alert in an attempt to coerce the Soviet Union to withdraw its military activities from Cuba. The pre-planned airborne alert missions took many of the bombers to the very edge of Soviet Territory and an ideal opening to carryout the hijack of the prized bomber. Through his handler, Sasha convinced his leadership in Moscow that it was possible to pull off such a bizarre scheme.

General Tushenskiy had moved to personally convince the Soviet Premier that the plot to *steal* the latest state-of-the-art American bomber by a very special and brilliant young agent was credible and could be accomplished. The scenario developed by the GRU with support of the KGB called for Sasha to drug and disable his bomber crew at an opportune time during one of their missions, and then he would fly the bomber into Soviet territory and land at a pre-planned air base. The general argued that if the scheme worked, it could prove to the leaders in the United States that the Soviet Union was equally superior and possessed the capability and craftiness to undermine the very heart of their prized strategic air war fighting system. The captured bomber would also provide an excellent tool for blackmail.

Tushenskiy was convinced that Sasha had devised an elaborate plan that was plausible and had an exceptionally high probability of success. He had assured the Soviet leader that the young GRU agent was fully capable of pulling off the scheme. The timing of the Soviet attempt to place nuclear missiles and medium bombers in Cuba and the resulting unexpected response by the United States was perfect. When President Kennedy ordered the implementation of airborne bomber alert missions, it provided the perfect opportunity for Sasha to initiate the hijack scheme.

Tushenskiy urged the Soviet leader, "Tavah'reeshch Premier, this would be a great victory for us. We would not only capture a U.S. bomber with the latest technology, but also one loaded with nuclear weapons! We could then accuse the president of the United States with an outrageous provocation and hold the American crew members as hostages. We could also claim that the pilot, our own agent, was not picked up after the crash and was presumed dead."

He had persisted, "Sir, this would not only distract the Americans, but bring to an end the outrageous allegations about our forces in Cuba. It would also clear the way for unlimited moves for our cause in the future. This would be an unparalleled triumph for you and the great Soviet Empire."

"And, Sir," he continued, "even though the world would not know the true story, the success of this venture will restore great confidence in your leadership and greatly embarrass the capitalist Americans."

Finally, he whispered to the Soviet leader, "Sir, if the Americans further persisted in their aims against us, you could shock them into reality by revealing the capture of their prized bomber and demonstrate to them and the world that we are capable of masterminding the greatest of feats!"

Becoming intrigued by the scheme, the Soviet leader approved the extraordinary caper and extolled high praise upon Tushenskiy for such a creative initiative.

He had also issued a stern admonition to Tushenskiy. "Comrade General, *do not* permit this mission to fail! You do understand the consequences of this if it is blundered and the real truth comes out?"

The Premier had kept the plot a tightly held secret except for only a few of his most trusted senior staff and those within the GRU and KGB whose support was required to make it a successful operation. The KGB leadership, dubious of the scheme, remained quietly supportive. They had effectively assisted the GRU in successfully *inserting* the young agent into the United States and had provided protection and support for his activities while he was there.

Tushenskiy and his KGB counterpart, General Kashevarov, were present at the designated Russian airfield on the ill-fated day that Sasha was to single-handedly deliver the bomber into Soviet hands. But as the extraordinary conspiracy unfolded, two jealous and errant KGB agents foiled the event by engaging a rogue Soviet fighter pilot to shoot down the B-52 before Sasha could safely land the bomber. The young agent-spy barely escaped the bomber before it crashed, killing his American crewmembers (The reader may wish to pursue *Requiem of a Spy*, Chris Adams, for the exciting background story).

Khodinka

General Tushenskiy rendezvoused with his young protégé at the VIP Portal of Khodinka Center. *The Centre*, as the GRU headquarters was commonly referred to, was the central operating location of the secret police intelligence agency. Located near the center of Moscow, Khodinka occupied a grossly large real estate complex. The Centre was completely surrounded by tall buildings on two sides with smaller ones on the two opposite ends of the complex. The lower story buildings accommodated takeoff and landings for the airfield located within the confines of the facility. Entry and exit portals were tightly secured and cleverly located within the surrounding buildings. Special access was strictly controlled. No vehicles except the staff cars of the ranking generals and others required for special work were allowed inside.

The General settled into the right rear seat of the sleek black *Zil* sedan and Sasha into the left behind the driver.

"Sasha, this could be a very serious incident for the world," Tushenskiy uttered in a throaty tone, the grim expression on his face reflected his apprehension about the sudden turn of events. "Let's hope that none of our people are involved."

His last statement alarmed Sasha.

"The Chairman has been very unsettled since the miscalculations in Cuba last year," Tushenskiy continued to muse in a barely audible voice glancing over at Sasha. "He has suffered badly from the embarrassment as well as the ridicule from the Politburo, our Eastern European Allies and the Chinese."

He sighed deeply and lowered his voice even more. "Surely the KGB wouldn't attempt such an act to vindicate the Chairman!" He turned his head, looking directly at Sasha. "Comrade, when the leader of a major government is assassinated, it can frequently have grave international repercussions. Let us hope that this one does not, at least where we are concerned!"

Sasha, still astonished by the assassination news, nodded politely to acknowledge the general's remarks as he absorbed the gravity of the assassination. He had spent over eight years in the United States as a Soviet GRU agent, serving undercover as a U.S. Air Force officer. He clearly remembered the election of President Kennedy, the events of the Cuban Crisis and his own near demise just a year earlier.

They rode on, mostly in silence, absorbed in their own private thoughts. Sasha felt an urge to express an opinion, but did not. The night was dark and wet. Few lights illuminated Moscow streets. The heavy limousine emptied the potholes as its huge wheels routed out the melted snow, making soft splashing sounds with each bumping encounter. Gazing out the window, Sasha took note of the all too familiar street scene. Even at this late hour, the sidewalks were crowded with Muscovites seeming to move aimlessly along. The bitter cold of night never deterred their quest for an opportune merchant or street vendor that might offer something they could afford. The better opportunities usually came late when the sellers became more anxious to move their meager stocks.

"What a contrast to the United States!" Sasha thought to himself. "What is it that Americans seem to do so well and with apparent little effort? How is it that they can be so fortunate? We have a much longer history, we have people just as intelligent and hard working and we are strong. What is wrong with our society?"

Sasha had often made these observations, but the answers were never forthcoming. The thoughts only depressed him and forced him to divert his attention to matters he could more easily accommodate.

It had been a little over a year since he had miraculously escaped the doomed B-52 bomber which had been shot down by his own people, and his fellow American crew members perished. Hardly a day passed that his thoughts didn't return to that fateful event and the years leading up to it. He and his crew had taken off in the nuclear bomb-loaded B-52 on October 27, 1962, along with dozens of other strategic bombers from around the U.S. to fly an airborne alert sortie.

The airborne alert missions flying up to the edge of the Soviet Union territories had served the purpose of President Kennedy's strategy to coerce them to back down from emplacing their bombers and nuclear missiles into Cuba. Sasha had spent those years in the United States serving his Kremlin Government and witnessing the American process. And then in the end, his own people destroyed what might have been a great triumph had he successfully delivered the prized B-52 bomber to the Soviet military. The enormity of President Kennedy being assassinated dramatically brought all of the memories sharply back to him once again.

He had often wondered if his mission on that day and the consequence of his bomber being destroyed by KGB deviates was the reason that the Soviet leader quickly agreed the following day on October 28th to remove all tactical nuclear weapons systems from Cuba. *"Did our government believe that my attempt to deliver the aircraft to the Soviet Union and the subsequent disappearance of the bomber and the American crew members might be revealed and the events escalate into an unwanted war? Or, did the Americans believe that the loss of my aircraft and crew was an unfortunate and unexplained operational failure, and the airborne alert missions had been successful in convincing the Soviet leadership that the United States would not tolerate the intervention into Cuba?"*

The Kremlin

His thoughts were interrupted as the limousine moved across the smooth wet surface of the ancient inlaid brick surface of Red Square and pulled through the portal entrance to within the Kremlin walls. The huge fortress first built of wooden construction in 1480 was rebuilt with red brick in 1516. It had served as the castle for Ivan III and Ivan IV. Later czars had moved on to elaborate palaces in St. Petersburg where the severe Russian winters were more kind. After the Revolution, Lenin also set up his headquarters in Saint Petersburg (formerly Petrograd then named Leningrad by Stalin and then history would find it renamed again, St. Petersburg, after the Cold War). The Kremlin became the seat of Soviet power under Stalin, who seemed to enjoy the ambiance and size of the huge complex. The more central geographical location of Moscow, the imposing size, great walls and controlled portal entrances also made for much better security.

The super secure Kremlin Command Center conference room was buzzing with chatter among the senior military and political leaders who had been summoned by the Chairman. A thick haze of acrid cigarette smoke settled over those gathered around the large horseshoe-shaped table. Suddenly the vault door leading from a private tunnel entrance abruptly opened, and in shuffled the rotund Soviet Premier.

The room fell silent.

His gray wool tunic was unbuttoned at the collar around his generous neck and fit loosely over the stolid and pale Soviet leader's shoulders and portly torso. His large head, completely bald, reflected the overhead lights. He made his way around the room, not acknowledging any of his staff as he passed by them, finally slumping down into the oversized chair at his designated place at the head of the table. He looked like anything but the leader of a super power. Taking in a deep breath and exhaling with a slow wheezing sound, he sat for a moment surveying the room, his face pale and expressionless. He moved his stare around the pensive faces before him, looking directly into the eyes of each of his generals and admirals. He did not particularly like or trust his Soviet flag officers. Ever since Marshall Georgi Zhukov, the Russian hero of The Great Patriotic War and the captor of Berlin, publicly denounced him before a meeting of the Politburo, he kept his generals and admirals at arm's length.

He sat for a long moment without further expression, and then he suddenly pounded the table sharply with a fat fist. The silent room echoed with the interruption. The seasoned of those around the table were not surprised by the outburst. Hardly anyone even blinked. They had often witnessed this same behavior and accepted it as an expression of his exertion of position and power over them.

"Are *we,* in any way, responsible for this assassination of the American president?" he shouted. "Do any of you have any information about this? Kashevarov, was the KGB involved? Tushenskiy, the GRU?"

General Igor Kashevarov, a political *survivor* and head of the KGB, hearing his name, fidgeted and nervously replied, "Nyet! Nyet! Tavah'reeshch Premier! We are clean on this tragic event. I am only aware of the brief circumstances from the news we have received from our Washington offices. I assure you, Sir, that none of our KGB agents were involved with this terrible tragedy."

General Tushenskiy looked confidently at the Premier and replied calmly and directly, "Nyet, Sir. We know nothing of the circumstances or those who may be involved."

"Good*!"* The Premier growled angrily, *"*I must never learn that the Soviet Union or any of our people were ever involved in this! Listen to me, Comrades, Never*!"*

He then turned to the Command Center senior controller. "Are you the one who called me, General? What more information do you have?"

Before General Butakov could collect his thoughts to respond, the Premier continued with his question. "What is the status of U.S. forces? Are they doing anything peculiar? Is there any indication that they suspect us?"

"Dah, Sir," Butakov quickly answered. "I notified you of the report of the assassination and, Sir, there have been no unusual activities with the U.S. strategic forces. In the first hour, our picket ships off the American coast detected considerable communications traffic, but there were no unusual responses by their bomber or missile forces. We are continuing to monitor them. But, Sir, we did overhear a radio broadcast announcing that their *Vice President Johnson* has already been sworn in as President of the United States."

"Hah!" The Soviet leader blurted. "The Americans don't waste any time! What do we know about this man, Johnson, Kashevarov?"

"Sir, we will have a complete dossier on him within the hour. But we do know that he is ten years or so older than Kennedy and that he was an apparatchik from the State of Texas."

The Premier looked around the table, his expression relaxing for the first time, revealing a grin and large widely spaced stained teeth. His eyes widened. *"Texas!* Maybe they have an enemy from within! Is that too coincidental, or not? Keep me informed about him. I want each of you to contact your commanders. Place our strategic forces on standby alert. Quietly, though! I do not want any unusual communications. Keep all of our movements silent! Just remain alert and cautious until we evaluate the situation. *No Slip Ups!"*

The plump and stodgy leader of the Soviet Union rose wearily from his chair and shuffled out of the room; his shoulders slumped. Turning back as he exited through the open portal, he growled a final admonition, "Comrades, remember, *'You needn't be afraid of a barking dog, but you should avoid a silent one!'"*

Sasha Katsanov was in awe of the proceedings as he sat along with other staff officers at the back of the Command Center. He had never been inside the Kremlin Headquarters before this evening. The interior of the massive structure reflected as much mystique as did the view of the high red brick walls on the outside that surrounded the ancient fortress. For that matter, he had never been that close to the Soviet leader before. He had only seen him from a great distance once when he presided over a parade from the reviewing stand high atop the Kremlin wall.

As he witnessed the events within the large command center conference room, he reflected on the series of events that brought him here. He had spent two years at Khodinka in intensive training to serve undercover in the United States as an *"illegal"* (secret agent). Most all of that, more often than not, now seemed like a distant dream. But, he could still kindle his thoughts to recall most of the details of the events of his training and the bizarre and provocative mission he was sent to accomplish. The extraordinary years he spent in the United States as an officer in their Air Force . . . a devout spy and *an enemy within* their own domain . . . and how easy it was to become *one of them.* But here he was, back home, an officer in the Soviet Air Force and assigned to special duty with the GRU. He had been promoted to his present rank of colonel at a very early age by his chief, General Tushenskiy. It was a reward for his exploit to attempt to hijack the American bomber, even though he did not fully succeed.

He had never been told, nor did he inquire, about what might have happened to the MiG 21 pilot that was *set up* by the two renegade KGB officers, General Anatoli Borodin and Colonel Dimitri Vetrov, to shoot down his bomber. He was reasonably sure that the errant pilot had met the same fate as Borodin and Vetrov. There was no forgiveness for traitors in the Soviet Union.

He had spent most of the past year since the disaster working at the Khodinka as a division chief in the strategic aviation exploitation directorate. Even though he was a junior colonel, working at least half-dozen levels below the GRU Director, it was not unusual for Tushenskiy to call directly to consult with his trusted young protégé on an issue, or just casually converse with him.

The injuries he had received from the beating by the peasants who set upon him when he parachuted from the doomed bomber into their collective farm had healed over the months. He wished that he had successfully delivered the American bomber. What a great coup that would have been! He also mourned the loss of his fellow crewmembers in the crash. In the bizarre situation, they had actually all become close friends of his . . . *comrades*. But in the end he was essentially responsible for their deaths, having rendered them unconscious during the flight with drugs in their coffee and water.

He was now married to Mackye Evanovich, the brilliant and beautiful widowed wife of Dimitri Vetrov, ironically one of the two plotters of his ill-fated bomber crash. She was, in her own right, a very successful KGB staff officer.

"Sasha!" He was stirred from his thoughts as Tushenskiy approached him following the meeting with the Chairman. "Are you ready? I am finished here."

"Dah! Dah! Sir! Sorry, General, I'm afraid I was caught up in the experience of being here in this magnificent place and witnessing the events." He immediately jumped to his feet and followed Tushenskiy toward the exit of Kremlin Command Center.

Walking briskly to keep pace with the general, Sasha offered, "Thank you for inviting me to come with you, General. I am very grateful for the opportunity to see the Chairman and to witness such an important meeting."

"Sasha, I am pleased to have you accompany me. With your experiences in the United States, it is important that you assist us in the deliberation of this unfortunate incident."

They departed the main building and walked out into the crisp and damp Moscow night to the waiting limousine. "What are your thoughts, Sasha?"

They entered the car and Tushenskiy motioned for his driver to depart.

Sasha, reflecting anguish, responded to the general's question. "Sir, I am very much disturbed with all of it. I was in the United States during the political campaigns for the election of President Kennedy. Most Americans were very impressed with his youth and his vigor, and I suppose that he earned great praise from them for the handling of the Cuban situation last year."

Then he asked, "Sir, do you believe that any of our people could possibly be involved with his murder?"

"I really don't know, Sasha," Tushenskiy replied with a sigh. "Ours is a very complex government and society. I sincerely want to believe that we are not involved, but after your own fateful personal disaster last year, I just don't know. Let us hope not. But I can tell you that the lens of the world and history are focused on this deed, and our government does not need even the slightest implication of involvement."

Sasha offered, "General, thank you again for this experience. Did I tell you that I once visited the White House and the Pentagon while I was in the United States?"

"No, you didn't. Tell me about it," Tushenskiy responded with surprise.

"Well, it was interesting," Sasha began. "When I first arrived in the U.S., my contact in New York escorted me to Washington as a part of my orientation. We joined a tour of visitors at the White House and then the same at the Pentagon. We walked around more or less freely through most of the open areas. We had a U.S. Marine guide at the Pentagon, but only a civilian female escort at the White House. It was a very surreal experience. I was most impressed by the size and magnitude of the Pentagon, and the apparent openness of everything. Everyone was also very friendly and casual. I found over the years that Americans are generally open and casual about most everything. We didn't see too much of the White House. It was a superficial tour, but it was interesting just to have the experience."

Tushenskiy smiled. "Sasha, for a young Soviet officer, you have truly led a very interesting life. By the way, how is your Mackye?"

"She is fine, Sir. Thank you for asking. She is working with western economic studies and research at the Lubiyanka Annex. She is a very serious and intense worker."

Mackye had earned her doctorate degree while Sasha was away conducting his activities in the United States, and she had become an expert in western economics and finance.

Tushenskiy grinned. "Sasha, when she gets the West's economics all figured out, tell her to work on our problems."

Mackye

Sasha arrived home at his apartment very late; Mackye was anxiously waiting. "Where have you been, Sasha? Have you heard the news? The U.S. president is dead! He was assassinated! I have been trying to contact you!"

He kissed her and held her tightly for a moment. "Yes, Mackye. I have heard. I have just come from the Kremlin with General Tushenskiy. I accompanied him to the Command Center to meet with the Chairman. I was in the same room with the Chairman, the Premier himself!"

Her sparkling eyes agape, gave a quiet gasp. "Sasha!"

Sasha continued, "Can you imagine? I heard him question the senior staff. I would not want to get between him and trouble. He is a very tough man!"

Mackye became even more excited. "Oh, Sasha, that is wonderful! Sit! Tell me all about it! Have you had dinner? Would you like to have some food while you tell me?"

It was exceptionally unusual for Mackye to demonstrate such excitement. Her early life and later KGB training was one of managing emotion. When Sasha met Mackye at the beginning of his training with the GRU, she had just graduated from Moscow University and had been selected as an intern to train as a political science instructor at the Khodinka Center. The two immediately found common interests in one another that eventually led to a strong bond of affection. Mackye, reared by her indifferent and widowed father, a career politician, was left mostly to fend for herself. She grew into a very beautiful, intelligent and inquisitive young lady. Her soft and pleasant demeanor belied her inner toughness. Vladimir Yepishev, *"Vlad"*, Sasha's assigned mentor and *handler* during his early training, became concerned with the evolving relationship between Sasha and Mackye and quietly arranged for her transfer away from Khodinka.

A few years later, during a brief return visit from the United States to Moscow for GRU de-briefings and indoctrination, Sasha arrived to find his mother, Tatyana, had been retained by the KGB for suspected anti-government sentiments. His father, although a ranking Soviet officer, was helpless to get her released. Sasha appealed to Mackye, with whom he had maintained an inconsistent and frustrated contact, and was then assigned to the KGB. She jumped at the opportunity to come to Sasha's aid but unwittingly inquired into a high-level and sensitive investigation.

Sasha's mother had been participating for years with the *krushki,* a State-banned underground intellectual circle, and had been turned in to the secret police by a jealous member. Even though she was the wife of a Soviet Air Force officer and a general, she was arrested and detained for questioning. Mackye successfully secured Tatyana's release, but she paid a price for her deed.

The venture resulted in her being blackmailed by a suave and corrupt KGB colonel, Dimitri Vetrov. Mackye was coerced into marrying the much older Vetrov in exchange for an agreement not to report her for an act of unauthorized prying into a KGB investigation. Otherwise, the incident could have easily led to her arrest and likely worse.

Later, Vetrov became aware of Mackye's lingering infatuation with Sasha and, over the years, attempted to foil the young agent's work through various means. His last attempt resulted in his own demise. He had coaxed his superior, General Borodin, an equally despotic KGB officer, to devise a plan to have the highly prized bomber, hijacked by Sasha, to be shot down by a renegade MiG-21 pilot. The whole notion of the scheme was to embarrass the GRU and Tushenskiy, and of interest to Vetrov, get rid of Sasha. Vetrov and Borodin were immediately arrested and executed. Several months later, Sasha and Mackye were married.

"Sasha, tell me all about it," Mackye pressed, instantly intuitive and suspicious. "Is it possible that our government could be involved in this tragic event?"

Sasha took a large swallow of the beer she placed before him and munched slowly on a plate of smoked fish, cheese and bread. He was not surprised by her perceptive outburst.

"I really don't know, Mackye," he replied. "Kashevarov was emphatic that the KGB isn't responsible, and I am reasonably sure that the GRU isn't. But need I remind you of our own experience just a short time ago? In a fit of jealousy, some of them tried to do away with me for their own selfish purposes. We have overzealous and errant agents everywhere. Each of them believes that their often-misguided feats will bring great rewards."

He paused with a sigh, "Mackye, I hope that we are not to blame for this terrible act, but the Chairman himself is noted for taking large risks resulting from bold ideas. The attempted infiltration into Cuba is a good example. Who knows? I do believe that if any of our agencies are somehow responsible, there will be hell to pay. I witnessed the Premier pound his fist on the table and warn the generals that they had better not be involved."

"I, too, hope that we are not involved, Sasha," Mackye lamented. "Our goals cannot be achieved in such a sinister way."

Sasha continued to sip his beer and nibble at the food. "You know, Mackye . . ." He drew a deep breath, "I have some concern that the Spetsnaz could be involved with the assassination. Although they belong to the GRU, I don't think even General Tushenskiy has complete knowledge of their activities. They are independent, scheming and calculated with exceptional skills in carrying out just such work. Mackye, I don't care for many of the KGB's activities, but the Spetsnaz can be even more treacherous."

"Sasha, I don't think you . . ." Mackye stopped short of objecting to his remark.

Sasha had been trained and indoctrinated for the most part of his life, but he had also witnessed and experienced the wrath of the foul deeds that the instruments of his government could inflict on individuals, even their own people. He had also benefited from observing an alternative social and political way of life during his eight years in the United States. Although he was never tempted by a desire to embrace the democratic and capitalistic motivations of Americans, the experience served to temper his devotion to the tenets of communism, especially the implements of Soviet authority.

Mackye was a devout ideologue and often took exception to Sasha's criticism of the Soviet Government, especially the tactics of the KGB. In spite of her own dreaded experience with Vetrov, she felt that the secret police were necessary to keep the Soviet people in check and evil influences out. But she also instinctively knew when to speak out and when she shouldn't. Sasha's exposure to another way of life in the United States and his near death experience at the hands of the KGB persuaded her to accept his feelings. This night was not the time to protest his thoughts or to engage in a philosophical debate.

Mackye smiled, "Sasha, you are exhausted from your day's experience and it's late. We need to go to bed and you get some rest."

He patted her hand and smiled back at her, "You are right, Mackye," he replied. "It has been both an interesting and stressful day. Let me help you put the dishes and food away."

For most of the remaining night he lay awake ruminating about the tumultuous events of the day and the past. The years he spent in the United States had made an indelible impression on him, and the assassination brought back deep-seated memories. Until this tragic event, he had all but let his American experience drift into the past.

"I must call my father tomorrow and get his reactions," he thought as he drifted in and out of restless sleep.

ONE

"There is no evil without good."

A Russian Proverb

November 23, 1963

Sasha first heard the news from Mackye. He had just concluded the phone conversation with his father he had promised himself he would make. General Viktor Katsanov had cut his teeth in the Soviet Army after Lenin's revolution and worked himself up through the ranks to the grade of lieutenant general. He was now retired and caring for his ailing wife. Sasha had missed being close to his parents during his extended period in the United States. He attempted now to be in touch with them as frequently as possible, and especially now he wanted to get his father's thoughts on the assassination of the U.S. president.

Mackye had called him on his secure phone line from her KGB office across the city. "Sasha, have you heard? The American police arrested a man last night shortly after the assassination of the American president. They have accused him of the murder."

"His name is . . ." She paused and tried to phonetically pronounce it . . . "Ozz . . . ah . . . vald . . . or something like that."

Sasha's direct phone to the Director rang. "Mackye, no, I have not heard that news. But thank you for the call, Dear, I must go! It's the general's phone. Later, goodbye."

He grabbed the red hand piece of the ringing telephone. General Tushenskiy's executive officer, Major Sitkov, summoned Sasha to the General's office. He departed immediately. Upon arrival, the aide admitted him in.

1

"Do'briy d'en! Sasha. Come in, sit down."

"Do'briy d'en! General."

"Sasha, the American police have arrested a man whom they believe to be the assassin of their president. His name is *Oswald, Lee Harvey Oswald.* Undoubtedly, he is an American for which we can be thankful. We are still collecting information."

Tushenskiy continued while Sasha listened to the sparse details of the news he had already heard a few moments before from Mackye. "Sasha, do you recall any talk or discussions by any of our people operating in the United States with whom you came in contact relative to such deeds as eliminating American leaders? Ever? We have some very zealous people over there, working for both the GRU and the KGB . . . Any thoughts about that possibility?"

Sasha responded immediately, "No, General, but my contacts with our own people were extremely limited and relatively low-level. There were only two, no, three of our agents that I met while I was transitioning through New York after I first arrived in the U.S. One was Russian and the couple who assisted me, I am sure, were Americans working for us."

Tushenskiy motioned for him to take a chair while he continued, "In Cleveland I only met two of our people; thereafter, only one contact agent met me at each location where I was stationed. The only exception was at the airfield in the state of Georgia where I was sent to pilot school. My contact there was Russian and presumably KGB, as was his wife. In fact, they had a daughter whom I had met here at Khodinka, and she came to the United States to attend college. She is back in Moscow now and works for Intourist at the National Hotel, but I don't know where her parents are. None of these people ever alluded to anything such as you have asked."

"Our organizations are spread far and wide," Tushenskiy responded. "Even in my position, or that of General Kashevarov, we do not know everything about our people. Your own experience can attest to that. We place considerable trust in our senior officials outside our country to make the proper judgments. Well, since you accompanied me last evening, I wanted to bring you up to date on the unraveling situation."

Sasha stood to depart the office and asked, "General, if this is an improper question, please tell me, but are our Spetsnaz agents operating within the United States?"

Tushenskiy mused for a moment. "Sasha, every category of agent of the GRU and the KGB operate all over the world. Yes, we have a small Spetsnaz detachment operating in the U.S., but their mission is not one of *peacetime* assassination. They are attached to the *rezidentura* provided by the Soviet Embassy in Washington and a few other locations. Their work has to do with intelligence collection of information vital to our government, and in the event of a war, to mobilize local support. Of course, should the United States move to engage the Soviet Union in open warfare, the Spetsnaz is prepared to take out key enemy leaders."

Tushenskiy paused. "Now all of that is highly sensitive, but, nevertheless, it is a part of our contingency planning. I believe that presently we have no more than ten Spetsnaz officers and perhaps a hundred men and women under them operating out of our embassy there. As you are aware, our agents bring valuable information back to us regarding U.S. and Western systems and tactics. There are likely several *special tactics* people among those assigned there, but you raise a good question. Perhaps I need an accounting of our activities in the U.S. That's a good thought, Sasha. Thank you!"

The day would once again run long into the night. The general's phone rang again. It was 9:00 p.m. and Sasha answered. "Dah, General?"

"Colonel, this is Major Sitkov. The general wishes you to come to his office immediately."

Sasha half-walked and half-ran once again to the building where the Director General's office was located. It was a crisp and cold evening, and the fresh air felt good on his face. He received these summonses frequently, but he intuitively *knew* that this one had to do with the American president's assassination.

When he entered Tushenskiy's outer office, the office staff was in high gear, answering telephones and looking busy. The aide ushered him into Tushenskiy's private office where a half dozen members of the GRU senior staff were gathered. Sasha recognized most of them. Several turned and looked somewhat surprised at his being there.

Tushenskiy entered his office from a private side door entrance. The concern in his face was obvious. "Sit down, Comrades."

He thumbed through the several papers he had carried in with him and sat down behind his desk. The others each took a seat in the various chairs around the spacious office. Sasha, in keeping with his junior status to the generals in the room, took a chair as far back as he could. He had not been in this arena of so many *heavies* in the general's office before.

Tushenskiy finally spoke, "Comrades, we may have a serious problem on our hands. The individual who has been arrested and now accused of killing the American president lived in the Soviet Union from 1959 until just last year—specifically, from October 1959 until January 1960—for a brief time right here in Moscow! He was also provided an Intourist guide or attendant, whatever, a Rima Shirokova. How many foreigners come into our country and are provided a personal escort? Comrades, this smells!"

The room was quiet except for an occasional stifled gasp or wheeze when one of the officers took a deep breath into his nicotine-filled lungs. In the typical manner of age-old Russian culture, Sasha could feel paranoia was setting in with those in the room. He could see the fidgeting of several of the officers as if they were about to burst out with an unsolicited denial, or *confession*, of any knowledge of this individual.

He continued, "I am informed that after the American was in Moscow for a week, he was told by Intourist that his visa was up and that he must leave. There is some mystery following this event. As the story unfolds, he apparently tried to commit suicide by cutting his wrist. The wound was superficial, but nevertheless, he was admitted to Botkinskaya Hospital for another week, the 21st to 28th of October 1959. During this time, he also renounced his U.S. citizenship to his Intourist attendant and asked that she seek asylum in Russia for him. Following his release from the hospital and after a further review of this very odd case, he remained in Moscow at the Metropole Hotel until he was sent to Minsk . . . Why Minsk we must wonder? Why not send him back to the United States? His visa had expired."

He looked around the room observing the impact of his revelations. "Do we presume the KGB arranged this? No one professes to know why to Minsk. Perhaps just to get him out of Moscow temporarily? Why? Who paid for his hotel and living expenses while he was here in Moscow? How about his hospital expenses? Did this so-called *derelict*, as our KGB friends are referring to him, have the means to live in two different Moscow hotels for almost three months? Is anyone curious that our KGB friends manage the foreign clientele at both the Berlin and the Metropole where he stayed? Who directed him to go to Minsk? Intourist? The KGB? Strange, no one seems to have the answers to these questions."

Tushenskiy, although angry, appeared to also be having some delight in teasing his generals, particularly his intelligence chief, with the abundance of information he had collected.

"This *mystery man* finally departed Moscow for Minsk on January 7, 1960," Tushenskiy continued. "But, Comrades, before he left Moscow by train, he was given 5,000 Rubles by Intourist to pay for his Metropole Hotel stay and train fare. While in Minsk, he was apparently very *busy*; he quickly met and married a Byelorussian girl, a Marina Prusakova, joined a hunting club and bought a shotgun. Now hear this, Comrades. He was an *eenastrah'nets!*" He repeated, "A foreigner!"

Tushenskiy then raised his voice for the first time. *"An American living in the Soviet Union marries a Soviet citizen . . .* and *just goes out and buys a gun!"*

He chuckled as if to find some cynical folly in the absurdity of what he was revealing. His mood stiffened quickly; he looked sternly around the room at his staff officers and continued. "This man was also provided a job as a machinist at the Belarus Radio and Television Factory. Let me quickly state that our friends in the KGB over at Lubiyanka are sweating blood right now over all of this, and," he added, "perhaps we should be also. How is it that a foreigner, an American and a former U.S. military man, a Marine, can apparently freely roam around our country for almost three years, marry one of our citizens, buy a gun and no one appears to be the wiser? This is just too bizarre!"

The room remained still. None of those present responded to the General's remarks. Only occasional heavy breathing and some wheezing could be detected.

Tushenskiy, in a low voice, not overly forceful, homed in on General Gurenko. "Mikhail, were any of your operatives aware of this man while he was in this country? Do you have any knowledge of this treacherous event in the United States? Are your operatives in the U.S. under control?"

Major General Mikhail Gurenko headed the GRU Third Department, *Spetsnaz*. Sasha had observed months earlier that Gurenko was a smoothly polished officer, apparently well-educated and did not reflect the appearance of a member associated with the dreaded reputation of the Spetsnaz.

The special force was the true elite of all the Soviet armed forces and very similar in nature to the *Nazi SS* during World War II. Its members were carefully recruited for their intelligence and athletic skills. They numbered in the tens of thousands and were dispatched in small units all over the world. The members were trained specialists in sabotage, espionage and assassination. Within the Soviet Union they were organized into traditional companies, brigades and divisions, but were also selectively placed within regular airborne, infantry, communications and armored units.

"The Spetsnaz members in these units are *sleeping agents*." Sasha had been briefed. "They are made to look like any other soldier by wearing the same uniforms of the unit to which they are assigned. In these special assignments they are ever ready to spring into action when hostilities break out and take the lead over the regular troops," he was told.

He had also learned that in foreign countries, such as the United States, they were usually assigned to work out of the Soviet Embassy and made to look the part of a bureaucrat or administrative staff. When called upon, their mission was to disrupt state governments, take out leaders and cause general chaos within the public sector.

General Gurenko had been the head of Spetsnaz for several years and held the full confidence of Tushenskiy. He was not a former Spetsnaz member himself. Tushenskiy, as did his predecessors, held a basic distrust for the career Spetsnaz soldier or officer.

Gurenko responded, "*Tavah'reeshch* General, I have no personal knowledge of this American or his alleged deeds, but I assure you that I will promptly conduct an investigation within my units. Sir, let me assure you that neither I, nor any of my officers would conduct nor tolerate such an act as this assassination without direct orders. And further, Sir, we would never recruit a foreigner into our ranks. That is a very dubious KGB tactic which we do not employ."

Sasha knew better than Gurenko's last statement. He had been accurately told that the Spetsnaz used any and every tactic, including the exploitation of foreigners to carry out their deeds.

Gurenko paused and continued, "Sir, if I might add, I would thoroughly question such directions if they were given to me. This tragic event is not in the best interests of our government or our future goals." Gurenko was also a shrewd *apparatchik*.

Tushenskiy appeared satisfied with the Spetsnaz chief's response. "Thank you, Comrade Mikhail, and please, I am not singling you out. Now, let me hear from the others of you. Do any of you have any knowledge of this man, Oswald, the fact that he spent almost three years in the Soviet Union? A former American Marine! Are we losing our edge?"

Unlike the Soviet Premier the evening before, Tushenskiy did not shout, pound his desk or berate the officers before him. His demeanor remained calm and pleasant, although seriously focused.

"He would have made a good American general," Sasha mused.

Each of the other GRU directorate heads and staff members responded, "Nyet, Nyet," to Tushenskiy's questions.

Sasha wondered how they were each *pondering* this international incident. Are they sincerely remorseful and sympathetic about the death of the American president? Are they concerned about the potential impact on the world at large and the Soviet Union in particular? Or, are they, most likely, really worried about their own skins right now?

Tushenskiy listened to each of his staff deny any knowledge of the assassination or the perpetrator, and continued. "Permit me to enlighten you even more, Comrades, about this *mystery man* who apparently roamed around our country for almost three years. He had arrived in Helsinki from London on 10 October 1959, likely by boat. We don't know yet how he got to London, perhaps by air or boat. He applied for a Soviet Tourist Visa on 12 October and was issued the visa on 14 October. The number of the visa was *40339* for those of you into details."

"But comrades," he emphasized, "the normal processing time for foreign visitor visas is one to two weeks. He received it in *two* days! I have a question for you, Comrades. Who expedited this foreigner's visa? And, why?"

Tushenskiy continued, taking delight in the fact that he had far more information than his senior staff officers. "The visa this man received was for a six-day visit. He departed Helsinki for Leningrad by train on 15 October and on to Moscow, arriving on the morning of the 16th. Our friends at Lubiyanka are still trying to figure out *who* besides Intourist was assigned to monitor him during his stay in Moscow. They do know that he stayed at the Hotel Berlin before he apparently cut his wrist to prolong his stay. He was then lodged at the Metropole after he was released from the hospital."

He pressed the issues. "The questions are numerous, Comrades. Why did he come to Russia? Who did he contact while in Moscow besides the Intourist people? Did anyone monitor his activities while he was staying in the Berlin, the Metropole? Why was he so coddled and looked after like a dignitary? Or, was this man under the control and management of the KGB all the time?"

None of the GRU senior staff officers spoke, quietly shaking their heads in response.

Tushenskiy made eye contact with Sasha. "Colonel Katsanov, you have had the opportunity to visit the United States in recent years. What is your assessment of this tragedy?"

The generals seated around the room, anxious to find a diversion from their own questioning, quickly turned their heads toward Sasha. Few were ever aware of Sasha's long-term escapade in the United States. Those who were briefed on his operation were also held to absolute secrecy.

Sasha, surprised at being called upon, quickly stood to respond.

Tushenskiy smiled. "Please be seated, Sasha. Give us your thoughts on what we are discussing here."

"Sir, I am afraid that I can offer little to that which has been discussed. I believe that the loss of the American president is indeed a tragedy. He was a recognized world leader, and it appeared to me that even after our disagreement over Cuba last year he has not held our government in contempt. Relations seemed to be improving. With regard to the accused assassin living in our country for such an extended period and with such apparent free reign, it should concern all of us! If the facts as you have revealed to us are accurate, there is much room for the United States to once again look upon us with great suspicion."

A bit nervous at finding himself the center of attention in the room with so much military seniority, he continued. "Through my studies and *brief* experience in the United States, I have learned that the Americans are a very benevolent society. They are not prone to over react to crises, but rather evaluate the circumstances rationally. So, I would not expect their politicians to initially jump to hostile accusations regarding this man's alleged relationship with our country. Sir, that is about all I can add to this very serious situation."

"Thank you, Sasha. I believe that we can all agree with your thoughtful comments. Comrades, I apologize for keeping you all so late this evening. I ask that each of you carefully monitor your own sources of information, and please advise me of anything you believe to be important. Dobre'niche."

As his staff members moved to depart the general's office, Tushenskiy motioned for Sasha to stay behind and closed the door. "Sasha, I have been giving these new developments considerable thought. What would you think about returning to the United States for a brief visit to assist me in analyzing this whole affair?"

Sasha's eyes widened as he looked at Tushenskiy. "Sir, I will do whatever you ask, but I am not sure what service I can perform over there. What would you have me do?"

"I am not entirely sure myself, Sasha. I have such suspicion of our KGB comrades that I have difficulty trusting any of them. And . . ." with a pause, he added, "frankly, that includes

Kashevarov. You may keep that latter remark to yourself. There are so many renegades among his operatives that I doubt he really knows what's going on out there. This assassination worries me. If the same thing happened to our state leader, and we discovered that one of our soldiers or citizens had spent considerable time in the United States just prior to such a crime, I am afraid that we would suspect the very worst. Our politicians and military would likely react irrationally. I do appreciate your assessment that it is unlikely the U.S. will do anything untoward, at least until all of the facts are in and they have thought it out. In the end, we need to remember, *'There is no evil without good.'*"

He paused for moment . . . "I apologize for the philosophical rhetoric. This isn't the time for that. Now back to your question. The most important part of your assignment will be to confirm or discount what we *believe* we already know. You can do that by making inquiries back along the pathway the American traveled . . . Minsk, Helsinki and even back in the United States. Don't bother with what might have occurred here in Moscow. I have other means of filtering that out."

"Yes, General, I understand and I wish to also thank you for the opportunity to attend this important meeting. I am grateful for the many opportunities you provide me, and I will do whatever you ask of me. If I can be of value by traveling on to the United States and reviewing the situation from there, I will be pleased to do so."

"Good. I will notify Intelligence. General Drachev will initiate the preparations. I will direct him to move with haste. How is your English these days? Do you practice much?"

Tushenskiy smiled and continued, "Sasha, I believe perhaps the best place in the United States to begin is with our embassy in Washington. I will advise General Kashevarov that you are going. He will provide you complete immunity from his KGB people there and wherever your travels take you. He should understand that perhaps we can assist in vindicating his people and our government. With the situation unfolding as it is, I think he will cooperate without any difficulty."

Tushenskiy further advised, "When you visit the embassies, advise the senior KGB agent of your presence and business, and show them a letter of introduction which I will provide you. You should then conduct yourself with the staff personnel as if you are an agent who is being newly assigned to the United States. You can be vague about your assignment and your eventual location. The *hounds* may quiz the hell out of you, but you can evade them. See if you can detect anything relative to the U.S. President's assassination wherever any information may lead you. The letter I will provide you will describe the purpose of your assignment and assist in gaining access and support of our government's activities."

He continued, "I will, of course, gain personal approval from the Chairman on all of this. I believe that he will support most any initiative to clear our government in this incident. You will also likely want to go to Texas and make contact with our GRU agents and the KGB who were present before or after the shooting. Bleed them of any information they may have."

Tushenskiy, thinking ahead as he spoke, continued to lay out his plan. "Lastly, I think you may wish to go to Mexico City. I have information that I did not want to reveal to the staff because all of it has not been validated, but it appears that this man, Oswald, visited our embassy in Mexico City perhaps as recently as one month ago. I would like to know what he was doing there and what was the KGB's interest in him?"

Sasha was surprised by this new revelation, but he didn't comment.

"Now, Sasha, I am not interested in face-to-face combat with the KGB. Kashevarov and I get along reasonably well," he smiled. "We have no choice, but as you know from your own near-fatal experience, they have a few agents who are zealous, misguided, out of control and can be very dangerous." Pausing, he asked, "How do you feel about this? Does it concern you to return to the United States? Do you believe that there is a possibility that you might be recognized?"

"General, I will do anything for our government that you wish, and, no, Sir, I have no difficulty with returning to the U.S. I should not be going anywhere that I might be recognized, but I will be cautious. I can be ready to depart as soon as the preparations are made."

And then he asked, "Sir, do you believe it possible that this assassination could be in retribution for the Premier's failure in Cuba last year? Our government was greatly embarrassed and we lost considerable credibility when the Americans literally backed us down. Would we go that far to inflict punishment, particularly at the heart of the United States?"

"Sasha, I am as concerned as you are. It is difficult for me to believe that any of our people would do such a thing . . . certainly not at the Chairman's level, but we have renegades at all levels with heady ideas and faulty logic on how our cause can be advanced. Our government was greatly embarrassed by the Chairman's ill-advised attempt to intrude aircraft and missiles into an ally's country, especially one so close to the United States. And then, just as abruptly, he capitulated to the American's retaliation; real or implied, nevertheless, he surrendered embarrassingly so. There are many zealots within our government who would do anything to get even, so to speak, even if they couldn't take credit or brag about it."

He sighed and continued, "Then there are our Chinese allies who undoubtedly found great joy in witnessing the Chairman's embarrassment. I am sure there are many among them that are suspicious of what role we may have played in the assassination of the U.S. president. Well, enough of my rhetoric, Sasha, you may wish to keep all of this in mind as you proceed with our plan."

"Thank you Sir, I will do my best to gather what I can."

"Good! Go home and get some rest. By morning, we will have a plan for you."

Tushenskiy shook hands with his young officer. "Thank you, Sasha."

TWO

"Any sandpiper is great in his own swamp."

A Russian Proverb

Washington

The Attorney General of the United States was in deep shock and remorse over the loss of his brother, the President, but he wasted no time in mobilizing the law enforcement and investigative agencies to determine if the assassination was conspired by other than the accused Lee Harvey Oswald.

To a gathered inner circle, he asserted, "I want nothing left to question in determining who or what factions were responsible for this crime."

He directed his attention to the law enforcement and intelligence agency chiefs in the meeting along with the Chairman of the Joint Chiefs of Staff, who had been invited to attend. "If a foreign government or power, organized or renegade, has had a part in this, I want you to go to the very roots of it! And, heaven forbid, if this cruel act was the result of a domestic conspiracy, we will deal with it by every means possible!"

The directors of the Secret Service, Federal Bureau of Investigation, Central Intelligence Agency and National Security Agency all set out to research their files. They proceeded to re-open all old leads to earlier potential threats against the President and dug deeply into the past of the man under arrest in Dallas.

Moscow

Concurrent with the meeting called by General Tushenskiy at Khodinka, General Kashevarov had gathered his senior staff in the KGB Headquarters at Lubiyanka. The dull gray stone complex of buildings became infamous over the years after Stalin relocated the Soviet Government headquarters from St. Petersburg to Moscow. The legendary facility with a huge statue at the entrance of the founding father of the Tcheka secret police and architect of Soviet labor camps and gulags, Filiks Dzerzhinsky, was located a kilometer from the Kremlin. The complex not only served as the headquarters for the dreaded secret police agency, but also was known for its dungeon-like prison cells and torture chambers. The mere whisper of *KGB* and *Lubiyanka* sent chills down the backs of Muscovites and conjured up visions of mystery and intrigue throughout the outside world.

The meeting here was a much different scene. Igor Kashevarov reflected one's vision of the typical mold of a tough Soviet general, short and squat with a full ruddy, grayish complexion. His thick salt and pepper hair, cropped short, sprouted from his head in all directions. A chain smoker, he fidgeted with a worn cigarette lighter he had proudly taken from a German prisoner during the war. He held it in the palm of his hand rubbing it constantly with his thumb as if he expected a magic genie to spring out. His manner was coarse and threatening, his language vile.

Kashevarov had accepted the dubious honor of heading the KGB even in view of the fact that he succeeded a long line of ill-fated KGB predecessors dating back to Lavrenti Beria and before him A. I. Rikov. At least seven of the fifteen previous secret police chiefs had been executed while serving in the position. Of the remainder, only three had actually survived to retire.

"Comrades, we are in a very difficult and potentially embarrassing situation! I want to get to the bottom of this immediately! I assured the Chairman last night that the KGB was clean on this Kennedy incident—that we had absolutely nothing to do with it. Now, I learn that the accused assassin is an American who roamed around Moscow and Minsk for almost three years!

Why? How? Which of you were aware of this? Has it become so common for Americans to *visit* our country that we accept them as if they were ordinary tourists?"

Kashevarov paused for a moment while his remarks settled on his staff officers . . . "Umnov! You are responsible for foreign visitor control! What do you know about this man, *Ozvald*?"

Major General Ivan Umnov headed Internal Security, which, amongst his other responsibilities, monitored and approved all visa applications, tracked foreign visitors and managed Intourist. The Intourist organization was a useful organ of the KGB who trained and made full use of all of their agents. Intourist intercepted all visitors to the Soviet Union and provided escorts during their stay.

"Comrade General, I must confess to a slight problem with monitoring the activities of the American, *Ozvald*. As you have already informed us, the American did acquire a visa in Helsinki under rather unusual circumstances. I am still attempting to determine how he obtained the visa in just two days instead of the usual seven to ten days we require in order to complete a background check."

"Slight problem!" Kashevarov shouted. "Slight problem, you say! The *'slight problem'* may be *YOU*, Comrade!"

Umnov continued, trying to find cover. He had endured this kind of wrath before and often, but not as a result of such an apparent gross lapse of efficiency. "With regard to monitoring his visit, Sir, we did intercept this man upon arrival in Moscow on 16 October 1959. An Intourist guide, Rima Shirokova, met him when he departed the train from Helsinki. She escorted him to the Hotel Berlin. The American told Shirokova that he was going to renounce his U.S. citizenship and apply for political asylum and Soviet citizenship."

"Intercepted Osvald in Moscow?" Kashevarov stood and walked around behind Umnov, fondling his lighter. The frightened Umnov may well have expected the KGB chief to put a pistol to the back of his head. "You idiot, you say you found him in Moscow? What about Helsinki? Let's not so quickly overlook how he got here in the first place! He brushed through your people in Helsinki as if he were an honored guest! Who do you have in charge there?

I want his name and his rotten carcass in my office as soon as you can drag him here!"

Umnov took a deep breath, not daring to turn and face his leader who continued to stand directly behind him and proceeded to relay the information he had hastily collected. "According to Shirokova, his application for asylum was refused several days later and he was told to leave Moscow on 21 October. The next thing we learn is that he apparently attempted to commit suicide by cutting himself on the wrist. He severed a vein and spent a week in Botkinskaya Hospital recuperating from his self-inflicted wound. Following that incident, he was granted a temporary residence permitting him to remain in our country, but was directed to move to Minsk. I have learned, however, that the man stayed on here in Moscow at the Metropole Hotel until early January before moving on to Minsk. I am unable to determine how he spent his time in Moscow before going to Minsk."

Kashevarov interrupted Umnov. "Very interesting, Comrade, but, *why*? Why did your office approve a temporary resident permit for him? Who authorized this? Who sent him to Minsk? Did you have in mind to recruit him? Did you use him as an agent or were you intending to use him as an agent? Why was I not informed of this affair?"

Umnov tried to interrupt, but Kashevarov who had returned to the head of the conference table, raised his hand to silence him. "Nyet! Permit me to continue, Ivan! Now, how is it that this American, living in Minsk, can go out and purchase a weapon, a shotgun? It amazes me that within a day of discovering that we had this lunatic freely roaming around our country for three years, apparently without the knowledge of anyone here, we now have all of this information. It is amazing to me that we immediately discover all of this information about him now that he has departed our country, returned to the United States and killed their president! Did it not concern you when he was here in Moscow and for the three years he lived casually in Minsk? And, NOW! NOW, you seem to know everything!"

Umnov turned pale at the barrage of questions and stammered as he tried to respond to the KGB chief. "Comrade General, I do not have the answers to those questions yet, but I assure you that I will get them! I am as concerned as you about this entire event."

Kashevarov continued to hold Umnov in his glare for an agonizing period, and then slowly moved his gaze around to each of the others at the conference table. "*Any sandpiper is great in his own swamp*, Comrades!" he uttered with a dry raspy gurgle.

"Now! I am ordering each of you, not only Umnov," continuing his tirade, "but each of *you*! Do you realize where our agency and where all of you stand in this situation? Do you?" he shouted. "Each of you have apparently sat snuggly in your own nests while an enemy sneaks your eggs from beneath you! Well, I will tell you that you are not safe within your own swamps any longer!"

He lowered his voice to a gruff whisper, "If you recall, just over one year ago, we had two senior agents who decided to act on their own without approval. In doing so, they committed a disgraceful crime against the State. Most of you know the consequence of their stupid act!"

No one had to be reminded of Borodin and Vetrov. Major General Borodin was executed before a firing squad within the confines of Lubiyanka, and Colonel Vetrov was unceremoniously shot in the head. There was not common knowledge even among many of the senior KGB officers about why Borodin and Vetrov were disposed of so swiftly. No one ever asked questions about the fate of comrades found guilty of *crimes against the State*. What each KGB officer did know was that each of their own lives hung on a thin thread, and it took little provocation to turn fate against them on any given day.

He moved on. "Now to you, Suvorov; were you aware that this man, *Ozvald*, visited our embassy in Mexico City less than two months ago? Did your people not report this to you? Are they asleep over there? What do we know about that visit?"

It was now the turn of Major General Suvorov, director of KGB foreign operations, to take the heat over the apparent *lapse* of security monitoring of the roaming American. "Comrade General, we . . . 'er, I . . . just learned of his visit to our Mexico City embassy today. I will be receiving a full report shortly. I cannot answer why this was not reported to me when it occurred."

"Comrades," Kashevarov interrupted again. "This is despicable! We tout ourselves as being the greatest intelligence organization in the greatest government in the world and we can't even be aware of one potential slimy spy in our midst! This will not be tolerated! Do you understand? Nyet! . . . Nyet!"

Finally in a calmer, but decisive tone, "Comrades, you have twenty-four hours to provide me independent reports on this renegade American who suspiciously showed up here, stayed for three years, then returned to his homeland and assassinated the President of the United States. If our hands are dirty, heads will roll. Get to the bottom of this; we cannot afford to be found in any way to be involved in this incident. Dismissed!"

Kashevarov, himself, had previously been spared personally by the Soviet Premier following the B-52 incident. Had the Premier himself, not intervened, the KGB chief would have undoubtedly suffered the same fate as his two agents and numerous former KGB directors who ran afoul of the Soviet leadership. It was only his quick and fortunate discovery of the two perpetrators, Borodin and Vetrov, and their prompt disposal that caused the Premier to *save him for another day*. But even the Soviet leader couldn't protect him now from another gaff such as this one that could bring worldwide embarrassment to the Soviet Union.

He was severely troubled. He knew that within the depths of the KGB there was a renegade element that had roots going back forty or fifty years. No one seemed to know who directed its activities, if anyone really did, or if they were simply an element of the agency's dark heritage. He knew for certain that Borodin and Vetrov had acted without his official sanction to have the American bomber destroyed, but he could not be sure if their act had begun or ended with themselves. Now, his KGB could be on the world stage, and he had no way of confirming or denying their involvement in this assassination. He *was* troubled!

Dallas

The Secret Service detail had remained in Dallas after the tragic assassination. The acting chief of personal protection of the President was permitted by the local police to meet briefly with Oswald at 11:15 on Sunday morning, November 24th. He had already been questioned by the local police and the FBI, placed in four different line-ups for witnesses, and visited by his brother, his wife, and his mother.

By the time Oswald met with the Secret Service, he was obviously fatigued from the previous day and a half of interrogations and very little sleep. Yet he responded to questions with guarded, but confident replies.

The accused assassin looked like anyone but a murderer. He was slightly built and appeared frail. His disheveled hair and colorless complexion gave way only to a single distinguishing feature——sharply focused penetrating eyes. Although exhausted from the experience of the day before and the non-stop questioning, he remained coherent and often belligerent.

"I will be glad to discuss anything with you after I talk to my attorney," he replied. "I want someone to contact my attorney, Mr. Aboud, in New York. Until I consult with my attorney, I have nothing to say to you." Since his arrest, Oswald had consistently referred to *his* attorney, *Mr. Aboud.*

The Secret Service questioning was interrupted by the Dallas police chief. "We are ready to transfer the prisoner to the county jail. Perhaps you can meet with him later."

The time was 11:19 a.m.

Two minutes later, at 11:21 a.m., a man named Jack Ruby stepped out of a crowd of reporters and onlookers, and shot Lee Harvey Oswald while he was handcuffed and being led out of the Dallas police department prisoner holding area. Ruby had apparently entered the underground parking area of the Municipal Building by way of an unsecured driving ramp on the south side leading to Commerce Street. Oswald died immediately.

Washington

CIA Director Jack McCloud gathered his staff. "Gentlemen, I want you to pour over every detail and path that leads you to where this man Oswald traveled. The FBI will provide us his bio, from birth to now, so I want you to follow every lead into every nook and cranny into every country on the globe and search out where, who, what and when. If the Bureau doesn't cooperate with you, let me know! We cannot continue to conceal information from one another."

"In just the past twenty-four hours," he said, "we have learned that this character, Oswald, has been all over the map in the last few years. He apparently lived in Moscow and Minsk for three years, has a Russian wife and child, visited the Soviet Embassy in Mexico City less than two months ago . . . and, we have just learned from State Department that he applied for a visa to go to Cuba while he was in Mexico City. It would appear that he had hatched an escape plan after he committed the assassination. This is unbelievable!"

As he spoke, his anger swelled. "I want you to get in touch with our people in Moscow, Minsk, Mexico City, and wherever th' hell else you need to, and collect every thread of information you can. Were we aware that he was a defector? How about our agency people in the embassy in Moscow? What did they know about him? Talk to Donovan, our station chief. If you are worried about secure communication, have someone meet him in London or Zurich. Debrief him, and do it quickly!"

The CIA Director grew even more agitated as the impact of the situation and his own questions mounted. "Don't be bashful! Talk to the KGB; blackmail one of those bastards if need be, and also find out *why we* were not aware that this character was living in the Soviet Union! Did the KGB have him in their net? Did he come back here as an agent? Did we know that he visited the Soviet Embassy in Mexico City less than two months ago? Were we asleep down there? Find out everything! God, what a disaster!"

The Director of the FBI began a methodical background investigation into the life of Lee Harvey Oswald. Prior to his being killed by Ruby, they had located the mysterious Mr. Aboud in New York, and he professed no knowledge of ever having known Oswald.

Surprisingly, as they began to dig, they turned up volumes on Oswald, which was amazing for a nondescript individual who apparently led a normal life until recent years. They found that during his three-year enlistment in the Marine Corps, between

1956 and 1959, his life took a turn. Not particularly bright, Oswald was a loner who resented authority and discipline. He was known to act secretively and alone in the most simple of circumstances. He apparently made no friends during his tour of duty with the Marines.

The Office of Naval Intelligence found that in his old unit, few even remembered him. Those who did recalled that "he talked a lot about Russia" and often "bragged about moving there when his enlistment was up." It was noted in his personnel file that he studied the Russian language while he was stationed in Japan and later in California. He once took the Army language aptitude test for Russian but was rated "Poor" and "Unacceptable for further training."

The Director, National Security Agency, Lt. General Lincoln Foster, had his sensor experts begin reviewing every intercepted communication from the Soviet Embassies and consulates in Washington, Mexico City, London, and Helsinki over the past five years. "Research all communications that we have on file from Moscow, Minsk, and Mexico City that might provide tips regarding Oswald's presence and movements."

"Look for code names," he instructed, "that includes any covers that this guy or the Soviets may have used in discussing him and any references to an American living in Moscow and Minsk. The Soviets like to talk a lot, so there has to be something in that mix. I *hope* that we can rely upon the CIA operatives in our embassy in Moscow and the consulate in Minsk to help us out. At least, *I hope* we can rely on some tangible evidence of this character's presence and activities while he was there. Three years is a helluva long time for an American to roam around inside the Soviet Union. We must assume that the KGB had him under surveillance, if not *control*. They don't trust their own people, much less a foreigner! Why didn't *the CIA* have a *tag* on him while he was over there? WOW! I can't believe all of this! It stinks! But I just don't know how bad! Get going!"

The U.S. Intelligence Community was in a frenzy. Their confident world of *all seeing* and *all knowing* had come crashing down, and under the worst of circumstances, the assassination of the President. Quiet finger pointing began to slowly creep across the various agency headquarters' staff groups. Imbedded animosity and jealousies deepened as more and more information surfaced. This was Washington bureaucracy at its worst.

The Chairman, Joint Chiefs of Staff, instructed his staff to *"run all the traps"* on Oswald's Marine Corps service. "Get everything you can on this guy. I want to know everything about him! I also want to know what the Soviets are up to. Are they doing anything funny? Moving any ships or aircraft around? Are they acting nervous? Get everything!"

Revelations

CIA operatives worldwide were alerted and ordered to . . . "look under every rock! Uncover even the smallest detail regarding a U.S. citizen by the name of Lee Harvey Oswald."

"My very first knowledge of the existence of Lee Harvey Oswald was when he showed up at my office in the U.S. Embassy in Moscow on October 31, 1959," the U.S. Consular responded to questions by the Moscow CIA Station Chief, Terrance Donovan. "He handed me his passport and told me that the purpose of his visit was to revoke his U.S. citizenship. He said that he had experienced an unpleasant life growing up in the United States. He had served in the American military, which amounted to imperialism, and that he was a Marxist. He made it clear that he no longer wished to be burdened by an American citizenship."

"What was your response?"

"I stalled him, which is our policy, by telling him that he should reconsider his decision while the paperwork for his citizenship revocation was being prepared. My hope was the Russians would expel him from the country because of his expired visitor's visa. He gave me his U.S. passport anyway and a handwritten note requesting that his citizenship be revoked and 'affirming his allegiance' to the Soviet Union."

"Did you counsel him on the seriousness of his decision and that he might not be able to ever return to the U.S.?"

"Indeed, I did. And I asked where he was staying so that we might get back in touch with him after he had thoroughly considered the consequences of losing his citizenship. He told me that he was in Room 212 at the Metropole Hotel, but that his decision was final and he wanted to get on with it. Of course, I was aware that the KGB managed all of the guests in the Metropole and felt that if they weren't using him for any of their pursuits, they would get him out of the country fairly quickly. They don't like loose foreigners hanging around."

"Did you notify my office of his presence in Moscow and his visit to your office?"

"No, I didn't. He seemed harmless and insignificant enough, so I initiated the necessary paperwork to revoke his citizenship and filed a report of the meeting proceedings and dispatched a notification to the State Department and the INS (Immigration and Naturalization Service) on November 2nd describing his request."

"Well, dammit, this *insignificant* asshole went back home and killed the President of the United States! Didn't you think his presence here in Moscow holed up in a KGB hotel was *significant?* What the hell were you thinking?"

Donavon walked around the room. "Okay, okay, I lost my cool. Sorry. During your meeting did you get the feeling at all that he was being managed by the Soviets?"

"No, I couldn't detect any coaching, but he did demonstrate reasonable intelligence and had a working knowledge of the provisions of Section 349(a) of the Immigration and Nationality Act regarding the procedure for surrendering his citizenship. He did tell me that he had spoken with a Soviet official and made a veiled threat that he could share with the Soviet Government any information they desired about his knowledge of U.S. military radar technologies."

"Holy shit! Did you report this?" Donovan shouted.

"Yes, I put that statement in my written report." The Consular again calmly responded, "We all know now, he was not ejected from the USSR. When he returned here a couple years or so later to revoke his earlier declaration, I was required to give him the documentation for Soviet citizenship revocation."

The CIA Station Chief could hardly contain himself as he listened to the *matter of fact* report being given on the accused assassin who had lived virtually under their noses for "years" in the Soviet Union. "Okay, go on. What else do you have on this character?"

"Well, I presume he was issued a *'Stateless Persons Identification Document'* by the Soviet Government to cover his continued presence in the country. The next time I heard from Mr. Oswald was by letter in February 1961, in which he stated that he had married a Soviet citizen and wanted to have his citizenship reinstated and requested a passport and visa for his wife. A few months later, while we were considering his case, we received a second letter dated May 25th in which he stated that his wife was from Leningrad, had no parents and they now had a baby girl. He assured me that his wife was willing to live in the United States."

"That's cute!" Donovan sneered. "Did he want us to pay his way back home with his *new family?*"

"No, sir, he didn't make any personal requests for support. So, as is our policy, we welcome U.S. citizens to come back home, and we reinstated his U.S. citizenship."

"Good Lord! Well, permit me to ask a dumb ass question anyway. Did you find his presence in Moscow and his request to revoke his citizenship unusual?" Donovan snidely asked.

"No, I did not. We had then, and we still have, a half dozen or so former U.S. military people who have defected while stationed in Europe. They usually entered through East Germany after being co-opted by Soviet agents. There are also a few known religious *kooks,* draft dodgers and others roaming around over here. The Soviets love it and use them where they can for propaganda purposes."

Neither the CIA nor the State Department was pleased with the events that dealt with Oswald in Moscow. They recognized that they had let him slip by any surveillance. They had not tagged his movements while he was in the Soviet Union and had no knowledge of his activities during the extended stay. Neither did the agency have any idea regarding whether he had been recruited and trained as an agent. Further, nothing was done to verify his loyalty before he returned to the United States. The CIA was in a deep depression. There were no excuses that could cover the faults. A new question arose. "How many other *Oswalds* are there roaming around the Soviet Union, and *who* is tracking them?"

Conjectures and speculation became a full-time industry as both the U.S. and the Soviet agencies tried to locate and *connect the dots* that had apparently been so frivolously scattered about. Both sides thought that it was highly unusual for an American citizen to be able to marry a Soviet citizen and to bring their child out of the country to the United States. U.S. authorities felt that the Soviets would not have so freely permitted him to return with a Soviet wife unless the KGB or GRU had planned to use him. Outwardly, the Soviets appeared to treat him as if he was just another confused American *beatnik.*

There were questions concerning his whereabouts during his stay in the Soviet Union, particularly his finances. "What about his apparent freedom of movement while he was there and so on?" Few answers were forthcoming.

As the hastily organized investigations proceeded, it was determined that Oswald visited the Soviet Embassy and the Cuban Consulate in Mexico City during late September and October 1963, less than two months before the assassination. The CIA, however, did not get around to notifying the FBI about Mexico City and the embassy and consulate visits until after the assassination. The fact that he had also made contact with Valeri Kotov, a senior KGB agent assigned to the embassy and a member of 13th Department—the division responsible for assassinations, sabotage and kidnapping—had somehow escaped notice!

The CIA Director again gathered his senior staff. "How in the hell did we get in this fix? We look like a bunch of bumbling *Keystone Kops!* There is going to be one *helluva* investigation and, without a doubt, a Congressional Hearing over this assassination, and we don't look very good! I predict some heads will roll over such stupidity! What is the FBI doing about all of this? Are they as screwed up as we are?"

The FBI was involved in a frenzy of hurried fact finding on its own. After all, the Attorney General was the dead President's brother. Newspaper, radio and television reporters were hounding every agent assigned to the case, and when they did not receive answers to their questions, they became very creative in developing their own stories.

Rumors in the U.S. media were in abundance with the mystery assassin who had lived in the Soviet Union for almost three years prior to his being accused of murdering the President. Then, *he* is killed by another equally mysterious individual. Soviet connections and conspiracy theories were read and heard from every source.

The FBI Director was not able to answer the flurry of questions hurled at him by an angry and frustrated Attorney General, nor could he respond to the aspersions cast at him by the CIA, Secret Service, local law enforcement agencies and the press:

"Did we debrief Oswald when he returned from living in the Soviet Union? Were we aware that he was in contact with a KGB agent by the name of Grechko in the Soviet Embassy in Washington? Was the FBI aware that Grechko was the KGB chief handler of illegal agents operating in the United States and was the paymaster for espionage work?"

The barrage of questions came from all directions and crisscrossed the various agency directors' desks:

"Did we know that Oswald visited Mexico City just two months ago and made contact with a KGB officer in the Soviet Embassy? Were we aware that Oswald applied for a Cuban visa while he was in Mexico City? Have we been tracking Oswald since he returned to the United States? Was Oswald a Soviet agent? Was he *ours*—a CIA or FBI agent or informant? Why did Oswald have an FBI agent's name, phone number and automobile license plate number in his pocket when he was arrested?"

The nonstop queries cascaded down on the head of every agency director, but there were few answers. The agencies became defensive with one another and battened down their individual information files, refusing to share collected data. Had an over confident bureaucracy betrayed itself?

At Ft. Meade, the National Security Agency (NSA) was busy reviewing collected communication files and classified signal information from their worldwide sensors dating back to 1959. Their *educated* hope was the detection of anything pointing toward Oswald: communications, possibly alias names, or any revealed Soviet interest in undermining United States leadership. The process was tedious and would take thousands of man-hours and months to complete.

NSA was also assisting the Joint Chiefs in determining Soviet responses to the assassination. Other than an increase in operational communications, nothing was detected. The new President and the Secretary of Defense were careful not to reflect any overt military actions during the time of the assassination crisis. Piecing together all of the curious parts of the large mosaic became a frenzied nightmare.

In a final flurry of anger and frustration, the Attorney General hurled a challenge to the intelligence agency chiefs. "I want to know what each one of you knew about this man, Oswald, and when you first heard about him!"

Meanwhile, under a dark cloud of anxiety, guarded fear, and suspicion, a sorrowful nation prepared to bury its President.

THREE

"All cats are gray at night."

A Russian Proverb

Dallas

The news blurted across the airways just at noon Dallas, Texas, time on Sunday, November 24th:

> *"Lee Harvey Oswald, the man accused of assassinating President Kennedy, was shot dead a little over a half-hour ago, at 11:21 a.m. Central Standard Time, while in the custody of the police in Dallas, Texas. Oswald was being escorted to a court hearing. The man arrested for murdering Oswald has been identified as a 'Jack Ruby'. He is now under arrest. Those are all of the details that we have at this time. Please stay tuned."*

A nation and world already in shock absorbed yet another incredible blow.

Moscow

Sasha arrived home from the meeting with Tushenskiy around midnight. Mackye was waiting anxiously. They had suddenly found themselves in the center of an incredible whirlwind turn of world events.

"Mackye, I'm sorry that I'm so late, but Tushenskiy has asked me to conduct some investigative work regarding the assassination of the American president. It will also require me to be away for a few weeks. I will have my office keep you informed about when I might return."

He quietly added, "Now, not to worry, this is not a dangerous assignment. It should be routine, but should any of your colleagues or anyone at Lubiyanka inquire about me or what I may be doing, just shrug it off. What you don't know, you can't reveal. Please don't worry, all of this will soon be over and back to normal."

Instinctively, Mackye asked, "Are you going to the United States, Sasha?"

"Perhaps, I'm not sure. The General is having a plan developed to determine what he would have me do. Don't fret, Mackye. All will be well with this."

The next morning, Sasha went directly to Tushenskiy's office as instructed. "Come in, Sasha. You know General Volnov."

Viktor Volnov was Deputy Director for Special Operations, GRU.

Sasha shook hands with Volnov and took a chair next to him. Tushenskiy paced around the office. "Sasha, we have developing news. There was no immediate need to call you so late last night, but the man, Oswald, accused as the assassin, has been murdered while in the hands of the American police. What do you make of that?"

Sasha did not respond. All of these events were unraveling too fast. "All of that happening in America!" He thought to himself, "That's not the way they conduct themselves over there! They are too *proper* and too *correct.*"

He looked at Tushenskiy. "Sir, that's incredible! Americans don't act that way. They are very much like us in such matters, extremely efficient and orderly. How could that happen? Did the police do this? This is astonishing! What all do we know?"

"All we know presently about this Oswald's apparent murder is that he was in the custody of the police where he was arrested in Texas, and an unidentified man came into the station and shot him dead," Tushenskiy responded. "This is becoming just too bizarre. However, enough about what is likely going on over there. Let's discuss your role in all of this."

Tushenskiy continued, "Sasha, we have devised a confidential plan. I want you first to travel to Minsk. Contact our office there. They will be expecting you and hopefully will have completed considerable background work by the time you arrive. You may have to spend several days there, but that will give us time to prepare your documents and travel plans to ease you out of the country and on to your other destinations. After Minsk, I would like for you to go to Helsinki. We have a GRU *rezidentura* at each location. They will be instructed to cooperate fully with you, as will the KGB and consulate personnel. If you encounter any lack of cooperation, contact me immediately. Do you have any questions at this time?"

Sasha paused. "Yes, General . . . uh, Sir, what is it that you wish me to do . . . I mean specifically, Sir?"

"Hah! You would ask the most important and difficult question first, Sasha. Your mission is really quite challenging. I want you to gather as much information from any sources you can about the U.S. President's assassination and now the apparent murder of his alleged killer, at least what is available from the American perspective. Provide me with your assessment. Try to determine if *anyone* in our government was involved in either or both of the incidents. Were other governments involved? Or, was it a single renegade attack? Did he have assistance . . . if so, from whom? Is there a possible cover-up by factions in our own system or in the U.S. Government? Sasha, that's a large order."

Tushenskiy paused and continued, "However, I believe that we need to move quickly now before too many facts are lost or covered-up. To be completely truthful about all of this, I frankly do not trust our friends at Lubiyanka. They certainly were not upfront about the American's long-term presence here in our country. I cannot believe that someone in there is not the wiser about all of this."

He paused . . . "Now Comrade, don't get yourself trapped by any of our KGB *friends*, or for that matter, *anyone* in the other places you visit. I simply want an outside appraisal and assessment. I'm not sure what I will do with the information you gather, but I, and for that matter, General Volnov agrees, that this is an important task to be completed. The KGB cannot be expected to honestly investigate themselves."

He looked at Volnov. "Viktor, would you please go over our preliminary schedule with Sasha?"

"As the general has indicated," Volnov began, "our plan is to have you initially travel to Minsk. So as not to arouse any unnecessary suspicions, you will travel via AEROFLOT as a regular passenger. When you arrive in Minsk, take a taxicab to the building address where our *rezidentura* is located. General Bekrenev is the GRU chief there and will provide you all the necessary local support you need. Once you have completed your review of the situation there, send us a preliminary report by GRU courier and provide Bekrenev with a copy. You will then proceed on an *Aeroflot* scheduled flight to Leningrad. Our people will meet you when you arrive and provide you with the necessary documents to get you safely through the scheduled stops on your *tour.*"

Volnov completed the plan. "We would like for you to travel to Helsinki, London, the United States, and then possibly to Mexico City, if you decide the latter location is necessary. Do you have any questions?"

"Yes, Sir, I will need a list of contacts at each location, phone numbers, code words and code names. Also, when do I depart?"

"You are ticketed on an 0700 flight tomorrow morning for Minsk," responded Tushenskiy. "Can you make it?"

"Yessir, I will be ready."

"Good," Tushenskiy smiled. "A car will pick you up at your apartment at 0500. General Volnov will accompany you to Sheremetevo II. He will provide you with everything you need during your ride to the airport. Turn over your day-to-day work to your deputy and take the afternoon to prepare for your trip, and, Sasha, I don't need to remind you of the confidentiality of this operation."

Minsk

Sasha shared little of the plans with Mackye, only that he would be away for a week or more, depending on the work that needed to be accomplished. He departed Moscow as scheduled and arrived at the Minsk airport late on the morning of November 26th. He debarked from the airliner and waited patiently on the tarmac of the antiquated airport and finally collected his suitcase. The lack of efficiency of personnel and services at Soviet airports had frustrated him since he arrived back from the United States. He proceeded out of the airport to the curbside. It was a brutally cold day. The air was heavy and damp. Patches of snow frosted automobile rooftops, and the streets were curb-deep with melted slush.

As he looked about for a taxi, a heavyset man in a tattered overcoat walked up to him, smiling. "Taxi, Comrade? I am not busy."

Sasha got into the musty smelling back seat of the worn-out sedan and instructed the driver to take him to 1016 Lishev Prospekt, the address of the GRU residence. As the taxi moved through the narrow grimy streets of the once war-ravaged city, he noted the sidewalks were busy with pedestrians. It wasn't much different from Moscow, he thought. Even on the coldest and foulest of days, people moved about, foraging for food and most anything that was available to purchase. He remembered how his own mother, even though his father was a Soviet general, would rise early several days each week to seek out perishables and staples for the table. He wondered if the Soviet Union would ever change. He had lived in the United States for over eight years and marveled at how well Americans fared. He never saw packed sidewalks in the U.S. such as these, particularly in the dead of winter. The overflow of pedestrians with looks of despair seemed to be getting even worse.

Sasha suddenly noticed several meters ahead on the particularly narrow street, two men standing prominently on either side opposite one another. Their appearance was unmistakable, dark fedoras, heavy wool topcoats, in contrast to the others loitering on the street. They were KGB!

Instinctively, he reached across the back seat and simultaneously depressed both rear door locks. He withdrew his *Graz Burya* revolver from the side pocket of his valise and placed the barrel of the pistol firmly behind the right ear of the driver.

"Turn off this street now! Drive fast and get out of this area or you're dead!"

The driver gasped and tried to look back at Sasha only to feel the cold steel of the revolver scrape against his cheek, but he continued at a deliberate slow speed.

"Comrade, what is this? What do you mean?" the driver yelped.

Sasha then shoved the barrel of the pistol hard against the nape of the driver's neck. "I said move! *Now*! Get out of here . . . *Fast!*"

The driver pressed the accelerator hard and the ancient vehicle bolted forward, brushing past the two men who were ostensibly waiting to jump into the cab on either side as it slowly moved past.

Sasha looked back and saw the two running after the taxi in an attempt to catch them. In a calmer tone, he whispered in the driver's ear. "Comrade, if you want to live, take me to the Soviet Consulate. Now! And quickly!"

As the taxi pulled to a stop in front of the consulate building Sasha grabbed the back of the driver's jacket collar and jerked it sharply.

"Hand me your operator's permit. Right there! Hand it to me!"

The frightened driver pulled his operator's permit card, with his picture ID, out of its plastic jacket fixed to the dashboard and handed it to Sasha. "Sir, what is wrong? Why are you acting this way? Are you crazy? Please, I must go!"

"Comrade, you remain here in your vehicle until I return, or I will hunt you down and kill you," Sasha responded in a measured, but firm voice. "Do you understand?"

"Yes, Comrade, I will stay until you return. You have my driver's permit."

Sasha returned his revolver to the valise, took his suitcase, *just in case,* and bounded up the steps to the door of the Russian Consulate. Once inside the musky building, he told the uniformed female receptionist to direct him to the security chief's office.

"NOW!" raising his voice in a convincing tone.

Sasha didn't hear the silent alarm that she pushed, and before he could react, two burly plainclothes security guards emerged from a side door, each grabbing one of his arms.

He attempted to wrench free. "You fools, I am Colonel Alexandr Katsanov, Moscow GRU! Stand back!"

Another dark-suited man, better and neatly dressed, stepped into the foyer where the two had Sasha held firmly between them. "Well, Comrade, who are you to make all of this *besporyadok*? You are on the hallowed property of the Supreme Soviet? What is your business here?"

"I am Colonel Alexandr Katsanov, GRU. I am here to see your chief, but I dare say that after the events of this day, you *know* who I am! Who are you?"

"I am Colonel Grigori Ostipov, deputy chief of intelligence here. What is your business? Do you have identification, Comrade Alexandr?"

Sasha shook free from the two holding his arms and presented his GRU picture identification card.

"Hmmmm. Thank you Comrade," Ostipov smirked, "but you have yet to state your purpose for being here, nor to explain your unruly conduct."

Sasha pulled the taxi cab driver's operating permit from his coat pocket. "This is your man, I presume. He carefully selected me out at the airport and was in the process of driving me into an ambush. I forced him to drive me here. Now, Comrade, you tell me what is going on!"

Ostipov nodded for the two security guards to step back from Sasha. "First, let me apologize for the zealous conduct of my security people, Comrade. We are often subjected to street people barging in here with their stupid complaints. Now, I am confused by what you are telling me about your taxi driver and an *ambush*? You are saying to me that you believe that our people are responsible for some street brawl that you found yourself involved in?"

"Colonel, I would like to meet with your station chief. I have business with him," Sasha demanded.

"Comrade, I am afraid that isn't possible. General Zetrov is away from the city at the moment," Ostipov responded. "How may I help you?"

Sasha was sure that Ostipov was lying. The KGB did not like being caught in the act of foul deeds, especially those gone wrong.

A lower level agent was always put forth to address the issue. "May we go into your office, Comrade?" he finally asked.

Ostipov shrugged and led Sasha into an adjacent office.

Sasha presented him the letter of introduction from General Tushenskiy. "Here, Comrade. Please read this."

"Ho! Ho! So we have a very special visitor in our city," Ostipov mocked. "Welcome Comrade! I am at your service. What can I do for you? Cigarette?"

"No, thank you. First, you may begin by keeping your *well-meaning* goons away from me," Sasha shot back. "And, while I was not going to bother your agency for any special support, I am going to call on you now to permit me to ask questions of you, your people and anyone else I wish to confront. I also want a free run of the city of Minsk while I am here. Any questions?"

Ostipov grunted an arrogant smirk and exhaled smoke from his nostrils. "Comrade Alexandr, I am afraid that you don't understand the ground rules. The security of Minsk is the responsibility of the KGB. We politely permit your GRU to have a *rezidentura* here, but Byelorussia and Minsk are the domain of the KGB. We work closely with the Byelorussian KGB and assist them in the protection of their great republic. So, I must humbly decline your request to, as you say, *have a free run of the city.* That simply is not possible. So, now what may we do for you?"

"Comrade Grigori, I regret that you do not have an appreciation for my presence here in Minsk. Do you wish for me to make a phone call to Moscow? I have little doubt that General Kashevarov will be pleased to accommodate my chief, General Tushenskiy, particularly under the present circumstances."

Ostipov's demeanor quickly changed as Sasha's words settled on him. He cleared his throat and reacted with a weak smile. "Colonel Katsanov, there is no need for you to *call Moscow*. I will grant you permission to walk about our city, but let me warn you, Comrade, watch carefully *where* you walk. We will tolerate no disruption of the peace and tranquility among our trusted Allies here in Minsk."

Turning his back to gaze out the window and exhaling cigarette smoke, Ostipov issued a warning. "Good day, Comrade, but just remember, *All cats are gray at night.* We would not want to mistake you for someone other than who you are."

Sasha departed the consulate. He was not pleased with the shaky beginning of his mission. He would have much preferred to establish a working relationship with the local KGB in order to ask questions, but now that was shattered. He had no sooner arrived at the first stop on his itinerary and had run square into an obvious KGB-devised *roadblock*.

"I should have expected this," he thought. "There are no secrets in Moscow. These bastards play rough."

Back on the street, he looked for the taxi, wondering if the driver had beaten a retreat. He noticed a crowd gathered a block down from the consulate building and then clearly made out the rear end of the taxicab. He walked toward the commotion.

Sasha took in a deep breath as he moved slowly through the mingling crowd and up to the parked vehicle near the curb. Inside, the driver was slumped over the steering wheel, his head and the interior of the car spattered with blood. He had been badly beaten.

"Well, he apparently tried to get away, but they caught him. They are no more than animals!" he quietly murmured. He got close enough to slip the driver's operating permit through the open window, on to the floor of the cab and walked away. No one seemed to notice his slight of hand. A police car, siren blaring, came up the street followed by an ambulance.

"Just another victim of KGB brutality. The poor bastard thought he was doing something for his country," Sasha breathed to himself as he worked his way from the scene. "No one will pay!"

Several blocks away, he waved down another taxi and continued his original journey to the GRU *residence*.

"Come in, Comrade Alexandr! I have heard much about you. I am Boris Bekrenev. I was expecting you a few hours earlier. Was your flight delayed?"

Sasha held out his hand. "I am pleased to meet you, General. General Tushenskiy sends his best regards. No, Sir, my flight was on time. The KGB had other plans for my arrival." He went on to explain the preceding events.

General Bekrenev was sharply dressed in a double-breasted suit. Sasha judged him to be in an age range of sixty, although he could have been older, slightly built with balding gray hair. He appeared to be tired but seemed genuinely pleased to meet Sasha.

His smile slowly turned to a frown as Sasha spoke. He took in a deep breath. "I should have suspected that they would be on to your visit. Those scum are into everything." His anger flared. "They are despicable bastards! I should have had our people meet you, but I thought that it would only arouse *local* curiosity. I apologize, Comrade."

He motioned for Sasha to sit down. "I get along reasonably well with General Zetrov, at least superficially. I believe that he is basically forthright with me, but there is an element within the KGB that is hard-core. Ostipov is probably one of those renegades. None of us know where, or from whom, they take their orders. Many of us doubt that Kashevarov is really in charge. Back in Moscow, he is the director in name, but beneath him there is a deep and dark level. It goes back farther than Beria or even Yezhof before him. They were two of the most treacherous of all secret police chiefs, and they left their indelible marks deep within the system. The remnants of their sordid past remain imbedded within the KGB, and they are blight on our process and our objectives."

Sasha listened. This was the first time that he had heard such a direct indictment of the KGB from a senior officer. Tushenskiy had expressed his concerns, but never with such a negative assessment. Most GRU and other Soviet military officers kept their personal opinions close to themselves. Bekrenev was different.

"Sir, I appreciate your concern, and I wonder with Ostipov acting as the front for General Zetrov, can we expect any cooperation from the KGB here in Minsk?"

"Zetrov is difficult to read. At times he is most agreeable and pleasant to work with. At other times he can become a brick wall. Today, he put Ostipov on display for you rather than face you directly. He may well feel that he will have to deal with you later. Ostipov is a *'wanna be.'* He is arrogant and brash, and one to watch. You put one over on him today, so you will want to watch your step while you are here, and for that matter, after you depart on the remainder of your operation."

Sasha sighed. "Well, Sir, I am not here to wage a battle with the KGB. My wife works for them. She is an international economics expert and above all of the intrigue, so I have an appreciation for the good work they can do. I don't understand the dark side, but I will attempt to do my assigned work without tripping over them."

"You will need to be careful, Comrade," Bekrenev said. "This assassination of the American president has many of us baffled. It is apparent that many within the KGB are twisted with the prospect of being implicated . . . whether they are or not. While you are here, my people will provide you all of the support that you need, and we will do our best to keep your path clear of obstacles. I regret your incident today. I should have been more alert. We often misjudge those within. You must be hungry. Come, let's have a libation and some food."

Over a tray of sturgeon caviar, saltines and vodka, General Bekrenev briefed Sasha on Minsk and the information he had been able to hastily gather regarding Oswald's stay in the city. "The American had received a residence permit in late 1959 to live in Minsk after having spent almost three months in Moscow. He moved here on January 8, 1960. Few of us, certainly not myself, realized that we had such a potential *celebrity* amongst us. The Byelorus KGB was obviously alerted by Moscow and put a track on him when he arrived. They gave him the code name, *Likhoi*. According to my sources, our own KGB permitted the Byelorus agents to place a full-time net around Oswald. Zetrov told me that they set up a special task force just to *watch* him after he arrived in Minsk."

Bekrenev frowned. "I thought this was both strange and unusual."

Then he speculated, "Why would they devote such an effort to this individual unless they had potential future use for him? Or did they suspect him of being a spy? Oh, and something special to note. On the day this fellow, Oswald, arrived in Minsk, he was met at the train station by two Red Cross workers and escorted to the Hotel Minsk. He was met at the hotel by two Intourist ladies who got him settled into his room. On the following day, your man, Oswald, was escorted to meet none other than the "Mayor," V.I. Sharapov, who welcomed him to Minsk, promised him a rent-free apartment, and warned him against "uncultured persons," who sometimes insulted foreigners.

"The mayor?" Sasha responded sharply. "That is curious! Why would the mayor of Minsk go out of his way to meet someone the KGB had characterized as a vagabond and ne'er do well foreigner?"

Bekrenev smiled and continued without responding to the question. "The city provided him an apartment which was well above the average working class level. He was given a job at the Gorizant Radio Factory, and I presume, was paid a reasonably good wage. He was also permitted to purchase a weapon, a shotgun. This was even more unusual. I have to presume that the KGB arranged all of this. I also admit, I have never before heard of such a thing. Our ordinary citizens undergo extensive security and political checks, and, more often than not, are denied a permit for even a sporting gun. Jobs such as in the electronics factory are usually reserved for loyal government workers whether they have a skill or not. All of these were very peculiar activities for a westerner freely moving within our midst. Now, with the sudden revelation of events, the KGB has sealed shut all information regarding him."

Bekrenev shared another element of information. "There is another interesting *coincidence* to all of this. The uncle of the young woman that the American met and married is Colonel Ilya Prusakova, the senior MVD official in Minsk."

"MVD?" She is the niece of the chief of the Minsk *Ministerstvo Vnutrennikh Del*—internal police?" Sasha reacted to the revelation. "Good grief! Do we know if there was any close connection between the American and the colonel? Did they ever meet?"

"Sasha, those questions will have to be answered by either the MVD or the KGB, but you can rest assured that *they both* were aware of what was going on. Interesting, isn't it, Comrade? Well, I wish you luck, Sasha, in finding out very much more than I have told you."

Bekrenev sighed, "Let's have dinner, Comrade, and speak of more pleasant subjects. I would like to hear more about you, and I understand that you spent some time in the United States. And then you need to get some rest. You have had a busy day!"

Over dinner, Sasha broached the sensitive question he had previously with Tushenskiy. "Sir, do you believe there is a possibility that our own Spetsnaz may be implicated in this assassination?"

Bekrenev studied Sasha's question for a moment. "Comrade Sasha, ours is a very complex government structure. Sometimes, I believe that we are far too large and complicated to be efficiently managed, much less to control. That goes for the KGB, with whom we in the GRU find at great fault most of the time. And, that goes for the GRU as well. I am sure that our Director General would like to believe that he is in complete control and has cognizance over every activity worldwide, but the truth is that General Tushenskiy suffers with his awesome and tenuous responsibilities. I have no doubt that he wonders each day about what is going on within all of his vast units . . . and who can be trusted and who cannot. The Spetsnaz is a special case for the GRU. They possess many of the unfortunate characteristics of the KGB's 13th Department."

Sasha was aware of the KGB 13th Department's operational responsibilities and reputation for assassination, sabotage and kidnapping.

"So, to answer your question, Comrade, I really don't know. I hope not and I am most sure that General Tushenskiy is taking every step to ensure that all of his units are clean in this assassination thing."

The following morning, Sasha joined Bekrenev for breakfast. "I spoke with General Tushenskiy last evening, Sasha," Bekrenev began. "I told him about your incident with our friends. He is very concerned about your safety. He told me that you had a near miss with these people just one year ago."

"That's true, General, but that was completely unrelated to what happened yesterday. I am not a special target on their list. At least, I *wasn't* until yesterday."

"General Tushenskiy told me that you are free to withdraw from this mission if you wish."

"No, General, I am here and I am going to complete what I can here in Minsk and move on according to the schedule."

"The General insists that that is your decision to make, Sasha. I will provide you everything you need while you are in Minsk and see you safely off to Leningrad. You will have a vehicle and my most trusted and skilled driver to move you around the city. There will be two back-up GRU agents following you wherever you go. They will not close in unless trouble is detected. So, you can assist them by trying to keep yourself reasonably visible as much as possible. That may be difficult, but stay in view from the outside as much as you can."

"And, Sasha," he continued, "I would advise you *not* to revisit the consulate. As you have learned, you are not welcome in Minsk, but you may wish to speak with the Byelorus KGB. They are generally more friendly and don't always go along with their Moscow counterparts. You will have to find that out for yourself. Now, here are the places where this man, Oswald, lived and worked, as well as the local drinking and social halls that he was known to frequent."

Bekrencv unfolded a map of the city that had been annotated with circles and notations with locations of interest regarding Oswald's stay in Minsk. He also gave Sasha a list of names and places.

"Thank you, General. I sincerely appreciate your hospitality and your support."

FOUR

"As you make your bed,
so you will sleep in it."

A Russian Proverb

The American

Sasha spent the next day driving around the city of Minsk and preparing to pursue the leads given to him in Moscow and by Bekrenev. Before setting out to contact former acquaintances of Oswald, he paid a visit to the Byelorus KGB Headquarters.

There, he identified himself and revealed his letter from Tushenskiy. "Well, Comrade Katsanov, you are on a curious visit to our city. We understand that you did not receive a very pleasant welcome from your fellow Muscovites. I regret that."

Colonel Baylin's greeting was pleasant enough and by far more receptive than that of his Moscow KGB counterparts, but nevertheless, it was apparent that he was on guard. He had been warned about Sasha's impending visit.

"There is little we can offer regarding the American, Oswald, who was here for a time," he said. "Because he was a foreigner, we opened a case file on him. It was entitled *Likhoi*, should you encounter that later. We determined after awhile that he was lackluster and harmless. At the request of our Moscow colleagues we permitted him to remain in Minsk. When he indicated that he was ready to leave our country, we welcomed the opportunity to assist him in departing. Regrettably, he took with him one of our citizens, but neither did we inhibit her departure. I am afraid that is all that I can tell you, Comrade, but please feel free to talk to our

42

people. Minsk is a friendly city, and if we may be of further service to you, please let us know."

Sasha was surprised by the apparent even-handed reception by the Byelorussian secret police, particularly after his encounter with the Moscow KGB counterparts. He wondered if they were toying with him or just playing him against their Russian *partners*.

Emboldened, he asked Baylin, "General, can you tell me why such special interest was given to this American? The mayor met him when he arrived in the city and provided him an apartment of above average class. He was given a job in a government factory. And I am informed he was allowed to purchase a firearm. All of this attention and the exceptional benefits seem most unusual for a foreigner, especially an American and a former member of their military."

Baylin smiled weakly, shrugged and stiffened. "Comrade, there are events that occur everyday in our lives that I do not fully understand. The American came to our city from Moscow. Your friends at the Consulate coordinated his arrival and visit here. I suggest that you pursue your questions with them."

"Sir, may I ask to see the Likhoi File?"

"Nyet," Baylin promptly replied. "That file is no longer here. The Moscow KGB retrieved it from us."

"When did they collect the file from you?"

"Enough questions here, Comrade. You should address any further inquiries to your local Moscow colleagues. Good day and enjoy your stay in Minsk." Baylin abruptly ended the meeting.

Sasha departed the Byelorus KGB office feeling some better about being in Minsk; at least Baylin did not turn him away and he invited him to look about the city, although he did reach his limit on questions.

He had his driver take him to the apartment building where Oswald had lived. The former neighbors all remembered the American well, and a few of them were eager to talk about him. Since the assassination, he had become a *celebrity,* of sorts.

Maria and Sergei Grechkovich lived above Oswald and told a story about the KGB requiring them to leave their apartment for a short period after Oswald moved in.

"They came to our apartment and ordered us to leave and to not return for two days," Maria Grechkovich said. "When we did return, they told us not to disturb any of the electrical wiring that might be visible. *It is for your own security*, we were told."

Sergei Grechkovich said he assumed that the KGB had installed surveillance receivers to monitor their new American neighbor. "The police agents came by several other times, mostly at night, and would ask us to leave our apartment and go to a local hotel room they had reserved for us. They told us not to come back until late morning. After the American departed Minsk, the secret police came back and evicted us again while they removed the electronics."

The Grechkovich couple also told him that Oswald was very temperamental and high strung. Once they accidentally flooded his apartment when the water line in their kitchen broke, and he flew into a rage, threatening to turn them in for intentionally harassing him.

"He implied that he had influence with the police," Sergei said.

Maria said, "Later, after he married Marina Prusakova and she moved in, he became a better neighbor."

Sasha next visited the Gorizont Radio Factory, or the Minsk Radio and Television Factory, as it was also called. There he found several *very talkative* former work mates of Oswald. One factory worker, who claimed to be a *close friend* of Oswald, was Pytr Gadarchev.

"I was once accosted on the street after work," Gadarchev seemed to brag. "And I was threatened with a factious blackmail allegation of trading in foreign goods if I did not agree to meet several times a week and tell *certain people* everything that I knew about Oswald's daily activities. I had to agree to do so even though I liked the American. Shortly after we heard that Oswald was accused of assassinating the American president and had been arrested, the secret police came to my apartment and demanded any photographs or other materials I possessed that related to Oswald."

"Later," he said, "two other secret policemen came back and took me to their Headquarters. They interrogated me for several hours. I told them that, as far as I knew, the American, Oswald, was an honorable man and a hard worker. He really liked living in the Soviet Union but held no grudge against the United States. I told them that he would make a loyal and trusted Soviet citizen. I also tried to assure them that I did not believe he had anything to do with the assassination of the U.S. president. They told me to keep my mouth shut and not to tell anyone that I ever knew the American."

He paused . . . "Why am I telling you all of this? I am telling you because I hate the KGB and everything they do to our people. Are you going to turn me in?"

"No, Comrade, I'm not going to turn you in," Sasha replied, "but can you tell me what you know about this girl that Oswald married . . . Were you aware that her uncle is Colonel Ilya Prusakova, the head of the MVD in Minsk?"

"No, Comrade," he said, "I know very little about the woman he married or her connections."

Sasha concluded the discussion with Gadarchev, "I wish to thank you for sharing your thoughts with me, Comrade. I will do my best to ensure that you and your family will be watched over."

He made a special note of the discussion with him. Something didn't ring true. He seemed too eager to talk, his responses implied that he knew more than he was telling, and he was perhaps even *coached* with too much information. He took down Gadarchev's address to give Bekrenev.

He met with Erno Telubchev and Alexei Zacharov, both of whom also claimed to be friends of Oswald's and worked in the same department with him at the factory. They confirmed Gadarchev's story of KGB interest in Oswald. They also said that there were at least twenty co-workers and neighbors of the American who were recruited by the KGB to monitor his every move and to note every conversation with him.

Telubchev whispered to Sasha, "I was warned just yesterday not to *wag my tongue* to anybody asking questions about the American, Oswald, and that I should forget I ever knew him. A police agent also came to Department 25 at the factory and told all of those working there to forget that an American ever worked at the factory."

He was a little surprised that he was having such open conversations with these former acquaintances of Oswald, but then it was very clear that they also despised the secret police. On the other hand, they did not appear to be afraid of them either, even to the point of being defiant. They seemed to feel protected by the quasi-sovereignty of their government, even though Byelorussia had its own KGB, trained and closely monitored by Moscow. He retained the grim reminder of the taxi driver who tried to obey.

They described their opinion of Oswald at one point. "He was very frail and not very *macho* for an American Marine," they said. "We expected that such a man should be very large and tough. He was really quite meek, although he did have a quick temper if someone roused him, but he was not very big or strong, physically. To the contrary, very few believed his story about his military background. And, then when we heard that he might have been the one who killed the American President, WOW!" They all laughed.

Sasha asked about the gun that Oswald supposedly purchased.

"Yes, he bought a cheap shotgun, but to my knowledge he only went hunting with it one time," Telubchev replied. "Then he told me he sold it for about 18*R* to Oleg Voroshilov who works here. He also bought a camera, but I never saw him use it."

"Where do you think he got permission and the money to purchase these controlled and fairly expensive items?" Sasha asked.

"I don't know," Zacharov replied, "but he also liked to spend money on food and drink as well. He bragged about eating meat and drinking wine every night. We just assumed that, he was being *taken care of* by the secret police. We have many strange activities within our country, and nobody asks questions."

"He spent considerable money on vodka, beer and girls before he married Marina," Telubchev offered, "and after that he still seemed to have money to spend. I don't know where he got it."

Sasha returned to the shotgun and Oswald's shooting skills with another talkative factory worker who joined the conversation. He was Oleg Voroshilov, the physical training and activities director at the radio factory to whom Oswald sold his shotgun. Voroshilov told Sasha that they once held a shooting contest and Oswald participated. He had bragged about his U.S. Marine training in weapons.

"But," Voroshilov shrugged, "he couldn't shoot well at all. He was just fair at best. Many of our employees who never had training or ever owned a gun out shot him. He told us that he was just out of practice. I made him an offer for his gun, and he sold it to me. He was a curious fellow."

The subject then turned to Marina Prusakova and Oswald's marriage to the 19 year-old drugstore employee. Voroshilov said that one of Marina's friends had told that Marina was a licensed pharmacist. The others couldn't actually verify her professional qualifications, but each agreed that she was very likely much too young to be a professional. They seemed to know little else about her—only that Oswald had met her at a dance party in March, 1961, and married her two months later in May.

"Was she a KGB agent?" Sasha probed.

"Hmmmmm, that is a curious question, Comrade. I don't know, but I doubt it." Zacharov replied. "She was bright enough, but she didn't display the coyness of a secret police agent. You ask a good question, Comrade."

The others responded about the same, but left the question open, shrugging that they hadn't thought about it.

"Her uncle was an MVD senior official, a colonel," Sasha offered.

They each looked at one another, shrugged at the statement, and did not respond.

"Was Oswald recruited by the KGB?" he asked.

"If so, he played a good game of acting dumb," Voroshilov chuckled. "He couldn't shoot, and he wasn't very athletic. At least he demonstrated to us that he was not good at much of anything, including his working skills."

The others snickered in agreement.

"Was he faking his shooting and athletic skills?" Sasha shot back.

Again, each of them shrugged.

Sasha thanked the men for their openness with him. He promised to keep the meeting and their names confidential, although he was sure that his every move was being closely observed. He felt comforted by the GRU agents trailing him along with the trusted driver. He left the interrogation of the workers with as many questions as he had asked. He already had the benefit of the information provided him before he left Moscow regarding the apparent shortcuts that Oswald was provided easily getting into the Soviet Union, the attempted suicide and the granting of a residence permit to live in Minsk, as well as purchasing a gun.

Sasha considered the information he had garnered from the acquaintances of Oswald. The unanswered questions bugged him.

"Where did Oswald get the apparent abundance of rubles he freely spent? How was it that his request to marry the Byelorussian girl, Marina Prusakova, was approved immediately after it was submitted when the average time for such approvals is three months or more? This was a *mixed* marriage, in the eyes of Soviet authorities, with the approval delays lasting much longer, if granted at all. Did Marina Prusakova's uncle and MVD official intervene and assist in the process? Was Oswald sent to the Soviet Union by the CIA or some other American group to marry a Russian woman, return to the U.S., assassinate the president or some other senior official, and then discredit the USSR for his act if he were caught?"

"Or was he a KGB agent, recruited in the U.S., brought to the Soviet Union for further training and sent back to do the deed? If so, was the Prusakova girl introduced to him with the intent that they marry to provide a cover? What would either secret police agency have to gain from the U.S. president's death?"

He mulled over the questions as he instructed his driver to take him around the city for a while. It was snowing lightly, and he wanted some quiet time.

"The answer to any of these," Sasha thought, "might shed some light on the American's conduct and the assassination. But the most important question is: "*WHY* has the KGB attempted to foil my visit here? And why have they warned anyone associated with Oswald to keep quiet and to turn over any photos or other materials associated with him? Is it their traditional paranoia or are they deeply involved in this thing?"

Back at the GRU residence, Sasha reviewed the highlights of his two days of questioning Oswald acquaintances with Bekrenev. "Sir, these details are for you to pass on to General Tushenskiy and for your files should something happen to me along the way. I am going to maintain a cryptic log of my findings since I was instructed that I am not to conduct an investigation but rather an assessment."

Sasha continued, "I am still amazed with the cordial, actually extravagant, treatment accorded Oswald here in Minsk. I was told that he was given 800 Rubles a month as 'humanitarian aid' while he worked along side the average citizens, making less than that in their full salary. I'm also puzzled, as we briefly discussed, that he was given an apartment virtually on the day he arrived—an apartment that was well above the amenities of the average worker."

"You raise many questions, Comrade," Bekrenev nodded, "most of which will likely never be answered."

He concluded, "General, not one of those I spoke with believes for a second that this man Oswald that they knew was capable of killing the U.S. president."

Bekrenev shrugged and shook his head, apparently not wanting to pursue the subject further.

"So, that's it, Sir," Sasha concluded. "Here is a list of the names of each individual with whom I spoke."

Bekrenev scanned the list. "Spasee'ba, Sasha. Well done! I don't know how you got them to speak so freely, but you did and the information is revealing," he smiled.

"General, I really didn't find it too difficult for them to visit with me," Sasha said, wanting to continue the conversation. "In view of the heavy-handed tactics of our government and the KGB that are used all too often on the people of Minsk, I believe that they welcome a friendly hand." He smiled, "Even one from Moscow."

Bekrenev appeared to ignore Sasha's comment. "There is one name here that could raise a question, Sasha; that is Pytr Gadarchev. You say he was very talkative?"

"Dah, Gadarchev was especially open and volunteered considerable information about Oswald and seemed to enjoy that he had been threatened by the KGB not to talk about the American. Do you know something about him?"

"Dah, I am sure that he is the son of General Gadarchev, Soviet Army," Bekrenev said, "but I don't know that the coincidence means anything. I will try to pursue that relationship and situation, if any, further."

Bekrenev appeared to be pleased with Sasha's work and assured him that there was a way to let the KGB know that if any harm came to any one of the Byelorussians that had met with Sasha, he would see to it that Moscow would be duly informed.

"Dah, spasse'ba, General," Sasha smiled with approval. "Each of his co-workers with whom I spoke were very generous and open to discuss the *'peculiar American'* they called him. I would only hope that our KGB friends will back off and cooperate on behalf of all of us."

Bekrenev did not respond to Sasha's comment and changed the subject. "For security and safety reasons," he moved on, "we have booked you on an AEROFLOT flight that departs Minsk for Leningrad at 0940 tomorrow morning, but we are going to put you on a flight that departs at 0700. I don't think our *friends* would attempt to do anything else stupid, but I don't trust them either. So, if you agree with this plan, we will proceed."

"That's fine, Sir."

"Good. My deputy, my driver and two back-up agents will see you to the airport. My deputy will escort you to the flight, exercise our *Official Business* option and see you safely aboard. You will be met in Leningrad by Colonel Vladimir Denisov and escorted to the GRU *residence.* Your documents should all be completed and ready for your journey when you arrive."

"Now, tell me, Sasha," he continued, "we did not get around to the subject last evening, but I understand that you have spent some time in the United States. What is it like?"

Sasha was caught off guard. He didn't know how much Bekrenev knew. "Well . . . Yes, Sir, I did spend a few years in the U.S. I am sure, as you know; it is much different than Russia or any of our Soviet Republics. The United States is a very open and, I would characterize, a frivolous country. The Americans live in a land of plenty, so to speak, and they are very self-indulgent. They have been very successful in their economic growth since the Great Patriotic War, but they have many problems as well. Racial bias is a major problem. The black people, in particular, are in a state of unrest. American politicians believe that they can be the policemen of the world. Vietnam is becoming a good example of that, as was their over-reaction to the small uprising in Hungary seven years ago, and then, of course, Cuba. Americans, in general, are true idealists. They have disdain for our social order of government, but don't really know what to do about it except to arm themselves against the threat of our government or any other who might try to impose their way upon them. Their alternative to other forms of government is to attempt to impose their own. The assassination of their president, I believe, may be symptomatic of their problems," he paused . . . "unless, of course, *we* had a hand in that terrible event."

"And," Sasha concluded, "Americans are also very materialistic. They appear to be rich in things that we are not, but I choose to be here. I hope that you might go there one day, General, and see for yourself."

Bekrenev didn't pursue any further line of questioning, only adding occasional comments.

"Dah, that is a good summary. Thank you, Sasha. Get some rest, Comrade. It has been my pleasure to host you during your visit to Minsk. I wish you well on the continuation of your mission."

"Do'briy niche, General. Thank you for your hospitality and generous support. I hope to see you again soon."

Retribution

Maria Grechkovich shook her husband out of a deep sleep. "Sergei! Sergei! Wake up! Someone is outside in the hallway. They're trying to open our door!"

Sergei Grechkovich wrested himself from a deep sleep and groggily moved toward the outside door of their third floor apartment. It was not unusual for errant passersby's or drunks to roam around apartment buildings looking for either their own or opportune doors to open. Just as Grechkovich reached the doorway, there was a loud crash and the flimsy door fell inward on top of him. Before he could roll from beneath the shambled pieces of the door, two burly men in dark suits grabbed him by the arms and stood him up against the wall.

"Sergei! Sergei!" his wife screamed. "What is it? What happened?"

A third giant of a man made his way to the bedroom and scooped up Grechkovich's wife in his arms. "Quiet, *Gespazhah*! Shut your mouth!" he growled as he put a gloved hand over her mouth. He then dragged her into the small living room where the other two intruders had her husband pinned to the wall.

The apparent leader of the intruders, holding Grechkovich's arm in his grasp, spoke with a muted growl. "Comrade, you have committed a terrible crime against the people, and we have come to punish you. You were ordered not to talk to anyone about the foreigner who once lived in this building. Unfortunately, you have violated that trust. So, Comrade, '*As you make your bed, so you will sleep.*'"

He nodded to his partner who took a slender bottle of clear liquid from his coat pocket, removed the cap and thrust it into Grechkovich's mouth. He promptly spewed it out. "Vodka! I don't want vodka to drink. Please let us go! Don't harm us. We have done nothing wrong. Please!"

The perpetrator smiled and forcibly shoved the neck of the bottle back into Grechkovich's mouth while his partner held his head back with a fist full of hair. Two front teeth were shattered in the process and the unwilling victim gagged and choked as he tried to swallow the vodka flooding his throat. His eyes bulged out at the torture being forced upon him.

Maria Grechkovich tried desperately to wrench herself free, but her captor held her fast and stifled her cries with a tight grip over her mouth. The three operatives obviously took pleasure in their work and the struggle of the helpless pair.

When they had all but emptied the contents of the bottle of vodka into their victim, the two dragged Grechkovich to a window facing the street side of the apartment building. With approving nods between them, they flung him headlong through the closed window, shattering the glass and framework. As the dull thud of his body struck the pavement below, Maria Grechkovich muffled a scream and collapsed into a lifeless heap onto the floor.

Satisfied with their work, the KGB thugs walked casually out of the dingy apartment. A few doors along the hallway that were ajar with curious listeners quickly closed.

Back on the street, they surveyed the lifeless body of their victim, and the leader smiled and grunted. "Another patriot with too much vodka celebrating a good day's labor for our cause," he chuckled as they departed their conquest.

The work of the three wasn't finished for the night. They had planned and mapped out their work carefully, and drove to a late night tavern where they had surreptitiously arranged for a meeting with Erno Telubchev and Alexei Zacharov, two former Gorizant Radio Factory colleagues of the American.

One of the operatives went into the tavern, rendezvoused with Telubchev and Zacharov and lured them out with a fictitious offer to make some easy money via the black market. The trio drove the gullible duo to a vacant warehouse. Once inside, the two were forced out of the car at gunpoint and strapped into heavy wooden chairs. Wads of paper were forced into their mouths and held in place with cloth rags tied around their heads.

The lead KGB operative spoke. "Comrades, you are both very fortunate. You both have committed a crime against the State. You have consorted with a known foreign agent, and you have proceeded to openly discuss your relationship with the foreigner with a nosy troublemaker. We are not going to kill you for your acts; we are only going to punish you so that you will not forget so easily that your first allegiance is to the people and the State."

With that, the other two revealed automobile battery cables, which they had coiled in the pockets of their heavy coats. Battery cables became a preferred weapon of torture by KGB agents assigned to carry out retribution. The cables have a connector on each end, which makes for a no-slip grip on one end and a vicious impaling device on the other end.

"Comrades," one of them sneered, "you will remember where your loyalties lie."

With that two of them proceeded to pelt Telubchev and Zacharov with the deadly cables. Each blow dug deeply into the flesh of the backs, legs and necks of the two unfortunate victims.

The beatings ceased when both men were unconscious and blood oozed through their clothes from head to foot. The thugs removed the manacles and gags from the two and left them in the warehouse to be found severely beaten if not dead.

Their next stop was at a small apartment complex flat where Oleg Voroshilov lived. Without warning or fear of their activities being interrupted by the police or neighbors, they entered the grimy courtyard of the apartment complex and kicked open the door of the ground level three—room apartment. Just as their previous victims had been caught by surprise, so was Voroshilov. He lived alone so there was no wife or children to deal with. Two of them quickly dragged him out of bed.

"Comrade Voroshilov, you once worked with the American foreigner at the radio factory, did you not?" the apparent leader asked.

Voroshilov was still groggy, attempting to find his bearings and make sense of the situation. One of the intruders slapped him hard with a leather-gloved hand.

"Comrade, did you hear my question? Did you know the American who worked with you at your factory?"

"Dah . . . Dah . . ." His thoughts and words came slowly. "Dah . . . Yes, I worked with the American. What do you want with me?" he pleaded.

"Comrade, did you purchase a gun, a shotgun from him?" The leader asked.

Voroshilov paused, trying to provide a right response.

Finally . . . "Dah, I bought the gun from him. I paid him a fair price. It was a legal transaction."

"Comrade, you know that it is illegal to possess a weapon of any kind without proper authority," the leader challenged. "Where are your papers? Where is the gun now? Do you still have it?"

"Dah, I do. Do you wish to see it?" Voroshilov replied.

"Yes, Comrade, bring the gun to me."

The two holding his arms in their grip released him and followed him into the bedroom. He retrieved the well-worn shotgun from its hiding place in the closet and handed it to the leader.

He inspected the gun. "Do you have ammunition for this relic, Comrade?"

"Dah, I have a few shells for it, but I have not fired the gun since I bought it," Voroshilov responded.

"Please . . . bring me one of the ammunition shells, Comrade." The leader of the intruders ordered in a softer tone.

Again, Voroshilov turned back to the closet and took a single .12 gauge shotgun shell from a box on the shelf. The lead spokesman then handed him the gun. "Insert the shell in the gun, Comrade."

Voroshilov was now even more visibly unnerved at what was transpiring. He tried to stay calm and manage his fears, but he began to shake.

"Put the shell in the gun, Comrade!" his captor firmly ordered.

Voroshilov opened the breach of the single barrel shotgun and inserted the shell.

"Good! Good, Comrade! Now, place the barrel under your chin. Let us see if the shell is real or if you are trying to fool us!" The leader smiled.

Voroshilov realized now that he had only one chance to save himself. He stepped back quickly and pointed the gun at the closest one of the three and fired. The blast struck the heavyset intruder in the midsection of his body, tearing a jagged hole in his topcoat. The man screamed, grabbing his belly and fell to the floor. Voroshilov threw the shotgun at the other two and made a move toward the open door, but the skilled KGB agents responded too quickly. They both drew their pistols and fired, hitting their prey three times each in his back.

The leader of the group shrugged his shoulders and motioned for his other colleague to help him drag their partner out of the building. Once again, a few of the windows in the other apartments were illuminated with lights, but no one dared to venture out much less inquire about the commotion.

"Comrade Gadarchev, you are to be commended for your excellent work of informing us about the conduct of the meddling amateur agent from Moscow and those who succumbed to his practical joke questioning." The words were spoken by KGB Colonel Grigori Ostipov. "You will also be pleased to know that each of the traitorous fools has been well taken care of and some of them more than others," he smiled. "It is also very unfortunate that our American *student*, Oswald, got out of control. We could have used him much more effectively than the stupid act he committed. Perhaps we underestimated him? In any event, he has drawn too much attention to us, and we must bring this foolish and dangerous investigative pursuit by the GRU to a close. My colleagues will soon tighten the screws on Comrade Katsanov," he sneered.

Handing the informer a thick fold of rubles, Ostipov smiled. "Here is a small token of our appreciation for your excellent work. We will also ensure that your father is made aware of your continued loyalty to your government. Spasee'ba, Comrade."

Judas *friends*, betrayal, force and brutality were a natural part of the KGB *active measures* process to impose absolute control over their subjects. If they achieved their objectives, well and good, or if they occasionally lost one or more of their own in the process, so be it.

FIVE

*"There will be trouble if the
cobbler starts making pies!"*

A Russian Proverb

Leningrad

Sasha stepped off the AEROFLOT Tu-162 and walked through the entrance into the terminal building. He looked up as he entered the doorway to find himself directly facing Mackye.

"What on earth?" he exclaimed. "What are you doing here?" He pulled her to him and held her tightly. When he finally released her, he grinned. "You sure are full of surprises! How did you get here? How did you know that I would be here on this flight?"

Mackye gave him a wink and a giggle. "It is my business, Comrade, to know your every move," throwing her head back haughtily with a grin.

He looked at her freshness approvingly. She had let her long blonde silken hair down from the more severe chignon style that she often wore, as did most Soviet professional women. He took her by the hand and moved away from the entrance, and held her again.

"I am so glad to see you, Mackye!" Sasha grinned. "It has only been a few days, and it seems like a year! Tell me, what *are* you up to?"

"General Tushenskiy called me late yesterday," she said, "and told me that you were to arrive in Leningrad today. He asked if

I would like to visit you before you proceed on to other places. I screamed, YES!"

"But," he whispered to her, "I wasn't supposed to be on this flight. How did you know?"

At that point, Sasha noticed a man standing very near them.

Mackye followed his gaze and turned. "Oh, Sasha, this is Vladimir Denisov. He intercepted me when I arrived this morning and waited here with me for your flight arrival. Colonel Denisov is your escort while you're here in Leningrad."

Sasha held out his hand. "Do'broye oo'tra, Comrade! Thank you for looking after my wife and for meeting me."

"Welcome to Leningrad, Comrade. I would like for us to depart the terminal now. You are not even supposed to have arrived here yet."

In the car, Denisov explained that Sasha would be staying in Leningrad for three days before proceeding on to Helsinki.

"You and your wife will be our guests at the GRU *rezidentura*. It is very comfortable and secure. Your travel and identification documents are about ready. I will brief you on your travel plans later. General Kalinin, my chief, will want to meet with you when we first arrive. After that, if the weather permits, perhaps you and Mrs. Katsanov can enjoy an afternoon and evening out in our beautiful city."

"Thank you, Vladimir; we sincerely appreciate your hospitality."

Arriving at the GRU *residence*, a beautiful old building located in the heart of Leningrad, Sasha and Mackye were shown to their apartment on an upper floor. It was lavishly furnished in the Old Russian style with a large window overlooking the chilly Neva River which meanders through Leningrad.

"Sasha, this is grand! I did not know that you rated such special accommodations. I am impressed!" Mackye reacted in mock jest. "Now, Sir, would you please tell me what you are supposed to be doing on this secret mission that Tushenskiy has sent you? Where are you going from here? Did Vladimir say Helsinki? Can I go with you?"

Sasha smiled and teased, "Mackye, Mackye. You are not supposed to ask questions. You are not even supposed to be here.

I am surprised that Tushenskiy permitted you to do this. Yes, I am going to Helsinki and perhaps a few other places, and, no, you cannot go. Further, you are not to worry, and no more questions."

A rap on the door and Vladimir Denisov was there to escort Sasha to meet with General Kalinin.

"Welcome to Leningrad, Comrade Alexandr. I hope that our welcome here was better than that in Minsk?"

Sasha shook hands with the Leningrad GRU commander. "Spasee'ba, Sir, much better, and I want to thank you for permitting my wife to join me here. The accommodations are very pleasant."

Kalinin was sharply dressed in a dark Italian silk suit, white shirt and blue necktie. He was tall for a Russian, Sasha noted, with a slender build. His graying hair was neatly trimmed, and he wore steel framed eyeglasses. Sasha's agent training had long since taught him to promptly take in the physical characteristics, including gestures of everyone he met. This was a basic secret agent modus operandi which he continued to diligently practice.

"Our pleasure, Comrade," Kalinin smiled. "I hope you enjoy your stay. I have spoken with General Tushenskiy, of course, and he has briefed me on your assignment. I fully support his initiative, and we here in my office will provide you everything you need to proceed. These times are difficult enough without our becoming involved in something like that U.S. problem. I hope that we are clear on that. Was your stopover in Minsk productive?"

"Yes, General, I believe that it was," Sasha replied. "I found the Byelorussian people very cooperative, even though the ones I met with had been heavily warned by the KGB to forget they ever knew the American, Oswald. The Minsk police were surprisingly cordial. The former acquaintances of the American were very open, perhaps too much so. I even wondered if some of them might have been prompted to feed me some garbage, but after I put it all together, I believe that I received a pretty good picture of the American's activities while he lived there. Our KGB friends, of course, were not very cooperative, to say the least."

"They are murderous thugs, General," Sasha continued. "I am sure that they killed or at least badly injured the taxi driver they set up to meet me at the airport. It was my fault that he failed to carry out their welcome for me, but I had no choice."

"Don't fret, Comrade. You may have saved your own life. They might have only intended to frighten you, but if you had resisted, they could have even killed you and disposed of your remains. Some of them carry their duties to the worst extreme and take great pleasure in doing it, even to our own people."

Kalinin paused . . . "Comrade Sasha, in that regard, I received a call from General Bekrenev. I have some unpleasant news regarding your visit in Minsk. Three of the Byelorussian factory workers that you spoke with and a former neighbor, I believe, of the American were paid a visit by the KGB after you departed. A man named Telubchev and one by the name of Zacharov were severely beaten and left for dead by their thugs. Both men will likely survive, but they will remember their misdeed of speaking with you. Another of those with whom you spoke, a man named Voroshilov, was killed. He was shot several times in the back. The fourth fellow, a man by the name of Grechkovich, the neighbor, I believe, is critically injured. They apparently rushed his apartment in the early hours of darkness and pushed him out of his third floor window. His wife was unharmed. I am sorry, Comrade. General Bekrenev also sends his regrets and cautions you not to take any responsibility for these unfortunate events unto yourself."

Sasha sank back into his chair, stunned. "The filthy bastards!" he murmured aloud. Sasha had once admonished himself for the use of vulgar descriptions and characterizations, even about the KGB, but over the year since he had arrived back in Moscow, the more he was exposed to their conduct, the more difficult it was to contain his animosity.

He was visibly shaken and furious. "They couldn't get to me so easily so they took out their vengeance on those poor miserable workers. Where does this all end? When will we find civility in this country? Has our government lost its focus and direction? I am ashamed and embarrassed!"

He jumped to his feet and walked around the room, banging his fist in his hand. "Has General Tushenskiy been informed of this? I know that he will go directly to Kashevarov and have it out with him! This is just too much!"

Kalinin held up his hand and beckoned Sasha to return to his chair. "I am sure that General Bekrenev gave him a full report on the events and the circumstances, Comrade. While you are still our guest here in Leningrad, I will speak personally with Bekrenev again and the Director General to determine what action has possibly been taken."

Kalinin poured vodka into two glasses as Sasha thought to himself, "Toying with me, indeed. They are getting more pleasure out of brutalizing those I make contact with than to attack me directly. Rotten bastards!"

"Salut, Comrade." Kalinin held up his glass. "I regret that your arrival here is greeted with such unfortunate news. We cannot always choose our destiny. Our government is authoritarian. We cannot change that, but I often regret that our system does not encourage genuine concern or love on the part of our rulers, not only for themselves and those around them, but especially for our people and all our neighboring people as well. Peace be with those who tried in good faith to assist you."

Sasha raised his glass. "Salut, Comrade General. Spasee'ba."

"Since the American apparently didn't spend any time in Leningrad," Kalinin offered as he sipped his vodka, "I suppose my main task is to see you safely out of our city and on to Helsinki. Is that correct?"

"Dah, General. I will need your support to get passage through the immigration people in Finland and the documents to cover me thereafter," Sasha replied.

He continued to seethe as the impact of fate of the people in Minsk cast a dark cloud over him. Then he thought about the name of one of them that hadn't been discussed. "Sir, did General Bekrenev mention the name Gadarchev to you when he reported the incidents in Minsk?"

"Nyet, he did not," Kalinin replied. "Did you also speak with that man while you were there?"

"Dah, Gadarchev told me that he was a good friend of the American, Oswald, and he was very open in his discussions about him, but curiously, he knew little or nothing about his new wife. General Bekrenev replied that he thought Gadarchev was the son of a Soviet general. Is that name familiar to you?"

"Nyet, but there are so many generals in our Army that I do not know all of them by name. It is strange though that his name was not mentioned. I will inquire about Gadarchev when I speak to Bekrenev. Hmmmm, I wonder if *he* received a *pass* because of his fortunate birthright. I will let you know what I find out."

"Now, to your schedule," Kalinin continued, "Your journey is fairly straightforward from here," he said. "Since you are fluent in English and have a good understanding of American customs, we are going to outfit you with a United States passport, a visitor's visa for Russia with all of the inclusive immigration stamps affixed that you collected along your route from the U.S., through London, to Finland. You are a returning businessman who has been marketing commercial communications equipment. You will be provided identification cards, equipment brochures and so on. We will also issue you sufficient currency, a credit card and airline tickets to get you through Europe and on to the U.S. What else do you require?"

"Sir, I believe that you have sufficiently covered everything," Sasha nodded. "When do I depart?"

"In two days," Kalinin said. "Take some time to be with your wife. Study the product materials we provided you so that you know your business. Review the latest news magazines from America in your apartment, and rest up for your journey."

There was a knock on the door and Colonel Denisov asked to come in. "Sir, sorry to interrupt you, but I thought you would find it interesting that the later AEROFLOT flight that Comrade Alexandr was officially scheduled to take from Minsk encountered *engine problems* and had to land at an airfield near Ostrov."

"Well! That is interesting!" General Kalinin sat up in his chair. "Ostrov is a very remote airport. Why would they divert there? I can't believe that they really thought our guest here was on that plane. Surely they monitored its departure and the passenger list. But . . . Ahhh! I would wager that our Minsk office left Comrade Katsanov's name on the later manifest list right on through departure."

Kalinin roared with laughter. "What a joke if they had that flight diverted in order to make another pass at you, Comrade! You are very popular with our KGB friends. Better watch your step! They don't like to be foiled, and you have accomplished that twice in just a few days!"

Kalinin continued to enjoy the moment. "Vladimir, this calls for a toast to our special guest! Please join us."

Sasha and his two hosts enjoyed two more rounds of vodka to top off the afternoon and celebrate the KGB's vacuous efforts, but the cheerful respite did not erase Sasha's thoughts of the fate of the Byelorussian workers.

The two days in Leningrad with Mackye were enjoyable and passed too quickly. He reluctantly shared with her what had happened to the men in Minsk. It sickened him to think about the atrocities, much less to tell Mackye about how they were brutalized by the KGB operatives. "Our *own* people!" he repeated more than several times.

He lamented, "Mackye, I quite often become discouraged with the strange tension between order and disorder in our country, between a superficial layer of control and a much deeper, darker and sinister element that churns silently beneath the surface. I wonder where we are really headed. Who is really in charge? There are so many enemies within that are of our own making."

Mackye expressed regret for the suffering of the good men in Minsk but remained the devoted and obedient communist servant and refused to even doubt the motives of her government.

Helsinki

Sasha bade Mackye goodbye, put her on a flight back to Moscow, and departed with his new identity on the short flight across the Gulf of Finland to Helsinki. Clearing immigration without difficulty, Sasha moved on into the airport waiting area.

"Mr. Scott? Welcome to Helsinki."

Sasha turned abruptly at the sound of English and his new identity.

"Yes, I'm Michael Scott, Thank you."

The stranger held out his hand. "Mr. Scott, I'm Christian Svendson."

"Nice to meet you, Mr. Svendson." The two shook hands.

"I see you are carrying a bag. Do you have any other checked luggage?" Svendson asked.

Sasha shook his head. "No, this is it."

"Come then, I have a car waiting."

Once inside the back seat of the car, Svendson indicated for the driver, Olaf, to depart.

"Good to meet you, Comrade. I am assigned to the Helsinki GRU office. You may be surprised that I am a Dane living here and working for your government, but my allegiance is to the Supreme Soviet. Your government has been good to my family and me, and I am grateful. One day, the Soviet way of life will rule the world."

Sasha was a little surprised by his Helsinki greeter and was guarded. He had already encountered too many startling events since he began his mission. "Do you have a code word to share with me, Comrade?"

Svendson chuckled. "The sky is *blue* today, Comrade, and you?"

Sasha responded. "It is *blue*, but it may turn *red* at sunset."

Svendson patted Sasha on the shoulder. "All is well, Comrade. I will see to your needs in Helsinki. Have you been to my city before?"

He observed Svendson to be in his early forties, blond and blue-eyed. His full head of hair was loosely brushed over a smaller head. He had a relaxed and friendly demeanor, unhurried.

"No, I haven't," Sasha replied, "but I have heard many good things about Helsinki and the Finnish people."

"Comrade, in accordance with your request, we have made arrangements for you to stay at the Hotel Torni where the American, Oswald, allegedly stayed while he was here. As you might suspect, it isn't one of our best hotels. Mostly vagabonds and lower class people stay there. How many days do you believe you will be in Helsinki?"

"No more than two days," replied Sasha. "That should be sufficient to conduct my business. How friendly are the KGB people at the consulate?"

"Oh, they run hot and cold. We never know what to expect from them. Do you want to visit the consulate?"

"Yes, I think I should go there first. I don't want to rattle their cage unnecessarily by making them anymore paranoid about my presence here if I can avoid it. Can we go there now?"

"Yes, we can. I will introduce you to my contact there. I think he is a colonel, who knows? He is always in the same baggy wool suit. But he is, as I would imagine, a KGB colonel, strident and arrogant. His name is Vilkov, Ivan Vilkov. We share a few vodkas and stories occasionally. He is mostly okay, just always suspicious of everyone and everything, I think even me!" he smiled. "Olaf, slight change of plans, take us to the Soviet Consulate."

The driver nodded in acknowledgement.

Sasha introduced himself and advised the KGB officer that he was on an informal inquiry visit to Helsinki. He made no secret that his office in Moscow had an official interest in the assassination of the American president and the possible connection with the American Oswald's stay in the Soviet Union.

"I would like to ask a few questions if I may?"

"Dah, Comrade," the KGB officer responded. "Come and be seated. We always welcome the opportunity to discuss business with our GRU friends. How can we help you?"

"Spasee'ba, Tavah'reeshch." Sasha, sensing a false tenor in the officer's cordial responses, nevertheless addressed him warmly. Vilkov shrugged and turned away from Sasha.

"Comrade, I will get directly to the point that concerns my director," Sasha began. "How is it that the American, Oswald, was able to secure a tourist visa to Moscow in just two days when the normal processing time usually takes up to ten days? How could your people have possibly conducted a proper background check in such a short time?"

"Comrade Katsanov, or shall I address you as *Mr. Scott*?" Vilkov countered.

Sasha was surprised by the fact that the KGB was already aware of his assumed identity name and was put off slightly by the arrogant response.

"*Katsanov* is fine for this meeting, Comrade," Sasha curtly replied.

"Fine, Comrade," Vilkov smiled. "First, I will advise you that I do not have a requirement to share any information regarding our

65

operations with you. But in the interest of our common purposes, permit me to inform you that many of our investigations are held in strict confidence, even to the GRU. In general, let me assure you that we always conduct thorough background checks on foreign visitors, and we never permit a visa to be issued until we are sure of an individual's reasonable credibility and intentions. In the case of this man, *Ozvald,* our people calculated him to be a run-of-the-mill American ne'er do well who wanted to visit our great country. We had no prior file on him, so there was no reason to hold up a visa for him for a brief six-day visit. We never want to offend harmless people who wish to visit our fine cities. This was merely routine for such a benign visitor. Does that satisfy you?"

"Comrade, I find it highly questionable that your efficient system of screening visitors would simply ignore *anyone,* especially an American and a former U.S. Marine, just because *someone* here decided that he was a casual tourist?" Sasha responded and continued. "This *run-of-the-mill ne'er do well,* as you have characterized him, was arrested and accused of assassinating the President of the United States, and now he has been murdered while in the hands of the American police. Does it now appear that he was *just a run-of-the-mill vagrant?"*

"Comrade Katsanov, we do not advise your agency on how to conduct their affairs, so we do not expect you to presume to advise us. Do you have any further questions?"

Sasha probed further. "Did you monitor his stay in Helsinki after he applied for the visa? Since the news of the assassination, and now that it is known around the world that this man lived in our country for almost three years, have you accomplished any further investigation of his stay here in Helsinki? Did he make any contacts while he was here?"

"Comrade, I have told you all that you need to know," Vilkov replied curtly. "His brief transient stay here was not unusual. We have no case here with this man. I suggest that you contact our headquarters in Moscow if you wish to continue pursuit of this issue. If you are finished, I have important work to accomplish. And remember, Comrade, *'There is often trouble if the cobbler starts making pies'!* You would be wise to concern yourself with your own trade and not engage in that of others."

Sasha and Svendson departed the consulate.

"Well, Mr. Svendson, that was informative, was it not?" Sasha said smiling.

"Not unexpected, Comrade," Svendson replied. "To say the least, our KGB friends are arrogant. They do not like to be questioned. They believe that only *they* can ask questions, but I think you did a good job of putting him on the spot. Where to now, Comrade?"

"Mr. Svendson, how did he know my assumed identity?"

"Sir, I don't know. That surprised me as well. I never under estimate them. Do you wish to go to the hotel now? Also, would you like to join me for dinner?" Svendson asked.

"Yes, dinner will be fine," Sasha replied. "Why don't we drop by the Hotel Torni first? I will check in and leave my bag."

Sasha registered and asked to see the hotel manager.

"Sir, I am Michael Scott from the United States. I am a journalist. May I ask you some questions about a guest who stayed here several years ago?"

"Yes, you may, Sir," the manager offered. "How can I help you?"

"Does your hotel register indicate that an American named Oswald stayed here in your hotel during October 1959? Specifically, I believe he stayed here five days, from the 10th through the 14th, and departed on the 15th of October 1959. Would your register reflect this?" Sasha asked.

"Sir, we had a visit by the police just two days ago, and they took our register for that period of time with them," the manager promptly replied. "I am sorry I cannot help you with that. Is there anything else I can assist you with?"

"Were these the local police who took the register?" Sasha asked.

"Yes, they were Helsinki detectives in civilian clothes," the manager answered.

Sasha knew without question, they were KGB operatives, or at least they were behind the Helsinki police's interest in Oswald's record of staying at the hotel. Otherwise, the local police would have no interest in the transient American.

"Do you remember the American in question?" Sasha asked.

"No, Sir. I do not. We have hundreds of foreigners who stay in our hotel every year," the manager replied.

SIX

"Cut down the tree that you are able."

A Russian Proverb

Close Call

Mackye moved along with the other passengers debarking at Sheremetevo II airport from Leningrad.

"Gaspazhah Katsanov, I am Anatoli Rubanov. This is Igor Yakushev. We were sent to escort you to your apartment."

She was startled by the sudden appearance of the two dark-suited men. "Who sent you?" she asked. "I was not expecting anyone to meet me. How did you know me and my name?"

"Madame, your administrator sent us to make sure you are safely seen to your home. Do you have a bag to collect?"

"Who is my administrator?" Mackye asked again, bluntly.

"We do not know him by name, Madame Katsanov. My supervisor instructed us to meet you and to escort you safely to your apartment." Rubanov replied.

Mackye quickly responded. "Yes, I have a bag to collect at the carousel, but I must visit the *tooal'et* first. Sorry. I will meet you there."

Before Rubanov, the one obviously in charge, could respond, she made her way boldly toward a ladies' room. Spotting a telephone near the entrance, she stopped, fed it a handful of kopecs and dialed the main operator at Khodinka.

"Ring me General Tushenskiy's office immediately," she quickly blurted. "This is Colonel Katsanov's wife. It is extremely important!"

Tushenskiy came on the line. "Mackye, is that you? Are you back in Moscow? How was Leningrad?"

"General, I am so sorry to intrude in your day," Mackye rushed her words for fear of being interrupted by her intruders. "Yes, General, I just arrived at Sheremetevo II from Leningrad and was met by two suspicious men who told me that they were directed to meet me and to escort me to my apartment. I know that my office would not send anyone. Are they your people?"

"No! Mackye, they are not my people!" Tushenskiy quickly replied. "Where are they now? Where are you?"

"I am at a telephone near the ladies' *tooal'et,*" she quickly replied. "One of them is watching me, and the other is standing near the baggage carousel. General, I am so sorry to bother you, but I am frightened of these people and did not know who else to call."

"Mackye, go into the ladies' room and stay there. Do not come out for any reason. Make a nasty scene if you must, but do not leave that facility until someone from my office identifies herself to you. Now, quickly go in there and stay."

Mackye acted as if she were having an animated conversation with a friend, laughed out loud a few times, then waved to Rubanov as she vanished into the *tooal'et.*

After an extended wait, the two became impatient. Rubanov then instructed his partner, Yukashev, to go into the *tooal'et* and see about Mackye.

As he reluctantly approached the entrance, a uniformed policeman suddenly appeared and blocked his way. "Nyet, Comrade, this is for females only. Your facility is down there."

"But my wife is in there, and she has been there for quite some time," Yukashev pleaded.

"Please, Sir. I will call for an attendant to see about your wife." The policeman used his mobile radio and summoned for support.

Six uniformed policeman responded and took the surprised Yukashev and Rubanov, who was standing some distance away, by their arms and placed them against a wall to search them.

Rubanov began cursing. "You idiots, we are special agents working on a case. Release us immediately. Here is my identification."

The police officer in charge inspected the KGB identification cards of the two. "We are sorry for this intrusion, Comrades. Please come to my office and we will straighten this out."

"But we cannot leave this area of the airport. We are monitoring a suspect," Rubanov pleaded.

"Sir, I am sorry for the inconvenience, but my instructions are to escort you to my office," the policeman in charge replied. "Come with us."

Rubakov and Yakushev, surrounded by the stern-looking police entourage, sighed as they were escorted away.

"Madame Katsanov," a voiced summoned from the entrance to the ladies' room. "I am Irina Popov from General Tushenskiy's office."

"I am here," Mackye replied from within one of the booths.

"Are you all right?" Irina asked, entering the room. "Here are my credentials. I am here to escort you to your apartment, and General Tushenskiy says that if you agree, would you collect some clothing and personal items and come be our guest at Khodinka for a few days?"

Mackye was still unnerved by the experience, but she readily agreed to go with her escort. "Yes, I think I will be pleased to stay at Khodinka if the General believes that it is best to do so."

Hotel Torni

Sasha looked around the seedy lobby and, for a moment, wondered if he should even stay in the old run-down hotel now that there wasn't much, if any, information to be collected. He finally decided that he would stay anyway.

Svendson took him to a fine restaurant where they enjoyed a pleasant dinner of reindeer steak with all the vegetable trimmings and Finnish beer. Afterward, Svendson dropped him off back at the hotel and they made arrangements for him to be picked up for breakfast at 8:00 a.m.

Sasha was tired. It had been a long day and he promptly fell asleep.

He couldn't get his bearings at first. Finally, fully awake, he focused on the shrill buzzing noise coming from the hallway. He grabbed the phone when it rang.

"Sir, sorry to disturb you," the voice urged. "We have a fire alarm. You must vacate your room immediately. Please use the stairway. The elevator is not operating. Please hurry, and come to the lobby."

Sasha quickly put on his trousers and sweater, grabbed his topcoat and valise, and departed the room. He joined other guests as they shuffled down the four flights to the lobby level.

"Please, everyone, outside immediately! Everyone must vacate the building!" A voice announced over a bullhorn, first in Danish, then Russian, and then in English.

The night was cold, and the hotel guests stood shivering across the street from the hotel while firemen and employees ran in and out of the building.

Finally, a fireman stepped over to the group and shouted in what he recognized as Finnish. "All clear!" he said. "There is no fire, just a false alarm. You may return to your rooms. We regret the inconvenience."

Sasha couldn't make out everything that was being said, but the grumbling and movement of the vacated hotel guests made it clear what was happening. He also picked up bits from different guests speaking in Russian and English as they all moved back toward the hotel.

Just as he reached the entrance, a voice behind him whispered in husky Russian, "Comrade, if you are wise you will return to Moscow promptly!" He turned quickly to face the *messenger,* but he had disappeared into the crowd closing in behind.

He bypassed the crowded elevator and climbed quickly up the stairway. The intuitive feeling he had as he made his way down the hall was confirmed when he saw the door to his room standing fully open. The room was dark and he stumbled over a chair and other unidentifiable objects as he fumbled for a light switch or lamp.

"Those filthy bastards!" He turned on the overhead light. "Fire alarm, my ass! That was all for me!"

The room had been thoroughly ransacked. The bed was turned upside down, desk was turned over, lamps were smashed and his clothes ripped to shreds and scattered across the room. They had destroyed everything that he had brought with him, including his suitcase. A single mirror on the wall above the toppled dresser reflected a crude message in paint or lipstick:

GO HOME FILTHY AMERIKIN!

"The clumsy idiots can't even spell," he smirked as he surveyed the damage. "The whole thing was a sham. They weren't targeting an *American*, they were after me. The message is just a cover-up."

Fortunately, he had taken his valise which contained his U.S. passport, Tushenskiy's letter, his revolver and his money.

He went back downstairs and reported the situation to the night manager who insisted on calling the police. Two hours later after a thorough, but innocuous meeting with the Helsinki police, he finally settled into another room for a few hours rest. Sleep was out of the question.

Svendson had given him his home phone number the night before, and shortly after daybreak, he called and told him about the night's event.

Svendson arrived shortly thereafter. "Comrade, I can't believe this! Are you sure that whoever did this did not believe that you were an American?"

"No, they know who I am!" Sasha angrily replied. "Look, let's forget it. I need to get outfitted in clothes. Do you know where I can get taken care of today?"

"Yes, Comrade, we will take care of that immediately. At least, you were able to keep your warm coat."

"Yes, you might say I was fortunate in many ways. I am going to check out of this place and take you up on staying at the GRU house until I leave." Sasha proceeded to the checkout counter to settle his account.

"Ah, Mr. Scott, I have a message for you. Here." The clerk handed him an envelope.

Sasha opened the envelope, looked inside and read the message roughly scribbled in English: *"Is your wife also safe, Comrade?"*

He froze and summoned Svendson. "Get me to the *rezidentura* immediately! I must call Moscow."

Sasha was escorted to the Communications Room at the GRU residence house.

He was put through immediately. "General Tushenskiy, please." His voice was tense.

"Sasha! Good to hear your voice," Tushenskiy answered. "Is all well with you? I was going to call you later this morning."

"Sir, I received a disturbing message at my hotel this morning." Sasha read the note, "and I wanted to determine if there is a problem."

"Sasha, there was a minor incident yesterday when Mackye arrived back in Moscow," Tushenskiy replied, "but it is under control now."

Tushenskiy described the airport incident with the KGB agents. "Sasha, I have provided Mackye with an apartment here at Khodinka. She will be safe in our care, and I will see that she is escorted to her place of work. She will also have protection throughout the day until she is safely back here each evening. Sasha, I apologize for all of this. I continue to underestimate their devious character. I have already had a serious conversation with Kashevarov about the unfortunate events in Minsk. He is on warning, and I have a meeting with him today regarding the incident with Mackye. Now, how about you? Are you okay?"

Sasha briefly described his night at the hotel.

Tushenskiy was livid. "Sasha, I am going to call this whole thing off! I want you to catch a flight back to Moscow today!"

"Sir, I had rather not," Sasha replied. "If Mackye is safe, and I know that she will be in your care, I want to proceed. There is something very mysterious about all of these interventions we are encountering from our friends at Lubiyanka. I would like to try to determine what is going on with all of this. I have not been directly life-threatened, only harassed. If it gets worse, I will advise you. Is there any additional news on the assassination situation that I should know?"

"No, Sasha," Tushenskiy responded. "You will undoubtedly be collecting much more the farther west you travel. If you wish to continue, go ahead, but if at anytime you feel bodily threatened, call a halt to your travels and come home. Do you understand?"

"Yes, General," Sasha replied. "I will be cautious and keep you apprised."

"Comrade," Tushenskiy continued, *"'Only cut down the tree that you are able to.'* Don't undertake more than you are able to manage. I will advise Mackye that you are well and safe. You, my friend, make certain you stay that way. *Da sveedah'neeya, Tavah'reeshch!*"

"Da sveedah'neeya, General."

Sasha hung up, knowing full well that the KGB had monitored their conversation.

SEVEN

*"Stormy weather cannot stay all the time; the red sun
will come out soon."*

A Russian Proverb

New York

As the Trans World Boeing 707 glided down through the clouds, Sasha could make out the skyline of New York City through the intermittent haze. When the aircraft finally pulled up to the parking stub at Idlewild International Airport, he began to feel stirrings of anxiety. He clearly remembered the first time that he arrived in the United States . . . ten years before. He remembered how tentative, but youthfully confident he was . . . fresh out of GRU training and fully prepared to take on the assignment that had been handed him. This time it was much different. He didn't have the same feeling of self-confidence. Somehow there was an aura of sinister darkness that was shadowing him . . . a darkness that was being cast by some of his *own* people.

He had walked the aisle of the jet airliner several times during the flight from London, attempting to look into every face for the sign of a KGB agent *giveaway* expression.

"Now, I'm afflicted with the paranoia bug!" he chided himself.

He had not detected anyone of suspicion on the plane, but he felt sure that *they* were somewhere about. Too much had already happened in such a short period of his journey. They wouldn't give up so easily on deflecting his mission, if they really didn't want him to continue.

"But, why?" he asked himself over and over. "If the KGB or some other agency in our government wasn't involved in this assassination or has some knowledge of it, then *why* are they trying to harass me into backing out? Maybe it's just embarrassment over the handling of the whole Oswald affair . . . after all permitting him to roam freely around the Soviet Union for three years! That in itself is incredibly bizarre . . . unless they were *managing* the situation."

The plane came to a complete stop and the passengers began to collect their belongings.

"Well," he murmured, "here *we go!*"

Once inside the terminal, the familiar queues of people lining up to go through the immigration and custom checks brought back old memories. He had his passport and a briefcase filled with product brochures reflecting the nature of his *business* travels. He was ready to re-enter familiar territory.

He confidently handed his passport to the immigration officer. "Welcome home, Mr. Scott. Let's see. You have been out of the United States for two weeks . . . Helsinki and London; business or vacation?"

"Business," Sasha replied firmly.

"Good, thank you. You may proceed to Customs after you collect your luggage."

Feeling more confident, he moved on to the baggage carousel and collected his single suitcase. After passing through the customs inspection, he was about to proceed to his designated rendezvous point to await his contact when he was suddenly confronted. "Mr. Scott?" one of the two men inquired.

"Yes?" Sasha responded.

"Mr. Scott," one of the men spoke. "We are with U.S. Customs and are required to make random inquiries of arriving business passengers."

Both men flashed badges secured in black leather folding wallets.

"Would you mind answering a few routine questions regarding your overseas travel?" the one apparently in charge asked.

"No, not at all," Sasha replied casually, but with an instant uneasy feeling about this sudden encounter.

"Good. Would you please come with us? It will only take a few minutes and you can be on your way," the spokesman beckoned him.

He followed the two into a nearby office off the corridor of the terminal. Inside everything appeared normal, a desk, lamp, four office chairs, the usual. But as he was about to take a seat in the chair to which he was motioned, he heard the distinct "*Snap!*" of the door being locked from the inside. He didn't react and continued to eye his two new acquaintances.

"This could still be on the up and up," he tried to reassure himself.

The spokesman of the two proceeded, "Please take a seat, Mr. Scott, and tell us where all you have traveled during your trip."

"Just London and Helsinki," Sasha responded.

"Did you happen to cross over to Leningrad while you were in Helsinki?" he asked.

"Well, yes, I did for one day," Sasha replied. "That visit is reflected in my passport along with my Russian visa."

"What is the nature of your business, Mr. Scott?" he was asked.

"I am with a communications-electronics firm. I was investigating some new and innovative technologies with the Nokia Company in Helsinki. If they get the high-speed communications technology perfected, then we may want to import their products to the United States. Would you like more detail?" Sasha explained.

He was prepared to *practice* all that he had quickly learned in Leningrad and studied along his flight.

The spokesman smiled, "No, *Comrade Katsanov*, we already know very much about your fictitious business, where you have been and where you plan to go."

Surprised at the sudden turn of events, but no longer shocked by such intrusions, Sasha felt trapped and glanced at the only door leading out of the small room. He didn't respond to the statement, only stared back at the two.

"Comrade Katsanov, welcome to the United States." The spokesman's words were firm. "We are here to make sure that you understand the *rules of the game* during your visit. First, our Chief does not believe that you have any legitimate business here, and he asked us to encourage you to return to Moscow."

Sasha suddenly stood up, pulled up his full six feet and two inch frame, and looked down into the eyes of the much shorter agent who was acting as the leader. "Comrades, your *Chief* knows full well why I am here and that I have official business to conduct for our government. So, I suggest that you unlock that door, and I will be on my way."

"Ho, Ho! Our comrade is a brave fool, Igor. Now, you listen to me, Comrade," the speaker replied, looking up at Sasha. "You have been warned for the last time. You have no business in the United States. This is KGB territory, and I should remind you once more, you left a very attractive wife back in Moscow . . . perhaps you had better return to her while you are free to do so and she remains safe."

Sasha lurched toward the agent, then quickly drew up short simultaneously pulling his revolver out of the inside holster in his valise. He dropped the valise and snatched the lapel of the operative who was speaking, pushing the barrel of the *Graz Burya* into the side of his neck. "Now, Comrade, would you like to repeat your warning to me about my wife?" he urged in a loud whisper.

The other agent stood by the door, silent and bewildered.

"Please, Comrade," the leader of the two in Sasha's clutch and the pistol at his throat, begged, "we meant you no harm, we were just sent here to advise you that it is not safe for you in the United States. Please, put the gun away before the police discover us."

Sasha released his grip, shoved him against the desk without speaking and turned sharply toward the door. He felt sure that they wouldn't further risk creating a scene. The once brave spokesman leaned against the desk and nodded for his colleague to open the door. Sasha departed without further exchange and headed in the direction of the waiting area. He moved at a measured pace and did not look back. He was unnerved by the incident and more so angry, but tried to remain calm.

"Again, they have threatened my wife," he murmured to himself, "but she is safe with Tushenskiy looking after her."

He took a seat near one of the terminal exit doors and opened a *TIME Magazine*, as he had been directed, fully exposing the outer cover.

A young woman sat down next to him. "Greetings, Comrade," she offered in a softly whispered voice. "You are late arriving here from your flight. Were you detained?"

The voice was persistent as her perfumed fragrance filled the air around him. He lowered his magazine and looked into the deep blue eyes of the very attractive auburn-haired female facing him.

"It is a very *warm* day for November, Mr. Scott," she offered.

"Yes, it is, but December should bring *much cooler* days," he replied.

He was still not sure of his greeter. *"Stormy weather cannot stay all the time,"* he offered further.

The woman smiled, *"But the red sun will come out soon.* Shall we go?"

Cautiously satisfied, Sasha looked about, did not see any signs of the two who had intercepted him and, without speaking further, followed the attractive and prim young woman out of the terminal. He couldn't help noticing that she was tall, slender and very well-dressed.

Outside the terminal, he breathed deeply. It *was* a pleasant evening for New York in November. The air was fresh and cool, and the stars shown dimly through the haze. The weather *was* much warmer than he had expected.

A car and driver were waiting; once inside the automobile, she said, "I am Paulette, Mr. Scott, I prefer to be called by my native name . . . *Tatyana,* but I must remain '*Paulette*' while I am in this country. Do you prefer to be addressed formally, or may I call you *Sasha*?"

He was surprised to hear the same name as his mother, *Tatyana,* spoken and for that matter, his *own.*

"I am very pleased to meet you, Tatyana, or Paulette," he smiled. "Tatyana is also my mother's given name. It's a beautiful name. I am surprised to have such an attractive agent to meet me. And, you may call me Sasha," he replied, "in private, of course," still a bit wary.

"Valori, this is Comrade Katsanov," she interrupted, introducing the driver. "Please move along cautiously and vigilant for awhile; we are in no hurry and don't need any company this evening.

"Dah," Valori nodded, glancing back at Sasha.

Sasha then briefly described the incident with the two who intercepted him in the airport, skipping over the details; to which she smiled and shrugged, "They are among us, Comrade."

Returning to his visit, Sasha asked, "When do I go on to Washington?"

Ignoring his question, Paulette wanting to know more about his encounter, asked, "Comrade Katsanov . . . Sasha, what did they say to you back in the terminal? Were you threatened?"

"Yes, they did advise me not to stay here but to return to Moscow," he replied. "I let my guard down," he smirked. "They fooled me with their professional dress, demeanor and false credentials. The apparent leader of the two spoke flawless English. I was impressed!"

"*Bastards*! *Scum*!" Paulette responded. "They crawl around everywhere in this country as if it were their own! We must wonder if our enemies move so freely around our own country. Well, at any rate, we thought that your arrival would go unnoticed, but they have ways of intercepting every communication we receive or send. But, they also *own* the communication systems which we rely upon. So, it is no wonder. Are you alright? Did they frighten you?"

"No, Paulette, they didn't frighten me as compared to some other experiences I've had with their thugs; I'm just embarrassed by being taken in so easily. They made the usual threats for me to go back home or to suffer the consequences. I'm not worried about them personally. I think I scared the hell out of 'em, at least momentarily, but I would like to report the incident to my superior back at Khodinka . . . because they also threatened my wife who is there. Is there a secure way to communicate a message back to Moscow?"

"Not from the New York area, Comrade," she replied. "The KGB owns all of our communications in this city. But," she said, "You can make contact from Washington. The GRU has its own coded Teletype and radiophone systems in the *rezidentura* there. I will travel with you by train to Washington whenever you are ready. We have set aside the remainder of this evening for you to rest here in our residence house. Are these plans agreeable with you?"

"Yes, they are fine," he replied. "I can use the rest, but I *am* also anxious to contact Moscow as soon as we can."

"Did the immigration authorities question you? I was very concerned that you might not even be on the plane," Paulette asked.

The driver drove cautiously around the city attempting to ensure that they were not being followed. Finally they arrived in a quiet suburban neighborhood not unlike the one he had stayed in during his first visit to New York City years before. He was prompted to ask about Frank, the GRU agent, who had met him back then and took good care of his initial introduction to the United States, but he thought better of it and really didn't want to engage in idle conversation at that point.

"This is it," Paulette smiled as Valori pulled up slowly to the curb in front of a neat and attractive upper middle class brick home. "We will be staying here until we depart for Washington."

Sasha thought to himself, "Boy, the GRU has come up in the world since my first visit, not only in the quality of agents, but also the living quarters!"

He followed Paulette into the house as Valori moved on away with the vehicle. Once inside the door, she promptly reset the security system. This was a clear indication that there was likely no one else in the house. The interior was even more upscale than the exterior and the grounds. She led him upstairs and showed him to a comfortable and well-appointed bedroom.

As she was showing him around, he felt a sudden twinge to ask about the house. "Does someone live here permanently? Is there a housekeeper?"

"No, to both questions," she replied, "but Valori, our trusted driver and security guard will be back here shortly after he parks the car. He will make his way in quietly and keep watch. We maintain this place which is reserved for our most important visitors . . . and, Sasha, you qualify."

He smiled.

"A house servant will also come in the morning," she continued, "and prepare our breakfast, but no one else will be here this evening besides Valori and ourselves."

She paused and snickered . . . "and, Comrade, you're safe with me. We wanted you to have a quiet and restful evening on the first night in the United States. Are you hungry? If so, I can have Valori order food in, or we can make the best of what is already in the larder. I can assure you that it is fully stocked. Can I make you a drink? Vodka? We have the very best, some of *our* very own brought in by courier."

Paulette was *cool,* confident and fully in charge of herself and her surroundings.

"Vodka would be great," he smiled. "I could use one to '*power-down*' a bit. And, . . ." he paused, "with ice, please. I am back in the United States." He suddenly felt uneasy and admonished himself. He had not wanted to sound so much at ease with his surroundings.

They sipped their drinks and exchanged information on their respective backgrounds. Paulette had grown up in Moscow and was selected for special language and agent training by the GRU, the same as he. She appeared to be exceptionally bright, self-confident and apparently a very trusted agent. After all, she had been sent to meet him. She was emphatic that she was very happy the KGB did not attempt to recruit her. She didn't offer any further explanation, but it was clear that she had the same disdain for the agency as did he. She said that her husband was a GRU communications specialist and is frequently called upon by the KGB to work with their equipment.

Paulette described the situation. "The GRU has its own communication facilities here in New York and in Washington, but we know for sure that our New York communications are closely monitored. We tease them occasionally with phony messages just to see if they are on the ball. My husband believes that we can communicate reasonably secure from the KGB jackals in Washington, at least presently. But he isn't sure how long we can maintain that since they have their own ways of detecting and intercepting telephone and teletype correspondence from everyone. He continuously discovers tampering within our systems," she sighed.

"To be quite honest," she continued, "the KGB rules supreme over the control of all our communications in and out of the country, so they are usually well-informed on *all* of our activities. The GRU has few secrets from them. That includes your presence here in the U.S. Your encounter at the airport is just one example of their knowledge of ongoing activities and their tactics. All of that just to prove that *they are in charge.*"

"We live in a tenuous world, Sasha," she said. "We should worry about ourselves as much as we do about our enemies. Perhaps we are our own worst enemy."

Sasha could have enlightened her considerably about his own experiences with the KGB, but instinctively knew that he could trust no one, not even this apparent GRU friend.

"Sasha, your wife is an economics specialist. Has she been to the United States to study?" Paulette asked.

"No, she has not. She has completed all of her studies in Russia," he responded.

"That's odd. She is an expert in western economics and she has learned *'everything'* from our own people . . . KGB people at that! Well, the reason I bring this up is that I have observed what I believe to be lucrative opportunities here in the U.S. for our government to exploit potential vulnerabilities in their banking, financial institutions and the stock market. Has she worked on any of these activities? Does she speak English very well?"

Sasha relaxed considerably after his second vodka and began to give way to the fatigue from the flight from Helsinki and London. "No, I don't believe she has had very much contact with any of those activities except academically."

He began to feel weary and didn't want to pursue any complex discussions farther. "Paulette, you must forgive me. It has been a long day. Can we continue this discussion in the morning? I am very interested in your comments and potential opportunities for our government, and I would like to hear more when I am refreshed. Do you mind?"

"No, not at all," she smiled. "Let's retire."

Sasha awoke very early but felt rested. As he showered and dressed, he could smell the preparation of breakfast coming from downstairs. The unmistakable aroma of bacon frying quickly brought back memories of his previous stay in the United States.

Paulette was already downstairs in the parlor reading the newspaper. "Good morning, Sasha. Did you rest well?"

"Dah . . . Yes. Thank you. I feel very well. And you?"

"Coffee or tea?" she asked, busily moving about the kitchen.

"Coffee, please," he replied. "Since I am in America, I suppose I had better begin to become a native. It's an American addiction, I recall. However, I do like coffee."

"How long were you in the United States during your last visit?" she asked.

He didn't know how much Paulette knew about him or how much she *needed to know.* "Quite awhile," he casually responded, "long enough to get accustomed to many American habits."

"Your English is quite good and *very* American," she replied. "You have either practiced considerably or you have been associated with people who converse quite well. Not a hint of accent."

"So is yours, Paulette, but my mother was an English teacher for many years. She taught me well."

Sasha decided to stay at the GRU *rezidentura* in New York for an additional day while Paulette assisted him in getting his wardrobe replenished and *Americanized.* The following day, she accompanied him on the train to Washington D.C. and to the rezidentura where she introduced him to General Boris Yurasov, the Washington GRU chief.

"Yurasov seems cordial enough," Sasha thought to himself as they exchanged small talk. He was medium in height, slight built, sharp facial features with gray green eyes and cropped gray hair. He wore heavy horn-rimmed glasses. His English was also very good.

Yurasov said that he had received a call from General Tushenskiy regarding Sasha's visit, but he offered no further details that Tushenskiy may have shared with him.

Paulette bid them goodbye. "I will follow up on our conversation, Paulette, regarding economic exploitation." Sasha offered. "That's out of my field of expertise, but I am sure that the Director General will have some thoughts. I will be in touch with you. Da sveedah'neeya!" He was provided with a comfortable room at the Washington GRU rezidentura which was located two blocks off 16th Street and not far from the Soviet Embassy. He asked Yurasov if he might contact Khodinka to inquire about the welfare of his wife, but was then assured that he, Yurasov, would make such an inquiry for him. This response did not put him at ease after having received the vague threats in New York, but he had no choice in the matter. He would await the results of the general's inquiry. His hosts had provided him with magazine and newspaper accounts from all around the country on the Kennedy assassination. He spent most of his first afternoon and evening carefully tracing and comparing the various stories. He attempted to merge the reported chronology of Oswald's suspected movements with that which he had collected in his previous stops. He thought to himself, "I wonder if the KGB and the U.S. intelligence agencies are making this same trek? There is little doubt that our KGB friends are hot on the Oswald trail and mine as well! I have to presume that the American CIA and the FBI are doing the same. With this Oswald character having lived in the Soviet Union for the better part of three years, the whole thing becomes very murky! It is still hard to believe that the ever vigilant and efficient KGB would ever allow such an oversight . . . unless maybe they were complicit."

The newspaper accounts of the assassination and funeral were voluminous; he poured over every paragraph, looking for any items that seemed to stand out from the various chronologies, opinions and early assessments. A quote in a *WASHINGTON POST* edition caught his attention:

> "The Assistant Attorney General told reporters today: 'The public must be satisfied that Oswald was the lone assassin; that he did not have confederates who are still at large; and that the evidence was such that he would have been convicted at trial.'"

"That is a strange statement coming from such a high-ranking official, and so soon," he thought. "Only two days after the assassin himself was murdered while in police custody. He made no mention of Oswald's killer, Jack Ruby, and the fact that he did the deed while Oswald was handcuffed and being held between two policemen. This is almost too absolute for an American bureaucrat. This whole thing gets more intriguing by the day! I thought the KGB was attempting a cover-up and now this curious and presumptive assessment by a senior American official?"

Several newspaper stories had begun to speculate on conspiracy theories including:

> *"Cuban participation, Khrushchev pay back, U.S. right-wing factions and organized gangsters, including Jack Ruby's questionable background as a night club owner and big time gambler."*

There were even whispers that the former vice president, who was now the President of the United States, might be involved. *"After all, it happened in Texas! And, the accused assassin was himself murdered two days after his arrest while in police custody, in Texas!"*

Sasha had all but decided not to visit the Soviet Embassy and risk another encounter with the KGB. There was no question that they knew he was in Washington and would not be cooperative anyway.

EIGHT

*"The tallest blade of grass is the
first to be cut by the scythe."*

A Russian Proverb

De' Ja Vu

The next morning was chilly and still dark outside his window on the second floor of the GRU *rezidentura*. There was only tea in the room, so he made himself a cup and retrieved the Monday morning *WASHINGTON POST* and *NEW YORK TIMES* newspapers placed outside his door.

Later, he would go downstairs for breakfast and meet with General Yurasov as scheduled. He scanned the front page. It had been a week since the assassination, and the headline and every news article in the paper continued to reflect one slant or another speculating about the events surrounding the death of President Kennedy and the subsequent shooting of Lee Harvey Oswald. As the days had passed, the stories continued to expand and elaborate on the minute details about the murders, and there were increasing conspiracy theory notions developed by zealous reporters.

Suddenly, his eyes caught an article in the lower left-hand column of the *WASHINGTON POST*:

> *"Families of Missing Bomber
> Crew Press The Government
> For Information"*

87

He began to read the article with casual interest at first and then he quickly plunged into the story. Not wanting to believe the unfolding details:

> *"Prominent criminal lawyer, F. Lee Baker, will represent the families of the missing U.S. strategic bomber that disappeared thirteen months ago during a Cuban Crisis mission. Baker has worked on behalf of the families of the missing Air Force crew members for the past six months in an attempt to force the government to open its files and reveal any information it may be withholding regarding the aircraft and the potential fate of the six crew members."*

He took a deep breath. "God, what on earth is this?" All interest in the Kennedy assassination news left him. He read on:

> *"Baker will address the issue before the Federal District Court in Alexandria, Virginia, on Wednesday, December 3rd, at 10:00 a.m."*

"That's tomorrow!" he muttered to himself and continued to read the news story:

> *"Judge Roswald Shrull, United States Federal District Court, Eastern District of Virginia, has agreed to hear the unusual case. Baker's petition will ask the court to direct the U.S. Government, the Pentagon and the Air Force in particular, as well as the Intelligence Agencies, to make all of their records available regarding the mysterious disappearance of the B-52 bomber and its crew members on October 27, 1962."*

He was in awe as he hurriedly shuffled through the newspaper to find Page A13 and read the remainder of the shocking article:

"Baker charges that the government has consistently refused to offer any reasonable explanation for the missing bomber and its crew other than it failed to return from a routine mission during the Cuban Crisis. Further, he says that Air Force officials will not confirm nor deny that nuclear weapons were being carried on board the missing aircraft. Fred Lee Baker, the controversial California lawyer, said that he agreed to take the issue forward and file an official complaint with the U.S. Government and Department of Defense on behalf of the missing air crew's families when he received a letter from one crew member's wife. He said that she and others claimed that they were unable to get anyone to shed any light on the potential fate of her husband or the other members of the aircrew. Baker also indicated that it has been more than a year since the bomber and its crew failed to return from its mission. Baker went on to say that after questioning members of the bomber unit in Puerto Rico where the crew and B-52 were assigned, there was a strong possibility that the aircraft could have gone down in Russia or some other Soviet territory. The crew members may even be being held as prisoners, " the attorney for the families went on to say.

He was aghast at what he had read. He slumped back on the sofa and felt mildly nauseous. He stared at the paper as the words blurred before his eyes. He couldn't believe what had suddenly erupted in his day.

Composing himself, he finished the article:

"The Pentagon refused to issue a statement or comment on the legal motion. Judge Shrull, however, in a brief comment to the press, said that this was a most unusual case and that he had only agreed to hear the motion filed by the attorney representing the families after he had been presented affidavits from individuals reasonably familiar with the situation. He would only elaborate further to the extent that this was a humane

> *issue and that there might be evidence that government agencies may not have provided the families of the missing aircrew members sufficient information to satisfy their questions."*

He felt the return of emotion as he was reminded of the loss of his bomber and his crew. He could only think about the five American crewmen on the B-52. They had been his trusted friends. He had drugged them with the strong sedative, *Doriden,* provided to him by Rudolpho Cardenas, his KGB contact in Puerto Rico. He had then headed the bomber toward the planned landing field near Kursk, a few hundred miles south of Moscow. While he had recalled various details of the event virtually every day since the ill-fated hijack attempt, the magnitude of it all now came crashing down on him anew.

He sat reading the words over and over. His thoughts took him back to the cockpit of the bomber and those last frantic moments as he was being fired upon by the MiG 21. He recalled how he had attempted to maneuver the B-52 to escape into the cloud cover below. He vividly remembered attempting to make radio contact with the Soviet air traffic controller, literally screaming and pleading for someone to call off the MiG fighter while he tried desperately to arouse the unconscious Bill Self, his copilot. But he could only vaguely remember the bomber virtually ripping apart and somehow he was ejected out and parachuted to safety.

He was semi-conscious when he landed in a cultivated field and was set upon by angry farm workers who apparently took him for an enemy aviator. When he awoke in the hospital, his first thoughts were about his crew. He had been promised that when he delivered the B-52 to his Soviet government, the American aircrew would be treated humanely as prisoners. He had been assured that they would be returned back to the U.S. under some arrangement similar to that of Gary Powers after his U-2 was shot down two years earlier. But his crew had all perished when the doomed bomber crashed and burned, destroying everything on board.

The telephone rang, bringing him back to his surroundings. "Dah?" he responded in a weak voice.

"Colonel Katsanov, Sir, this is Major Lobanov. General Yurasov is ready to see you now. Sir, did you have breakfast? Are you well?"

Immersed in his thoughts, Sasha had lost track of time. He quickly looked at his wristwatch. It was 8:05 a.m.

"Dah, dah," he responded wearily. "Nyet . . . I am fine, just a little tired this morning. No, I have not eaten. Please, tell the General I will be right down."

Bold Move

When he arrived at Yurasov's office, the major showed him in. "Do'broye oo'tro! Comrade Katsanov," Yurasov greeted. "Come in, please and be seated. Tea or coffee? Are you well this morning? Major Lobanov said that you did not come down for breakfast."

"Nyet, General. I am fine. I got absorbed in reading the newspapers and allowed the time to slip away. I apologize for being late. I will help myself to a cup of coffee if I may?"

"Dah. Please do. It is all there before you. Tell me, Comrade, what are your plans today? Oh, but before that, I spoke with the Director General overnight, and he told me to put you at ease about the safety and well-being of your wife. She is fine and being well cared for."

"Thank you, General," Sasha responded. "I very much appreciate your asking for me."

Yurasov asked, "Do you have a specific schedule for your visit here in Washington? How may we assist you? What about the KGB? Are you going to visit those rascals over at the embassy while you are here?"

He began to think fast and replied, "Well, initially, Sir, I had decided that I wouldn't go to the embassy, but perhaps I should. I have reviewed and noted most all of the background reading that you have kindly provided, so maybe a visit there to introduce myself would be in order. Hopefully, that would help to keep the air clear regarding my visit to the United States, and I might learn something additional. Do you think that I might go there today?"

"Dah, I think it might be arranged. I will call and see if we can see General Zotov this afternoon. But, Comrade, don't count on *learning* anything from those people," Yurasov smirked, "Anything else?"

"Well, Sir, tomorrow I would like to take care of some collateral business." He paused.

Instinctively, he knew that he needed to be more explicit about his *collateral* business. He quickly continued, feeling for words as he spoke. He knew that he had to be truthful or risk unnecessary questioning.

"General, there is a legal case which is to be conducted in the U.S. Federal District Court here in Alexandria, Virginia. I would like very much to go to the court building and observe the American legal process. The case, according to the newspaper, involves a petition to the U.S. Government for the release of information about a missing bomber aircraft that occurred during the Cuban event last year. As you are aware, Sir, my duties at Khodinka are involved with aircraft technology exploitation. This court hearing may very well provide me with unsolicited information on U.S. aircraft operations."

Sasha was reasonably sure that Yurasov was not aware of his previous agency work in the U.S. and his involvement in the attempt to hijack and divert the B-52 bomber back to Russia. He had been assured that his entire operation during all the years he worked in the United States had been kept in the closest compartmented secrecy. He waited for Yurasov's response.

"I have no objection to either of your pursuits, Sasha," Yurasov responded. "And I agree, I believe that in the interest of maintaining good relations, paying a courtesy call at the embassy is a good idea." He continued, "I would also like to bring you into our confidence and have you meet with one of our special agents who works within the American intelligence community. He is one of our GRU recruits, but by agreement, he is required to also report to General Zotov. As you know, Zotov, in addition to serving as the KGB Station Chief, is also head of the agency's Third District, and has cognizance over all *illegals*."

He continued, "*Stork* is the agent's code name. He has been closely observing the activities within the U.S. intelligence community since the assassination and may be able to assist you with what they have concluded."

"Sir, that is a good idea," Sasha responded. "I will be pleased to meet with him. Do you believe that he will be able to speak freely without KGB influence? To say the least, they have not been very cooperative with me since I began this trip."

Yurasov sighed, "We operate in a curious environment, do we not? They spy on us and we spy on them . . . a very dangerous game for all! Don't concern yourself, Sasha, he is *my* agent and *my* property, and he will speak openly to you. I would like to arrange for us to meet with *Stork* tomorrow evening if he is available. Will you be completed with your visit to the American court hearing by early evening? If so, Stork may be able to add a data point or so to your information collection. Now, I wish to caution you on your visit to the embassy today. As you are well aware, the KGB counter-intelligence people are extremely sensitive about this Kennedy assassination thing. They are actually paranoid. They really don't know if they are involved or not."

He smirked and continued, "It has been a bit humorous, watching them flounder about with all of this, but if you wish to go there, you have a very legitimate reason to do so. You have the Director General's letter that should serve to protect you, but I doubt that it will get you very much more information than either the newspapers or we have provided to this point. I wish to keep confidential your meeting with our agent, *Stork*. Semenov will also maintain confidentiality."

Yurasov then frowned, "Now, with regard to your visiting a U.S. legal court, that is another issue. We are very careful not to expose ourselves in this country unnecessarily nor to provide any opportunity to be accused by U.S. officials of . . . 'er *spying*, if you will. I *hate* that term! Keep in mind that you are in this country illegally with an undercover name and identification. Should you get tripped-up, you would be on your own and there would be hell to pay. Let me think that one over."

Sasha listened carefully, particularly to Yurosov's admonition. The last thing he wanted to do was to get cross-wise with a senior GRU officer for misleading him about the real reason for his interest in the court activity.

"Sir, I understand," he said. "If you wish, I will be pleased to transmit a request to General Tushenskiy to ensure that he is in agreement with my initiative to go to the U.S. courtroom and observe."

He felt sure that Tushenskiy would approve a routine request, but he was not sure about how he would react if he knew what the court case was really about. He might feel it too risky.

"No, that will not be necessary," Yurasov replied. "I can make such approvals here. Show me the newspaper article describing this legal case."

Sasha reached for the *WASHINGTON POST* on a nearby table and pointed to the article on the front page.

The general acknowledged, "Dah . . . , yes. I did read about that, but didn't that event occur during U.S. air operations in the so-called Cuban Crisis?"

He paused. "Well, if you believe that there would be some value in visiting the courtroom and observing, then I do not object. Again, I caution you to be on your toes. Simply ride a taxicab to the location and innocently go in there. If you are questioned or challenged in any way about who you are or your interest there, then politely leave and do not pursue it further. You do understand?"

"Yes, Sir, I understand completely." Sasha breathed a quiet sigh of relief.

"And, of course," Yurosov said, "I expect you to provide me with a report of your observations and conclusions. I will advise the Director General that I have approved your request to make this side excursion while you are here and that I believe that it fits your job responsibilities back home. Now, I will see if we can get in to see Zotov at the embassy today. I have some other business to attend to over there, and I will also be interested in observing how you are received."

"Sir, I would be pleased to have you accompany me. I will also be comforted with your presence," he smiled.

General Yurasov winked. "Good."

Major Lobanov knocked on Sasha's door. He handed him a box, "Sir, your appointment at the embassy is on for 2 p.m. The articles of disguise in the box are required in order to accompany the General to the Embassy. I suggest one of the wigs that fits you well, a moustache and the clear horn—rimmed glasses."

He then handed him a wool fedora and a heavy tweed topcoat. He added with a smile, "Please also wear this hat and coat, Sir."

Sasha was confused. The KGB already knew his identity. "Why the disguise?" he asked.

"Sir, these should provide you sufficient *mackarova* against the FBI surveillance cameras that watch over our embassy visitors," Lobonov responded. "General Yurasov is a well-known Russian Trade Ministry official, so he will be dressed as usual. Please come down to the General's office about 1:30." He inspected the contents of the box; wigs, moustaches, stick-on eyebrows, and various clear lens eyeglass frames. He chose a dark-haired wig, much darker and considerably longer than his own hair, a matching moustache and a pair of glasses. Standing before the bathroom mirror, he changed his appearance from Mike Scott, communications equipment salesman, to *Mr. whomever?* Amused at himself and feeling a bit foolish, he reported to Yurasov's office. "Ahhh, Sasha, you look great!" Yurasov smiled. "We will leave by way of the garage. Someone may observe our departure, but our automobile windows are darkened and I enjoy occasionally giving the snoops something to worry about." "Our *rezidentura,*" he smiled, "is an official Soviet *Trade Mission* property, but the U.S. secret police still watch over us. Occasionally they may follow us, especially if it is my personal vehicle. In any event, you may be assured that you will get your photograph taken when we get out and walk into the embassy. They will then spend hours trying to figure out who you are . . ." Yurasov chuckled, "They will pour over thousands of photo profiles to identify you."

Once inside the embassy, Yurasov guided Sasha to the office of the Chief, Third Division, Lt. General Igor Zotov. A heavy odor of stale, pungent cigarette smoke cloaked the office of the senior KGB officer in charge of U.S. domestic surveillance. He was wearing a crudely tailored wrinkled gray suit. His dingy white shirt collar revealed its persistent wear. Yesterday's or last week's food stains remained steadfast on his faded necktie. Zotov's greeting was cool, matter of fact and unenthusiastic. "Welcome to the United States, Comrade Katsanov. I have been informed of your visit." It was obvious that the KGB station chief was not pleased with his presence in the United States or the Soviet Embassy. This was KGB territory! "Thank you, General." Sasha saluted smartly and held out his hand. Zotov ignored both Sasha's salute and his offer to shake hands. He nodded an acknowledgement to Yurasov, turning away toward his desk; he motioned to two expensive over-stuffed chairs. "Good to see you, Boris. Please, Comrades, sit. What can I do for you?" Yurasov spoke. "As you are aware, Igor, Comrade Katsanov is visiting the United States at the direction of General Tushenskiy and with the concurrence of your chief. Comrade Katsanov's assignment, as I am sure you are also aware, is to conduct an unbiased assessment of the preliminary findings surrounding the assassination of the American president as the tragic event might interest the GRU. He will review all of the American open source literature, newspapers, magazines and so on, and other media commentary regarding the incident. He is to compile a report of his observations and any significant findings and provide them to the GRU and KGB chiefs." Yurasov's voice took on a firm tone. "He also has the authority, Igor, to speak with any of our people . . . GRU and KGB here in Washington and elsewhere whom he believes will contribute to his findings and report."

Zotov stared across the room and didn't acknowledge. He casually lit a cigarette and turned his eyes sharply toward Sasha as the heavy smoke spiraled above his head. He held his gaze for a time, exhaling smoke from his nostrils and in a raspy voice, barely above a whisper, smirked, "and *what* are your qualifications, Comrade Katsanov, to conduct such a comprehensive mission for our government? You do not appear to be old enough, much less have the experience, to address such matters." Then he asked, "Why were you chosen to do this and for what purpose?" "Sir, General Tushenskiy requested that I make this visit to the United States," Sasha began, "and as General Yurasov has described, to collect any information that I can about the events leading up to and surrounding the assassination of the American president.

I . . ." Zotov interrupted, exhaled a deep cough to clear his throat and with his voice still grating and firm, "And does your Director General believe that *You* are more capable of conducting such a research and collection of information than *We* are?" Sasha was about to respond when General Yurasov intervened. "Igor, it is not Comrade Katsanov's responsibility to explain why he was assigned to conduct this task. We must honor the GRU Director General's request to provide our support to his mission. Your own KGB chief is cooperating with the GRU Director General's initiative." "Dah, dah, Boris," Zotov cut in. "I am aware of our chief's mutual agreement with all of this nonsense. Nevertheless, I am not at all pleased with such meddling for any reason. But, Comrades, permit me to inform you that General Kashevarov reported to the Chairman and the Politburo just today that our Polish *friends* have reliably confirmed the criminal assassination deed was the result of a conspiracy instigated by several wealthy pro-fascist and racist individuals in the south of the United States." Turning his attention back to Sasha, "So, Comrade Katsanov, permit me to tell you . . . Nyet! *To Warn You*! Do not cross any lines that are not open to you. I do not care what you believe your orders to be. From my point of view, you are not welcome here. If you are smart, you will recognize, based on what I have revealed to you, that your assignment is at an end. You should, therefore, promptly return to your place of duty in Moscow. If General Tushenskiy is as wise as he is touted to be, he will act accordingly, lest he finds himself in some difficulty." Zotov wheezed and coughed again, this time with a loud gurgling roar. Sasha took a measured breath as Yurasov was about to protest Zotov's statement. He boldly reached over and put his hand gently on General Yurasov's arm. "General Zotov, with due respect, Sir, permit me to inform you that I am here to carry out my orders. I have been so directed by the Chief, GRU, and with the concurrence of your chief, General Kashevarov. And further, permit me to advise you that General Tushenskiy received personal approval for my assignment from the Premier." Sasha paused, "Now, Sir," not sure how far to go with what he had started. But, surprisingly, he was full of confidence as he addressed the much older and tough KGB officer before him. Zotov's eyes widened in disbelief as the young officer continued, "I am sure,"

Sasha said, "That you are well aware that I have been continuously harassed by your people at every stop since I departed Moscow on this assignment. Several of those interventions bordered on being life threatening. Further, my wife has also been subjected to questionable tactics by some of your operatives at the airport in Moscow. These were obvious attempts to frighten me into abandoning my assignment and returning home. But, I wish to inform you, Sir, I am not returning to Moscow until I have fulfilled what I was ordered to do or my general recalls me."

He breathed deeply and finished, "General Zotov, I do not understand what appears to be an attempt to cover up ill deeds by either your people or by some other members of our government. I sincerely hope that is not the case, Sir, because our great government cannot afford such embarrassment for whatever reason. Thank you for your time, General." He turned to General Yurasov. "General, Sir, I apologize for my conduct here, but I hope you understand." Sasha stood and saluted the stunned and red-faced Zotov who sat speechless and flushed. Yurasov also stood and moved toward the door. "Good day, Igor." Zotov remained still with a fixed glare at Sasha. As the two reached the door, he finally responded in a barely audible throaty growl, "General Yurasov, I will be making a full report regarding the conduct of this arrogant officer. I hope you will be inclined to do so as well."

Turning his glare to Sasha, "Comrade Katsanov, I do not wish to see you again, and I advise you to watch your self carefully as you stumble around this country. You may recall the old Russian proverb, my young Comrade, something about '*the tallest blade of grass is always the first to be cut . . .*' Lest you forget, we are in charge of the harvesting here!"

NINE

"The appetite comes during the meal."

A Russian Proverb

Lubiyanka

"Oleg, come in. Sit." General Kashevarov curtly responded as his Assistant Director of Aktivinyye Meropriatia, Major General Oleg Petrov, entered the office. Unfazed by the gruff tone of his superior, the gnarled old veteran unceremoniously tossed his heavy coat and his gray wolf skin fur hat on an adjacent chair and slowly eased himself down into another.

"Oleg," Kashevarov began, "as you know we continue to have a very serious situation on our hands regarding the events surrounding the assassination of the American president. My friend, Tushenskiy, seems determined to become a hero in the eyes of the Chairman and to solve the American mystery killing all on his own."

Petrov was a career KGB operative. He had been a trusted lieutenant to Lavrenti Beria, the most notorious and feared of all former KGB chiefs. Petrov was not a politician, rather a survivor, and much older than his present boss, Kashevarov. His craggy features and crude manners reflected the persona of the hard-core villainous agent, which he was. He was also a highly experienced and skilled tactician whose responsibilities for directing the active measures program which included executing the most sordid and vicious assaults on those who became a target of *the system.*

Petrov smiled, showing two rows of dark yellowish stained teeth. "Comrade General, we have put numerous impediments in the way of the GRU and their young investigator already, and we have sent strong messages to several of our citizens in Minsk who found pleasure in cooperating with him. We have only toyed with both he and others thus far."

He shrugged and continued, "So it will be my pleasure to tighten the screws considerably to get their attention and especially that of the GRU chief himself. You do not need to issue any instructions, Comrade. I will take it from here."

"Dah, Oleg, I have exchanged messages with Zotov in Washington, and he has already had an unpleasant encounter with the young upstart colonel. We need to get all of this under control."

Petrov didn't respond, he only grinned and nodded as he lifted his rotund body from the chair. The meeting was over; neither cared much for engaging very long with the other. Breathing heavily, he slowly put on his heavy wool topcoat and fur hat. He seldom wore his military uniform, much preferring to look the sinister agent part he enjoyed portraying.

"Oleg . . ." The KGB Director General, somewhat troubled by Petrov's words, said in a hushed voice as his senior henchman prepared to depart, "you need not report back to me. I wish to know nothing more about any of your work on this case and, Oleg, *no* fingerprints. *NO* fingerprints!"

Petrov smiled cynically and leaned toward the unsettled KGB chief, his foul breath engulfed his words, "*The appetite comes during the meal,* Comrade. Was it just one year ago that this young shrimp barely missed his calling? Perhaps it is time to boil him for good!"

His parting comment confirmed that Petrov had more than likely been in collusion with Vetrov and Borodin when they conspired to shoot down Sasha's bomber. He was certainly aware of the event.

Chilling Recount

Sasha slept fitfully. The encounter with Zotov coupled with the news article concerning the court hearing on the missing bomber and aircrew—*his bomber and aircrew*—troubled him deeply.

Yurasov understood his frustration and anger with Zotov and had humorously chided him on their return from the Soviet Embassy. "Comrade Sasha, you are either a fool or a very brave young officer. You took on the senior KGB official in the United States . . . and one of the most feared, I might add. Of course, I will have to report the event to General Tushenskiy, but I will do so in your favor."

"General, I apologize if I embarrassed you," Sasha replied, "but I am afraid that even Comrade General Zotov does not understand the gravity of the harm his agency and his agents often cause our government . . . and especially to our own people. And, Sir, his last remark amounted to a threat to *our* Director General."

Yurasov had not responded to his remark, and Sasha did not pursue the issue further. Yet, the veiled threat to Tushenskiy troubled both of them.

Attempting to refocus his thoughts, Sasha retrieved the morning newspapers from outside his door and began to scan them for any additional slants on the assassination and the scheduled hearing. Most of the articles on the assassination continued in the same vein. A few reporters attempted to arouse speculation about conspiracy theories. There was always at least one or two pointing to the Soviet Union and Khrushchev, speculating that they might have supported the assassination as a way of *getting even* with the United States for the embarrassment over Cuba. Others raised the possibility of Castro's involvement, and there were a few subtle inferences to an internal U.S. conspiracy. One article featured a vague allusion to the *Texas connections* surrounding the tragedy.

"Maybe the Premier was correct on the night of the assassination, that it was too coincidental for the president to be killed in Texas," he mused. "The very conservative state and home of the vice president would definitely fall in line with Soviet thinking and past history of succession."

He finally found a brief article referring to the court hearing on the missing bomber on page two of the Metro Section of the *POST*. It had already slipped off the front page. The article simply re-capped the one from the previous day's paper.

When he opened the closet door, the strong choking odor of Zotov's foul cigarette fumes stung his nostrils. His clothes had brought with them a lingering reminder of the unpleasant human being and the meeting.

He went downstairs to the dining room and ate breakfast alone, avoiding having conversation with anyone. Major Lobanov dropped by his table. "Comrade Colonel, forgive the interruption. The General wished me to give you this special telephone number to contact us here at the *rezidentura* should you have an emergency. As you would expect, all of our standard phone numbers are monitored either by the American secret police or the KGB."

He grinned, "We are well watched over, but so far this special number is still safe. Have a good day, Sir."

"Spasee'ba, Major," Sasha replied.

Back in his room, he donned his topcoat and departed the GRU residence via a side door exit. It was cold and damp with a few snow flurries in the air. The weather reminded him a little of Moscow, but that is where it ended. The streets were relatively clutter-free and the buildings were architecturally sharp and considerably more inviting than any of those in the Soviet capital. He walked over to 18th Street, glancing back frequently to see if anyone might be following. After attempting to determine that he was not being observed, he hailed a taxicab.

"Take me to the Smithsonian, please . . . the main entrance on Jefferson Drive," he requested.

He entered the Smithsonian Museum main building and went directly to the men's room. Once inside, he stepped into a stall and fitted on another one of the wigs from the selection provided to him at the GRU residence. He took a dark blue necktie from his suit jacket pocket and exchanged it with the bright red one he was wearing. Next, he put on the dark-rimmed clear eyeglasses. He inspected his appearance in the mirror, approved of the disguise and departed the restroom, carrying his topcoat over his arm. He exited the building through the rear exit on the Independence Avenue side.

The transformation had taken no more than five minutes. He walked north a few blocks, looked about several times, attempting again to make sure that no one was following him and waved down another taxi.

"I'm as paranoid as my fellow comrades," he muttered to himself as he entered the taxi.

"The Federal District Court Building in Alexandria—I believe it's located on Duke or Queen Street," Sasha directed. "I'm not quite sure."

The interior of the taxi had a faint stale odor similar to that of Zotov's strong cigarettes. The only difference was that the driver had obviously used a cheap sweet aromatic spray which commingled with the pungent tobacco scent. The combination only worsened the interior breathing space.

"Yeah, I know about where it is. We'll find it. Going to court?" the driver grinned as he lighted another cigarette. Sasha didn't respond. He rolled down the window slightly to let in the cool fresh air and allowed his thoughts to be absorbed with what he might possibly expect when he arrived at the courthouse building.

"Should I be doing this?" he pondered. "Will I even be permitted inside?" He had no familiarity with American courts. Such exposure had not been a part of his prior experiences during his stay in the United States.

He asked the driver to drop him off a block past the courthouse entrance. It was 9:35 a.m. and twenty-five minutes before the scheduled beginning of the court hearing described in the newspaper.

His curiosity was building. "Why would they be conducting a legal hearing concerning a military aircraft that disappeared over a year ago?"

He observed a number of people arriving in taxis and private automobiles, ostensibly to attend the same court hearing. He casually moved toward the steps to the court building, carefully observing the face of each individual entering. He didn't know who might show up or what might transpire at the proceedings, but he felt compelled to be there.

This is just too bizarre, he thought to himself, as he started up the steps to the entrance. "I can't believe the timing of all of this. Here I am back in the United States as a result of their president being killed and then walk right into this incredible past event in my life! This is too bizarre!"

He followed the trail of those entering the courtroom, casually nodded to the uniformed police officer at the door, and confidently moved to a row of seats about midway down the aisle on the left-hand side. He sat down and perused the people already gathered. Near the front and to the right side, a group of mostly young women and a handful of men were huddled together in conversation.

He couldn't make out their faces, but he was sure that the women were some of the wives of his ill-fated B-52 crew. He had not known the crewmembers' wives very well and had only been around them at a rare social function or so that he had more or less been forced to attend. This had been intentional. He really didn't want to become too familiar with anyone on a personal basis. At the tables on the left and right front before the judge's bench were men in business suits. He had never been in a courtroom before, but he recalled similar scenes on television during his years in the United States. These were the lawyers representing the respective sides in the hearing.

Suddenly his eyes caught the backs of the unmistakable blue uniforms of several U.S. Air Force officers seated at the front of the courtroom directly ahead of him.

As one of the officers turned to speak to the other seated beside him, he immediately recognized Colonel Blair. Colonel William Blair had been the commander of the B-52 unit he had been assigned to in Puerto Rico. He also noticed the stars on his uniform epaulets. His former wing commander was now a brigadier general. Blair was speaking to Lt. Colonel Jack Lambert, his former squadron commander. Then he recognized Colonel Chris Ward, the operations officer of his squadron. This was all too surreal. He felt a rush of anxiety.

"Damn! I have to get out of here! There too many people who know me!" he began to fidget. "If I should get recognized, it would be the end of the world!" Even with his thick wig of hair and false eyeglasses, he felt nakedly vulnerable. His desperate thoughts were suddenly interrupted by the firm voice of the court bailiff.

"Ladies and gentlemen, please rise! Judge Roswald Shrull, United States Federal District Court, Eastern District of Virginia, presiding."

He was hemmed-in by people on both sides of the row in which he was seated. He felt mild panic and started to excuse himself to those next to him and leave, then just as suddenly he decided to stay. He gradually calmed himself. "I'm going to stay. That's why I came. No one will recognize me in this disguise. I'll slip out when the session breaks up." He began to relax and concentrate on the proceedings.

The judge entered the courtroom from a rear door. Clothed in a black robe, he observed the room for a moment as he took his seat. He was a tall erect man, likely in his fifties, Sasha observed, with a youthful face, horn rimmed glasses and a fringe of graying hair. He appeared unhurried as he spent several seconds shuffling through papers.

Finally, he spoke in a clear distinct voice, "Ladies and gentlemen, this is an unusual hearing today. I have only agreed to take up this issue because of the strong concerns and convincing arguments put forth to me in the plaintiffs' formal petition. I am not sure where this procedure will lead us, but I am willing to hear the arguments of those represented by the complainants in the case and by the Government's representatives. The issue in the hearing is unusual because it deals with a military aircraft and its crewmembers who were declared missing a little over a year ago while conducting air operations during the Cuban Crisis event."

He paused and looked down at the attorneys sitting at adjacent tables, "I wish for each of you to understand that it is not the standard norm for civilian courts, or even Federal District Courts, to address such incidents as this. However, as I have stated, I agreed to hear the complaints in this case after carefully reviewing the written and oral arguments put forth to me. Now, does the counsel for the plaintiffs have a formal statement to make?"

The noted attorney, F. Lee Baker, stood and addressed the judge. "Yes, Your Honor, if it pleases the court, we do have a statement."

Sasha observed the lawyer's dapper dress: three-piece striped gray suit and brilliant red necktie. He had read a brief biographical profile on Baker in the newspaper—confrontational, challenging, insulting, were but a few of his descriptive characteristics, the paper cited.

"Proceed, Counselor," the judge directed.

Baker took his time as he casually swaggered around to the front of the table at which he had been seated. His tone of voice had a touch of arrogant solicitation.

"Your Honor, as you have so correctly observed, this is a highly unusual hearing. And, Sir, like you, I only agreed to represent the plaintiffs in this hearing after carefully listening to each of their stories and conducting considerable research to verify facts in the case. But I must confess, Your Honor, I ran into numerous roadblocks and even a few brick walls when I attempted to gain any reassuring information from our government, the Pentagon and the Air Force, in particular. But, Your Honor, I had much better success with other agencies as my staff and I persisted in our research."

Sasha could see the Air Force officers slightly shaking their heads and the lawyers at the table in front of them frown at one another. It was apparent that there was disagreement and discomfort on the part of the military and government representatives in the room. The smug arrogance reflected in the lawyer, Baker's, tone was cutting.

"Your Honor," Baker continued, "we have with us here this morning several wives and family members of the Air Force crewmembers who disappeared along with their aircraft over one year ago. Now, we all understand that air accidents frequently occur, but in the case of this particular aircraft, a bomber heavily loaded with nuclear weapons was on a highly important and carefully monitored mission when it disappeared without a trace."

Sasha listened intently as Baker developed his case. "This bomber and its highly dedicated and patriotic American crew, as well as all of the other aircraft and crewmen participating in this extremely well-planned and calculated mission, were each undoubtedly monitored and tracked by every electronic means our government and our allies have at their disposal."

He paused, took a deep breath and continued, "And Our country was on the verge of war with the Soviet Union over the events in Cuba, and thousands of brave young men and women were called to arms. This particular aircraft and crew took off with another similarly configured bomber and flew a very closely coordinated *buddy* route. That is to say, Your Honor, the two bombers took off within seconds of one another and flew very close to each other for many hours. One aircraft, its call sign identification was *Apache Two-Zero,* suddenly disappeared from the face of the earth. There was no call for help from the crew; no radio communication of any kind to indicate that there was a problem."

Sasha shuddered when the lawyer mentioned *"Apache Two-Zero."* A hundred anguishing memories flooded his thoughts.

"I need to get out of here. I don't need this!"

But he didn't dare make a move or draw any attention to himself and risk being noticed by any number of people who might be in the courtroom.

Baker continued to develop his case. "The mystery question, Your Honor, is how did this particular bomber amongst all of the other hundreds of aircraft flying on the same day in relatively the same region of the world, and all in radio contact among themselves, and with numerous ground stations, simply disappear without anyone else being the wiser? The apparent answer is that we don't know. But what we do know is that had it not been for one particular wife of one of the crewmen, this incident would have become just another statistic."

He turned suddenly and faced the families sitting on the benches to his left, "This young lady, Caitlyn Adams-Self, the wife of the copilot had by accident heard a rumor that the aircraft commander of that doomed bomber had been previously questioned by the FBI. At the time, she had no idea what the subject of questioning might have been," he paused . . . "and, Your Honor, neither did I. Ms. Self along with several other wives and relatives are here with us today."

Sasha was frozen in his seat. He was unsettled and became slightly nauseous as he scanned the wives and relatives of his doomed crew members; not only Caitlyn his co-pilot's wife, Jacque', his navigator's wife, whom he had enjoyed dinner with the two of them numerous times. He couldn't move. He could only listen in disbelief.

Baker continued to make the most of the opportunity. "After listening to her story," he said, "and learning of the apparent indifference on the part of the government to both her and the other wives of the missing men, I began my own pursuit of any details that might be even faintly associated with this questionable tragedy. I first visited the senior commander of the unit in Puerto Rico to which the aircrew was assigned. When I met with Colonel William Blair, now Brigadier General Blair,"

He turned and faced General Blair sitting on the front row bench to his right, "The wing commander of the unit, he was reluctant to talk to me about the missing aircraft and crew or any of the details related to the incident. When I mentioned to Colonel Blair that there was a rumor floating about that the aircraft commander of the missing bomber, a Captain Michael Scott, had been questioned by the FBI just prior to the mission, he put me off and suggested that I seek to verify my rumors somewhere else."

Sasha became further agitated and tense when he heard the lawyer introduce the name, *Michael Scott*, his undercover pseudonym for over eight years. He remained fixed on the unraveling events. He could do little else. *"Why on earth did I choose to return to the United States with the same name?"* he stirred within. *"How stupid!"* he sighed deeply.

"Your Honor," Baker continued, "I filed several document requests with the Department of Defense and the Air Force regarding the missing bomber and the alleged story on the aircraft commander and was rebuffed virtually at every turn. No one was willing to discuss the incident and persisted in covering it with security classifications."

Baker scanned the table where the government's lawyers were seated. "Finally," he said, "I challenged the Attorney General's office to the point of them granting a meeting for me with the FBI

Special Agent in Charge in San Juan, Puerto Rico. He was gracious enough to permit me to interview two of his agents, Manuel English and Jack Young. Your Honor, since you have granted me the privilege of subpoenaing these two gentlemen, I will wait until they present themselves for testimony before we elaborate further on that issue."

Sasha searched around the courtroom for the FBI agent, English. He couldn't spot him. He clearly remembered the meeting with the agent which took place just days before his fateful mission, but he felt at the time that it turned out to be routine and that English reflected no suspicions.

"What could have happened?" he wondered. "Did the FBI get something out of Charlie, his handler, after they arrested him or the OSI secretary who forged his Top Secret security clearance forms? What's going on here?"

Baker continued with his statement, "Your Honor, I will also call General William Blair of the U.S. Air Force and later, a Mr. Ron Butler from the CIA. This completes my formal statement, Your Honor, but permit me to quickly add, six brave aviators who were serving our nation in a critical time of need mysteriously disappeared over one year ago. I believe that their families deserve to know as much as there is available about the circumstances surrounding the apparent loss of their loved ones. To date, they have received nothing more than letters of condolences without any words of explanation."

"Yes, go on Mr. Baker," the judge acknowledged.

"Your Honor," Baker continued, "We need to determine if the Pentagon and the Air Force have exhausted every possible means, including what international aid they have requested, to determine the fate of these men. That is my purpose in addressing this court, Your Honor. Thank you."

"Thank you, Counselor," Judge Shrull nodded. "Does the Government wish to make a statement?"

A tall bespectacled, well-dressed, distinguished looking man with thinning gray hair rose from his chair at the table to the left of the courtroom. His dark blue suit with a matching gray tie was considerably more conservative than that of Baker's *attire*.

"Thank you, Your Honor. I am Zachary Hollis, Deputy Chief Counsel for the Department of Defense. I do have a statement for the court. First, I wish to introduce Brigadier General Daniel Stauffer, Deputy Staff Judge Advocate, U.S. Air Force and Jacob Mason, my research assistant and sensitive information security expert, who join me here this morning."

Each of the men nodded and Hollis continued, "Your Honor, we appreciate the opportunity to participate in this inquiry. First, on behalf of the United States Government, I wish to express our regret and sincere sympathy to the families of the missing airmen we are discussing here today. Our hearts also go out to the family of our late president. The tragedy of his loss and that of these young airmen are inexplicable. The circumstances surrounding the mysterious disappearance of the aircraft in question, and the crew, remain a profound mystery."

Hollis looked over at the family members seated on three rows to his left and continued, "I want to assure the court that for the past year the U.S. Government and the Air Force have exhausted every means and traveled down every avenue in an attempt to resolve this mystery. We have also attempted to provide the families with every element of information resulting from our attempts. We simply cannot provide an answer to the disappearance."

Hollis then turned his attention to Baker seated at the adjacent table to his right. "Now, with regard to counselor's assertion that there is a question regarding the credibility of the aircraft commander of the missing aircraft, there is no evidence to the effect that Captain Michael Scott was anything other than a highly competent Air Force officer, pilot and loyal American. We, too, are interested in the testimony of the FBI agents and others, but I caution the court that it is quite possible that some of the testimony may very well take us into some sensitive areas of security classification which we cannot openly discuss in this forum. Therefore, I would ask the indulgence of the court to the point that if my associate, Mr. Mason, detects a potential breach of security, he will so advise us, and I will ask for a motion to recess and discuss the situation."

"So granted, Counselor, Proceed," the judge replied.

"Thank you, Your Honor. I wish only to comment further that the plaintiffs' attorney's veiled assertion that the aircraft commander of this B-52 bomber is under some strange suspicion is an insult to him, his family and the government he faithfully served. Those assertions serve no useful purpose whatsoever. Further, we do not believe that a hearing of this kind will in any way assist in solving the mysterious disappearance of the bomber and its crew of American patriots. But we will cooperate with this hearing in any way possible to bring this unfortunate situation to closure. Thank you, Your Honor." Hollis returned to his seat at the table.

The judge then directed his attention to Baker. "Thank you, Gentlemen. Mr. Baker do you have witnesses at this time?"

"Yes, Your Honor," Baker responded. "I wish to call Special Agent Manuel English of the Federal Bureau of Investigation."

TEN

"Any fish is good if it is on the hook."

A Russian Proverb

Reflections

The Bailiff walked to a side door and Special Agent Manuel English entered the courtroom. He was led to the witness stand and stood while he was sworn in by the clerk.

Sasha recognized the darkly handsome and pleasant agent dressed in a brown sport jacket and tan slacks. He had visited with him in a room at the Ramey Air Force Base, Puerto Rico Officers' Club a few days before he and his crew took off on the fateful mission. They had concluded the meeting amicably, and he felt that he had satisfactorily answered English's questions. The fact that the FBI agent was now in this courtroom rekindled his memory and heightened his concern.

"What have they possibly uncovered?" His thoughts raced in search of all that had occurred during his extraordinary first stint in the United States.

He focused on the lawyer, as Baker nonchalantly moved from his position at the table and eased to within a few steps of the witness stand and spoke.

"Agent English, I have advised the Court that we have met previously and that I have invited you here to perhaps assist us in better understanding certain of the events that occurred at the base in Puerto Rico, before the disappearance of the strategic bomber. Therefore, I will go directly to the crux of the issue."

Baker paced back and forth for a moment. It was apparent that he enjoyed the center of attention. "Agent English, would you tell us about an inquiry you were requested to conduct by your agency office in San Juan, Puerto Rico, about one year ago?"

"Yes, Sir," English replied. "My office was advised that there was an inquiry underway into suspected misconduct in the application and granting of security clearances to Air Force officers stationed at Castle Air Force Base, California. The focus of my inquiry was directed toward one of those officers, a Captain Michael Scott, then stationed at Ramey Air Force Base. I met with Captain Scott to determine if he was aware that his request and the approval of his Top Secret security clearance had been falsely administered. By falsely administered, I mean that the required background checks on his past were never conducted and the final disposition forms for his clearance had been forged, apparently, we learned, by a secretary working in the personnel office at the base. The secretary, Ms. Lisa Quintero, mysteriously disappeared immediately after base investigators discovered the discrepancies during a routine compliance inspection."

English adjusted himself in the witness chair and continued, "I visited with Captain Scott and questioned him about this allegation. He professed no knowledge of the situation, nor did he know the secretary. He also denied any knowledge of a civilian male who had resided near the base and had been arrested by our agents for suspicion of being a foreign agent."

Baker interjected, "Did you discuss your inquiry with the senior officials on the base in Puerto Rico?"

"Yes, Sir, I did," English said. "Agent Young and I paid a visit to Colonel Blair, commander of the bomb wing, on October 27, 1962. We informed Colonel Blair of my previous meeting with Captain Scott and that other questions and serious concerns had arisen since that meeting. I requested a further meeting with the captain, a formal meeting and one that would possibly be under oath. I also advised the colonel that we were prepared to exercise a warrant for Captain Scott's arrest if the meeting proved such action necessary."

"What was Colonel, we should say, *General* Blair's reaction to your visit?" Baker asked snidely.

"Well, Sir, he was visibly disturbed," English responded. "He characterized Captain Scott as one of the top officers in his wing and did not want to believe that he could be suspected of anything untoward. He also advised us that the captain had just departed on an airborne mission and would not return for at least twenty-four hours. I asked if it were possible to bring him back sooner, and the colonel said that it was not because they were on a Cuban Crisis mission ordered by the president."

"What did you do then?" Baker persisted.

"The colonel offered to provide agent Young and myself overnight quarters to await Captain Scott's return," English replied. "I reported the situation to my S.A.C. in San Juan, and he agreed that we should remain at the base and wait out the captain's return."

"And?" Baker asked.

English responded, "I received a call from an officer in the wing command center very early the next morning and was asked to come to Colonel Blair's office. When we arrived, the colonel told us that they had lost contact with Captain Scott's aircraft and that no one had heard from the bomber in several hours. He was concerned that there could be a serious problem. Of course, as we know, the aircraft and crew did not return to base."

Sasha felt as if he were observing all of this unfold from some far away place, not sitting in this courtroom. It was more like a stage play, and he was watching a story about someone else. He remained glued to his seat, his thoughts crisscrossing the events of his past life.

"What can they do?" he thought. "Even if they get anything out of Charlie or the secretary, there is no place for them to go after that."

Sasha's thoughts continued to rationalize the situation. "The bomber is gone; the crew is dead, and *Mike Scott* dead. For that matter, Captain Mike Scott never existed. There is nothing to pursue. There is no evidence that the bomber did anything other than crash at sea, and, certainly, there is no evidence to indicate that the aircraft flew into Soviet territory. I feel very badly about the crewmembers and the suffering of their families, but we are at war and this is a consequence of war. I wish I could do something for the families, but time will heal their wounds."

He would have liked to leave the courtroom right then, but he stayed put.

Baker pursued his line of questions with English. "Agent English, will you describe for us what this Captain Scott was suspected of, beyond the apparent discrepancies in his security clearance paperwork? Was there something else?"

"Yes, Sir, there was," English replied. "Between the time I met with Captain Scott and then with Colonel Blair, the Air Force OSI and the Bureau conducted a background check on the officers whose security records were in doubt. Each of the officers checked out okay with the exception of Captain Scott. I will get to Scott in a moment, but it appeared that the secretary, Lisa Quintero, who perpetrated the caper with the clearance paperwork was making a few dollars on the side. She was apparently expediting the clearance approvals on officers who were impatient to get their security clearances, or who were aware of something in their past that might have jeopardized their background check."

English smiled ever so slightly. "She apparently had a little private and perhaps profitable business going, but with regard to Captain Scott, we hit a brick wall. The personal references he listed in his background questionnaire were either bogus or could not be located. There were several names listed as relatives that were apparently fictitious and others that were also either false or could not be traced. The whole process required that he have an insider to make sure that his background questionnaire did not get to an investigator to follow up. That is where the secretary came in to play. We believe that she was paid handsomely for her work, either by Scott himself or an intermediary working on his behalf. Her sudden influx of ready cash was confirmed in a sworn statement by one of her coworkers, a Ms. Summer Lee. I have provided a copy of Ms. Lee's affidavit to you."

"Is that all, Agent English?" Baker persisted.

"No, Sir," English responded. "Our investigation uncovered a curious coincidence. In Cleveland, Ohio, the city that Captain Scott listed as his home of record, we discovered that a male with the name, John Michael Scott, with the approximate same date of birth as that of Captain John Michael Scott, was killed in a brawl near his twentieth birthday. His body was claimed by an unrelated and unknown person or persons and buried privately. Our investigators further determined that the deceased Scott was a street person with no known relatives."

"What did your investigators conclude from that coincidence?" Baker asked.

"They concluded that with the coincidence of identical names of two people from the same locale with similar birth dates and with one deceased, there is a possibility of a ploy to assume an identity. This has been used in the past by underworld connections and by foreign perpetrators to introduce agents into the United States," English concluded.

"Agent English, are you implying that there is a possibility that Captain Scott was somehow a foreign agent?" Baker snidely asked.

"Sir," English replied. "I am saying that we had intended to question Captain Scott along those lines when we visited Colonel Blair and discovered that the subject had departed on a flight. The evidence we had strongly suggested that the subject might very well have been using an assumed name. Of course, we could not confirm that, nor for what reason."

"One last question, Agent English," Baker implored. "When did Captain Scott enter the United States Air Force and from what city?"

"John Michael Scott entered the Air Force from Cleveland," English responded. "He had ostensibly applied for aviation cadet training after completing two years of academic work at Milner College. We visited Milner, however, and found no record of anyone by his name ever attending school there. In conclusion, Mr. Baker, the Bureau believes there is a strong possibly that Captain Scott was an imposter of some sort. However, we have no conclusive findings that can provide proof to that assertion."

"Thank you, Agent English. I have no further questions, Your Honor," Baker smiled confidently.

"Thank you, Mr. Baker," the judge acknowledged. "Mr. Hollis, do you wish to question the witness?"

"No, we do not, Your Honor," Hollis responded.

"Do you have another witness, Mr. Baker?"

"Yes, Your Honor. I would like to call Brigadier General William Blair."

Sasha watched as his former wing commander walked erect and confidently to the witness stand and took the oath. He recalled that the last time he saw Colonel Blair was at the pre-departure briefing just before he and his crew took off on his fateful mission. This all seemed like a distant dream or an illusion. For that matter the entire eight years he spent in the United States posing as an Air Force officer and pilot had faded considerably with time. This court proceeding was bringing it all back, and all too vividly!

He listened as the lawyer, Baker, questioned General Blair. "General Blair, will you tell the court what your relationship is to this hearing?"

Blair described his position as commander of the B-52 unit stationed in Puerto Rico during the Cuban Crisis a year earlier and about the execution of the airborne alert missions that were flown in response to the Soviet excursions in Cuba.

"General, how well did you know Captain Scott and the members of this crew?" Baker asked.

"I knew Captain Mike Scott reasonably well," Blair began. "Not personally, but perhaps I was more familiar with his reputation as an exceptionally intelligent, dedicated officer and excellent pilot. He was among, if not *the* most professionally dedicated and skilled officer and pilot in my wing. He was also the youngest aircraft commander in the unit. His age and lack of equivalent experience to the older pilots, however, never deterred him. He excelled in every aspect of his flying skills and leadership with his combat crew. I rated him as a superior performer, professional and loyal. I did not know each of the other crewmembers on Captain Scott's crew except once again by their professional performance under Mike Scott's leadership. We all regret the loss of those exceptional young men and our heartfelt sympathy goes out to their wives and families."

"Thank you, General. Was Captain Scott married?" Baker asked.

"No, at least not to my knowledge," Blair replied.

"Did you send letters of condolence to the wives and or families of the missing crew members?" Baker asked.

"Yes, I did, to each one," General Blair confidently replied.

"Did you write a letter to Captain Scott's next of kin?" Baker persisted.

"Yes, I am quite sure that I did." Blair replied.

"To the best of your recollection, General, was that letter delivered?" Baker asked.

"I presume that it was," Blair replied and asked, "is there some question to that effect?" He was obviously becoming irritated with the line of questioning and Baker's arrogant tone.

"General Blair, my research reveals that the letter you wrote and sent to Captain Scott's next of kin was returned and stamped, *Return to Sender*. This implies that the person to whom the letter was sent either did not live at that address or perhaps did not even exist. What do *you* think?" Baker continued to dig.

"I have no idea, Mr. Baker," Blair looked pensive. "I merely wrote a personal letter to each of the crewmembers' families expressing my sincere regret and distress with the apparent loss of their loved ones. That is all that I could humanly accomplish at the time."

Baker raised his eyebrows in mock jest. "Your Honor, if it pleases the court, I would like to submit for the record, an affidavit from the United States Air Force casualty office, which states in part:

> *"The Air Force Finance and Accounting Center has been unable to locate the next of kin of Captain John Michael Scott, missing and presumed dead, in order to remit the proceeds of his government insurance policy and to close out his personal financial records."*

Sasha watched as Baker handed the clerk the document from which he had read. He felt a glow of perspiration as he listened to the lawyer describe the document.

General Blair sat stone-faced and did not respond.

Baker pursed his lips with a smile. "Okay, that's enough on that subject so let's move on. General, do you believe that the United States has done everything humanly possible to determine the fate of the aircraft and crew?"

Blair paused for a moment. "Yes, I do. I am confident that every effort has been made to determine the cause and the estimated location of the aircraft's disappearance. Our government and our allies in the area have combed every inch and researched every communications recording to determine the fate of the men. We can only conclude that whatever occurred was a prompt and disastrous emergency, and the aircraft crashed into the sea. But today, Mr. Baker, I regret that you are attempting to create some mystique with this aircraft accident and the sad loss of these brave men. I don't know what is to be accomplished by all of this other than to bring the sadness and despair back to the victims' families."

Baker frowned and looked around the courtroom for effect. "General, are you aware that there was a British frigate positioned along the southern coast of Italy, and that the surveillance radar on that ship detected a large unidentified aircraft image flying away from the area where your bomber and crew were supposed to be? And, are you aware that when the aircraft was queried on all available radio frequencies, it did not respond, but continued to fly east and northward across the southern end of Italy and presumably across the Adriatic Sea toward Soviet controlled territory?"

Blair was visibly vexed. "Yes, I have heard about that report, but I, along with the others who were made aware of it, put no credence to any logic that it might have a relationship to our missing bomber. There were hundreds of aircraft, both U.S. and friendly allies, flying in that region during the operational period, and it could have been any one of those. But importantly, there was no logical reason for our bomber to be headed in that direction, and even if for some completely unknown reason it was, there is no doubt that the crew would have responded to queries by the tracking ship."

Baker smiled and looked at the government lawyers. "Thank you, General, no further questions."

"Mr. Hollis, do you have any questions for General Blair?" the judge asked.

"No, Your Honor," Hollis replied.

"You may step down, General Blair. Thank you for your cooperation," the judge responded. "Mr. Baker, do you have any further witnesses?"

"Yes, Your Honor, as I alerted your court earlier, I have a sworn witness affidavit, which I wish to have read, then submitted to the record of these proceedings. But first, Your Honor, I want to assure you that I have permission of the office of the Director, Central Intelligence, the CIA, if you will, to present this sworn testimony in open court. As the document is read, the court will notice places where names and locations are redacted for security reasons. Therefore, if Your Honor or the Air Force representatives have any concerns for the security or sensitivity of the information in the document, they have been put to rest by the CIA, which has cooperated fully and agreed to the testimony of my next witness. If your Honor pleases, I would like to call Mr. Ronald Butler."

The Defector

Once again the bailiff proceeded to the side door of the courtroom and escorted a well-dressed man with grayish dark hair and medium height to the witness stand where he was administered the oath.

Baker proceeded. "Mr. Butler, will you please state your name, place of employment, your position and purpose for being in this court?"

"I am Ronald Butler, assigned to the Central Intelligence Agency. I am a Special Investigations Officer and Russian linguist presently working with foreign defectors. I have been requested to attend this hearing to read the testimony of a Soviet volunteer defector who came to our attention in March of this year."

"Thank you, Mr. Butler," Baker acknowledged. "Would you please proceed with the deposed affidavit you have cited?"

Judge Shrull interjected, "Mr. Hollis, have you been provided a copy of this deposition, and do you agree to its submission before this hearing?"

"I have, Your Honor," Hollis responded, but apparently not too happily so. "And while we are surprised by its content, we are perhaps concerned even more so about the authenticity and integrity of the deposed individual and the substance of his disposition. We have no grounds, however, to pose an objection."

"Thank you, Mr. Hollis," the judge acknowledged. "Mr. Butler, you may proceed."

"Yes, Sir," Butler replied and began his statement. "The defector mentioned, has provided several depositions during the interrogation phase of his agreement to cooperate with us. The following deposition concerns an account of one of several interesting events he has related to us. As to validity, accuracy and authenticity of this particular account, we can only take his uncorroborated word. I quote the deposition as follows:

> *I, Alexei Ivanov, which is not my actual name, do hereby give this deposition voluntarily and of my own free will."*

Sasha froze. "What on earth is this? What is going on here? Who have they found? What could he possible know?" He fidgeted as he continued to listen to the reading of the deposition:

> *"Having lost confidence in my government, I freely left my country of citizenship in January, 1963. I departed from the confines of East Germany on 14 January after considerable deliberation with my conscience and the possible consequences of my act which will undoubtedly be considered treasonous by my government. Before I arrived on assignment in East Germany in late November, 1962, I was assigned as a Soviet Air Force officer serving in the grade of major. In mid-October of 1962, I became a part of a special task force sent to (redacted) air base several hundred miles south of Moscow. My duty as an aircraft maintenance officer was to prepare the base facilities for the arrival of a special aircraft. The aircraft, I learned, was of U.S. origin. It was to be a strategic bomber with an American flight crew. However, the strong rumor was that one of our own people, a Soviet agent, was flying the aircraft. The bomber, we were told, was an American*

> *B-52G aircraft and that it was fully loaded with nuclear weapons."*

His heart pounding, Sasha felt as if he was going to explode. There was nothing he could do except to try and control his turmoil and remain still. He listened as the story unfolded:

> *"We were not told how this aircraft had fallen into Soviet control, nor why it had an American crew with a Soviet pilot. It was quite odd. We were heavily briefed not to ask questions and not to remember anything we saw or the work we were doing. It was my task to supervise my people to make ready one of the large hangers on the airfield to accept the incoming bomber aircraft. We heard that all personnel and their families normally assigned to the base were relocated elsewhere until the operation was completed. My colonel told me that there were numerous important military officers present at the base for the event. He warned that we must stay on our toes and do our work professionally. To prepare for the aircraft's arrival, we retrofitted a tow bar from one of our own large transports to fit the incoming aircraft. I was told that the plans for making the tow bar operate properly were provided to us by the secret police. We did not ask about their origin, but it was obvious that the photographs and descriptions were taken from an American military aircraft maintenance technical book for their B-52 bomber. All of the language in the instructions was in English."*

He distinctly recalled the day he visited the maintenance training facility at his base in California and casually picked up several Tech Orders on the B-52 bomber. He gave them to his handler, Charlie, for disposition.

"They obviously reached their destination!" he was able to confirm as he listened to the defector's incredible story.

"We worked for several days preparing for the arrival of the aircraft, and finally the scheduled day arrived. It was 28 October 1962. Everything was prepared and in place. The security forces were everywhere, both military and secret agents. We were all being watched and our work monitored closely. As we eagerly and patiently awaited the arrival of the aircraft, suddenly my colonel called me aside and told me that the scheduled exercise was over. The bomber was not going to arrive after all. I did not question him nor did he reveal to me the reason for the change of plans. He told me to prepare my men for return to our home base as soon as possible and take with us all of our equipment and any evidence that we had ever been at that base. That is all I know about this event."

Butler concluded, "Sir, that is the deposition we took from the defector known as Ivanov."

"Thank you, Mr. Butler. Are you prepared to validate the substance of the defector's story?" Baker asked.

"Sir," Butler responded, "there is an old proverb, actually a Russian proverb; *'Any fish is good if it is on the hook'!* Our Mr. Ivanov is *on the hook*, so to speak, and we will take him at face value until his story is otherwise found lacking.*"*

"Thank you," Baker smiled. "Now, would you enlighten us further from your experience at CIA or from any other sources what this defector's story might have been all about?"

"Well, Sir," Butler continued. "Our agency was aware of the event concerning a B-52 bomber that disappeared last year during the Cuban Crisis operation. The date that our defector gave us in the deposition corresponds exactly with the date the bomber disappeared. The part that he related about there being a Soviet agent at the controls of the aircraft had us baffled. That is until you brought us the story about the FBI inquiry at the base in Puerto Rico, and their interest in one of the pilots that flew an airborne alert mission on that same date and into a region not many hours from Soviet territory. Our people are presently working with the FBI on the details of their findings."

Butler proceeded to elaborate, "Our defector, Ivanov, and we presume, most of the people involved in the special project at the Soviet air base, were reassigned, as well, to various distant locations. This was likely in order to distract them and lessen the opportunity to relate to where they had been or what they had worked on. This is a typical Soviet tactic. They go to great lengths to break up units and redistribute both military personnel and civilians in attempts to divert attention and interest in sensitive projects. Ivanov was reassigned to a military base near the western border in East Germany. He apparently has never been a zealous communist. He has told us that he is not married and that his parents are no longer living. He also said that he was fascinated with the west and saw an opportunity to get safely across the border into West Germany, so he made his move. One might suspect that he was sent over to become a double agent, and we are always sensitive to that ploy. However, it is also the fundamental practice of the Soviets to hold a tight string on their agents by making sure that they have control of a spouse, children or other close family member back home while the agent is dispatched to another country."

Sasha could relate to the agent's conjecture. While he was away in the United States, he knew very well that his mother remained under surveillance and was an easy prey for the KGB if he had elected to conduct himself other than what he was assigned to do.

Butler continued to validate the bizarre story. "Now, regarding the credibility of the defector's story about this particular event, he seems to have all of his facts straight, including locations, times, dates and so forth. It would appear to be almost too coincidental for his story not to have some credence. The huge question we have is what happened to the *mystery* bomber that was supposed to land at the base that was being prepared? We have three speculative propositions. First, was there really an American bomber that had been captured by the Soviets? Two, if there was a bomber in Soviet hands, was it sent to another base as a cover tactic, and the base where our defector was working was a decoy? And third, did the bomber crash enroute to the recovery base?"

"To summarize, Sir," Butler continued, "the first proposition seems highly questionable to most everyone, but again there are a number of coincidental factors to consider the merits of such a thing happening. If the second proposition is correct, how did the Soviets take control of the aircraft? If one of the pilots was an agent, how did he overcome the other crewmembers? Or, *was he* one of the crewmembers? And where is the flight crew today? Finally, if this bomber is in Soviet hands, there is no doubt that they could easily cover up the whole escapade. Whether they have it in their possession somewhere or it actually crashed enroute, we all know that their government is capable of masking anything they wish. Sir, that completes my summation."

"Thank you, Mr. Butler," Baker smiled. "You have been extremely informative.

"Your Honor," Baker addressed the judge, "this completes my witness list."

"Thank you, Counselor. Mr. Hollis, do you wish to question the witness?" the judge asked.

Hollis was in consultation with his colleagues; he looked up at the judge and responded. "No, Your Honor, but I would like to reserve the opportunity to return to Mr. Butler and some of the other witnesses later if time permits."

The judge gave Hollis a studied look, "Mr. Hollis, it appears that the plaintiffs have completed their arguments, and I understand that you do not wish to call any witnesses; therefore, I am prepared to call for summations. This is likely your last opportunity to address this witness or any of the others."

"We understand, Your Honor," Hollis responded. "May I have a moment with my colleagues?"

"Yes, you may have the next hour and half," the judge replied. "The court stands adjourned for lunch until two p.m. If there are no further questions of the witnesses after we return, then I will call for closing arguments. Thank you, Mr. Butler. You may step down, but I request that you return to the court this afternoon and remain until there is a determination of your further service. Again, we thank you. Court is adjourned."

ELEVEN

"A wolf won't eat a wolf."

A Russian Proverb

Full Disclosure

Sasha sat immersed in his thoughts. "This is unbelievable! It's like a cascading avalanche. Everything with the destroyed B-52, the traitors and the events thereafter were all efficiently taken care of. How did this disloyal officer possibly defect?"

He was startled and then he became suddenly aware that he had become absorbed in his thoughts and was almost alone in the courtroom. He stood and tried to appear nonchalant as he casually walked out into the corridor. It was a little after twelve-thirty. He needed to go somewhere to think over what he had witnessed. He departed the court building and moved down the sidewalk absorbed in thought. Several blocks away, he spotted a small diner. He looked around inside briefly, didn't recognize any of those he had observed in the courtroom, and took a booth at the rear.

Ordering a sandwich and hot tea, he pondered the extraordinary events of the morning. "The lawyer has accomplished an incredible investigation. Tracking down the FBI agent, pursuing the U.S. intelligence sources, and the uncanny luck and timing of the defector falling into his hands has put the entire event into perspective. Still it's curious why the U.S. military appears to be reluctant to cooperate with the lawyer's findings. Perhaps they're embarrassed? Or, maybe they just don't want to give credence to the lawyer's linking all the loose parts together."

The waitress brought his ham and cheese sandwich and hot tea as he continued to muse to himself. "I can't conceive of anywhere else they can go. The defector certainly was not aware that the bomber was shot down and destroyed. If he were, he would have already told them. Unless, someone is holding back, either the CIA people or the defector himself . . . perhaps for more money or a better deal, or whatever they offer these traitors? Well, at least they can't go much further, he thought confidently to himself. I am sitting right here in their midst, and no one is the wiser."

He finished his lunch and made his way to the cashier. As he passed one of the booths, he noticed a man sitting alone eyeing him as he passed by. Giving the man only a momentary thought, he paid his check and walked outside. The weather had turned colder with a brisk wind and sleet mixed with light snow.

"Moscow," he murmured and shivered as he pulled his topcoat collar up around his neck and headed back toward the courthouse.

Back inside, he found a seat roughly in the same place where he sat that morning. Looking around, there appeared to be more people inside the room than in the morning session. Several rows of seats on his side were filled with men and a few women, all dressed in an array of casual attire. He reasoned that these were newspaper reporters. They had obviously heard reports of the hearing that morning and were sent there for a story. The wives and family members of the crew had returned and were clustered back in their front row seats on the right side. He didn't want to look in their direction. The memory of his loyal and trusting crewmembers filled him with guilt and depression.

The Air Force officers and the government lawyers had taken their seats, and Baker had returned to his table. The bailiff called for everyone to stand while the judge returned to the bench.

Judge Shrull spoke, "Mr. Hollis, does the Government wish to question the CIA witness further?"

Hollis responded, "No, Your Honor, as I indicated earlier, we have been provided a copy of the defector's affidavit and do not believe that there would be any benefit in questioning Mr. Butler further."

"Very well then, at this time, I will call upon the counsel for the plaintiffs to give his closing argument: Mr. Baker."

Baker rose from his chair and paced back and forth for a moment, eyeing the lawyers at the government's table.

"Thank you, Your Honor," he replied with a wry smile on his lips. "There really isn't very much I can add, Your Honor, to the incredible revelations that we have all heard this day. But I am shocked that it has taken a full year, the alertness of a bereaved wife, and some rather rudimentary work on the part of an ordinary lawyer such as myself, to bring all of this to the attention of this court and the American people. Where has our military and our government been all of this time? Why did these suffering families have to resort to finding someone outside of their military community to assist them in finding some closure to the tragedy that has befallen each of them?"

Baker continued to pace back and forth in front of the judge's bench, glancing at the government lawyers, eyeing the audience and paying special attention to the wives and families.

"Your Honor, it doesn't take a rocket scientist to piece together all the parts of this mosaic. We have a highly suspicious Air Force officer under investigation at the very time he was taking a flight crew of loyal and patriotic young Americans on a very dangerous mission. There is mounting evidence that he was perhaps a spy or even a traitor. To the contrary, there is every possibility" . . . Baker raised his voice. **". . . that he was not an American at all!** Your Honor, we have heard the testimony of a trusted agent of the Federal Bureau of Investigation. He told us of their pursuit of an Air Force officer who had either bribed a civilian employee to falsify his military records to acquire a coveted top secret security clearance, or someone else working on his behalf allegedly paid that same employee to gain the security clearance for him."

Baker moved over to the table where the government lawyers sat and stood half-facing them and continued, "Then, we have the testimony of the commander of this suspect Air Force officer who told us that he thought the officer was one of his very best. He trusted him, and rightly, he should have. He should have, of course, unless there was reason otherwise to do so. And, when the bomber being commanded and flown by this mysterious officer disappeared, the commander wrote letters of condolence to each of the crewmember's wives and families, including Captain Scott. But, Your Honor, strangely, the General's letter which was sent to Captain Scott's next of kin was returned because it could not be delivered."

With a spring in his voice, Baker proceeded to hammer his case. "Next, Your Honor, we have the extraordinary testimony of Mr. Butler of the CIA, including the deposition of a defector, describing an event that is almost too incredible to believe. But, there is no reason to dispute the defector's story. The details he described are just too coincidental not to believe. He could not have told such a bizarre tale unless he was there during the event he described. He said that an American bomber, a B-52, was inbound to a Soviet base and that a Soviet pilot was in command of the aircraft. He said that he assumed the remainder of the crewmembers were American. The date of the event described by the defector was the same day that the bomber carrying the men whose families are here in this courtroom disappeared. All of this is just too coincidental."

He paused, making the most of the situation that he had well in hand, "Your Honor, the B-52 bomber that departed the base in Puerto Rico on October 27, 1961, was, without a doubt, hijacked by the aircraft commander, Captain John Michael Scott, who was either a Soviet agent or was acting on behalf of the Soviet Government. He delivered the bomber and its innocent crew into the hands of the Soviet Union. And, Your Honor, I believe that it is entirely possible that those American aviators on board that bomber may very well be prisoners in the Soviet Union this very day!"

Several audible gasps and murmuring stirred the courtroom.

"Order! Quiet, please! Continue, Counselor," the judge admonished.

"Thank you, Your Honor," Baker smiled approvingly at his work. "I apologize for issuing such an alarm, but I challenge the United States Government to refute any of this and to prove otherwise. Thank you, Your Honor."

"Thank you, Counselor." Judge Shrull was also visibly moved by Baker's accusation. "Those are extraordinary allegations, Mr. Baker, and I sincerely hope that there is a more reassuring account and explanation of the events that you and the witnesses have described."

"Mr. Hollis, are you prepared to summarize?"

"Yes, we are, Your Honor," Hollis stood and addressed the judge. "Sir, as you have so correctly concluded, we have heard some extraordinary testimony here today. Those testimonials have played well into Mr. Baker's own exceptionally stretched imagination. It is also quite apparent that Mr. Butler and his agency are reasonably convinced that this defector they have in their possession is telling a credible story. We do not hold that same position, and we believe that this entire affair should be rightfully turned over to the Department of Defense for further investigation and validation of the presumed facts presented us by the plaintiffs' lawyer."

Hollis's argument, although articulately presented, could not measure up to the compelling evidence presented by Baker. He continued, "Your Honor, this court is not the appropriate forum for such a sensitive inquiry. We urge you to dismiss these proceedings and hand over all of the documented testimony to the Secretary of Defense who, I am assured, will in turn open a full investigation surrounding the disappearance of the Air Force B-52 bomber. He will coordinate his investigation with the Attorney General and the Director of the CIA."

Hollis appeared to condescend. "While we on the Government's side feel some embarrassment with the revelations presented here today, we also believe that we have been intentionally left out of the game, so to speak. Perhaps, that in itself has been to intentionally cause embarrassment to the U.S. Government."

He concluded his argument, "Again, Your Honor, we are as concerned as anyone to determine what happened to this aircraft and its precious crew of American airmen. We believe that in order to bring all of the parties together, the appropriate responsibility should rest with the Secretary of Defense, not in a courtroom. Thank you, Your Honor, we have no further comments."

Baker promptly raised an objection, "Your Honor, the Government's request is ridiculous! They have had their opportunity to address this matter, and the evidence reflects that they have not acted in good faith. Instead, they simply tucked the missing bomber and its crew in a file cabinet somewhere in the Pentagon and closed the case on six missing airmen. Those

American men may very well be rotting away somewhere in the Soviet Union, except of course, *Captain Mike Scott*, who has likely been given a medal and a promotion in the Soviet Army!"

Sasha flushed. He could feel the heat in his face and the sweat pop out on his brow as the prophetic words of the lawyer ricocheted through his body. His thoughts flashed back to that day when he waked up in the hospital room with Mackye and General Tushenskiy at his bedside. He sighed and bowed his head as he recalled the General lauding him for his exploits, awarded him with the Order of Lenin and promoted him to colonel in the Soviet Air Force.

Baker continued with his objection, "Your Honor, it is imperative that you provide a ruling on this hearing that *does not* hand the responsibility back to the place where it has been buried. I recommend that the appropriate authority is at the highest level of our government which must take seriously the evidence we have uncovered and provided this court and get to the bottom of this sad situation. Thank you, Your Honor."

The judge studied the two tables of lawyers for a long moment, before responding, "Collectively, you have given this court a very complex problem and one that I must take some time to review and study before I can conclude what I believe is in the best interests of all the parties, but mainly the families left to suffer through all of this." Turning his attention to the assembled members of the families, "My heart goes out to each of you. I will attempt to render an opinion within one week. Court is adjourned."

Sasha felt drained. He slowly departed the courthouse with the others, remaining a far distant from the families and his former Air Force superiors. Outside, he walked slowly down the street; his mind was a jumble of thoughts when suddenly he felt the presence of someone close behind him. "Interesting session, wouldn't you agree, Comrade?"

Disciplined to sudden intrusions, he did not turn to face the voice. He continued on down the sidewalk. The man behind the voice moved along side him.

"Comrade," he smirked in a crusty voice, "your disguise almost fooled me when you departed the Smithsonian this morning. First, you entered the building and then a different person departed. But the different person had on the same shoes and the same walk as you. So I came along with you to this court building. I thought that if it were so important to change your identity to go somewhere, that the somewhere must be very important for me also."

Sasha turned his head slightly and recognized the man he had seen briefly in the booth at the restaurant at lunchtime. "What is your business with me?" he asked in a directive tone of voice.

"Comrade Katsanov, let us walk down to a quiet place, and we can talk."

He knew that he had little choice. The intruder was KGB and would dog him until he conceded. "Fine. You lead the way," Sasha replied.

"Dah," the intruder smiled, speaking with a clearly detectable Eastern European accent. "Let's go back to the quiet little place where we had lunch."

They entered the restaurant, moved toward a booth and sat on opposite sides of the table. Sasha sized him up as *not* being one of Zotov's *first team.* He was dressed in a wool sport jacket and mismatched trousers. His topcoat had seen better days. He appeared to have applied an industrial grade gel to hold his thick head of hair in place. "But," Sasha conceded to himself, "he did skillfully track me across Washington!"

They each ordered tea and the stranger spoke quietly.

"Comrade," the stranger challenged in a quiet voice, "what business is this American courtroom session to you? Are you studying American law procedures? I was very surprised to follow you here."

"Why are you following me in the first place?" Sasha responded in a grating voice.

"Comrade, we just want to make sure that you are protected while you move about the United States. After all, you are traveling about with *questionable* identification. If some smart U.S. secret policeman decided to question you, you would be in very much difficulty. So, you see, I am your security blanket."

The stranger was taking pleasure in chiding his prey. "Comrade, we were led to believe that you are here on other business. Why did you go to this courthouse today?"

Sasha regained his confidence. "My friend, it is none of your business, but I came here because I had heard that you have a defector loose in this country and that he is blabbing all over the place. I thought maybe your people needed some help keeping track of these loonies that leave our country for a few American dollars and spread bogus stories. That doesn't help our credibility, you know!"

The stranger flushed. "Comrade, we are aware of all the traitors who are lured to the United States, and we watch them carefully. With regard to this crazy you refer to today, we will find him soon enough and take care of him. It is obvious that his story is a complete lie designed to get more money from his CIA protectors. We will eventually get him anyway and teach him a lesson, or perhaps give him better stories to tell. We do not need your help to do that. Now, Comrade, what was your real purpose in coming here this day?"

Convinced that his new friend was a lightweight, *although a good tracker*, Sasha strung him along, "Comrade, to tell you the truth, I had a day off in my schedule and I do have an interest in American law proceedings and came down here to witness a session," he chided the agent further, "but little did I know that the proceeding would reveal some of your own agency's clumsy work. It appears that the CIA has a hot one in their clutches. I would think your chief, Zotov, would be better served to watch after traitors like him rather than me. I must be going, Comrade. I hope you also enjoyed the day in court. And, you and your people should remember, *'A wolf won't eat a wolf!'* Thank you for the tea."

Sasha smiled, grabbed his topcoat and quickly departed, leaving the agent to pick up the tab and pay the bill. He knew that he wouldn't try to skip out without paying and risk getting picked up. Outside, he hastily found a taxicab and headed back to the GRU residence.

TWELVE

"Once burned by milk, you will drink vodka."

A Russian Proverb

Faux Alarm

Yurasov was not at the GRU residence when he returned. That saved Sasha from having to recount the day to the general. He needed time to reflect on the courtroom revelations and what if anything, to do about them. He certainly couldn't discuss his role in the missing bomber affair with Yurasov. He needed also to move on with his assignment of tracing the strange assassination mosaic.

From his room, he called Major Lobanov. "Alexi, would you make airline reservations for me to travel to Dallas on Thursday with a follow-on open ticket to Mexico City?"

He would like to move on as quickly as possible, but he was sure that Yurasov would still want him to meet with his agent, Stork, before he departed.

"I might as well cover all of the bases, Dallas and Mexico City, while I am in this hunt," he concluded. "But I would much prefer to return to Moscow, Mackye's safety and discuss the courtroom event with General Tushenskiy. This assassination trail will lead us nowhere."

His heart was really not into tracking the assassination events any further. The courtroom drama and the persistent KGB harassment had left him distracted and depressed. And, he really had not uncovered any revealing information beyond that reported and conjectured in the news media.

"It's apparent that the KGB probably had some curious connection to it," he continued to muse to himself. "Either they are somehow involved in the assassination or they are so damned paranoid as a result of the complexity of their activities that they don't know what the hell is going on. Either way, they don't want me here."

He endured another night of fitful sleep and consternation. The phone rang as he was getting dressed. It was Alexi.

"Do'broye oo'tra, Comrade Colonel, General Yurasov would like for you to join him for breakfast at 7:30 in his quarters."

"Dah, I will be there, Alexi. Spasee'ba."

He looked at his watch. It was 6:45 a.m. He had time to quickly scan the newspapers. There was the usual continuation of assassination coverage and more speculation. He skipped over those articles for later reading and hurriedly searched for news coverage of the court proceedings he had witnessed.

He found the story on Page Two. The event was not reported in exceptional detail, but it was reasonably accurate and without embellishment. The speculation about the missing bomber being flown by a suspected Soviet agent was only given scant mention. The reporter apparently was not impressed with that angle presented by the lawyer, Baker. The writer was intrigued with the testimony of the CIA agent and the affidavit of the Soviet defector. Most of the news story was devoted to that portion of the proceedings. In part it read:

> *"We must wonder how many other defectors from the Soviet Union are in the custody of the CIA or FBI? And, can their stories be trusted? We can only speculate whether this Russian officer is telling the truth or merely spinning a yarn for money and notoriety. And, are there U.S. defectors doing the same thing in the Soviet Union?"*

He was pleased that the reporter sought to develop the story in that direction rather than to highlight the suspected "Soviet agent pilot" plot implied by the lawyer. He wondered if Yurasov had read the story? He concluded that he had.

He rapped on the door of General Yurasov's quarters. Alexi responded, "Do'broye oo'tro, Tavah'reeshch Colonel! Vaidee'te."

"Ah, Do'broye oo'tro, Sasha," General Yurasov greeted as he entered the room. "Did you rest well? I am sorry that I was away last evening when you returned. I had to attend a very boring trade mission affair. How was your day at the courtroom?"

"Good Morning, General," Sasha greeted. "I enjoyed a very interesting day, thank You. Have your read the newspaper account, Sir?"

"Dah, I did. What was your impression of the CIA's testimony about one of our defectors?" Yurasov asked.

"General, I must say that it moved me greatly," Sasha replied. "It is both an interesting and disturbing story. The agent who gave the account was very convincing. I don't know whether to believe the story or not."

Yurasov smiled. "Sasha, you will encounter many troubling events here in the United States. Remember, the Americans are also very good at *mackorova*. Their intelligence and secret police agencies use their news media to relate stories to their advantage. Perhaps there is some truth to the defector's story. I only read the newspaper account. You observed it being told. Perhaps it was an attempt to divert some attention away from the assassination stories which continue to dominate, and with wild speculations becoming more and more bizarre. With regard to this *defector,* keep in mind, Comrade . . . money is a great attraction in return for information whether it is truthful or not."

"It is possible, Comrade General," Sasha replied. "The CIA officer, however, made the story very convincing, but permit me to tell you about another experience with my visit to the courtroom. As I was departing at the end of the day, I was intercepted by a KGB operative who had tracked me there. And, Sir, this was in spite of my walking several blocks out of the way, dodging into a building and disguising myself. He was astute enough to track me. I found him to be a dolt, but I must give him credit for successfully trailing me. I was more or less forced to join him for tea and attempted to divert his attention from me to the defector story revealed in the courtroom. He expressed embarrassment and was anxious to report the event to his superiors. I departed and had no further trouble with him. I believe, in the end, that he was sent to merely observe my movements, nothing more. I continue to be surprised at their interest in me."

Yurasov considered Sasha's story for a moment. "Hmmm . . . that is interesting, but after your exchange with Zotov, I am not at all surprised. You are very much a curiosity to our KGB friends, and you may find yourself dogged throughout your visit. Did you learn anything else interesting at your American courtroom visit?"

Sasha responded casually, "No, Sir, it was an interesting process. I found it very surprising that a story such as one about a missing aircraft could find its way into a legal court proceeding." Wishing to dismiss the account further, he continued, "I was hoping to learn something about American aircraft operations, but the whole event turned out to be something of a charade. It appeared to be a show with an effort to embarrass our government with a drummed-up story about a Soviet officer defecting."

"You may be right, Sasha, but the Americans are not stupid. That courtroom affair very likely has more merit than you give them credit for. I was very intrigued by the scenario about an American bomber being stolen by one of our people. That is truly wild!" Yurasov shrugged as he beckoned Sasha. "Come, let's eat."

They sat down at a very elaborately prepared table and Yurasov continued, "Sasha, I spoke with General Tushenskiy last evening. He found your encounter with General Zotov very interesting, and he asked me to caution you to remain very careful. You have already had a few close calls with our friends, and he wants you back home safely. He did laud your bravado and commended you for not allowing Zotov to severely thrash you. Everyone, even his own people, despise Zotov. So, you are not free of him. He will continue to attempt to harass you by having you followed, intercepted and so on, but maybe the defector story will send them in another direction. Who knows?"

Sasha listened and nodded in response, "Dah, Sir, I will be careful."

"Oh! And, Sasha," Yurasov continued, "the Director General said to tell you that your wife continues to be fine. She is being driven to and from her place of work each day."

"Thank you, General, that is good news," Sasha replied. "Perhaps as you know, these thugs have also unfortunately harassed her. I continue to find it strange that if the KGB has nothing to hide, why all of the paranoia?"

"Good question, Sasha," Yurasov frowned, "but they are by their own nature, schizoid most of the time. Now, I understand you wish to move on to Texas and continue your journey. I have set up a meeting with our friend, *Stork*, for this evening if you are still interested. I don't know what more he can offer regarding the internal workings of the American secret police and the assassination, but it may be of some use to you."

"Yes, General," Sasha replied. "I would like very much to meet with him. Anything he can share with me will be helpful. The newspapers have begun to run in circles with their stories. Sir, I am sure that General Tushenskiy has shared with you his concern for our own government's possible involvement with the assassination. He is particularly concerned with the fact that the assassin resided in Moscow and Minsk for the better part of three years until just recently. That is the principal reason for my coming here, to attempt to glean any additional information from both sides. I must say, our own KGB friends are not very pleased with my presence . . . anywhere!"

"That concerns all of us," Yurasov shrugged. "Whether the man in question had any connections with the KGB or not, it is still very embarrassing that he lived in our country for such a long period with apparent immunity. If *we* are involved in any way, and I truly hope that we are not, it could result in terrible consequences. While the Americans are vulnerable in many ways, they are not stupid, and as we witnessed with Cuba, they can only be pushed so far. Let us hope that we have no connection with the assassination of their president. I have made arrangements for us to meet with *Stork* at 8:00 p.m. We will depart here at 7:15. You will need to put on a few articles of disguise. I will do so as well."

Yurasov smiled, "Did you mention paranoid?"

Back in his room, Sasha donned one of the wigs, a matching moustache and the clear horn-rimmmed glasses. He went downstairs to meet Yurasov who was dapperly dressed and also fitted with a wig. It was gray and very thick in contrast to his short, cropped hair. They departed the GRU residence in a dark green late model Chevy that had been pre-positioned on the street outside.

Yurosov drove. "We're going to park in the underground lot of the Essex Hotel and then catch a taxi on the street side," he gestured with his hand. "I don't think we are being watched tonight, but just in case."

The general directed the cab driver to take them to the Tivoli Restaurant in Arlington. The large dining room was dimly lit, very busy with customers and noisy with conversation and the clatter of dishes. He spoke to the waitress, and she led them to a booth in the back of the room where a man wearing a dark jacket over a blue sweater was already seated.

Yurosov greeted the man, addressing him as *John* and motioned for Sasha to move into the inside seat in the booth.

"John, how have you been?" Yurasov asked, sitting down next to Sasha.

"Fine, Sir," he replied, "and you?"

"John, this is Roger, an associate of mine with whom I would like for you to have a discussion and perhaps answer some of his questions."

John casually glanced in Sasha's direction and nodded. No one shook hands.

"Roger?" Sasha thought to himself. "I wish Yurosov had told me what my *name* was going to be!" He observed John to be around forty years old, clean cut features and no doubt an American.

Yurosov began in a clear, but hushed voice, "John, Roger is interested in any activities you have observed within your area of work regarding the assassination of the president. Specifically, what do you know about any unusual or special investigations, meetings or conferences are the agencies conducting relative to the incident?"

A waitress arrived with menus and water and Yurosov asked her not to come back for their order until he signaled for her.

John responded to Yurosov's questions; "Do you mean is there a flurry of activity surrounding the incident? Damn right there is! Every agency has its tail in a crack. Finger pointing is aimed in every direction. The Attorney General is screaming at every department head in Washington. And, some heads may very well roll over this thing. Everything that could go wrong, did! There is egg on everybody's face. This guy Oswald came *diddie bopping* back from three years in the Soviet Union and kills the president of the United States. Apparently no one from here was tracking him while he was there . . ." he smiled, "but I'll bet your guys over there were. And," he sneered, "apparently no one picked him up when he came back to the U.S . . . your people or the intelligence gurus here!"

He paused, slowly looked around the restaurant, keeping his voice just above a whisper and continued, "I can't tell you a great deal about what is going on behind closed doors, except that every agency is on high alert. They're stumbling all over each other, each one trying to fix blame away from themselves. That goes especially for the Secret Service, whose chief, by the way, decided not to make the trip to Dallas. He sent his deputy! The FBI, rumor has it, had a file on this Oswald character as did the Office of Naval Intelligence. It's apparent that both agencies knew that he had expressed communist sympathies while he was still in the Marines and that he had left the country after his discharge, but no one in either place bothered to follow-up . . . *out of sight, out of mind . . .* so to speak, much less to track him when he returned from the Soviet Union."

It was apparent that John was growing increasingly nervous as he revealed what he knew as he continued, "Also the immigration people didn't show any interest in him either when he passed through, even though he brought back a Russian wife and kid. Neither did the FBI or the ONI share any background information on the guy with the CIA before he left the U.S. It's very apparent that these *intell* agencies work behind some very high walls and have been inflicted with their own *subjective reality*. They're in a convoluted mess."

Sasha also sensed a certain measure of embarrassment or maybe disappointment in John's tone as he characterized the situation inside the U.S. intelligence community where he apparently worked.

"None of the agencies want to claim any significant knowledge about Oswald," John seemed to sneer, "or to take the blame for failing to know what he was up to. I understand from ONI sources that they have had a long-standing concern about the vulnerability of U.S. Marines since they guard the embassies and come in direct contact with you people all the time. Oswald was a Marine, you know, but I have not heard of any linkage between that particular concern and his military background. Who knows? In any event, there is a lot of paranoia going around. It's the old *woulda, coulda, shoulda* that always sets in after a major screw-up."

Sasha asked, "What about the U.S. interest in the Soviet Union and any potential part they may have played in the incident?"

John continued, keeping his voice to a near whisper. "Yeah, there is some interest! The U.S. Intelligence Community, the FBI and the Dallas police included, would be delighted if they could somehow pin this on the Soviets or some outside connection. On the other hand," he paused, "If that somehow should happen, it could also open a *Pandora's Box* that probably no one really wants. In any event, I don't need to tell you that that is another very high wall to breach. You guys do a great job of blocking out information or at least deflecting it."

He paused again, continuing to nervously scan the restaurant as if he expected someone to catch him in the act. "Of course, it's too early to determine if they can get a credible defector to come forward who knew what was going on with Oswald while he was out of the country. I am sure, as we speak, that big bucks are being shown around for somebody . . . anybody, to step up."

It was apparent and somewhat amusing that John tried to occasionally disguise his vocabulary in an attempt to reflect a not well educated and run of the mill background, but he succeeded poorly. Neither was there any doubt that he *was* educated, polished and experienced in his field, either the CIA or one of the other intelligence agencies. In any case, he was definitely an American. "A credible defector?" he wondered. "Why is he doing this—money, politics, ideology? Who knows why people betray their own?"

John continued; he appeared to urgently want to get his story told, drumming his forefinger on the table to make a point. "There's one more detail that I learned today; one of the investigative agencies, I don't know which, discovered a very interesting event in the news media television film that was tracking the whole motorcade. They noted that it appeared that the driver of the president's limousine turned in his seat from behind the wheel and fired a shot over his right shoulder from a pistol he was holding in his left hand. That's not been verified, but it's a story floating around the community. If that's true, then who was he firing at? The president was sitting directly behind him and to his right. How could he possibly know where the shot came from that hit the president and the Texas governor? Could the driver have hit the president in the forehead, blowing the back of his skull off? They have a big mystery on their hands."

Sasha and Yurasov listened intently to this latest revelation, waiting for John to speak further.

He looked at them both and nodded, smiling, "I believe that in the end, the U.S. will be just as happy to pin the assassination singularly on Oswald, especially now that he is dead. Dead men don't talk. The Ruby guy is a bit of a mystery. They can probably write him off as a zealous *kook*," he smiled and then smirked, "unless of course, *he is your guy*, and then there is new twist about the driver."

Yurosov glanced at Sasha without comment.

"But, let me say this," John appeared to sigh, "This assassination could have been prevented if the U.S. agencies had been on their toes; whether you guys or any one else was involved. It appears that not just one, but every one of them failed in one way or the other."

He leaned against the back of the booth, smiling with the satisfaction of his conclusions.

Yurosov waived for the waitress, they ordered sandwiches and concluded the meeting with small talk, occasionally clarifying one remark or the other. As they prepared to depart, Yurosov took an envelope from his jacket pocket and handed it under the table. John leaned forward and took it, casually putting it in his coat pocket.

Sasha sensed it before it happened. Two men quietly and swiftly moved up to the booth. One firmly pushed John next to the wall on his side and sat down beside him. The other squeezed in on the outside of the seat next to Yurosov.

"Sit still and don't any of you attempt to move!" One of the men whispered firmly as he opened a leather wallet revealing a badge. "FBI, gentlemen; please sit where you are while we sort this out. Each of you place your hands on the table!"

Looking at a very flushed and pale John, the spokesman of the two whispered, "Sir, may I see some identification? Use just one hand, retrieve it slowly and place it in front of you."

Glancing at Yurosov and Sasha, who was tightly pinned against the wall, he whispered sternly, "The two of you keep your hands still. I will get to you shortly!"

With a sudden impulse, Sasha grasped the edge of the table and shoved it with all his might into John and the other agent on the opposite side, and then he quickly sprang up and literally rolled over the back of the booth and into the unoccupied seat behind him. He didn't miss a beat as he dodged, half-crouched and made his way through the milling people and waitresses to the front entrance. He expected any second to hear gunfire and feel a bullet in his back before he burst out onto the street.

Peeling off his wig, moustache and eyeglasses, he darted into a pitch-dark alley and ran as fast as he could. Stumbling over trashcans along the way, he tossed his disguise articles into the darkness. He crossed over the street at the end of the alley and ran into another one, dodging packing crates and bags of trash. Emerging from that alley, he hailed a passing taxicab.

"National Airport, please," he said, surprised at how calm he was after the lightening fast and potentially life-threatening experience. He sat back in the cab and began to assess his situation.

He quickly concluded that *John,* or *Stork,* or whoever he was, is dead meat. "He is a goner. They can't hurt Yurosov. He has diplomatic immunity. Even if they try to pin the payoff of money to a defector on him, they can't do anything except scream for his deportation. Now, what do I do?"

He had directed the cabbie to take him to the airport in order to get as far away from Arlington as possible and to get as close to as many people as he could. The airport would be ideal. He would then catch a shuttle bus or another taxi to a nearby hotel and contemplate his next move.

Once inside the airport terminal building, he strolled around to get his bearings. He located the baggage pickup area on the lower level and a nearby bank of hotel listings and phones. He direct-dialed the Airport Marriott Hotel.

"Hello, I have just arrived in DC and need a hotel room for the night. Can you accommodate me?"

He was instructed to collect his luggage and to look for the shuttle bus at curbside. He mused, "I'll tell the shuttle driver that my luggage did not arrive with my flight and that the airline would deliver it later."

Once inside his hotel room, the unfortunate events of the night began to settle on him. "What to do next?" He called the desk clerk explaining his luggage dilemma and asked for a toothbrush, toothpaste and a shaving razor, ". . . *pending the arrival of my luggage,*" he explained.

It was 11:00 p.m.—too late to call the GRU residence even with the special telephone number. The police authorities might very well have it tapped as well. He would wait out the night and contemplate his next move. He felt secure in that the "*John*" fellow could not identify him, and Yurosov would not reveal his identity under any condition. He turned on the TV to see if there was any local news about his *eventful evening.* There was no mention of anything about it. He went to bed and finally to unsettled sleep as he tried to rationalize his situation and to develop a plan. He had sufficient cash in his wallet along with a credit card to get him around locally, but he would have to retrieve his passport and other paraphernalia in his valise.

"I am in a serious bind without a passport!" he smirked.

The next morning he showered, shaved and dressed. His clothes were not too worse for the wear considering the night before. He checked out of the hotel and took a taxi to the northeast corner of DC and just across the line into Silver Spring, Maryland. He had the driver let him out in a seedy neighborhood near a corner convenience store and found a pay phone.

He called the *rezidentura,* dialing the number Lobanov had given him. "Lobanov, please."

After a brief delay, "This is Lobanov, how may I help you?"

"Alexi, how are things there?" he asked in a soft voice.

"Comrade Katsanov! How are you, Sir? Where are you? One moment, Sir, for the Director!" Lobanov was careful not to use any military rank with names, after all the *rezidentura* was an official *trade mission* office.

"Sasha! Where are you? Are you all right?" Yurasov quickly asked. "I have been extremely worried about you!" Yurosov expressed genuine concern.

"I am fine, Sir. I have been worried about *you*!" Sasha quickly responded.

"Sasha! You must get back here soonest! I have the most hilarious story to tell you! I will send a car for you. Where are you?" Yurosov was obviously relieved and all was apparently well.

He relaxed considerably. "Sir, thank you, but I will take a taxi, and I will be there very shortly."

Yurosov was anxiously waiting in the anteroom when Sasha arrived. He quickly embraced him. "Sasha! Are you okay? What happened to you? Where have you been? I have been frantic about you!"

"General, I am very sorry. I thought . . ."

"Let's go to my office," Yurosov interrupted and nodded to Lobanov, "Have some tea brought in." Sasha followed the General into his office.

"Sit, Comrade, let me share a wild tale with you! But, first, I must congratulate you on a magnificent feat of brilliant athletic skill! What an escape! Where did you learn that trick? What physical ability! Never mind, permit me to tell you what happened!" Yurosov was filled with excitement.

"Within a minute after your smashing departure, which by the way caught our two intruders by complete surprise and shocked them speechless, two DC policemen showed up. They asked us not to move. I didn't know what to think except that we were all goners!"

Yurosov couldn't contain a burst of laughter. "The police asked what was going on and wanted to see identifications. Sasha, you will love this! Our two intruders were *not* FBI agents. They were two of Zotov's clowns!"

Yurosov couldn't stop laughing. "Sasha, they only had one badge between them, and it was a poor fake!" He cackled again! "They had to reveal their Soviet Embassy credentials. They told the police that they were playing a practical joke. I showed them my Russian Trade Commission ID and Stork showed him his driver's license and nothing more. The cops were not very happy. They asked about the commotion and about the *'guy that ran away.'* We brushed it off as we were just having some fun. They left us with a warning and departed."

Yurosov continued to enjoy the story. "That is when I laid into the two from Zotov's office. I told them who I was and you should have seen their shock. Then I told them that I was going to not only have it out with Zotov, but I would report the whole episode to Moscow and have their hide stripped from their bones. They could have crapped in their pants when they discovered my identity and how they had blown it. They thought I was just one of the staff escorting you around. They were, and I am sure still are, scared silly. And, Zotov will get his due when I see him this afternoon." He chuckled at his own excitement. "I called General Tushenskiy last night and gave him all the details, so I am sure that Kashevarov is already getting it. But, Sasha, my friend, if you had not made your move, caused the ruckus and prompted the police to get involved, those thugs would have had a heyday scaring the hell out of us. I am still not sure that our man, Stork, is still with us. He left promptly and got out of there. We may have lost his services for good!"

Sasha sat in awe of the revelation by Yurosov. He couldn't believe what he was hearing. Finally, he spoke, "General, just how far will the KGB zealots go to do-in our own government? Zotov deserves to be shot! He could have endangered all of us and everything else we are here for. He has betrayed us. How will you deal with him?"

"Comrade Sasha, I dare say that he is already being dealt with. I am going over this afternoon just to gloat over his inept stupidity. I have no doubt that he will claim that his men operated on their own. That is the KGB way. If some severe harm comes to those two cheap thugs without Zotov himself catching it, I will join Tushenskiy in doing everything I can to see him done in! We have had enough!"

Yurosov, smiling, held up his cup of tea. "Let's toast our KGB colleagues. *Salut*, Comrade! And as my father used to say, *Once burned by milk you will drink vodka!*"

Sasha smiled and responded, "Salut!"

THIRTEEN

"A fly will not get into a closed mouth."

A Russian Proverb

Dallas

Sasha departed Washington on an afternoon Braniff Airlines flight. He couldn't get the restaurant event with Stork off his mind. "If he was an American intelligence agent on the take from us, what other and how many American agents are working with us? Could an American agent have been involved in the assassination?' Was Oswald their *pawn* and the KGB not directly involved at all? Or, did Oswald really act alone in the assassination?"

Questions began to multiply, especially after discovering that the Americans also have traitors within their own country.

He arrived at Love Field in Dallas at sundown. He had an eerie feeling having read about President Kennedy landing at this airport just over a week before and then his body was flown out of the same airport only a few hours later after he was assassinated. As near as he could tell, he had not been tailed. He had scanned the passengers up and down the isle, but he could never be sure. Collecting his bag, he selected a local motel at random from the directory posted in the Departure Area and took a taxi to its location on Harry Hines Boulevard. As he settled in for the night, he had recollections of Texas when he was sent to San Antonio for Air Force basic training. "That was a *lifetime* ago," he lamented, "and here I am again in a place so near and yet far from *reality.*"

The next morning he went to the motel office, purchased the *DALLAS MORNING NEWS* and returned with it to his room. He scanned the front page for any eye-catching articles relative to the assassination. Most of the news had been reduced to rehashing and speculation. He then turned to the *Classified Ads Section*. He ran his finger down the *Used Cars* column until he came to the ad insert he was looking for: *"Like new, 1959 4-door Chevy Bellaire. Call Phillip to see and test drive. 672-6848."*

He dialed the number. A male voice answered. "Is this Phillip?" Sasha asked.

"Yes, this is Phillip."

"Phillip, I'm calling about your ad for the '59 Chevy; Do you still have it?"

"Yes, I still have it, but I am expecting someone who is very interested in buying it to come by this morning. You may want to call back later in the day to see if it's still on the market."

Sasha responded, "Phillip, I am a Bellaire fan and if it's in good shape, I'll be willing to pay top dollar for it. What color is it?"

"Its two-tone blue, but I will have to let the earlier caller have a look first," Phillip countered.

"Okay," Sasha concluded, "but I sure would like to see it. I am looking for a blue two-tone. I'll call back later."

He hung up, left his motel room, walked a short distance to a *7-11* convenience store and redialed the same number from a pay phone.

"Hi, Phillip," Sasha responded when the phone was answered. "Where did you want to meet for coffee this morning?"

"Hey, how are you?" Phillip replied. "Where are you? I'll come by and pick you up."

"I'll be at curbside at Love Field in half an hour," Sasha replied, "if that is okay with you. What will you be driving?"

"That's fine," Phillip said. "I'll be in a black Ford sedan with the headlights on. Pick you up in half an hour."

All of that done, Sasha went back to his room, collected his bag and valise, checked out of the motel and had the clerk call a cab to take him to Love Field.

A black late model Ford with the headlights on pulled up to the curb; Sasha put his bag in the back seat and got into the front seat next to the driver. They shook hands and drove off.

"I'm Phillip, Phillip Ford," the driver spoke, smiling.

"Mike Scott," Sasha responded. "Did the buyer show up for the *Chevy*?"

Phillip chuckled, "Yes, I believe he is with me now so I think we can close the deal, and by the way, call me Phil."

"Good, Phil, good to find you and where are we headed?"

"Comrade, we are going to work out of an apartment I rented nearby after I was notified you were coming and that I was to be your contact. I don't live here. My work is over in Ft. Worth, but you may already know that."

"No, I was not given any background information about you, Phil," Sasha replied, "except how to contact you through the newspaper ad. I will be direct now though. Are you GRU or KGB?"

"I am GRU, Comrade," Phil said, "and thank God! I'm an aeronautical engineer assigned to collect data on U.S. military aircraft developments, testing and manufacturing. I've been in the U.S. for ten years and working at the Convair plant, now called General Dynamics, near Ft. Worth for the past six years. Have you seen any of my good reports?" he smiled.

"Yes, yes, I have indeed," Sasha replied. "You have provided us with some exceptional data on the U.S. B-58 supersonic bomber and the development technology on the new F-111 fighter-bomber that is scheduled to be coming along soon. I am very pleased to meet you, Phil. If we have an opportunity while I am here, I would like very much to discuss your work and what you see coming in the future."

Phil was Russian, probably fifty, medium height, stocky with a full head of black hair, graying at the temples. He had a big toothy smile and seemed to be a cheerful sort. There was no hint of an accent in his speech. He had been well schooled. Sasha immediately felt comfortable with him. He moved on to his current task. "You are aware of why I am here?"

"Only vaguely," Phil replied. "I was contacted to meet you when you arrived and to assist you while you are in the Dallas area. I presume you are here as a result of the assassination of Kennedy, is that correct?"

"Yes, I am. The Director General pulled me away from my primary duties in the aircraft exploitation section and sent me out to back track this fellow, Oswald, to the degree I can. Our KGB friends in Moscow, and for that matter everywhere else, are jumping through their *rear-ends* over this assassination. The fact that this character, Oswald, was under their care in our republic for three years has them going crazy. Tushenskiy wants me to attempt to see if there is any possible direct correlation between Oswald's three-year escapade on our turf and the assassination. Thus far my trip has resulted in little more than what has been reported in the newspapers. Our people in New York and Washington had nothing to offer."

Phil pulled the car to a stop in a shady park area near the small Bachman Lake just north of Love Field.

"Phil," Sasha asked, "are you in contact with the KGB in this area? Or have you had any since the assassination?"

"I mostly stay clear of those guys," Phil replied. "but I have had some interaction with one who calls himself *Paul*—Paul Pearce; that's his cover name. He is their communications officer here. I am sure that they have a fairly active operation in this area because of the large military and defense operations in Texas. Paul and I occasionally have a drink or two when I meet with him to dispatch a courier pack to Khodinka. Otherwise, we seldom engage one another except for me to make use of their communications network to make a phone call back home. It would be much better if I didn't have to rely on them at all, mostly because they aren't *user—friendly*."

"Have you spoken with your contact since the assassination?" Sasha asked.

"Yes, I have," Phil replied. "I saw Paul yesterday when I went over to drop off a courier packet for mailing and to check into the apartment. Later, we had a couple of drinks at a bar and talked for an hour or so."

"Do you sense any connection between the assassination, this fellow, Oswald, and the KGB?" Sasha pressed.

"I'm really not sure," Phil said. "He really didn't say anything specific that I detected which would lead me in that direction. That sort of intelligence deduction is out of my field of work, so I probably wasn't that tuned in. I think that Paul might have wanted to talk more about the assassination than he was free to do so, but I'm not sure. He talked about the newspaper speculations and the conspiracy theories going around, including the rumors that there was more than one shooter. He did comment that it would be greatly humorous if the assassin turned out to be one of their own intelligence agency people, CIA, Secret Service or one of the others. I couldn't determine if he really knows anything beyond the news reports. I'm sure they're running in circles just like everybody else, unless *they are* in the middle of it? What are your thoughts, Comrade?"

"Well, I will share with you," Sasha replied, "our fellow countrymen bastards have attempted to sabotage my every step since I left Moscow." He went on to describe in brief detail the various impediments and threats that he had encountered.

"That's incredible!" Phil exclaimed. "They are a vicious bunch, but it's hard to believe that they would attempt to intentionally go after you, especially since you were sent out here by the Director General. Who knows, they may very well have used this stooge, Oswald, as their trigger man . . . maybe even along with others here in the U.S. With regard to all of this, what is your purpose in being here anyway, Mike . . . 'er, and is that the name you wish to be called?"

Sasha shrugged, "Mike is fine. My given name is Sasha, but we had better stick with Mike, lest we screw up in public."

He was absorbed in his thoughts and Phil's comments about his Dallas KGB contact. "Phil, with regard to why I'm here, it is my intention to hold over here for a few days, look and listen, see what I can learn and then decide what to do next. So far, with the exception of the excitement provided by our KGB thug friends, it has been a fruitless mission. They are either completely innocent, or they have pulled off a very large and successful cover-up. Frankly, I am ready to head back home as soon as I can determine something to report. Speaking of home, when were you last back there? Do you have family here with you? Back there?"

"I have my wife here with me," he said, "but my son and daughter are back in Moscow in school. We have not seen them in three years. It is not a happy situation, but that is our lot in life,

I suppose. The KGB, of course, controls how many in one family that can be out of the country at any one time. That is for obvious reasons as you know. So, my two kids are in school back there. The truth of the matter is that they are really being held hostage by the government to keep me in line. The only contact we have with them is by way of the KGB courier system, and we never know if those guys are being fair with us. Sometimes we don't hear anything for months at a time. I am about ready to tell Khodinka that it's time for me to leave here. I like my work very much and living here is a great experience, but the family worry and frustration is often overbearing."

"I can understand," Sasha responded. "I have been in a similar situation. I, for one, wonder how long our government and the U.S. will continue on this surreptitious path?"

Returning to the subject at hand, he asked, "Phil, do you think your friend, Paul, would talk to me?"

"Hmmmm, I don't know if he will or not, Sasha. He is friendly enough, but who knows, it might be just an act he puts on with me. I will be pleased to give him a call. You are more familiar with how those guys operate than I am. It could get us all in trouble, but I sure don't mind making a call if you want me to."

"I think that it might be a good idea," Sasha responded. "Are we going to your apartment from here?"

"Yes, we can go on over there. I just pulled in here so that we could talk without concern for being overheard by *prying ears*. I am about as paranoid as any when it comes to who may be watching or listening. Who knows, our friends may very well have already bugged my apartment and the telephone. What a life we live!" Phil shrugged and frowned. "Maybe we have met the enemy, and it is us."

"I agree," Sasha nodded. "Well, let's see if your contact will meet with me. Since they may have your place bugged, maybe you should try to call him from a pay phone. Why don't you suggest a meeting for dinner somewhere and don't mention that I will be with you. You can introduce me at the restaurant."

"Fine with me, Sasha," Phil responded. "I'll call from that *7-11* pay phone and we'll see what develops."

Phil had a smile on his face when he got back into the car. "We're all set, I caught him before he quit for the day. He'll meet us for dinner at 8:00 at a restaurant we use for a *yavka* from time to time. That will give us a few minutes to freshen up and get over there."

Sasha felt a little uneasy as he and Phil waited in a booth at restaurant for Paul to arrive. He didn't know what to expect. "Is this guy worth the trouble of meeting or not?" he wondered. "Will the meeting open a pile of trouble for him . . . and, for Phil, as well? Too late now; this must be him."

He moved out of the booth slowly as Phil stood to greet the man nodding to them as he approached.

"Paul! We meet again," Phil smiled. "Permit me to introduce you to Mike."

Sasha shook hands with the man as he sized up his features. He was Russian for sure, dark complexion, thick black hair and stocky built. He judged that he was in his mid-forties, maybe fifty.

Sasha and Phil had concluded that the restaurant booth with its high padded backs was sufficiently benign and reasonably safe to talk reasonably free of detection. "I have had confidential meetings here before," Phil had said.

Now, he had to carefully *feel-out* Phil's KGB contact. "Paul, I am pleased to have the opportunity to visit with you," Sasha began in a soft voice. "Phil tells me that you are very supportive of his activities here. I am also GRU, and I am here under orders from my Director General and with the concurrence of your Director General. This is a letter of introduction."

He handed the letter from General Tushenskiy to Paul. He read it carefully and looked at Sasha. "Very impressive, Comrade, what do you wish from me?"

"Paul, I will be very direct," Sasha began. "It has been my intention to attempt to retrace the journey of the American who spent several years in our country before he came back here to this city and assassinated the President of the United States. I am sure that your people are equally concerned about how the sequence of the events could have evolved with such apparent simplicity . . . unless, of course, *we* . . ." Sasha paused to observe Paul's expression, "Unless, of course, *we* participated in the process."

Paul seemed to study Sasha's statement for a moment and calmly responded, "Comrade," he said, speaking quietly, "most of all that I know, I have read in the newspapers and observed on the local news. *If, we* are involved, it is not at all apparent where I work. We were as shocked as the Americans. We are a small office, only four people and no one else has visited us recently, nor have I heard of any outside agents coming into the area. The visit of Kennedy to Dallas was treated with routine observance by our *rezidentura* here. Now, of course, there could have been some agency people from elsewhere who came into the city without our knowledge. I am just the communications officer and do not get involved with *other* activities, but neither have I received any messages to that effect. I have also been taught to live by the Old Russian adage, '*A fly will not get into a closed mouth.*'"

All three smiled at the familiar proverb.

Paul quietly added, "It's common knowledge, however, that there are a number of wealthy Texans, oil people, who were very vocal about their dislike for their president. The newspapers have reported such. It is my judgment that this man, Oswald, was either the assassin or a fall guy and that he was himself killed to keep him quiet—from whom, we don't know—perhaps those Texans who despised Kennedy."

Sasha countered, "Then, my friend, how does your agency account for the fact that this man, Oswald, visited our embassy in Mexico City just a few weeks before he returned to Dallas to do his deed?"

Paul looked surprised. "How do you know that he visited our Mexico City embassy?"

"It is common knowledge back in Moscow and with our people in New York that Oswald made contact with our embassy in Mexico City and the Cuban Consulate as well, and applied for a visa to go to Cuba just three weeks before he killed President Kennedy," Sasha replied.

"Okay," Paul smiled. "You have done your homework well, Comrade. I have no secrets to keep from you. You are fully aware that my agency does not favor working with the GRU. I don't have a problem with it, but my residency chief despises your agency and its intrusion into our territories. The communiqués that I have monitored have advised that we are to keep clear of you. I am sticking my neck out by even talking to you,"

His self confidence seemed to wane for a moment and then the continued, "but getting back to the issue, I do not believe that my agency had anything to do with this fellow Oswald or the assassination. As I said, there are strong rumors around that American right wing zealots hated this president, and there is a story going around that the man, Jack Ruby, who killed Oswald, is strongly aligned with those zealots. Also, it is said that Ruby may well have killed Oswald to keep him from talking. Perhaps you are aware that there is also a story going around that there was possibly another shooter. Allegedly, the president was shot in the back of the head as his car drove past the building where Oswald was positioned, but . . . and, a big *but* . . . the back of his head was blown off which indicates a bullet hit him from the front. I just thought you might want to speculate about that for awhile."

Sasha nodded and interjected, "Paul, what have your people learned about a story that the driver of the president's limousine may have fired a shot himself, looking back over his shoulder, just after, or about the time the president was hit?"

Paul smiled and nodded slowly, "Comrade, my director did comment on a rumor that's floating around in the local law enforcement circles. The story goes that a television camera may have detected the driver firing a pistol shot back over his right shoulder, maybe in response to the sniper, maybe not?"

Sasha and Phil listened without comment.

Paul was getting antsy and appeared eager to shift the conversation. "Comrades, what have you learned about *why* our government permitted this man to live in our country for such a long period? Did we have an interest in him? If not, did we monitor his activities?"

Sasha smiled at Paul's attempt to switch roles. "Paul, I am fully aware of the animosity between our agencies. I have experienced it! It is regrettable. We have the same objectives, but there are factions within our government represented by some devious evildoers—perhaps some are even at the highest levels—that should cause all of us to question their motives. I have experienced every possible obstacle since I began my assignment to come here. Several innocents have been injured and some have even been killed by *your* agency people after I visited with them. Does that surprise you? And," he sharply added, "Yes, I am aware of the story about the president's suspicious wounds. It could mean that this Oswald character had some assistance, doesn't it?"

"I am not aware of anything about anyone being injured as a result of your prowling around, Comrade." Paul rebutted. "You should be careful not to make such accusations!" He was obviously becoming agitated.

Sasha shrugged, "No need to go any further with that. It is important, however, that we all understand our respective situations. Can you tell me, after this fellow, Oswald, returned to the U.S. from Minsk? Do you know if your people made any contact with him?"

Paul seemed to calm down and studied the question before he replied, "Comrade, to my knowledge, our agency people did not make any direct contacts with the man here in Dallas. We felt very sure that the FBI was closely watching him and did not want to get into such a situation, but now it is apparent that no one in the U.S. Government was even aware, much less monitoring Oswald either. We do know that he contacted the local Russian Émigré Society and met with them several times. We monitor their activities closely, of course, but so does the FBI, and we found nothing unusual with his contacts there," he smiled. "And apparently the FBI didn't either. Our opinion was that he was a *flake* and not worth our attention. Neither did our headquarters," he smirked, "and apparently neither did the U.S. agencies determine anything suspicious about the character."

Paul looked at Sasha sternly. "Getting back to your Mexico City question, yes, he did travel to Mexico City and contacted our people there, but first he visited the Cuban Consulate and requested a visa to visit that country. He apparently had two stories. One, he said that he was unhappy with the United States and wanted to help with Castro's revolution, and two, he said that he wanted to travel through Cuba to return to the Soviet Union. The Cubans granted him a provisional visa, pending final review and approval by our people before he could actually travel. He was told to come back in thirty days. This was not unusual on their part. Our concern was that the CIA was using him as a ploy and our people went along with his potential game." He paused . . . "Comrade, now I have told you all that I know as well."

Sasha ignored Paul's attempt to close the discussion. "Have your people sought to engage the U.S. law enforcement or investigative agency people who are likely all over this city looking for evidence, motive, Oswald contacts, etc.?"

"Nyet, Comrade," Paul replied, showing some agitation. "We have no business with American police agencies."

Sasha persisted, "Does your office have a U.S. agent working with you?"

"Nyet! I have nothing more to say," Paul was now red in the face and noticeably irritated with Sasha's questions.

"Thank you, Comrade," Sasha replied with a slight smirk. "One last question: has this man, Jack Ruby, ever contacted your office here? Had you heard his name before he killed Oswald?" Sasha paused . . . "Is he one of ours?"

Paul flushed and hastily moved out of the booth, "Comrade, I have told you all that I know. I must go."

Sasha stood, held out his hand, "Paul, thank you for meeting with me. I appreciate you sharing your understanding of the events. Phil tells me that you have been very supportive of his important work. We appreciate that, and I will provide a report on your good efforts when I return home."

"Spa'see'ba," Paul didn't return the handshake and smirked, "Don't do me any favors, Comrade; have a safe trip home."

On the way back to their motel, Sasha advised Phil that he wanted to look about the area himself. "I am aware that my mission is to investigate our own government's possible involvement with this assassination. In that regard I am going to try to determine if our people have otherwise stepped over the line."

"What do you mean, Comrade?" Phil was puzzled. "What *area* are you going to look for?"

"Phil, you live in Ft. Worth," Sasha replied. "Oswald supposedly came back to Ft. Worth when he returned from Minsk.

Do you know where, or who, he came back to live with? A relative's home? Friends?"

"No, I have stayed away from showing any interest in this whole matter," Phil replied. "That's out of my business area."

"Will you assist me in researching and determining who and where he came back to stay or live with?" Sasha asked. "I am sure the local newspapers must have tracked all that down by now."

"Yes, I will try to assist you, Comrade," Phil replied with a deep exhale. It was apparent that he wanted to get away from all of this and back to his job of technical information gathering. He had already made it clear that he did not like police work.

"Good," Sasha replied. "Do you keep a backlog of newspapers, especially those since the assassination?"

"As a matter of fact, I do have all the news items from the papers concerning the assassination," Phil nodded. "They are at my home in Ft. Worth. I can retrieve them for you."

"Are you comfortable with me coming to your home?" Sasha asked, "Or would it be better to secure another place for me to stay? How far are we from Ft. Worth?"

"It's a half-hour drive," Phil said. "I think it best if you work out of a motel room over there; how long do you intend to stay?" Phil demonstrated some anxiety. This was not his cup of tea.

"Okay," Sasha replied, "Do you think we can get over there without being tailed by this local KGB crowd for say, just a day?"

"We can try," Phil sighed. "Hopefully, after Paul reported back to them and told 'em you're leaving they'll back off. As a matter of good judgment," he quickly added, "let's depart this apartment now, tonight, and head on over there. We can return here for your departure."

"I'm ready," Sasha replied.

They hurriedly left the apartment and headed to Ft. Worth, taking a circuitous route and being ever cautious of any suspicious automobiles behind them. When none were detected after an hour and a half of meandering, Phil found a small motel in west Ft. Worth a block off Camp Bowie Boulevard and not far from where he lives. He said he wouldn't call his wife since he knew they had his phone tapped. Sasha suggested that they take turns watching overnight by peeping out the window for any suspicious vehicles that might pull up to the motel office.

The next morning, they scanned the area as best they could. Phil went out to a nearby McDonalds and picked up coffee and breakfast sandwiches. While he was gone, Sasha donned his wig, moustache and eye glasses disguise he had in his bag and strolled around the area. He didn't detect anyone that appeared out of place or suspicious.

Phil returned and they mapped out a plan while they ate. "I need the newspapers to review," he suggested to Phil. "Do you feel safe in going home to retrieve them?" he asked.

"No, I don't," Phil replied. "They know by now that we are no longer in Dallas and I am sure they have my house under surveillance. I suggest that I call my next door neighbor—they're nice people—and ask he or she to go over and tell my wife that I called. I would like for her to take my newspaper file to the library and leave it there for me to pick up later. They are good folks and won't ask any questions . . . my wife will know how to 'cover' the situation; she's trained."

"I will leave that up to you, Phil," Sasha replied. "This is your territory."

Phil called his neighbor from the motel room phone. He had a casual chat, made up a story about the newspapers and hung up, smiling. "All's well," he said. "We'll need to kill some time and then go to the library sometime later today . . . we'll need to be patient."

Sasha, not pleased with having to wait, shrugged with a smile.

They spent the morning watching the television news and chatting about how to proceed. Finally, Phil said, "Let's go and take our chances. You stay in the car." As they pulled up the library, he said, "No one seems to have followed us, so I will go in and collect the newspapers."

He returned in a few minutes with a folder of papers under his arm, got in the car and tossed them to Sasha. "I suggest we go back to the motel. You review the news reports and we'll plan our next step. Keep an eye out for anybody on our tail."

Sasha took the folder and nodded in agreement.

Back in the motel, he scanned the assassination news items; there were hundreds . . . reports, quotes and speculation. He created a suggested plan to look around the Ft. Worth area where Oswald supposedly stayed from the time he, Marina and the baby arrived. Phil looked over the various addresses in Sasha's notes and marked them on a city map.

"I would like to drive by Oswald's brother's address first," Sasha said. "That's where he went first when they arrived here. Is that very far from here?"

"No," Phil replied. "7313 Davenport Avenue is just a few miles to the northwest. Okay, let's go."

They arrived at Davenport Avenue and Phil scanned the house numbers. "There it is, 7313," Phil pointed. "I'll drive by slowly, and you check it out, although it looks pretty closed up from here."

"Pull up, Phil," Sasha said, "and I'll go see if anyone is home. If his brother, Robert, is there, I'll see if he will talk to me."

Phil shook his head as Sasha got out of the car and walked up the door. It didn't take long. He returned and said no one was home, or at least wouldn't answer the door.

"Okay, where next on my list?" Sasha asked.

"West 7th Street," Phil replied. He was getting pensive. "Comrade Mike, do you believe looking up this trail of places where that guy lived is of any value? What if you do meet someone? What will you say to them?"

"I'm not sure, Phil," Sasha said with a shrug. "I just feel as though while I'm here I need to justify my trip by doing more than meeting with some KGB lightweight."

"Okay, Comrade, I'm with you," Phil replied. "Let's go to the next stop . . . 7th Street."

Phil drove to 1501 7th Street. "There it is right there, Mike," Phil pointed to the small apartment house. "It looks pretty shabby."

"I agree," Sasha shrugged. "Okay, Phil, I'm not going in there. He only stayed here a month and then moved on to another place, an apartment, on Mercedes Street." Sasha was quiet for minute and then he said, "Phil, this is a wild goose chase. I also made a list of several places where he worked off and on, but I have already experienced talking with his former co-workers . . ." Referring to his meeting with those back in Minsk and the unfortunate results

161

to those pitiful men. "He lived in a dozen or more houses and apartments all over this side of Ft. Worth. There is one more over here that sounds interesting. It's on Byers Avenue . . . know where that is?"

"Yeah, it's on the map just north of the Trinity River," Phil replied. "It's not too far. What's your interest there?"

"There's a neighbor there, a Mrs. McCarroll, who lived next door and has spoken fairly freely with reporters. She might be willing to talk to me."

"Okay, Comrade," Phil exhaled, sounding a little more frustrated. "We'll go over there."

Phil located and drove to Byers Avenue. As they approached, they noticed several automobiles parked on both sides of the street. "Oops," Phil said abruptly, "We don't want to intervene here. There's too much traffic. I see at least one police car. We're outta here!"

"Agree, let's go," Sasha replied, eyeing the line of vehicles up and down the crowded street. "The media and I suppose the police as well, are showing some interest here. Okay, Phil, just one more stop, if you will bear with me," Sasha continued. "Let's go to the last place he lived before he allegedly did the deed."

"Okay," Phil said, "That's over in the Irving side of Dallas on West 5th Street. A Mrs. Ruth Paine put Marina and the baby up there while Oswald traipsed off to New Orleans and then to Mexico."

"That's right, Phil," Sasha smiled. "You have done your homework as well. Okay, let's just drive over there. I can at least say I saw the place he departed from to go and kill the president."

Sasha lamented further, "Oswald was back here in the U.S. for a year and a half. He moved around to a dozen or more places in the local area, worked off and on, mail-ordered a hunting rifle, and went to New Orleans, Louisiana for a month. He came back and made a trip to Mexico and visited both the Soviet Embassy and Cuban Consulate, came back here and then supposedly shot and killed the U.S. president. I say 'supposedly', Phil, because the jury is still out."

He continued after thinking through his words, "He did kill the policeman he ran into . . . Tibbets . . . was that his name?"

Phil pulled on to West 5th Street in Irving. "That's the Paine house over there," he said, pointing to the small white tract house where two cars were parked in front. "Comrade, that one vehicle, the black one, is an unmarked law enforcement car. So, we're on our way out of this neighborhood."

"I agree, Phil," Sasha nodded as they drove slowly down the street. They were not alone. Several other automobiles, likely sightseers were cruising down the street in both directions.

"Well, that's it, Phil," Sasha exhaled deeply. "I've done my thing . . . met with your KGB contact, for what that was worth, and attempted to trace where this lunatic jumped around Dallas after returning from Minsk and I have little or nothing to show for it, except for the trail of misfortune imposed by those black KGB bastards along the way back in Minsk."

"Don't fret, Comrade," Phil smiled. "When such a tragic event like this happens, thousands of never before heard from people come out of the woodwork. In the case of our own government, paranoia grips everybody from top to bottom. We look inward for guilt even where there is no evidence. After all, that's why you are here. Our Director General sent you on this chase to attempt to confirm or deny our government's involvement. Is that not paranoia?"

"Phil, you're correct," Sasha nodded. "I am still mystified by several parts of this event, mystery, whatever we call it. This idiot lived in our country with apparent immunity. That's strange in itself. Then he comes back to the U.S. and bounces all around with apparent immunity from his own government in spite of bringing a Russian wife with him. He leaves her and a baby here while he goes off to New Orleans and openly demonstrates his anti-American feelings. He then comes back to Dallas, buys that rifle . . . and some of the police believe he tried to kill some retired U.S. general named Walker. I guess Walker was a radical right-winger, they say. Then after he is arrested following the killing of the president, he is gunned down in front of the police by another questionable character. Bizarre, Phil, bizarre!"

"Many questions to be answered, Mike," Phil replied. "Many questions . . . there will be investigations and hearings for months and years to come, and predictably just as many questions will remain unanswered. Where to now?"

"Well, we have everything we brought with us," Sasha replied. "I suppose we go back to the apartment here in Dallas, get some food, rest and make reservations for me to depart first thing in the morning."

FOURTEEN

"Chickens are counted in the autumn."

A Russian Proverb

Dallas

"Thank you for the good work, Comrade," the Dallas based KGB chief smiled. "Perhaps when our young GRU friend runs out of ghosts to chase, he will quietly return to Moscow. If not, we may assist him in doing so. By the way, is this GRU agent friend of yours, Phil, a concern to us? Does he get in our way or do we need to give him *lessons* in operational protocol?"

"No, Comrade," Paul responded, "Phil is not a problem to us. He works quietly over at the aircraft plant and sends his dispatches back to Moscow through us. He is a good man and serving our government well."

"Nevertheless, Comrade, we may need to remind him of who is in charge here." the KGB chief replied. "You know, maybe just a little nudge to keep his attention," he smiled. "Tease him a little for attempting to secretly engage with this young upstart from GRU."

Paul departed his chief's office feeling unsettled by the remarks. "They get considerable joy even out of making our own people miserable," he mused to himself. He was sympathetic to Phil and worried, but he dared not tip him off, lest he get tripped up himself. Just let things be and hope nothing happens to his friend.

Moscow

Working late as usual on a wintry Moscow evening, the Director General answered his personal phone, "Dah, Tushenskiy here."

"Tavah'reeshch General, this is Lt. Colonel Tarasov at Lubiyanka Centre. Forgive me for interrupting your important work, Sir, but General Kashevarov wishes you to come to his office this evening if it is at all convenient. There is a matter of urgent business he wishes to discuss with you."

"Dah . . . Colonel," General Tushenskiy acknowledged. The irritation in his voice was clear. "Can you tell me the nature of this *urgent business?*"

"Sir, I am not informed of the subject to be discussed," the caller replied. "Only that my General requests your presence."

Well aware of the KGB's all too frequent tactic of inflating the importance of subject matter, Tushenskiy sternly requested. "Please put General Kashevarov on the phone, Colonel."

"General Tushenskiy, Sir . . . that is not possible. He is presently in conference with his senior staff and has directed that he not be disturbed. May I inform him that you will depart shortly to come to Lubiyanka?"

Further agitated by what amounted to a *demand* to go see his KGB counterpart, Tushenskiy replied, "Dah, dah, Colonel, tell your director that I will be on my way shortly."

Tushenskiy buzzed his aide, "Oleg, I will be going to Lubiyanka. Please have Igor bring my car around to the portal. You may also tell the staff to go home for the evening, you as well."

Arriving at the Exit Portal, the Director General walked quickly to the open rear door of his black shiny Zil staff car. The November night was bitter cold with wisps of snow swirling around. He noticed immediately that it was not his personal driver holding the door open.

"Where is Igor?" Tushenkiy asked testily. "Who are you?"

"General . . . Sir, Igor was summoned home to see about his wife who has taken ill," the driver replied. "I am Semyon, Sir. I work in the motor pool also. I am prepared to take you to Lubiyanka."

Something didn't feel right. He was always kept informed about his staff, but the night was cold and he was already irritated by Kashevarov's request to come see him.

"Sitkov should have told me that Igor wasn't on duty. That's not like him . . ." he thought. Grumbling an expletive, he nodded to the driver and climbed into the comfortable warm back seat of the leather-upholstered limousine.

The driver maneuvered the sleek Zil sedan through the Moscow night pedestrian traffic and in and out of slushy potholes as the Director General of the GRU pondered the events of his day and the abrupt call to meet with the KGB chief. The grind of life in the world of the Soviet was always tenuous and uncertain.

Suddenly the heavy automobile appeared to stall, then lurch forward and stall again as if the accelerator and the brake were being tapped alternatively. The driver pulled the vehicle over to the curb.

"General, we seem to be having an engine problem," the driver nervously advised. "Please, I will check it out."

Tushenskiy didn't respond and remained seated while the driver got out of the car and raised the hood.

And then in an instant, a shadowy figure dressed all in black, jerked open the right front door of the Zil, leaned inside and quickly fired three shots from a revolver into the helpless general.

Both the driver and the killer disappeared into the cold darkness as curious Muscovites surrounded the limousine and peered in at the blood-spattered uniform of the Director General of the GRU.

General Kashevarov was initially shocked at the treacherous way Oleg Petrov had *apparently* carried out his pledge to no longer *toy* with the GRU's persistent meddling in the KGB's affairs. On the other hand, the KGB chief no longer had to be jealous of the brighter and Kremlin-favored Tushenskiy.

Dallas

Sasha was exhausted. He had not been totally dissatisfied with the meeting with Paul, the trekking around Ft. Worth or any of his mission. The Minsk visit was a classic KGB retaliation against innocent people.

"Even a few members of the KGB have a conscience," he thought, referring to Paul as he drifted off to sleep following a busy day.

The phone in Phil's room waked him from a sound sleep. The clock on the nightstand indicated that it was 6:20 a.m. He was still exhausted from the day before trekking all over Ft. Worth with Sasha.

In a sleepy voice, he answered, "Hello."

A dry, deep voice responded, "Comrade, you may inform your guest that his leader is dead and if he is smart, he should prepare to return home immediately. His mission is completed." The call was terminated and the dial tone came on.

Phil, now wide awake, sat up in bed and tried to reconstruct the call. Getting his bearings, he put on a robe and went to Sasha's room. "Mike, Comrade! Sorry to wake you, but we need to talk," he urged.

Sasha turned over and stared at Phil standing in the dimly lit doorway. "What is it, Phil? Is it morning? What's up?"

"Mike," Phil replied. "I just had a strange phone call, and the caller said to tell my guest that his leader is dead and that he should return home himself before something else happened. His mission is complete."

Sasha sat up straight. "What? What did you say?"

Phil partially repeated what he had heard on the phone, adding, "What do you think that was all about . . . a prank phone call?"

Sasha didn't respond. He was trying to clear his head and absorb Phil's words. Finally, he spoke, "Phil, did Paul and the KGB people here know that you rented this apartment?"

"No, I didn't tell Paul or any of them that I was living over here temporarily," Phil said. "I had no need to. As far as he was concerned, we drove over from Ft. Worth, but as I said before, they have found me before when I was not at home and out of town or something. They always seem to be able to track me down. Now . . ." he thought for a moment. "I did give my wife this number in the event of an emergency. They may have tricked her into giving it to them. I will call her and confirm that."

While Sasha tried to think through what appeared to be some very bad news, Phil called his wife and, sure enough, she told him that someone who said he was from the office had called and needed to locate him immediately. She gave him the phone number at the apartment. Phil relayed the information to Sasha. Putting two and two together, the KGB *knew* that Sasha was there also.

Sasha stared at his friend. "Phil, this is the worst possible news. If *it was* the KGB that called you, and no doubt it was, it means that either General Tushenskiy has met with some terrible accident or it is another of their crude jokes. How do you call out of here to get back to Moscow?"

Phil smiled weakly and shrugged, "The most direct way, *actually* the only way, my friend, is through our *favorite* friends. They *own* the telecom system as far as we are concerned."

"Damn!" Sasha cursed. "Well, I suppose that we can call your man, Paul, and see if there is anything unusual going on."

"Yes, I can do that," Phil responded.

They drank coffee and talked until Phil figured that Paul would be in his office. He made the call. The conversation was brief, and Sasha listened as Phil received the fateful news. "General Tushenskiy was killed . . . mysteriously. He was shot dead during an ambush on his staff car last evening while he was in route across Moscow."

Sasha sat stunned. The suspicion of the first phone call was confirmed. His first thought shot back to Zotov and the direct threat regarding Tushenskiy and this investigation mission of his.

"Perhaps Zotov is one of those who lurks within the KGB *underground* element?" he pondered, sighing deeply. "Tushenskiy had casually mentioned once that Zotov, Borodin and an *old guard* KGB survivor, Oleg Petrov, were *all one of a kind.* But, I never gave a thought to one day running head on into Zotov and apparently neither did Tushenkiy see his fate in the hands of the bloody bastards! Where does this all end?"

Still trying to comprehend the news and the fact that his trusted leader was dead, it was even more troubling as he wondered about Mackye. Would she be safe now that the general was no longer watching over her well-being? He was in a dilemma.

The Contract

Semyon, Tushenskiy's substitute driver, and the shadowy figure who assassinated the GRU Director General, sat at a table in the dark corner of a seedy tavern on Arbot Prospekt. In the hour since accomplishing their murderous deed, the two had considerably dulled their senses by downing the better part of a liter of vodka.

"Semyon, where is your man? I want my rubles!"

"Shhhh!" Semyon admonished, putting his fore finger to his lips. "Boris, be quiet! There are too many people here. He will come. He said that he would meet us here within two hours after we completed our job and pay us our money. Be patient, Comrade, have another vodka. Soon you will have many rubles."

"Dah, Dah!" Boris loudly shouted. "Soon, I will be a rich man! *A rich man*! *A rich man*!" He sang as he stood and danced around Semyon and the table. The other patrons raised their glasses in approval and clapped to the beat of Boris' heavy-booted dance.

"Quiet, Boris! Sit down!" Semyon tugged at Boris' coat sleeve. "We must not attract attention. You know the secret police are everywhere, even in here! *'Chickens are counted in the autumn.'* Shhhh! Quiet!"

"Okay . . . alright, Semyon!" Boris growled as he collapsed into his chair, downed another slug of vodka and grinning asked his cohort, "Tell me, Semyon, how did you take command of *your general's* staff car and drive him to me? Does he not have a special driver?"

"Dah, he does," Semyon frowned. "Igor is . . . or, *was*, his regular driver. I delivered a phony message to Igor, telling him that his wife had taken suddenly ill. I told him to go to her immediately and that I would cover for him. It was easy to convince him. When the general's aide called to bring the car around, I just responded as if all was well. The general was a little surprised and maybe upset, but he did not object, so I drove him to our rendezvous spot," he sighed. "Now, I must run from the army. They will be looking for me."

The two burly men in heavy dark leather jackets and fur hats were given scant notice as they made their way through the din of smoke, smell of alcohol and late night revelers to the table where Semyon and his comrade, Boris, were seated.

"Comrades!" One of the men addressed Semyon and Boris. "I see you are here as we agreed. We are also pleased that you accomplished your job as planned," he smiled. "Congratulations."

Semyon looked up, grinning, "Do'briy ve'cher, Comrades. Yes, we have been having a few vodkas while we waited for you. Sit down, please."

"Nyet, Comrade," the man replied. "We must leave this place to conduct our business. There are too many nosey people in here."

Boris protested. His words were slurred. "Nyet, Comrade. I want my rubles now! My job is done!"

"Shush! Boris!" Semyon responded. "Yes, Comrades, we are ready to go with you and complete our contract."

The spokesman for the two men nodded and motioned for Semyon and Boris to follow them out of the tavern. As they departed the second of the two handed the waitress a wad of ruble notes to cover the vodka bill and to forget they had been there.

Outside, Semyon and Boris were guided toward a black Lada sedan and instructed them to get into the rear seat. The vodka had taken its toll and the two of them collapsed into the snug back seat. They drove off into the chilled dark night.

When the sedan came to a stop, Boris was jostled awake sufficient to protest again, "I want my rubles! Pay me my rubles! I have done your dirty work! Pay me now!" he slurred.

"Dah, dah, Comrades. We have arrived. Please get out," the man driving responded. "Come with us and we will settle our contract with you."

Semyon and Boris climbed unsteadily out into the cold. It was pitch dark. The pavement was wet with grime. No lights were visible in any of the buildings along the street.

"Where are we?" Semyon asked. His mouth and throat were dry. His words were forced. The cold air aided in sobering him from the effects of the vodka.

"Come this way, Comrades," one of the men instructed and took Semyon by the arm while the other guided Boris. They made their way into a damp and murky alley between two buildings.

"Okay, Comrades, we can now settle our contract with you," one of them spoke in the darkness.

Semyon had now sobered enough to recognize it was a trap and shouted, "Boris, run! This is a trap!" But his arm was in the grip of his captor who slammed him against the building wall and then on to the wet alley pavement. The other man was ready and quickly pushed Boris down on top of him. One of the captors switched on a bright flashlight and, simultaneously, both men pulled out P-6 silencer revolvers in their jacket pockets and fired half dozen shots each into the two heaped before them. Several of the bullets met their mark into the heads of the two ensuring instant death.

"Your contract has been settled, Comrades," one of the men smirked as they walked back to their sedan.

Mackye

The funeral for General Tushenskiy was to be conducted with full military honors. Mackye was still in full shock from the tragedy. There was no way she could contact Sasha. She needed desperately to talk to him.

"Was he aware of Tushenskiy's death?" she wondered. "Where was he and what danger might he also be in?" She was sure that the Tushenskiy's murder was the work of those who wanted to send a strong message to everyone.

It quickly became whispered common knowledge that Tushenskiy had met a violent death by an unknown assassin, but it was not discussed publicly, only that he met with an unfortunate *accident*. The Soviet powers attended to his funeral with the highest honors accorded that of a war hero.

The funeral services were done in haste. The KGB Chairman attended and spent an unusual amount of time with the widow and family members. He was too obvious in showing his sympathy which was unusual for a KGB general, even for one of their own. *Pravda* and *Izvestiya* newspapers, in typical form, gave only scant mention of Tushenskiy's death and also attributed it to *an unfortunate accident*.

The Soviet Premier had quietly ordered a "full and thorough investigation," but those on the inside knew that the MVD which was charged with the inquiry would be closely *monitored* by the KGB. Eventually they would issue a report without any specific findings, or perhaps, some derelict would be singled out and executed for the crime.

In the case of Tushenskiy, however, the two perpetrators were themselves agency operatives and had already been dealt with. This was the routine manner in which the mysterious deaths of Soviet senior leaders were handled. The families were frequently pacified with trumped up honors and accords for the deceased, and they would be rewarded with very lucrative annuities. Soon the whole affair would be forgotten. The Chairman, himself, likely did not want to know what happened or why.

Mackye was startled out of a restless sleep by the abrupt ringing of the telephone. "Mackye! It's me! How are you? Are you okay? Is all well with you? I am sorry to wake you at such an hour!" Sasha's voice and questions riveted through her ear.

"Sasha! It *is* you! Are you okay? Where are you? Have you heard the tragic news?" she gasped.

"Dah, dah. I am fine. I am okay," Sasha quickly replied. "Yes, I have heard the bad news. I am still in shock. Are you being looked after?" Sasha rushed his words. "I can speak only for a few minutes. I just wanted to hear your voice and reassure myself that you are well. It is so good to find you!"

"And you, Sasha! I am fine. When will you return home? Please make it very soon!" Mackye urged.

"I . . ." the phone connection clicked dead. "Mackye? . . . Mackye!" They each held on to the telephone hand piece listening for it to reconnect before finally hanging up in frustration and anger.

Mackye did not go back to sleep; she finally got up, drank tea and dressed to go to the KGB Centre' Annex where her office was located. With her briefcase in hand, she stood outside in the brutally cold morning and waited on the snowy sidewalk in the scant shelter of the Pedestrian Exit Portal of Khodinka. Her thoughts continued to be totally occupied by the few seconds phone call she had received from Sasha.

"At least he is safe," she thought. "He sounded fine. He must come home soon!"

A black sedan pulled to the curb and the driver motioned her to get in.

FIFTEEN

"The sun will shine into your yard again."

A Russian Proverb

Dallas

Sasha's thoughts were a blur after he spoke with Mackye. He had a dull headache and was considerably depressed. "This journey is finally at an end! I've not discovered anything regarding the KGB's potential involvement in this tragic escapade or, for that matter, the role of any collective group, Soviet or U.S."

Still he couldn't get the whole assassination event out of his thoughts along with that of the death of Tushenskiy. "The Oswald character was no doubt a misfit and a derelict, and he was recognized as such by both our government and U.S. authorities. I think there is little question that the KGB had plans for using him somewhere. They had coddled him far too much to not have had something in mind. The only problem was that they failed to recognize how unpredictable and dangerous he could be. Then there is the incredible angle with this man, Ruby. *'Who'* set *him* up to do in Oswald? Was it an American leftist or right-wing crowd that egged on Oswald, goaded Ruby and whoever else that might have been involved? *Or, was it our own KGB?"*

He continued to contemplate the conceivable possibilities. "The KGB bastards are already out of their minds with paranoia. They have killed General Tushenskiy to get him out of the way and to get even. There is no doubt that they have me targeted next, or even Mackye."

174

He knew in his own thoughts that "The chaos following Tushenskiy's death would virtually eliminate any interest within GRU regarding what I might have to say when I return."

His appearance in this caper had stirred up far too much trouble *'somewhere'* within the KGB, and he was fortunate to still be alive himself, he mused. "They have won." With regard to General Tushenskiy, "there is no way that he *'just got killed'* by an errant thug no matter what the story line is. No *sane* person would attack a Soviet Military limousine, and in the middle of Moscow! Even if he was a drugged-up dissident, the police would have easily captured him. The KGB has had their way."

He was sick and saddened with all that had happened. He wasn't really concerned about his own safety in returning—he had already been faced with about every challenge they could hand him—but he *was* worried about Mackye. She was now virtually alone to look out for herself. She would not get much attention from the GRU staff with all the confusion at Khodinka in the wake of Tushenskiy's death.

"It's time for me to hold up the surrender flag!" he heaved a sigh, measuring his options. "I will also ask Phil to pass the word to his KGB contacts that I am returning home, never to return."

Phil had already made flight arrangements for him to return via New York to Helsinki and said that he would get the word to Paul that he was leaving—-returning to Moscow. The GRU rezidentura staff in Helsinki would assist in getting him back into Russia. He would get a communiqué to them when he arrived in New York.

Sasha was filled with excitement and mixed apprehension as he got into the car with Phil very early the next morning. It was going to be a chilly wet day in Dallas. The low overhanging clouds made it seem even darker. Phil pulled out onto the street and headed toward the airport. Sasha noticed through his side view mirror that a car parked at the curbside a block down the street had turned on its headlights, pulled out at the same time and appeared to be following them. "Turn right at the next street, Phil," he said. "I think we may have company behind us."

Phil nodded and turned right at the next intersection and then again back to the left at the next street. "Yep, he's trailing us," Phil acknowledged, monitoring the vehicle through his rearview mirror. Then he looked ahead.

"Let's check him out," Phil smiled as he pulled up next to a white and blue Dallas Police cruiser at a signal light. He motioned for the officer to lower his side window.

"Yes, Sir," the officer responded, the rain peppering in through their open windows. "Can I help you?"

"I'm not sure, Officer," Phil replied in his best Texas drawl . . . "I'm taking my friend here to catch a flight at Love Field, and it appears that car behind us may be following me for some strange reason. I have made a couple of turns off the main streets and back on again and he has stayed with me. I just don't feel comfortable this time of the morning with it still dark and all."

"Thank you, Sir," the officer replied. "I'll check him out. You be on your way and drive carefully, this is a nasty morning."

"Thank you, Officer, we feel much better now," Phil said as he smiled and winked at Sasha, and they proceeded on their way. "Our friends just may be making sure that you were really departing."

The officer turned on his flashing lights and edged his patrol car in front of the dark colored sedan which had come to stop a few car lengths behind Phil and Sasha.

Arriving at the airport, Sasha bade Phil goodbye, "Thank you, Comrade, for all your support. I am sincerely grateful to you and wish you well here until you can come back home. I will make it one of my first priorities to contact your children and other family members and reassure them of your well-being. Da sveeda' neeya." He bounded out of the car. Neither had given another thought about the car they thought to be following them.

The weather had turned much worse with the rain coming down hard, but that didn't dampen Sasha's spirits. He was going home!

Phil pulled away from the curb at Love Field and headed south toward the airport exit. He heard the rumble of thunder as he merged into the traffic flow. "Only in Texas can it thunder and rain so hard in the cold dead of winter—in Moscow, we would be up to our bottoms in snow!" He murmured a fleeting thought about *home*.

The traffic was heavy and the rain didn't help. He wanted to get out of Dallas and back to his more familiar environment in Ft.

Worth as soon as he could. He would turn in the rental car back there and take a cab home. "All of this is over with," he breathed to himself. He had not enjoyed the past couple of days. "I'm just not into this secret police work." He was feeling relieved already.

The traffic signal light turned red as he approached the intersection of Airport Boulevard and Mockingbird. As he slowed to stop, a car directly behind skidded into the rear end of his car with a hard jolt.

"What th' hell!" he murmured looking into the rear view mirror.

As he moved to open the door and inspect the damage, two men in raincoats quickly jumped out of the vehicle that had rammed him. One climbed in on the front passenger side while the other pushed Phil back into the car and behind the steering wheel. Then he got into the back seat.

The heavy-set one in the front seat pushed a pistol into Phil's right side. "Let's move! Turn left here!" he ordered. "Go east and stay on Mockingbird, *Do Not* speed, and don't run any traffic lights! Do you understand, Comrade?"

Phil thought at first that he was in for a robbery, but now knew immediately that he was in far more serious trouble. He glanced down at the P-6 silencer-fixed revolver, the KGB handgun of choice.

"Keep your eyes on the traffic, Comrade!" the one in the back seat whispered, cuffing the back of Phil's head with the back of his hand. Through the rear view mirror, Phil was sure that he recognized that one. He had seen him at the KGB residence here in Dallas.

"What's the game, fellows?" Phil tried to act calm.

"This is no game, Comrade. We don't play games. You apparently have been the one playing around. Just do as I say, no funny tricks, and don't get cute by flagging down another policeman," the one with the pistol responded firmly. "Take it nice and easy and when you get to Greenville Avenue, turn right."

Phil drove on knowing full well that sure tragedy lay ahead unless he made a move. As he crossed over Preston Avenue, another police cruiser moved along side him. "Don't give it a second thought, Comrade!" The one in the front seat whispered loudly as he thrust the revolver hard into Phil's side.

He turned off Mockingbird onto Greenville and headed south. It was getting daylight and he noticed in his side view mirror that the car the two had been riding in out of the airport was trailing close behind with only the single driver visible. It had an unmistakable large dent in the left front fender.

"Turn left at the next street," the gunman in the front seat ordered.

Phil made the turn and gradually increased the speed of the car up to 30 mph, making sure the trailing vehicle was directly behind.

"Slow down, you fool! You're going too fast for this weather," the gunman shouted and jammed the pistol again into Phil's side.

Phil then quickly spun the car into a sharp left turn in the middle of the street and jammed on the brakes. The trailing car rammed into the left rear of his vehicle and the gunman was thrown against the dashboard. Phil caught them all by surprise. He quickly opened his door and ran down the street yelling, "Help, Robbery! Help!"

They were in a seedy part of Southeast Dallas near Fair Park. He ran into a small grocery market that had just opened for the day, moving quickly past a surprised clerk behind the counter, through a rear door into a store room and finally out the back into a wet filthy alley. He kept running, brushing past a few winos in doorways and others pilfering in the trashcans and rain-drenched discarded packing boxes.

As he came to the end of the alley, he heard sirens screaming. "The police," he thought. "I hope I killed some of those bastards," he murmured as he searched up and down the street for a taxi. "To hell with the car," he smiled. "Something told me to use a fake driver's license when I rented it. Thank goodness, I did!"

He walked on more slowly, catching his breath and finally spotted a beat up looking black Plymouth sedan with white "TAXI" bulb mounted on the top. He opened the right front door and jumped in, handing the surprised driver a "Twenty". He was soaking wet, but he couldn't have cared less. "Take me to the bus depot!"

It was Phil's lucky day. Few ever escaped the diligent wrath of the KGB. The escape and evade training that he had taken to avoid capture by the enemy had been effective against his *own* people! He also knew that he would now have more trouble ahead unless he made plans to leave his assignment and *very soon*! He would call the New York GRU rezidentura and leave a message for Sasha.

New York

Sasha was again met by Paulette. She greeted him warmly and promptly asked if he had heard the news about Tushenskiy.

"Dah, I have, Tatyana, 'er *Paulette*," he replied. "I'm sorry; I can't break old habits, Paulette," he said smiling. "What information do you have regarding what happened?"

"Not very much," Paulette said. "We have been advised that he was apparently called to a meeting with Kashevarov at Lubiyanka late one evening and departed to go there around eight p.m. Along the way, his staff car pulled over to the curb and someone opened the door and shot him several times. No one at Lubiyanka was aware that he was called to a meeting. They also deny that anyone there called him. I am told that they even deny the circumstances of the murder as I described it to you."

"What about his driver? Was he also killed?" Sasha pressed.

"That is also a mystery, Sasha," she said. "His regular driver was called away to see about his wife who was reported to be ill and a substitute driver apparently drove him. The substitute driver is no where to be found."

He wasn't surprised by what he was hearing. "Was Igor's wife, that's his regular driver's name . . . was Igor's wife really ill?" Sasha asked.

"We do not have any information relative to that, Sasha. That is a good question," she replied.

"There is no doubt that the whole affair was a set up to ambush the general," Sasha responded. ". . . A phony late call to come to Lubiyanka, Igor's wife supposedly ill, a substitute driver and he cannot be located. The KGB is all over this! Someday they will bring our government down and all of us with it. This is sickening. Do you know if there are any results from an investigation?"

"No, Sasha," Paulette replied. "I have told you all that we know here. The KGB operatives here in the consulate are silent on the subject and will not respond to any questions about '*the tragic incident,*' they call it! Does that surprise you?"

"No, no, it doesn't, Paulette." He looked at his watch. "What time is my flight to London?"

"You have just about an hour before you board the plane. Are you hungry? I need to bring you up to date on another event. Our office received a call from Phil in Dallas. He called from a bus station and was trying to get back to his home. It seems that after he let you off at the airport, he had a big encounter with our KGB friends there." She related Phil's story.

"Is he alright?" Sasha asked. "Those dirty bastards don't give up. What is he going to do? Obviously he can't stay in that area. They're mad now, and they'll get to him again."

His thoughts continued to be on departing as soon as possible, but the news about Phil didn't help. "I'll report this as soon as I get to Moscow. Perhaps you should also try to relay the story to Khodinka. It may already be too late to save a good man like Phil . . ." he paused. "And, his family! Paulette, we need to act quickly and try get him out of there!"

"I will get a communiqué to Moscow as soon as I get back to my quarters. In the meantime, should I tell Phil to pack up and leave?"

"He may already be doing that," Sasha nodded. "He's pretty savvy, but make your calls anyway."

"I will as soon as I drop you off at your terminal," she replied.

"Paulette, are you coming home to Moscow soon?" Sasha asked.

"Perhaps," she smiled, nodding. "Perhaps, we never know what our next move is to be, do we?"

"Oh, Paulette, I almost forgot with all of this going on," he frowned. "Would you do me a favor by monitoring the news in the *WASHINGTON POST* over the next several weeks? There should be an article regarding a court hearing and a judge's ruling about an investigation of a missing U.S. bomber. You do have access to the Washington newspapers, don't you?"

"Yes, we do, Sasha. I will look for it," she replied.

"Good!" he smiled, as the car pulled to a stop. He reached into his brief case for the clipping about the hearing.

"The article will be concerned with this story," he said, handing her the clipping. "When something turns up, would you send it to me along with returning this clipping by the first available courier? Well, I must go. Goodbye, Paulette. Hope to see you again, soon."

"Da sveedah'neeya, Sasha." She bade him goodbye, kissing him on each cheek and smiling, *"the sun will shine into your yard again."*

Reflections

Sasha tried to relax and find some sleep once the aircraft was airborne, but it was out of the question. His thoughts were preoccupied with Tushenskiy's murder and now the well-being of Phil. "He is a goner, for sure, if he doesn't get out of there!" he worried to himself. "Damn! Every decent human being that I have come in contact with has ended up on the wrong side of those vicious murderous bastards!"

He got out of his seat and walked the aisle several times to determine if he had *company* on the long flight. He detected no one who looked the part. In the back of his mind, he relished discovering *one of them* on board the flight. He would have no difficulty sitting down beside him and shoving a knife into his ribs. Finally settling into his seat, his thoughts were a jumble of inter-related events and reflections.

"I wonder where we are all headed with this life we live?" he mused to himself. "While the United States occupies an enormous and obsessive amount of our time and energies, our leaders cannot seem to control the excessive betrayals within our own society. The divisions among our institutions and our people more often than not make us our own worst enemies."

He pondered the questions in and out of fitful sleep as the noise of the jet engines whined on. "Are we too driven? Is the United States such an evil enemy that they threaten our very being? Do they have a quest for absolute world power? Is it our mandate to defeat them before they defeat us?"

He couldn't find comfort in his seat as the time dragged by ever so slowly. This trip had created even deeper doubts and more questions about his government and the Soviet leaders' objectives and motives.

"My loyalty has always been absolute," he had never before doubted. "My father is a loyal and devoted Soviet officer. I have taken every challenge seriously and worked hard to perform to the standards put before me. Yet, my life has been threatened several times, and always by my own people. Now, my loyal and devoted leader has been murdered . . . more than likely by thugs who are a part of our own government. Is the United States any better? Their president was murdered apparently by one of their own, even though it might have been with our assistance. Who knows, or even their own? Rumors had already begun regarding the wounds that the president suffered . . . he was allegedly shot from behind, yet his head wound indicated that a bullet entered the front portion of his head, thereby exiting the back and taking half of his skull?"

Serious doubts now evolved. "During all of my years of being assigned in America, I would have never believed that such a thing could happen in that country. There may be many questions about Kennedy's murder that point back to us. I can understand that. Why? How . . . did we permit such a derelict as Oswald to freely enter our country and live openly without someone closely managing his activities, or did they? Why else would the KGB powers, or who ever within that quagmire, want to interfere with an investigation initiated by the GRU, if they are clean? And, why would they kill the Director General . . . unless they themselves were implicated or *worried* that some of their own were involved in the Kennedy assassination?"

Sasha had drifted into philosophical thought before. His mother had gone even further in doubting and questioning the Soviet government and its aims.

"Perhaps she was much wiser than our zealous convictions would permit us to understand," he thought. "She cautioned me several times about '*the enemy within*' our '*own walls*,' she would say."

He finally arrived back in Moscow. It was late in the afternoon and he was exhausted. He had moved smoothly through London and Helsinki. Svendson, his GRU contact, had collected all of his

American identification and papers, returned his Soviet passport and promptly put him on an Aeroflot flight to Moscow.

It was cold and bleak when the plane arrived at Sheremetevo II. He looked around the arrival lounge for Mackye among the waiting greeters and then scanned all around for a familiar face. Finally, he spotted General Drachev and Major Sitkov coming toward him. As he moved through the crowded lobby to meet them, he could see dour expressions of deep concern on their faces.

"Something is wrong!" He knew it. They had the *look* in their eyes.

"Do'briy d'en, Comrade Sasha," Drachev spoke. "Welcome home."

"Do'briy d'en, General," Sasha replied as they shook hands.

"Sasha, we must have a private discussion before we depart the terminal. Please come with us," Drachev motioned toward an office door with a uniformed guard posted at the entrance.

Sasha instinctively knew that further bad news was coming. "General, what is it?" he asked. His first thoughts were that *they* had gotten to Phil back in Dallas.

"Come, Sasha, let us go into this office," Drachev urged. "Please be seated. Sasha, we have the gravest of news. Your wife, Mackye, is missing. We cannot locate her anywhere. She has been missing since yesterday. She apparently departed for work early in the morning, left by the pedestrian exit portal which was her normal pattern. No one has seen her since. She did not report for work that day and has not been in touch with anyone as far as we know."

Sasha reeled at the news. He felt faint. The combination of fatigue from the lengthy series of flights and Drachev's words made him nauseous. He didn't reply. He couldn't. He promptly jumped to his feet, reeled with dizziness for a moment and walked slowly around the room.

Drachev stood and took his arm to steady him. Sitkov handed him a glass of water. He shook his head and waved it off. He finally moved back to the overstuffed chair and eased into its soft cushions. No one spoke. Drachev allowed the shock to settle into Sasha's thoughts.

He suddenly stood again. "General, who is investigating this?" he asked. "What information has been collected? Who picked her up and took her to work? Was he the regular driver? What do we know?"

"Sasha, the MVD has the case," Drachev replied. "They have been required to report back to General Sokolov and to me whenever they have information or at the end of each day."

Sasha turned quickly. "General Sokolov? . . . General Sergiy Sokolov? Is he here? At Khodinka?"

"Dah, Sokolov is the new acting Director General," Drachev responded. "We are very pleased to have him come back to GRU Headquarters. We all hope that the Premier will wisely confirm him to the post permanently. He is anxious to meet with you and sends his heartfelt concern for what has happened. These have been very difficult days for us all and now to have this terrible thing to happen with your wife."

"Sasha, we are all so very sorry, but we are doing everything possible to locate her and bring her safely back." Drachev was at a loss for words.

Although relieved with the news of General Sokolov now being in charge, he was chilled and sickened inside with concern for Mackye. Sokolov had been assigned by Tushenskiy as his senior mentor when he was first recruited out of the Aviation Academy by the GRU. He was colonel then and a trusted and competent officer.

"The GRU will continue to be in good hands with him in command," Sasha commented.

He then turned his frustration back to Mackye's disappearance. "The *MVD* is in charge of the investigation? Are they to be trusted to help us? General, the KGB direct every step that the MVD idiots take! Can the GRU not go look for her? I have no trust in the MVD whatsoever, or their dubious masters either! I cannot stand by to wait. I will find out who is responsible for this! I have been threatened and interfered with by KGB interlopers at every step along the way since I left Moscow. Some innocent people I met with were killed because of me, and others were beaten and tortured. And now, General Tushenskiy is dead and my wife is missing . . . and," he paused. "She may also be dead while we wait for the same treacherous bastards who are charged to find her. I am going directly to Kashevarov and the Premier himself if necessary to find her! Sir, may we get out of here!" he said finally. "I must see General Sokolov as soon as we get to Khodinka."

Drachev was also visibly shaken as he spoke, "Dah, Sasha, we are crushed and furious at what has overtaken us. Yes, we will first visit with the Director General and from there determine our next step. Sasha, we are all so sorry for this. With General Tushenskiy's tragic murder, I am sure that the attention of all of us was deflected. We let our guard down."

"Our guard down?" Sasha mocked. "Our guard is down against our own people! General! I am sorry, sir, but I have witnessed the murderous acts of the KGB for far too long. Something must be done to control them and to weed out the scum that betrays us within our own walls!"

Few words were spoken during the 28-kilometer ride into Moscow. Sasha gazed out into the snow-covered barren fields along the highway, remaining deep in his private thoughts. Sitkov sat up front with the driver, and Drachev sat quietly with Sasha in the rear seat. He could add nothing more to the discussion.

Betrayed

Mackye woke up with a splitting headache and her mind a jumble of confused nightmares. Unaware of where she was, she slowly raised her head and looked around the starkly furnished room. She immediately discovered that she was not wearing the dress she remembered putting on to go to work. She was in a gray smock and it was soaking wet from perspiration. As she moved to sit up on the side of bed, her head throbbing, she felt and then saw the wet profile of her body imprinted in the dingy sheet. She sat up trying to rationalize her bearings and what could have happened since she last remembered standing in the portal at Khodinka waiting for her car. She vaguely remembers getting into the back seat after the driver motioned for her to hurry out of the brutal cold. She had quickly opened the rear door and climbed in. She did remember a man already seated in the car. He pulled her inside and held her tightly while holding a damp pungent cloth over her mouth and nose.

Moving slowly, she was dizzy and nauseous, and couldn't clear her thoughts of the bad dreams which seemed to have lasted for days. She had envisioned Sasha and herself being thrown into a jail cell. She had dreamed that she clearly saw her former husband and KGB deviate, Dimitri Vetrov, standing outside the cell laughing and taunting them. She watched as the guards came in and beat Sasha into unconsciousness before dragging him away.

Finally she shook herself awake enough to look around the room once again, hoping that this was also a dream. She had no idea how long she had been there or whether it was day or night.

"Where am I? What is this place?" she wanted to scream out loud. She barely remembered doing just that when she thought she woke momentarily the first time from the deep sleep hours or maybe *days* before, but no one had responded to her call.

There was no window in the room, only a door with a very small observation slit near the top. She could not see anyone peering in, but she felt the eyes. The walls were pale blue. The only furniture was the bed and a single folding chair. A combination lavatory and commode were fixed into one corner. Above it was a small stainless steel mirror attached permanently to the wall.

The only discernable scent or odor in the room was that of a strong disinfectant of some kind. A single stark light bulb was fixed into the high ceiling. It apparently remained on constantly. After sobering to her surroundings, she again felt the sticky wetness of the dark gray smock.

"Where are my clothes?" she cried softly to herself. Her purse, wristwatch and briefcase were also missing.

The door suddenly opened and a female dressed in a dark uniform dotted with brass buttons, but without insignia or identification otherwise, entered carrying a tray. "Do'broye oo'tro, Gaspazhah, your breakfast."

Mackye noticed that she was not alone. A uniformed armed guard stood visibly just outside the door.

She did not respond and continued to sit on the side of the bed. She reasoned that it was morning after the greeting and delivery of the breakfast tray. The intruder placed the food tray on the end of the bed and noticed the wet stain and grunted. She departed without further comment.

Mackye reached for the mug of steaming tea, her hand shaking almost uncontrollably. She steadied the cup and sipped the tea slowly. She finally nibbled at a piece of dry toast. The rest looked and smelled inedible. She was weak, but not so much as to force feed herself. She finally found the strength to get up and walk to the lavatory and dab water on her face. She looked into the mirror and was shocked at her appearance. Her face was pale and drawn with dark circles beneath her eyes. Several damp strands of her blonde hair had pulled free from either side of the severe chignon she had carefully put in place when she last prepared to go to work. She felt nauseous and made her way back to the bed, turned the soggy pillow over and settled her head onto it.

The door suddenly opened again and the same matron or whoever she was, entered, handed her a clean dry smock and placed a stack of sheets at the foot of the bed. When the door closed, Mackye moved over to a corner of the room out of direct sight of the observation slit in the door and changed into the dry smock. She had not been chilled from all the moisture, rather her entire body felt as if it were on fire. "What on earth have they done to me? What have they poisoned me with?" Mackye murmured in tears. She spread the clean sheets over the bed and lay down feeling somewhat comforted by the change of clothes and bedding.

After awhile, the door suddenly opened again and two men along with the uniformed female entered. "Do'broye oo'tra, Gaspazhah Katsanov," one of the men greeted.

Again, she did not respond, only stared at the three as she slowly sat up on the side of the bed.

The one who greeted her, continued, "Madame Katsanov, we are very sorry for the circumstance in which you find yourself, and we apologize for the crude manner in which you were brought here. But, as you know, these are very troubling times in our country and we cannot be too careful."

Mackye stayed seated firmly upright on the bed and stared at the one speaking.

"Madame Katsanov," he continued, "It is my unfortunate duty to inform you that you are temporarily under arrest for some questionable activities in which you were allegedly involved a few years ago. Do you recall intervening in a case involving a prominent high level officer's wife who was suspected of participating with the *krushki* underground dissident group?"

Mackye shuddered as she heard the statement and tried desperately to provide a firm and defensive response. "Comrade, first of all, I do not know who you are and I do not know where I am being held. I do know that I have been kidnapped, NOT merely arrested as you say. I was taken from the very entrance of GRU Headquarters where I reside. I am also a staff officer in the KGB. With regard to your accusations, they are preposterous! I will also advise you that if I am not released to return to my place of work and my private life, there will be hell to pay for all of you that are involved in this gross miscarriage." She raised her voice to almost a shout. "You are holding a Soviet Government official against her will!"

The speaker ignored her plea, "Madame, please, you are being well cared for. We mean you no personal harm. We know who you are, where you are assigned to work and we know who your husband is. But I am charged with following up on back investigations which were never properly adjudicated. Will you tell me, did you intervene in such an investigation which I have described?" the speaker pressed.

"No! No, I did not participate nor intervene in any such venture which you have described!" Mackye spat out the words.

She knew very well that he was referring to the event that involved Sasha's mother and her arrest for suspected activities with the unlawful intellectual group, *krushki*. It was obvious that the KGB was now going to use the incident of her involvement to some advantage with Sasha's present activities, the GRU or both.

"Madame, you are now married to the son of the woman in whose case you tried to intervene. Is that not true?" he asked.

Mackye was fully alert and fiery mad. "You stupid fool. I have no idea what you are talking about. This is nothing more than a trumped up story and I warn you, heads will roll when those who are looking for me, find you!"

"Madame," he persisted, taking a sheaf of papers from his valise, "Will you please review this document and consider signing it? If you do so, everything will go so much more easily for you. I hope you will take time to consider your situation."

They departed the room and Mackye leaned back on the bed and against the wall. She was shaking uncontrollably in convulsive tears. "I cannot believe this! My own government! My own government! Here I sit in a prison and being charged with such a ridiculous and stupid *non-event!* That corrupt bastard, Dimitri, must have filed a written report before he forced me into his wretched web of deceit. The filthy and corrupt dead bastard has come back to haunt me. Twice I have been betrayed by him and now even after he is dead!"

"Sasha, Sasha where are you?" she screamed, threw the folder of papers, scattering them across the room and fell across the bed, sobbing uncontrollably.

SIXTEEN

*"Lord rescue me against friends;
against enemies I can rescue myself."*

A Russian Proverb

Khodinka

Drachev escorted Sasha directly to General Sokolov's office. "Sasha! Sasha! Comrade," Sokolov greeted him warmly. "It is so good to see you after so very long. You look exceptionally fit! Come in! Come in!" he exclaimed, beckoning him into his office, hugged and bussed him on both cheeks.

Sasha looked at an older and graying Sokolov. It had been seven years or more since they last saw each other. Sokolov had been a colonel and special assistant to Tushenskiy. He had worked closely with Sasha during his agent training. He was a polished officer and much like Tushenskiy in many ways. Sasha had liked and trusted him as much as he did his former leader.

"It is also good to see you, General," Sasha smiled. "Congratulations on your appointment as acting Director General. The Chairman has made a wise choice, Sir, and I hope that he confirms you into the position very soon."

"I am so sorry to have to greet you with such terrible news, Sasha," Sokolov replied. "We are at our wits end. I am in contact with every senior police official to find your wife as soon as possible. There has not been a clue detected as to her disappearance. We are absolutely shocked that she could have disappeared literally from right before our eyes. A witness said that he saw her get into her car right at the Exit Portal."

"Thank you, General, I am devastated. Sir, there is background that you should also know." Sasha looked at Drachev and the Sitkov.

Sokolov motioned for his aide to leave the room. "May General Drachev remain?" Sokolov asked.

"Yes, General, of course," Sasha responded and proceeded to briefly describe Mackye's background, commencing that he had known her since his training days here at Khodinka.

Sokolov acknowledged with a smile, "Yes, Sasha, I remember that you and she got off to a good start."

Sasha continued to give an account of her attempt to assist his mother when she was arrested for suspicion of participating in the *krushki*. "I just happened to be back here from America for debriefings when this all happened, and I called on Mackye for advice."

He described how Mackye had inquired into his mother's arrest and how she was first threatened for her intrusion in the investigation. Then she was blackmailed into marrying a KGB operative named Vetrov, and he told about Vetrov's role in plotting with a KGB general, Anatoli Borodin, who was a KGB exchange officer assigned to GRU. "Your successor when you departed GRU Headquarters for another assignment, General," Sasha interjected.

Sokolov frowned, "Yes, I recall Borodin very well. General Tushenskiy was not pleased to have him assigned here. He didn't trust him, but he had no choice. The KGB persisted."

"As I am sure you are aware . . ." Sasha hesitated and looked toward Drachev, then back to Sokolov and decided to continue, ". . . the two conspired to have the American bomber that I was delivering shot down."

Neither looked surprised at the revelation and he continued, reminding him finally how Vetrov and Borodin were summarily executed by their own agency people for their ill deed.

"Yes, Sasha, General Tushenskiy briefed me on most of the details about your work, skilled efforts and the aircraft tragedy, as well as the ill-guided people that intervened as you have described," Sokolov acknowledged. "General Drachev was brought into it also. I am not, however, familiar with the story about your mother's difficulty and Mackye's role in that. Tell me more."

Sasha proceeded to discuss the details of his mother's arrest regarding her participation in the banned intellectual group.

"Mackye was assigned to KGB Headquarters then and merely responded to my request to see if she could assist in clarifying the situation," he said. "My father, in spite of his position, could not buck the secret police. Mackye, as I have said, was successful in securing my mother's release, but I didn't discover until later that in doing so she paid a price. She was first threatened, as I indicated, with interfering in an investigation, and then blackmailed into having to marry that bastard, Vetrov. Otherwise, she would have been arrested herself."

Sokolov listened as Sasha revealed his concerns. "General, I am suspicious that Mackye's disappearance is directly connected to my visit back to the United States regarding the murder of their president. The KGB has harassed me at every turn and several people have either been killed or badly injured as a result of my making contact with them regarding that tragic event. I was threatened by those people continuously."

He wanted to emphasize even farther his conviction that Tushenskiy's murder was tied directly to the KGB and Kashevarov, but he held back due to Drachev's presence in the room and unsure how far he could go with Sokolov. He knew that sensitivities at the senior levels of government were not to be pressed too far.

"Yes, Sasha, I want a full report on your journey and the problems you encountered in due time," Sokolov interrupted and moved the discussion along. "I have received only brief sketches from our rezidentura chiefs since I arrived here, and I want to hear all of it from you, but first, we need to find Mackye."

Sasha nodded and decided to make the most of his opportunity to speak, "Yes, Sir, Mackye must come first. But permit me to say that I do not doubt, for a minute, that General Tushenskiy's murder is also a result of his sending me on that journey . . . and now I am sure that they are directly responsible for Mackye's disappearance. Considering all of the harassment that I encountered on my visits from Minsk to the U.S. and back, I feel sure that *they* must presume that I turned up some evidence that links the KGB to the Kennedy assassination. General, I will not let this stand! The Chairman himself approved of my mission, and General Kashevarov was directed to provide KGB support and cover for me throughout. We know the results of *that support!*"

Sokolov did not appear to be fazed one way or the other by Sasha's emotional assertions and replied, "Sasha, I know that you are very disturbed. I will do everything within my power to find your wife. The accusations you make are very dangerous. You want to be careful not to express them too loudly or to the wrong people. We share your ill feelings toward many of those in our government who often decide their own courses of action," he said. "I don't have all the answers, but those of us who believe in our great country and our goals must work together to rid ourselves of those enemies within. Sasha, *did you* discover any linkage between the KGB and the Kennedy assassination?"

"No, General, I did not," Sasha replied, "The mystery remains regarding *why* and *how* did an American, and a former U.S. military man, enter our country so easily, marry a Soviet citizen and proceed to live here in a relatively comfortable style for over three years . . . unless *someone* in our government was using him? And then that same American goes back to the U.S. and kills their president? When time permits, Sir, and at your pleasure, I can provide you a complete report. I believe those questions require an inquiry lest the Americans do it for us!"

He had permitted anger to enter his tone of expression and paused considering whether he should go farther, then proceeded. "Sir, did you know that General Borodin and General Zotov, KGB 3rd Division in Washington had been very close colleagues?"

"I have heard rumors to that effect," Sokolov responded, "but I try to steer clear of KGB inside activities, and especially the most sordid of stories about some of their work. It is difficult enough to work with them. What is your point?"

"As you know, General," Sasha continued, "General Zotov warned me off my assignment while I was in Washington and further added a direct threat against General Tushenskiy if he did not back off his pursuit with my presence over there."

Sokolov's expression flushed. He wanted no further part of this line of discussion. "Thank you, Sasha," he abruptly interjected.

"I sincerely appreciate the update. I know that you are exhausted. Please, we have an apartment all arranged for you. Try to eat some food and rest if you can. I have an appointment with the Chairman this evening, and you can rest assured that my main topic will be your wife, Mackye. We will find her, and safely so, Sasha. Get some rest, but before you depart, how is your father and mother?"

"My father is fine and in good health when I last spoke with him," Sasha responded, "but my mother is not well and in failing health. She has always been a serious worrier about our lives and times and it has greatly affected her health."

"I am sorry to hear about your mother, Sasha," Sokolov frowned. "Your father was a loyal and devoted officer. You should be very proud of him. He has served our government well."

They shook hands and Sasha departed. He felt little better after his meeting with Sokolov. He was dead tired and emotionally drained when he finally arrived at his apartment to get some rest. A hot meal was soon delivered along with vodka to soothe his body and nerves, but he touched nothing and collapsed into the bed. He knew that he needed to call his father but didn't want to get involved in all the details requiring a long conversation. And then, the thought of Phil hit him.

He bounded off the bed, picked up the phone and called Sokolov. "General, in all of the turmoil over Mackye, I forgot to mention that our GRU agent at the aircraft plant in Texas near Dallas, who goes by Phil, at least that's the name he used, could be in grave trouble with the KGB. They tried to do him in after he dropped me off at the airport there. Have you heard anything about the incident?

"Nyet, Sasha, I haven't," General Sokolov replied. "I will inquire. Thank you."

After the phone call, he drifted in and out of troubled sleep.

Sasha awoke to a knock on the door. It was Major Sitkov. "Do'broye oo'tra, Colonel, did you rest well?"

"Dah, Oleg, come in," Sasha sleepily responded. "What time is it? Any news from General Sokolov?"

"The General wishes to see you as soon as you are fit to do so, Colonel," Sitkov replied.

"Good!" he said. "Give me a few minutes to clean up and get dressed. My clothes are a mess, but they will have to do."

Sasha began to hurriedly locate his trousers, shirt and jacket. He quickly showered, shaved and headed to Sokolov's office.

"Good Morning, Sasha," Sokolov greeted. General Drachev was already seated in the office and nodded.

"Sit down and, please, pour yourself a tea," Sokolov offered. "Sasha, we have some encouraging news. First, I am advised that Mackye is well and not in any danger. You were correct in your judgment about what might have happened to her. Presently, she is being detained by *our friends* on the very charge you mentioned . . . *interfering with a police investigation,* the incident involving your mother some years ago. Of course, we know that is a sham. General Kashevarov says that he was not even aware himself that his goons had arrested her. But again that is not unusual; people get arrested all the time and are held incommunicado. He is trying to get more details on the situation and will report back to me as soon as he does."

Sasha was furious and had difficulty controlling himself. "General, this is an outrageous crime against all of us . . . Mackye is a staff officer in the KGB, she is my wife, she is a loyal and trusted Soviet citizen and government official. How corrupt can we possibly be? Did you consult with the Chairman, General?"

"Yes, Sasha, I did," Sokolov replied. "It took a phone call from him to Kashevarov to get this far. I must confess, though, that the Chairman is so distracted with other matters that he gave scant sympathetic interest in this issue other than to contact Kashevarov and request that he work with me to resolve this . . . *incident,* he called it. He is still troubled by the murder of General Tushenskiy, that investigation and the ongoing internal inquiries about how we might have been implicated, if at all, in the American president's assassination. His troubles are great, but so are yours, and *ours,* Sasha. I expect a call from Kashevarov at any time. Have you eaten?"

Sasha sat for a moment, absorbing the news. He knew that he was helpless to do nothing other than to be patient at this point. While he was overcome with anger, at least Mackye was reported to be safe.

"Thank you, General. I am not hungry," he finally responded. "I can appreciate the Chairman's distractions. At least we have been told that she is safe. At least *they* say she is. Do we know where she is being held? Will formal charges be brought and why the secrecy?"

"Sasha, I don't have the answers to your questions," Sokolov wearily replied, "but the Chairman *is* most interested in what you discovered on your journey. He would like to have as complete a report that you might provide as soon as you can put one together. I know under the circumstances that your mind is not on that, but if you are up to it while we await further news, we will assist you in developing one . . . At least a preliminary for now."

Sokolov pressed. "What you have to tell us may very well take some pressure off the Chairman."

"General, I am not sure that what I have to report regarding our government's potential role in the Kennedy assassination will be of much relative use," Sasha shrugged and relied. "I am afraid that I have not concluded anything that puts everything in order," he said. "It is much like a box of puzzle pieces, but many of the pieces are missing. Perhaps there are two boxes of puzzle pieces, one in the U.S. and one here, with some in one box that might belong in the other in order to complete the mosaic? I will do my best to try to sort out what I have discovered or observed."

"But, Sir," he continued, "what I do feel compelled to report is the corrupt interference by the KGB bastards throughout my travel. I am afraid that will not set well with the Chairman much less General Kashevarov. I believe that it is very important for me to go into considerable detail about their atrocious acts and deeds, most of which were leveled directly against our own innocent people."

"Fine," Sokolov acknowledged. "I want you to take the necessary time to render a complete report and your assessment. I would, however, like to have a brief outline and synopsis that I might take to the Chairman as soon as possible. Such a report might very well assist in relieving his anxiety and help with getting his support in releasing Mackye."

"Yes, Sir, I can do that now if you wish," Sasha said, "and, Sir, have you had any reports on our man, Phil, in Texas?"

"No, Sasha, I have not," Sokolov replied. "I have our Washington people working on your report to me about him. I will keep you posted. General Drachev will escort you to an office where he will have some scribes take down your commentary. If you feel compelled to comment on the KGB interference in this initial rendering, please do so. Do not spare any details no matter how assertive or sordid. You will be given an opportunity to review and agree to all that is written down before I deliver it to the Kremlin. Thank you, Sasha. When I receive any further news, I will call you immediately."

Reflections

Mackye walked around the small room after the visitors left, kicked at the papers scattered on the floor and reflected on her situation. "We are living in a flawed and corrupt nation. The betrayal of all of us has become a way of life. Allegiance and loyalty to the government mean nothing. How can it be that I am snatched off the street like a common criminal, drugged and brought to a jail cell? The only crime that I have committed has been to commit and dedicate myself completely to my country and my government. And now, I am being persecuted and offered an opportunity to *confess* to wholly created and false charges. We have become a nation of lies, deceit and corruption."

She sat back on the bed, bewildered with her situation. "First, there was Sasha's training handler, Vladimir, a sneak and a scum who had the power to transfer me from Khodinka. Dimitri Vetrov blackmailed and seduced me into a corrupt marriage of horror and then he helped create the plan to destroy Sasha and the prized bomber he was delivering. He got what he deserved, a bullet in the skull. Tushenskiy is murdered . . . and, by whom and for what reason? Now, this? I am being held in jail like a common criminal and being coerced to sign papers of *confession*. Where is this corrupt underground power and where does it begin and end? I cannot believe that it reaches to the Chairman or even to the KGB General Director . . . but perhaps it does! Meanwhile, we are fooled into believing that they all mean well for the *good of our people*."

There was a sharp knock on the door and another uniformed female brought in a food tray. She observed the papers scattered on the floor, shrugged and left without speaking. Mackye was hungry. She couldn't remember when she had last eaten, but she was afraid to touch anything for fear it was either drugged or poisoned. She drank the tea earlier, but now she feared that even it might not be safe. She picked up the apple and munched it slowly. She knew that she needed to keep up her strength or she would be even more vulnerable to those who were holding her.

She had heard many stories about the political prisoners being held in the gulags in Siberia. She wondered how many of them were really dissidents and plotters against the government, or were they victims just like herself, arrested and carted off for minor offenses or whatever the reason? "Then there are those such as these matrons or whatever they are?" she wondered. "Are they also prisoners or simply bound to the system without conscience or voice? Do they go home at night and report who is here? Our system is so miserably flawed, our people so galvanized into a single-minded culture."

"*WHY* am I here?" she cried within. "What is this for? It can't be for something I may have innocently and in good faith intruded into years ago!"

She was full of despair and felt totally helpless. She was unable to let anyone know where she was. "Is anyone even concerned or looking for me? She remembered a phrase from her mother's book of verse: *'Lord, rescue me against friends; against enemies I can rescue myself.'*

Strategy

Sasha dictated the highlights of his recollections and after they were typed, he reviewed the text. He had decided to leave out the sordid details of the work of the secret police in Minsk and only mention that he was interfered with and harassed at virtually every turn of his assignment. He would save the atrocities for a later, more comprehensive report. Also, he would never report witnessing the courtroom drama regarding the missing B-52 bomber.

Handing it to Sokolov, "Sir, I have provided a summary of my findings herein. I will go into considerable more detail later including the brutal and unforgivable events in Minsk to which General Bekrenev can validate. The portions regarding the attempts to hinder me personally are minor and incidental so I have only commented about them in broad terms. I don't want to jeopardize Mackye's safety any further by antagonizing anyone."

"I agree, Sasha," Sokolov replied. "I do want the Chairman to know what goes on within that agency and with some of its people. Your observations here apparently vindicate our government from any direct participation in the assassination. That is good and the part about the American roaming around our country for three years validates that our friends at Lubiyanka are not as perfect as they tout themselves to be."

Sokolov advised Kashevarov that he was delivering Sasha's preliminary report to the Kremlin and invited him to attend the meeting.

"Dah, I will meet you there," the KGB chief acknowledged. "Should I be concerned about anything that your young *spy* is reporting, Sergiy?"

Sokolov took some delight with Kashevarov's timorous question. "Comrade General, you will be relieved to know that Colonel Katsanov did not discover any apparent *direct* participation by your people or our government in the tragedy with the American president. I must warn you that his findings reflect that the accused assassin wandered around within our republic for several years and also enjoyed apparent freedoms that even our own citizens do not enjoy."

Sokolov concluded, "You must be aware that there were some indisputable brutal acts of violence against several citizens in Minsk ostensibly as a direct result of Comrade Katsanov's visiting with them. The details of those crimes will not be a part of this initial report to the Chairman in order that you may have an opportunity to conduct your own inquiry. At some point, however, Comrade General, perhaps your agency should be prepared to respond to those accusations. And lastly, Comrade, I have an agent working at an aircraft plant in the United States—in Texas near Dallas. Your people have already attempted to do him harm. I suggest that you call off any plans to interfere with him personally or his family. Do we understand one another?"

Kashevarov was silent for a moment and then in a grating voice, "Comrade, you Razvedupr people should not be so sensitive to the necessity of our police work. I will be in attendance at your meeting with the Chairman!"

Sokolov smiled with some modest satisfaction as he placed the phone back in the cradle.

SEVENTEEN

"A word is like a sparrow when it flies out; you cannot catch it."

A Russian Proverb

Reprieve

Sokolov presented the Chairman an outline reflecting Sasha's preliminary report of findings. The KGB chief, Kashevarov, was in attendance. The Soviet leader was moderately pleased with the carefully crafted summary, which did not include any specific evidence of wrongdoing by his government in the assassination of the U.S. President.

After scanning the paper, however, he turned his attention to Kashevarov. "What are the details about this man who murdered the American President and the fact that he apparently wandered around our republic for several *years* before he returned to America and did his deed?"

Kashevarov fidgeted in his chair. He would have preferred not to be at the meeting after all but he had dared not excuse himself.

He was now on the defensive and nervously responded, "Tavah'reeshch Chairman, my people are continuing to investigate the details of this American derelict who visited our great republic for a time. Sir, we have found no evidence that he was anything but just that, a harmless derelict, and perhaps a person who was seeking a better way of life than that in his native America. My initial impression is that he conducted himself in a very proper manner while he was living in Minsk. He was productively employed; he married a Byelorussia lady and started a family before he returned to the United States."

"Dah, Comrade," the Chairman grunted. "When you complete your full investigation, please advise me. Now, what is this in the report that alleges your people interfered with the GRU agent that I approved to conduct an inquiry into the activities of this vagabond American?"

"Again, Tavah'reeshch Chairman," Kashevarov replied, "I continue to investigate those allegations. I do not believe that any of my people interfered in any way with this GRU agent's activities. To the contrary, I am convinced that we cooperated with his assignment in every way possible. I do not have any reason to believe otherwise. With General Sokolov's permission, I wish to speak directly to his colonel and determine what he means by *interference*. I shall also report those facts to you, Sir, as soon I have them."

The stodgy Chairman cut his eyes to Sokolov. "Sokolov, can you tell me what is meant by these vague statements in this report that imply interference by Kashevarov's people? Are you and the KGB feuding again?"

"Tavah'reeshch Chairman," Sokolov quickly responded, "In deference to Comrade Kashevarov's beliefs, Colonel Katsanov will provide a complete report on his encounters very soon. It will be corroborated by other credible officials. However, Sir, the officer is severely stressed at this moment with the recent questionable arrest and incarceration of his wife. He returned to Moscow to discover this very grievous and unwarranted personal shock. I beseech you, Sir, and Comrade Kashevarov, to please correct this miscarriage of police conduct and release Madame Katsanov as soon as possible. We should never condone such treatment of our loyal citizens."

The Chairman looked back at Kashevarov and waited for a response.

"Tavah'reeshch Chairman," Kashevarov confidently replied, "my people are required to act on all questionable conduct by our citizens. In the case of Madame Katsanov, I am advised that some time ago, she did in fact, intervene in a police case where she had no business. My agents are merely following up on that incident to clear the record. I will have a complete report shortly."

Sokolov, visibly flushed, chose his words carefully. This was not the time or the place to directly confront the KGB chief. He looked at Kashevarov. "With due respect, Comrade Kashevarov, I do not believe you wish for us to discuss here the many details of that case *or* the relative aspects of that particular incident. The important issue here is to resolve the status of Madame Katsanov."

Kashevarov knew full well that Sokolov was referring to the previous conduct of his renegade agents Vetrov and Borodin. Without looking at Sokolov, he responded, "Comrade Chairman, with respect for Comrade Sokolov's concern for the welfare of this Soviet citizen and whatever she did or did not do, Sir, I believe that we can resolve this without troubling you further."

Frowning, the Chairman eyed both and then moved unsteadily out of his overstuffed chair. "Good!" he grumbled as he shuffled out of the conference room. "I do not wish to be bothered further about any of this."

After the Chairman departed, Kashevarov whispered to Sokolov, "Comrade, when your colonel decides to *create* his *more comprehensive report*, I hope that he will exercise extreme caution in characterizing the so-called *interference* or any other untoward activities by my people. Such faulty judgment could be counter-productive. Meanwhile, I will see to the disposition of his wife. Oh, and do not trouble yourself, Comrade, about your man in Texas. That incident was a misunderstanding. He will be well looked over by my people in the area."

Kashevarov winked and whispered, "Do we understand one another, Comrade?"

Sokolov understood the implications of Kashevarov's challenge. "Dah, Comrade, this can be worked out," he replied, comprehending fully that . . . *"If we cooperate together, Mackye will be released, there should be no report mentioning 'KGB interference,' and Phil, in Texas, will be safe."*

Sasha had been summoned to General Sokolov's office at mid-afternoon and was waiting there alone with measured anticipation. He did not know what to expect. Suddenly, the door opened.

"Mackye! Mackye!" Sasha swept her into his arms.

Neither spoke for another minute or so. He led her to the sofa and helped her to sit down. She was pale and drawn. Sokolov entered the office smiling. He had already greeted Mackye when she arrived.

"Sasha," Sokolov said, "I am informed that your apartment is ready whenever you and Mackye are ready. The kitchen will bring in your dinner. But, please, no hurry. You are free to stay right here as long as you wish."

"Thank you, General," Sasha acknowledged. "Sir, we are deeply grateful to you for your personal intervention and all you have done to secure Mackye's release and return."

"And Sasha," Sokolov said, "I am also assured that our man, Phil, in Texas is well and no harm will come to him. Thank you for informing me about him."

Sasha smiled, "Spasee'ba, General."

The Mosaic

Sasha and Mackye remained secluded in their apartment at Khodinka without venturing out into the Moscow winter cold and dismal weather. She recovered slowly from the harrowing experience of the kidnapping arrest and related to Sasha the details of the experience that she could piece together. He suggested that she should put in writing as much as she could recall and add to it as events surfaced in her memory. "It might be of some value later, who knows?" he told her.

Sasha began to meticulously write his full report. The earlier impromptu characterization to Sokolov that his findings and observations were much like a box, or perhaps two boxes, of puzzle pieces became more of a reality as he outlined the various events of his trip. The comfort of the cozy apartment in contrast to the outside cold and drab Moscow weather along with the company of Mackye made for a good working environment.

"Mackye," he pondered, "I am not so sure that I can come to any clear conclusions regarding our government's possible involvement in the assassination of the U.S. president. There is an abundance of suspicious activities, not the least of which was the KGB's consistent treacherous conduct."

"Sasha, it is not so important that you make any conclusions," she countered politely. "That is someone else's responsibility. You must document as many facts as you can and supplement the facts with your observations and strong opinions. You obviously cannot provide much information or credence to what the agencies or people in the United States have done, but *you must* carefully describe what you observed and also identify those in our government who attempted, for whatever reason, to sabotage your assignment."

A little irritated, she gave him a firm look. "You can do nothing less, Sasha. The facts must speak!"

As he reviewed the details of each phase of his recent adventure, they began to take the form of an irregular mosaic with some important pieces either missing or not matching the others. He reconstructed the chronology in an attempt to connect the pieces that matched and left the others off to the side to address later. The most consistent part of the journey was the ever-vigilant KGB and their tactics to warn him off the assignment.

Sokolov reviewed the highlights of the draft of Sasha's report:

"Upon arrival in Minsk to meet with General Bekrenev, I was intercepted at the airport by an eager taxi driver. In retrospect, I should have been more alert to the potential for foul play. Indeed, foul play it turned out to be as the taxi was a setup to ambush me enroute to the rezidentura . . . I forced the driver to escape interception by two secret police-looking interlopers. From that intervention, I went directly to the Soviet Consulate and encountered an arrogant and hostile KGB Colonel Grigory Ostipov who proceeded to warn me about my conduct while in Minsk. The taxi driver's reward for not delivering me into the hands of the agents on the street was a severe, if not fatal, beating.

At the GRU rezidentura, General Bekrenev was most cooperative and provided full support. I visited the Chief, Byelorussia KGB and surprisingly found reasonable cooperation there as well. I conducted interviews with several of the American, Oswald's, co-workers and acquaintances. The result was numerous questions and many facts: How and why was the American permitted to live so comfortably in Minsk? Why did the Mayor of Minsk personally meet him when he arrived from Moscow? Why was he provided such a good job, particularly for a foreigner? How was it that he appeared to have more disposable rubles than his regular employment would have provided? His standard of living was well-known to be above that of his counterparts. He purchased a shotgun, which even for Soviet citizens requires a special permit from the MVD. He purchased a very expensive camera. He married a Soviet citizen, apparently bypassing the normal waiting period for foreigners. When he finally departed Minsk for the United States, his wife was permitted to freely go without the required exit visa. Of particular note, his wife's uncle is a Soviet MVD colonel.

In Leningrad, I was advised that after my departure from Minsk, all but one of the citizens I had met with had been questioned and then brutally tortured. They were severely beaten, and one was shot to death. The one not sought out and punished for unexplained reasons went by the name of Pytr Gadarchev. He is allegedly the son of a Soviet general. I found him to be much more curious about my interest in the American than providing information. My suspicions are that he is an agent and may have had a larger role with the American than merely that of an acquaintance.

My journey through Helsinki was met with equal interference. I received a verbal warning from the local KGB security officer to "be careful." My hotel room was ransacked; I determined that the American, Oswald, had virtually bypassed all of the normal requirements for obtaining a visa to visit the Soviet Union. Prior to my arrival, the police had confiscated the hotel registration records that reflected the American's stay. While there I was also advised in an anonymous handwritten note that my wife might be in danger. General Tushenskiy confirmed that she had been intercepted at Sheremetevo II by two individuals who turned out to be KGB agents; they had attempted to lure her away.

In America, I encountered similar attempts to foil my work, mainly in Washington DC, I was threatened by General Zotov, the KGB station chief. He made it clear that I was not welcome, warning me "not to overstep his authority." His agents attempted to harass GRU Chief, General Yurasov and myself while we were meeting in a public place. I did learn from one of our undercover agents in Washington that the American intelligence agencies were in considerable turmoil following the assassination. The CIA, FBI, NSA and ONI were all quarreling, finger-pointing and fault-finding amongst themselves, and accusing one another of withholding or not sharing vital information known to them about the American, both before and after the assassination. (Note: I presumed that the American intelligence agencies are in much the same difficulty and under as much scrutiny as are we). There were also strong allusions in the newspaper reports and from the GRU agent that U.S. "right wing" factions might be responsible for the assassination and the subsequent murder of the assassin.

During my visit to Texas, a cooperative KGB operative confirmed that reports before and after the assassination alluded to right wing involvement. He confirmed that the American assassin had visited our embassy in Mexico City just a few weeks before he assassinated the president. During that visit, he visited the Cuban Consulate and secured a provisional visa to go to Cuba. It was while I was in Texas that I was informed General Tushenskiy had been murdered. Following notification of his death, it was my decision not to travel further to Mexico City.

Finally, it was my mission to attempt to determine if any elements of our government were directly involved in the assassination plot against the President of the United States. It would be entirely appropriate, even prudent, for me to report that I found no such evidence of any of our people to be involved in any way. The truth must speak for itself, however. I was constantly warned and harassed throughout my journey by our own government's agents, even though I was under direct orders from the GRU Director General and with approval of the Chairman. Innocent people with whom I visited and questioned were later tortured and even killed, and my wife was first threatened and then kidnapped and arrested by the secret police. Lastly, although well outside the boundaries of my directions, I find the fact that the Director General, GRU, was murdered under the most suspicious of circumstances during this stressful period casts an additional dark shadow of mystery over us. Each of these unwarranted and suspicious interventions surrounding an investigation and the cruel acts committed are closely coupled with the established fact that the American suspected of the assassination, lived openly for several years under the eyes of our police agencies and enjoyed every privilege and many beyond those granted to our own citizens.

In conclusion, I offer three propositions based on the experiences of my mission:
First, the most superficial of facts speak strongly to the possibility of some sort between the American, Oswald, and this government's secret police. Clearly, he was given special treatment from his entry into the Soviet Republic and virtual carte blanche to do as he pleased during the period of his entire three-year stay. His

liberties were far greater than that of a Soviet citizen. Perhaps it was only the KGB's intent to 'use' the misfit in some future way they found beneficial and not to have him carryout such a dire act as he did.

Second, collusion, or not, the American, Oswald, did apparently carry out the assassination, perhaps even with the help of others.

Third, if it can be assumed that there was 'no' collusion between the American and this government's secret police intelligence interests, then all of the attention given to him was incidental. The subsequent interest in my inquiry and the abhorrent conduct of the KGB was a result of their inherent paranoia and lack of knowledge and control over their vast enterprise of activities.

Finally, to the benefit of our Government, I found it extraordinary that the U.S. intelligence agencies apparently failed on all counts to monitor one of their citizens, who should have been profiled as a potential problem, was permitted to leave the U.S. for the Soviet Union, stay for a protracted period and then freely return with a Soviet wife and child without question or concern for his purpose, conduct or loyalty.

Respectfully, Viktor A. Katsanov, GRU

Sokolov studied the report, including the numerous supplemental details provided by Bekrenev, Yurasov and others.

"Sasha, I wish to congratulate you on the meticulous detail you have applied to your report," he began. "You are to be commended for performing such an important mission for your government."

He then paused for a lengthy period, thumbing the pages of the report back and forth, including the supporting documents from his generals. He finally exhaled a deep sigh as he looked at Sasha.

"Comrade, I must tell you that I am having considerable difficulty about how parts of this report will affect the leaders in the Kremlin, not to mention Lubiyanka. As you are quite aware, there is a delicate balance of power in our government. From my perspective, I must respect that balance and make certain that my actions do not inadvertently skew it one way or the other."

Sasha sensed what was coming. He was visibly dismayed and blurted out an impromptu response, "General, you requested that I submit a full and unfettered report."

"I know, Sasha," Sokolov said, "and that is just what I expected you to do, but as you well know from your own personal experience and unfortunate encounters, there is a dark enemy within our complex society. None of us, and I believe not even the Chairman, is fully aware of the perilous world that lies within our own walls."

He continued to study Sasha for a moment and finally advised, "For your protection and that of us all, Sasha, including Bekrenev, Yurasov and others who assisted you, I am going to edit your report before it goes forward. I will retain the original in my personal files for the time being. I regret to do this, Comrade, but it is for the good of all of us at this time. Perhaps at some period in the future, I will be able to reveal its entire substance. I hope you understand, and I also exhort you to keep the details of your report in confidence to yourself. Trust me, Comrade and remember: *A word is like a sparrow when it flies out; you cannot catch it.*"

Sasha stood, burning with anger and disappointment. "Yes, General, I trust you as I do all of my superiors, but Sir, innocent people were tortured and killed because of me and the investigation I was directed to conduct. I was promised by General Bekrenev that *'there will be hell to pay'* if any of the people in Minsk were harmed. To my knowledge, there was not even an inquiry! And that was only the beginning, your own colleague and friend, General Tushenskiy . . . murdered . . . and no doubt by these same vicious swine. Have we lost our conscience, General?"

Sokolov did not react or respond, only stared at his young officer for a moment and then in a soft tone, asked, "Sasha, tell me this; do you believe that the assassin of the U.S. president acted alone, and if so, how can it be explained that the man, Ruby, you mention, just walks in to the police station with a weapon and kills Oswald who is surrounded by policemen? What would be his motive, unless he was directed by an agency to keep the man Oswald from revealing the perpetrators?"

Sasha was caught off guard by the questions; he thought that Sokolov was ready to conclude the meeting. He was further surprised by the apparent interest in more of the details and his opinion.

"Sir," he finally replied. "The Americans will have to decide if he was the lone assassin or not. As for the alleged assassin, he was a pawn of both our government and the Americans." He continued, "Lastly, Sir, the man Ruby is and will likely remain a mystery . . . leaving even more conjecture to a conspiracy theory."

"Spasee'ba, Comrade," Sokolov nodded without comment.

Sasha stood, saluted and departed the office.

EIGHTEEN

"The end is the crown of any affair."

A Russian Proverb

Arc of Betrayal

Mackye's spirit and demeanor had changed considerably since her recent experience. She herself had begun to have serious doubts about her unfailing loyalty and defense of the Soviet style of government. She sat for hours reflecting on her kidnapping and the past unfortunate episode with Vetrov, trying to contemplate the future. She could not yet muster the energy or interest to return to work. Sokolov had sent a note advising her that he had contacted her supervisor at the KGB, and she was free to take whatever time she required to regain her health. He also told Sasha that they could reside in the apartment at Khodinka as long as they wished.

Sasha returned from his meeting with Sokolov.

Looking for a beam of hope, she happily greeted him, "Sasha, what was the general's reaction to your report? I was beginning to get concerned. It's late."

She needed only to read his expression to comprehend unpleasant news.

"Mackye, I have more than likely condemned myself. I committed an unpardonable act," he related how he had reacted to Sokolov. "I have been for a long walk attempting to rationalize all that has happened and trying to comprehend the meanings. But, even the cold reality of the night air cannot clear my thoughts and the fact now that even Sokolov has betrayed my confidence. He is frightened, Mackye. My report frightened him. I could see the look on his face as he poured through it, reading some of it and skipping much of it. He simply didn't want to look at it. And then, I lost control. I shouted back at him."

Sasha gauged Mackye's reactions. She had grown immune to shock experiences and said nothing. She waited for him to speak further.

"I know now that he did not even want me to write a report," Sasha continued. "He did not want anything documented. I believe that he wants only to move on from here, forget the work I did and what I encountered, forget what happened to you and of greater importance, forget *the why* and *the who* of Tushenskiy's murder. He is not the confident and good officer that I once knew. He has become a captive of the system. He has become weak and afraid for himself as most of the other paranoid bastards are!"

"Sasha, *shush!*" She tried to calm his tone. "Did you mention to him about your experience at the American court proceedings?"

"No, Mackye, hardly!" he countered. "That would have totally unnerved him. That saga would require far too much background explanation, and under the present circumstances, he couldn't handle it." Sasha smiled, "He might even put me in jail or worse to shut me up!"

They both laughed, attempting to find some sick humor in all that consumed them, and he quickly returned to serious conjecture.

"Mackye, our government and our lives are caught up in an arc of betrayal. There is an erratic circle of deceit, corruption and viciousness that encompasses the whole Soviet world we live in. I never thought that I would think this way, but we have reached the point of not being able to trust our leadership on any level. We must watch our every step, look over our shoulders and be wary of what we say and do. I have begun to feel that after all of this, I may also be succumbing to paranoia. Perhaps we should move on. I am not sure to where, or even how, but then again, after my conduct today, the choice may not be mine!"

There was little sleep for either of them that night. Sasha heard nothing further from Sokolov and after several days, their emotions about the event began to slowly abate.

He spent much of the next several weeks catching up on the activities in his office and again getting absorbed in the work he once enjoyed. He had not seen General Sokolov since that fateful day. Mackye had been contacted by one of Sokolov's staff members and offered a position at Khodinka commensurate with her experience. Some normalcy was slowly being restored to their lives. Neither of them had ventured back into the earlier discussion or returned to the subject of what might lay ahead for them or how they might even prepare for the uncertain future.

Sasha received a pleasant note from Paulette in New York along with a clipping of an article from the *WASHINGTON POST* newspaper.

"Judge Renders Ruling On The Missing Bomber Issue," the heading of the article read. Sasha quickly plunged into the story:

> *"Federal Judge Roswald Shrull issued a ruling concerning a recent hearing dealing with the government's handling of a case involving a U.S. strategic bomber which was declared missing during the Cuban Crisis operations well over a year ago. Judge* Shrull *ruled that an inquiry into the case brought by dependent families of the missing aircrew members had to be jointly addressed by both the Defense Department and the Department of Justice to further investigate. In his summary, Judge* Shrull *concluded that the questionable circumstances surrounding the missing bomber and its crew, and the questions posed by the plaintiff's lawyer warranted a much more in-depth review than his court was capable of conducting."*

That was it, no details or conjectures about the previous hearing. Sasha studied the words in the brief synopsis over and over. He finally satisfied himself that whatever became of such an investigation, he was now so far removed from it, emotionally and otherwise, that it really didn't matter. He would let it go and hope that he was never again reminded of the terrible experience.

He remained philosophical. "Let the Americans figure it all out," he concluded.

FINAL BETRAYAL

The direct phone to the Director General startled him. He quickly snatched the hand piece, "Yes, General! How are you, Sir?"

"Fine, Sasha. Can you come to my office? I have something of importance to discuss with you." Sokolov's manner appeared pleasant, but businesslike.

"Yes, General," he responded. "I will be there promptly."

He was more than mildly concerned. The once close relationship between himself and Sokolov no longer existed. He had not spoken with the general in over a month since the traumatic meeting about his mission report.

"What can this be about?" his thoughts churned as he put on his coat and fur hat.

Not a day passed that the event of his abrupt behavior and perceived questionable situation didn't nag at him. In all of his years, he had been the consistent obedient officer and never questioned any of his superiors. He had attempted to rationalize, "Sokolov isn't Tushenskiy. He is new in the job, trying to get a handle on all of the issues. Following the death of Tushenskiy and my unpleasant report, he has been under considerable stress."

The call troubled him. His confidence in his work, his superiors and the direction of his government had been severely fractured. He arrived at Sokolov's office.

"Well, time to face it," he breathed to himself.

The aide showed him in.

"Come in, Sasha," Sokolov greeted. "Please, sit down. Tea?"

Sasha saluted smartly and Sokolov shook his hand warmly. He acted as if all was well between them.

"It's good to see you," he said, smiling. "I understand that you are getting back into the business of your office. That is good. How is Mackye? Is she enjoying her work here? I have been meaning to call and check on you both, but as I am sure that you are aware, I have been extremely busy getting into this job."

"Yes, General, thank you." Sasha was pensive. "We are fine. As you know, I have been very busy as well just catching up and Mackye is quite pleased with her assignment here. We appreciate all that you have done for her."

"Good, Sasha! Good!" Sokolov was cordial and animated. "Sasha, when you were in the United States, you got off well with Yurasov while in Washington, didn't you?" he asked.

"Yes, General," Sasha's thoughts began to race. *"What now?"* Sasha continued, "Yes, I did. General Yurasov was exceptionally pleasant and supportive. As you know, we shared an interesting experience together, you might say."

Sokolov smiled, "Yes, I recall from your report. Sasha, how would you and Mackye like to go to the United States where you would become Yurasov's deputy at the . . ." he paused and smiled again, "The Russ*ian Trade Commission?"*

Sasha stared at Sokolov. His thoughts were in high gear, spinning in all directions. Before he could respond, Sokolov continued.

"You and Mackye are perfect for the assignment. You are proficient in English and know the United States and Americans well. And," Sokolov continued, "Mackye is an expert in economics. The two of you will make a great team and can assist our efforts there very well."

The proposal took him by complete surprise and he didn't know how to react or respond. He paused for a long moment as he absorbed the surprising offer.

"Sir, I am very surprised by this. I don't know what to say." Sasha finally replied, puzzled by the sudden turn of events.

Concurrently, his mind quickly assessed the impact of the proposal, *"This is it!"* he calculated. *"This saves face for both Sokolov and Kashevarov. I am out of the way and their consciences are clear."*

He was tempted to burst out with a testy response, but caught himself and replied, "General, I am honored to be considered for such an assignment. I have no doubt that Mackye will also be pleased and honored to be chosen for such an important duty, but may I talk to her about it first before I respond?"

As he spoke, his thoughts continued to spin in his head. He knew better than to act on a passing impulse and ask what an alternative might be. Simultaneously, he was feeling a large burden within being released.

"Dah! Please discuss this with Mackye. It is a great opportunity for you both. I shall attempt to make sure that she is provided with a position of considerable responsibility to fully employ her skills. I have no doubt of course that you will become invaluable to General Yurasov."

Back in his office, he called Mackye and asked if she could return to their apartment early that evening. He met her there.

"Mackye, we have been living behind these walls of the Centre for over a month. I have an idea," he said. "The weather is very pleasant for a change so why don't we go outside into the city tonight and treat ourselves to dinner? I have been told about a new restaurant, the *Dushanbe*, which some Afghani migrants have opened. The food is supposed to be very good, and we can even stroll over there. It's just across the bridge."

"Well, Sasha, you are full of surprises! If you think it is okay for us to leave the Centre, then, let's go!" Mackye responded with unusual enthusiasm. "I will be ready in a minute!"

They departed the exit portal and were outside the *walls* for the first time in over a month. The evening was very pleasant for December, cold and clear, but without the chilling wind. Sasha knew full well that everyone who entered and departed Khodinka was monitored by the secret police on the *other side,* but he felt confident that they were finally safe from any further intrusions. Sokolov's offer was a perfect way to remove him from KGB concerns. They strolled casually, hand in hand, and moved along with the always busy throng of pedestrians, and headed toward a bridge which leads across the Moscow River.

The new restaurant, Dushanbe, was pleasant and the freshly installed interior decorations colorfully reflected the origin of its managers. As with the seldom new experiences for Muscovites, the place was crowded with those seeking diversion and pleasure. It seemed forever since Sasha and Mackye had found some peace in their surroundings. Even the noise and laughter was a welcome relief which they enjoyed with pleasure. Mackye was relaxed and had begun to find a pleasant renewed meaning to their lives.

She was shocked by Sasha's description of Sokolov's demeanor and took the news of the offer to go to the United States cheerfully and with considerable relief for Sasha. He had been worried about how she would react.

"Good!" he exhaled with joy. "I will tell Sokolov that we are ready to go!"

He was suddenly jubilant, "Mackye, you will enjoy the United States. It will be a great adventure that we can share." He raised his half empty glass of wine, "To our new future!"

After the pleasant dinner and upbeat conversation about their forthcoming venture, they departed the restaurant and joined the others who were out for fresh air on the crisp night and moved back across the narrow and crowded river bridge walkway.

A bright spot light suddenly caught them directly in their faces with a blinding shock. It all happened instantly.

"MACKYE!" Sasha screamed as he saw the impending disaster. He reached for her arm, but was thrown off balance by several others who were jammed between them.

The last thing he remembered was a glimpse of the familiar chrome encircled *star* logo on the grillwork of the massive *Mercedes* tractor truck as it plunged into them. He was shoved aside and fell to the pavement as he flailed and grasped in vain for Mackye. It was now suddenly pitch dark. There were screams of panic and muffled cries of pain from those mangled by the behemoth machine, and then gradually only whimpering and groans.

The truck which had been guided with accuracy toward its intended targets was just as quickly placed in reverse by its driver, backed away from the carnage it had caused and sped away leaving a dozen or so crushed beneath its wheels and against the bridge railing. Among those was Mackye.

The end is the crown of any affair . . .

EPILOGUE

"The legend is still fresh,
but hard to believe."

A Russian Proverb

Several Years Later

The distinctive ring of his private telephone sitting among the others on the desk gave him a momentary start. He promptly reached for the hand piece, "Katsanov!"

"Sasha! How are you?"

The voice was unmistakable. Even after almost six years, her native Russian had retained the distinctive hint of an American accent, "Galina! Is that you? How have you been? I have been meaning to call you every day since I returned! Are you okay? Are you well?"

"Yes, Sasha, I am very well, thank you. And, how are you . . . *General?* I have heard through the system that you have been rewarded for your continued excellent works. Congratulations! Where have you been? I have not heard from you in such a long time, I cannot remember when! Are you well? I heard about your wife's horrible accident. I am so sorry. I tried to contact you then, but you disappeared."

A flood of memories brought the surprise phone call back into perspective. He had met Galina when he first arrived at Khodinka for training. She was a hostess in the cafeteria, and he sought frequent opportunities to chat with the attractive blond and blue-eyed girl. That is, until his handler, Vlad, decided that a

219

friendship was developing and had her transferred away from the Centre. Vlad had accomplished the same feat later with Mackye. By incredible coincidence, Galina showed up in the United States while he was on assignment there. The daughter of a KGB agent also on duty in the U.S., she had been granted a student exchange visa and enrolled in an Alabama college. Sasha and she had enjoyed pleasant, but irregular, patterns of time together as their schedules permitted. Galina eventually completed her college work and returned to Moscow. When Sasha returned via his ill-fated bomber experience, they saw each other rarely with him finally marrying Mackye.

"Galina, It is so good to hear from you. Yes, I have been away for sometime. Actually, I've been out of the country for a few years. Time and distance can heal some things, others it cannot. It's a long story. Thank you for your thoughtful words, though."

He paused, not wanting to drift into a somber mood, "What are you doing these days, Galina? Are you still managing the important activities at the *National?*"

"Yes, I am now the assistant general manager of the hotel," she replied, "and continue to be challenged with the many responsibilities attendant to that. Anatoli Kuzlov is a very bright and pleasant man to work for. I have learned a great deal from him over the past several years, Sasha, and one of the reasons I am calling you, of course, other than to mainly find and check on you."

Sasha detected the almost forgotten sincere sweetness in her voice. "I think you might be interested in some of the guests who are presently visiting Moscow and staying here at the National, she told him, "but I would prefer not to discuss that over the telephone. Is it possible for you to drop by the hotel sometime whenever you are free? It would even be better if we could have dinner and visit longer."

Sasha thought about his day for brief moment, "Galina. I would love to see you. If you're free, why don't I come by around eight this evening? We can have dinner and get caught up."

"Good! Sasha, I am free and will be in my office. Come there. It will be so good to see you."

Sasha reflected on the past and Galina for a moment. "She has always been a very good and loyal friend. She is much different than was Mackye. She never got caught up in the politics of the government or the intrigue of the agency spy business, but then again, she *is* working at that elite KGB rat hole, the National."

The old National Hotel located on Tversskaya Prospekt, was built in 1903 and had 231 guest rooms. It had been used by the KGB for decades to house and entertain foreign dignitaries during their visits to Moscow. The lobby and lounges were furnished and decorated in expensive and charming old Russian art and fixtures. The rooms were equally well-furnished and comfortable. The grade of the room assigned to a foreigner was usually based on the visitor's stature, *or* what the intelligence agency wanted to *extract* from the guest. Each room had sophisticated monitoring and surveillance equipment. The devices, well imbedded and hidden from even the most well trained snoop, consisted of highly sensitive radio receivers, video cameras and noise discriminators. Some of the best equipment could null-out music or radio and television noise to record conversations. All of the telephones were bugged for both direct listening and recording. The hotel surveillance control room had the sophistication of a major intelligence command center and was manned 24 hours a day. The hotel's 300-meter proximity and five-minute walk to Red Square and the Kremlin also made for ideal surveillance from the elaborate listening posts located therein.

The KGB also used the Savoy, Berlin and Metropol Hotels for the same purposes, but not as extensively as the National. Each had essentially the same elaborate capabilities to monitor selected guests in the same manner.

Sasha and the GRU had, from time to time, also made use of the KGB hotel facilities, to exploit foreign visitors who may have important information of interest to their activities. He thought for a moment about Galina's mention of the foreign visitors in whom he might be interested.

"Galina has always been no-nonsense," he smiled, "so she must have something of interest to share with me. She isn't a trained operative; at least, I don't think she is! And I hope not!"

he continued to ponder the surprise phone call and returned to addressing the pile of bureaucratic papers scattered before him.

He cleared out the routine matters on his desk and prioritized the remainder to review in more detail later. The clock on the wall just above Lenin's portrait showed that it was almost seven p.m. He called his father, Viktor, to let him know he was home and all was well. He worried considerably about him since his mother passed away. Viktor was now in his late sixties and continued to work in the Ministry of Defense as a senior staff officer. He continued to be well respected among his peers as a seasoned strategic planner, but time, stress and the loss of his wife, Tatyana, had hastened his aging.

"Dobre Di'en, Father. How was your day?"

"Oh, fine, fine, Sasha. How was yours?" The daily routine of exchanges always began the same.

"It has been just another day of dealing with incompetents and ever-increasing challenges," Sasha began and then he asked, "Are things going well within the MOD? Have we decided when we are going to cease tolerating the insolence and warmongering of the United States and demand more concessions?" He had a chiding hint in his question.

"I don't know, Sasha. We should be more aggressive with them about their meddling in Vietnam. They have no business forcing themselves into an internal civil matter halfway around the world from their own shores. People are dying on both sides, but mostly the poor Vietnamese who are caught in the middle. If our government were to insert itself into political situations such as the U.S. has in Indochina, and, for that matter, the way they did in Korea, we would be ridiculed all over the world as warmongers."

"Yes, unfortunately, you are correct," he replied. "Well, Father, I just wanted to see how you are. I have a dinner meeting shortly over at the National. I will call you in a day or so and make plans for dinner soon. Take care of yourself. Eat well and be strong. Do'briy niche."

"Do'briy niche, Sasha, it's good to have you back home, Son. Take care of yourself."

Sasha hung up the phone feeling depressed, not only about his father, but the world situation in general. He had just returned from doing his government's deeds in the United States. His reward: *"Losing his wife, Mackye, to murderous thugs within his own government."*

He was back home and nothing had changed; the Soviet Government was continuing on its devious path and making no progress on behalf of its people. There were increasing food shortages and growing dissatisfaction with the government. The military forces were growing weary of training and playing war games. Morale was at its lowest and desertions were at an all time high. There were more soldiers serving time in prison camps than in the ranks. He marveled at how everything seemed to come all too easy for Americans. During his more recent assignment, he witnessed the same easy and free way of life that he had before even though now they found themselves embroiled in the quagmire in Vietnam.

He pushed the button on the corner of his desk and a young major promptly opened the door. "Yes, General?"

"I'm leaving now, Georgi. No take home paperwork tonight. Leave these as I have stacked them and take the others. Is my car ready? I am going to the National for dinner."

"Dah, General. I will take care of your office. Yuri is waiting with your car. Goodnight, General."

"Goodnight, Georgi, and are you continuing with your studies? I want to put you high on the next nomination list for promotion. Don't let me down. Hold off the girls and the vodka. They can come later." Sasha slapped his young executive officer on the back as he departed his office.

Sasha's sedan was waiting at curbside with the engine running when he exited to the street. He was feeling good on this evening; Galina's call raised his spirits.

"Yuri! How was your day?"

"Very quiet, General," his driver replied, "Just routine duties, very quiet, Sir."

"Good," Sasha smiled as he eased into the car. "Let's go to the National Hotel, Yuri."

Yuri pulled the sedan up to the curb in front of the hotel entrance and the doorman opened Sasha's door. He tapped his driver on the shoulder, "Yuri, I hope to be ready to depart by 10:30. Go have your dinner and not too much vodka. Okay?"

Yuri smiled. He liked driving for his general. He had risen from conscript to non-commissioned officer and had learned *the ropes* early on, discovering that by obeying orders and staying out of trouble, he might eventually find favor in the Soviet Army. The duty was far better than life on the collective farm where he had lived with his parents since birth. Now, at twenty-eight, or *nine*, he wasn't really sure of his exact age, he was assigned to drive for a general who worked at the super secret Khodinka Center, and he knew that General Katsanov liked him. Yuri was not married and with the extra perks provided by his *masters*, he fared quite well with the girls in Moscow. He looked at his watch. He had two and a half hours to call one of his favorites, drive her around in the shiny sedan, have a few vodkas and treat her to dinner.

The doorman tipped his hat to Sasha as he entered the lobby of the hotel. "May I direct you, Sir?" he asked.

"No, thank you," Sasha replied and headed toward the administrative offices off the main lobby.

He nodded to the secretary sitting at her desk just inside the main office area, and walked to the door with ASSISTANT GENERAL MANAGER, in bold letters across the glass upper half. He knocked.

"Come in," Galina responded. She was already around to the front of her desk by the time Sasha entered and closed the door.

"Hello, Galina."

"Sasha, it is so good to see you! My, you look so handsome in that silk suit! Are you sure that you are still a soldier?"

They embraced warmly, and Sasha kissed her on each cheek.

"It is so good to see you, Galina. You are more beautiful than ever. Your eyes are bluer and hair more silken than I ever remember!"

"Thank you, Sasha, and you as well. Your work and your lifestyle apparently agree with you. Please sit down."

She motioned him to a pair of comfortable chairs.

"Your office is that of a very important *apparatchik*!" Sasha smiled, "You are doing very well, Galina! I am proud of you. Do those goons from Lubiyanka treat you well?" He was referring to the KGB operatives who managed and controlled the hotel.

"I can deal with them," she looked at him, smiling. "They know *who* is in charge here. Sasha, let's chat for a moment before we go to the dining room. Would you like a vodka or something else to drink? Tell me how are you? You have been away for a very long time and again, Sasha, I was so sorry to hear about your wife's accident. How terrible!"

"Nothing to drink, thank you. I'll wait until dinner." He paused, "Galina is your office secure to talk?"

"Yes, as secure as I like to think it is," she smirked.

Sasha looked at her with a stern expression, "Mackye's death was no accident."

Galina gasped slightly, putting her hand to her mouth.

Sasha patted the back of her hand. "It's okay now. That entire story can wait until anther time, Galina. My assignment was both challenging and interesting, but it is good to be home. I will tell you more about it one day. Now, what about these hotel guests you mentioned? Or were you just trying to lure me into your lair?" he smiled, trying to lighten up the meeting with Galina. "But, first, how are your parents? Where are they?"

Galina's father had been Sasha's KGB handler while he was attending Air Force flight school in the United States, and it was through that coincidence that he and Galina had become reacquainted.

"They are fine. At least I think they are. I don't hear from them very often. I have only seen them twice in over eight years, once in London and once in Madrid. It is sad, but it is the life my father has chosen, and he doesn't seem to want to come home. Sasha, I know that you know more than you have told me. I know that my father works for one of the secret agencies. Is his job safe? Will the government not permit him to come home? I hardly know him or my mother any longer and only rarely receive a letter from them." She was on the verge of tears.

"Galina, I can only tell you that your father has a very important job with our government, and he is performing a great service. I really do not know very many of the particulars, but I am sure that sooner or later he will be reassigned back here one day. These are very difficult times, and we need loyal and trusted people like your father. You must trust the system and try to understand that his duties are very important to our future."

Sasha patted her hand again as she wiped away tears.

"I'm sorry," she replied, turning her head away toward the window. "I know not to question things that I'm not supposed to know about. I see many things that go on here in the hotel, but I do not question them. I just do as I am told. We all do."

"Galina, you have a right to question," Sasha attempted to console her, "but not to persist. Things will be fine one day."

She regained her composure, "Sasha, there are several strange foreigners staying here at the hotel: two Americans, three Brits and four Frenchmen. Actually there are three Americans. The third is a very nice lady whom I hope to introduce to you. She is from *Texas*! The KGB made the routine arrangements for all of them except the American lady. The others are not in special VIP rooms, but they are taking exceptionally good care of them. Their expenses are all being paid for by the agency. What I find unusual is that they are pretty scruffy looking . . . more like western *hippies*. They are probably in their early or middle twenties and are very arrogant and rude. Cocky, I would add—loud and rowdy. I would also think too young to be very important to intelligence agents. I'm equally surprised that the police are allowing them to show off the way they are . . . drinking and very noisy in public areas of the hotel. The reason I am calling your attention to them are the two American men. It is very unusual for Americans to be in Moscow or anywhere in the Soviet Union. Don't you think?"

"Yes, that does seem strange, Galina, but we have certainly had Americans here before. How long have these been here? Are they *tooree 'sts* or *Stood'e 'nts*?" he asked.

"They are students, Sasha. I am sure of that," she said, "and I believe attending school in England. I don't want to act like an agent myself, but I thought since you spent several years in America, you might be interested in their presence here. The two Americans and the Brits really cozyied-up to me when they discovered I speak English, but I try to avoid them whenever I can.

They drink too much and chase every female that comes into the hotel. But, I don't know why, the KGB furnishes them all of the companionship they can handle——every night! It's disgusting!"

"I don't know that I should meet them, Galina. Do you know who their *senior keeper* is?"

"Yes, at least the one that manages *special guests* for the hotel" she replied. "He is Vladimir Popov. He keeps a permanent suite here. He is in Room 200. That is on the floor just above their Control Room. Sasha, I really don't like working here, but I am captive. Intourist will not reassign me to any other hotel and the manager, Surov, likes my work." She quickly flashed a smiled, "So, *General*, you are my guest. Are you hungry? Can we go to the restaurant?"

"Yes. I would have preferred to have dinner elsewhere," Sasha smiled, "but I presume you must be here for a certain part of the evening."

"Yes. Surov is away this evening, so when we have special guests, either he or I must be on duty. Shall we go?"

Galina led the way out of the office complex, into the lobby and on to the hotel restaurant. The hostess sat them at a table for two near a window facing the street. Sasha ordered a double vodka and Galina asked for a glass of white wine.

Looking out onto the street, Sasha observed, "Galina, do you notice our people as they seem to walk aimlessly up and down the sidewalks, despairingly and without purpose. Our country and our people's daily lives are so sad and with little to look forward to as each succeeding day comes along."

"Yes, none of us can ignore it, Sasha; I am so lucky and even embarrassed and apologetic at times for my good fortune."

As they sipped their drinks, chatting, there was a shout from across the dining room in clear English. "Galina! Galina! There you are!"

Sasha looked up to see two men with full beer glasses in hand moving toward them. The shout came from one with a large toothy grin. He was bearing down on their table.

"She whispered, "Those two are the two Americans. Be prepared!"

"Galina, introduce me as Mike Scott from America," he quickly responded, using the cover name that was his back in the United States.

"*Wellll*, Galina, we didn't know you were still hanging out here this evening," the grinning toothy one slurred. "Oops, Sir, I'm sorry to intrude, but *Galina Girl* is a good friend of ours."

He offered a sweaty handshake, "I'm Billy J. Clanton from the USA and this is my buddy, Strom Talmont. Do you *speaka th' English*, Comrade?"

Sasha eyed the two as Galina looked down at the table, blushing with embarrassment.

"Yes, I do *speaka th' English*, my friend," Sasha shot back in perfect diction. "I am from the U.S. as well. What can we do for you?"

"Oh well, really *nuthin'*" he grinned. "We just wanted to say hello to Miss Galina, our sweet hostess. Where are you from in the U.S., Mr . . . er' . . . Did you say your name?"

Sasha didn't respond immediately. He eyed the two. Each was dressed in worn wool trousers and an over-sized baggy sweater. Both had scraggly beards and long hair. Billy J., the talkative one, had kinky dishwater blond hair and a stringy month or so growth of facial hair. It could hardly be called a beard. The other one had rail thin features and wore horned rim glasses. He had dark hair with a high thinning forehead.

Sasha finally spoke, "I'm Mike Scott, from the Chicago area; over here on business. Where are you fellows from?"

"*Wellll* . . . I'm from the little rural state of Arkansas . . . and, darned proud of it! And my friend, Strom here, is from Ohio. Don't we make a pair . . . Ohio and Arkansas! Strom studies Russian and speaks it pretty darned well. *Wanna* hear him say *somethin'*? Speak some Russian, Strom," Billy J. grinned. "May we visit for a minute?" he asked as he pulled a chair from an adjacent table. Strom likewise dragged over another chair and collapsed into it, grinning as he mumbled something like, *"Spaseeeee' Bo!"*

"What brings you *fellas* to Moscow?" Sasha asked, interrupting his attempt at humor, continuing to study the curious pair.

"We're *stooodunts* . . . *would'ja* believe it?" Billy J. grinned as he slurped a swallow of beer. "We're even more than that, Mr.

Scott, we're Rhodes Scholars and *goin'* to school at Oxford. *Ain't* that uh hoot! Is this not a great world we live in or *ain't* it?"

"That is pretty neat, but what brings you to Moscow? Are you studying here?" Sasha pressed.

"*Noooooo . . .*" Billy J. smiled and took another draw of beer from his glass. "We're here as guests of the Supreme Soviet *guvernment*. I wrote a letter to the embassy in London and told 'em that some of us were pretty fed up with the U.S. intruding in Vietnam, and we would like to come over here and help the Russians to express both theirs and our feelings about the American atrocities going on over there. I was about ready to skip to Canada myself before I got this Rhodes Scholar appointment. I'll be damned if I was going to let them draft me and send me to that jungle to get my ass shot off. Ol' Strom here and the rest of us feel the same way. We're for a one-world approach to societal differences and killing innocent civilians *ain't* the way to get there. I met President Kennedy once when I was still in high school, and if that bastard, Oswald, hadn't killed him, I believe that he and Johnson would have had us well on the road to a worldwide peace-loving society. My buddy, Strom, here has some great ideas about one-world global government. No more nation-building. All of us should be just one happy world country. Strom will be famous one day for his theories. And, I *wanna* to tell *You*, Mr. *Shhcot*."

The beer, pot and whatever else was beginning to tell on Billy J. He was on a roll. "I *wanna* tell you!" he slurred. "My goal is to get to be president of the United States one day, and if I do . . . Yeah! *When* I do! You'll see just how Strom and I will change the course of world history. No more Cold Wars and no more Vietnams! Matter of fact, the Soviets have it right already . . . equality for all the people. Fulfill people's legitimate needs and they're happy. The U.S. has a lot to learn from these Russians."

"Well, that is all very interesting, Billy J.," Sasha said, "but America has operated quite well on a philosophy of democratic process and competitive capitalism, and I am not so sure that your theories will sell." Sasha was enjoying baiting the two intoxicated *intellectual theorists*.

"*Wellll* . . . let me tell you, people are like sheep, Americans especially," Billy J. replied. "They're soft and vulnerable, and with the right leader and philosophy, they can be turned into most any direction you want. Unfortunately, Ol' Lyndon Johnson has done screwed up his opportunity and, consequently, Vietnam is a disaster. The damn Republicans got us into that mess and now they're laughing their heads off."

"Pardon me, Billy J., but I thought that President Kennedy initially got us into Vietnam?" Sasha chided.

"Oh, bull shit, Mr. Scott! If you will forgive me, Galina," he objected, rising up half out of his chair, "That war-mongering Eisenhower crowd put us in there. MacArthur and that bunch of World War II militaristic bastards couldn't wait to get back to fighting and oppressing little people. But . . . Hey! Strom, myself and our other school buddies have organized a big U.S. anti-war protest march tomorrow. You *oughta* join us! You, too, Galina! Hell! We're *gonna* rock the ol' Kremlin's walls. The Russians will eat it up and just maybe some of those military geeks back in the U.S. will get the message!"

He staggered to his feet, "Okay, Strom, *ol'* Buddy, let's go get a fresh fill up and let these folks have their supper. See you guys tomorrow. Hope you'll come to the big rally!"

Sasha and Galina watched as the two maneuvered themselves unsteadily out of the dining room, bumping into tables, patrons and anything else in their way.

"Now you see what I mean, Sasha," Galina offered. "What possible value could those scruffy idealists have to the KGB?"

"Well, they are certainly interesting, Galina, but as you know, our secret police friends exploit every possibility: derelicts, pseudo-intellectuals and opportunists alike. These characters here, of course, play well into their hands . . . Young students and draft-dodgers disparaging the U.S. over Vietnam," Sasha mused, "and who knows, these two may be of even greater value to them at some point in the future . . . after they get back home and develop more fully into *mature* idealists and *sociologues.*"

"Oh, Sasha!" Galina interrupted, "there's the lady from America, I mentioned."

"Mary, Mary!" she summoned in a loud whisper; waving to the fashionably dressed lady that had just entered the dining room.

"Oh, Galina," she responded as she nodded to the waiter that she would be going over to the table where Galina and Sasha were seated.

"Mary, so good to see you," Galina greeted her excitedly. "I was just telling my friend, Sasha here, about you being here in the hotel. Come join us."

As she approached the table, Sasha rose with a smile and a nod as he observed the well-dressed, pleasantly attractive and very fair blond.

"Mary, this is my friend, Sasha Katsanov; Sasha . . . I mean, *General Katsanov*, I'm pleased to introduce you to my American friend, Mary Rodgers," Galina said with a smile as she reached out to give her a gentle hug.

She looked back at Sasha with a wry grin, "Forgive me, Sasha, I am still in awe that you have risen up so far in importance in our government, but you are still 'Sasha' to me."

Sasha smirked at Galina's comment as he continued to study her friend, extending his hand in greeting. "I am very pleased to meet you, Mary. Please, will you join us?"

"Thank you," Mary responded, as she held out her black leather gloved hand to Sasha. "I am very pleased to meet you, General, and yes, I would be delighted to join you if I am not intruding. This is a *very cold* dining room."

"Yes, it is," Galina quickly interjected, "it's not a very friendly environment, I'm sorry to say, but it's so good to see you; I was wondering where you might be today and how your work is proceeding."

Sasha eased out a chair for Mary on the opposite side of Galina so that they faced one another and he was between the two.

"Oh, let's not talk about it," Mary frowned. "No, just kidding," she smiled. "I wrapped everything up today and I will be departing for the States tomorrow."

"Oh, no, Mary! Not so soon!" Galina exclaimed. "I have enjoyed you being here so very much, and we haven't had that much time to visit or to see Moscow."

"I know, Galina," Mary smiled, "but, hopefully I will be coming back one day."

"Where is your home in the United States, Mary?" Sasha inquired, "or where do you work, I should ask?"

"I am from Dallas, Texas, General," she responded. "I both live and work there."

"Please, Mary," Sasha patted the back of her hand. "It's *Sasha.* Don't permit Galina to try to impress you."

"I am impressed," Mary smiled. "I have never before met a Russian general, but I also imagined them as being much older and rugged, and not very *gentile*. You don't fit the image I had in mind."

"Mary," Galina injected, smiling, "Sasha is a rare exception to the pattern you imagined. He is not *that* old, nor is he rugged. He has excelled far beyond his age and peers, and has been so rewarded."

"Thank You, Galina!" Sasha smirked. "Now let's get on with something more pleasant and enjoy the company of our special guest. Mary, will you join us with something to drink?"

"Thank you, Sasha," she smiled. "I would like very much a sweet red wine. I have sampled theirs here in the hotel and found it to be very pleasant."

Sasha motioned to the waiter and ordered *aoktop.*

"So that's how you pronounce it, *'a-o-k-top'*," Mary smiled repeating, phonetically. "I'll remember that next time."

As they talked, he couldn't help but to admire her fair *Scandinavian* complexion, soft blond hair and emerald green eyes, and asked, "Are you originally from Texas, Mary?"

"No, not originally," she smiled. "I was born and grew up in Michigan, and moved on to the south and southwest with a previous marriage and work."

What is your profession?" Sasha asked.

"I am a banking and financial specialist," Mary replied, "and I am here in Moscow with a small consortium of Europeans; British, German, French and Swiss, studying and conducting research on Russian banking, financial and economic business practices. The group I represent in the U.S. is very interested in perhaps extending and expanding our business ventures to Central Europe, including, and especially, Russia, but I must say, this visit to your country has been a struggle to establish a dialogue with your banking people. They seem to be very suspicious, even paranoid, about my presence here and my questions, in particular. You would think I am a *spy*. They don't seem to avoid my European colleagues that much, however."

"They probably do think you are a spy," Galina responded in a serious tone. "That's one of the reasons they arranged for you to stay here in the National Hotel, so they could keep tabs on you."

"Galina may be right, Mary," Sasha shrugged with a slight smile. "Ah, here is your *aoktop;* may I propose a toast to our very special guest?"

"Thank you, Sasha and Galina. You are both so kind and cordial," Mary responded as she held up her glass and then sipped its contents. "Neither of you fit the Russian demeanor that I have witnessed this past week. It is such a pleasure to meet both of you. Cheers!"

"Cheers!" Galina and Sasha responded in unison.

"I am also impressed, actually amazed, at both of your English language and speaking skills," Mary said, shaking her head. "Sasha, you have no accent whatsoever and Galina, your English is so fluent as well. Do they teach English language in your schools?"

Galina smiled, "Well, we both have had the wonderful experience of spending some brief times in your country and learned to converse while we were there."

"You were both in the United States?" Mary asked with a surprised expression.

"No, not at the same time," Sasha responded. "Actually, Galina was fortunate to attend college in the U.S., and I was there on business off and on over several years."

"So you are a spy," Mary chided smiling. "No, just kidding. We live in an international world today and it isn't surprising to find English-speaking people everywhere we travel."

"Speaking of international visitors, Mary, have you met the two Americans, I should say, shabby looking *so-called* Americans staying here at the hotel?" Sasha asked.

"Oh, spare me!" Mary blurted with a frown. "Oh dear, yes, I have met them . . . so to speak! They invaded my table the first evening I was here. I was shocked at both their appearance and their arrogance. Frankly, I was frightened. I started to call hotel security, then I recalled a ploy I have used before back home. I took out my cell phone and pretended to call in a loud voice, *'Aleksai! Please come to the dining room, Now! I am being accosted!'* They stepped back with startled looks on their faces, apologized and vanished. I have seen them a few times since, but they totally ignored me."

"That's fantastic, Mary!" Sasha chuckled. "You have learned well, Dear Lady. I am proud of you." He continued, changing the subject, "So, you depart tomorrow?"

"Yes, I have British Air flight to London, departing at ten a.m. out of *Sher-e-me-tyevo* Airport. Is that how you pronounce it?" Mary asked.

"Yes, that's close enough, Mary," Sasha smiled.

"Great," she smiled. "I may learn to speak Russian yet!" They all chuckled.

"Oh, excuse me," Galina suddenly interrupted, looking across the dining room at one of her staff members motioning. "I'm being summoned. I'll be right back."

Galina departed the dining room while Mary and Sasha continued to chat.

"May Galina and I see you to the airport?" Sasha asked.

"Oh, no," Mary responded. "Moscow Bank has arranged transportation for all of us in the visiting group and made it clear that we *must* travel together, and in their care."

"I understand," Sasha shrugged. "It's only one of the many *adversities* of *our ways* here."

"Oh, that's alright," Mary replied. "You both have been so kind and generous to me this evening. Let's have another aperitif, may we? These are on me."

"Great idea," Sasha smiled as he motioned to the waiter. "No, you are our guest, Madam," responding to Mary. "Another sweet red and a vodka," he told the waiter. "I'll wait and order for Galina when she returns."

As they chatted, the wait staff began to bring the pre-ordered dinner to the table she had arranged—okroshka, a cold vegetable, egg and spice soup, along with *ykra*, red salmon caviar. Then the main course, *otbivnaya*, grilled beef steaks with boiled potatoes.

Finally, the dessert—*tvorog*, cottage cheese covered with berry jam.

Sasha asked the waiter to hold Galina's entrées until she returns.

They continued to chat, exchanging backgrounds and small talk as they enjoyed the sumptuous dinner provided by Galina.

"My," Mary sighed. "I have learned and enjoyed so much, visiting your country. You have been gracious, and I have enjoyed meeting you and your friendship so much more."

"I feel the same, Mary," Sasha replied, smiling. "I will look forward to your returning, and soon. It has been such a pleasure to meet you," he continued, reaching to pat the back of her hand. "I feel sure that we will meet again. This has been far too pleasant to permit it to be lost. Oh, do you have a business card?"

"Yes, I do," she smiled. "I'm glad you asked," opening her purse. "And you?"

"Yes, I have one also," he replied, reaching in the vest pocket of his jacket.

As they exchanged business cards, Mary asked, "Do you think you might return to the United States one day?"

"One never knows, Mary," he replied. "I hope so. We are living in a very dynamic world these days, and one never knows what opportunities might present themselves."

"So true, Sasha," she replied with a slight smile and questioned, "Well, I wonder if Galina will be returning for her dinner?"

"We never know," Sasha replied. "She holds a busy and complex position here at the National."

"Well, Sasha, my new best friend," Mary sighed, "I'm afraid I must go very soon. I have to get a dispatch to my office in Dallas and prepare an early departure in the morning."

"So soon?" Sasha frowned.

"Yes, I'm afraid so," Mary replied with a weak smile. "Please convey my hearty thanks and appreciation to Galina, and tell her that I will see her before I depart in the morning."

"I understand, and I will be pleased to tell her, Mary," Sasha smiled. "May I see you to the elevator?"

"That's very thoughtful of you," Sasha, "but what about Galina?"

"I will go to her office as soon as I see you to the elevator," he smiled.

He escorted Mary to the lobby and the elevator, continuing their conversation along the way. He returned to the earlier comments regarding the unusual guests at the National Hotel. "Back to these two offensive Americans that made a move on you, Mary, I want to apologize on behalf of my country. I am frequently amazed with what our system permits and so much that it does not."

"Oh, don't give it another thought," she replied.

"Well, I find it interesting," he continued, "that not too long ago, we had an idealistic American come to our country, spend a few years here, and then he went back and assassinated your president. Now, we have another one who says he is going back to *become* your president! *Only in America, Mary, Only in America!*"

They both chuckled at the faux humor.

When the elevator door opened, Sasha hugged Mary gently and kissed her on each cheek. *"Da sveedah'neeya,* Mary," he smiled. "This has been a very special evening with a very special lady. I look forward to the next opportunity."

"Goodbye, Sasha," she smiled, her emerald eyes glistening.

CODICIL

As you have come to the end of this saga, perhaps you have discovered an unusual approach in addressing many of the issues surrounding the assassination of President John F. Kennedy. Much has been written over the years about the assassination of the president; even more will be forthcoming as the fiftieth anniversary of the tragedy engulfs the recurring subject. One only needs to search the internet to find thousands of references to facts, allegations, speculation and satire addressing the catastrophe. No doubt you have been struck by the considerable illustrations of the harsh realities within the Soviet Union during the period of this historical tragic episode. In that regard, we chose to address our researched factual elements of the event, to convey the many impressions drawn from the principal author's conclusions experienced from over five years of post-Cold War travels within the former Soviet Union states, including Russia, Ukraine and Byelorussia. During those journeys, I met and interacted with hundreds of former military, government and just plain citizens, who, in too many cases to innumerate, were completely open and frank regarding their lives and the frequent vile experiences they witnessed and many personally endured.

We offer no apology for revealing, in a narrative sense, examples of some of the hardships and the brutality suffered by their citizens during the era of the Soviet Regime. Also referred to frequently in our story are examples of historic paranoia which was prevalent throughout era and which I personally witnessed and experienced in the many business connections during my venture.

In concluding this narrative of a tragic event now a half century in the past, we wish to briefly add this footnote of some current facts and incidents which closely couple with the history and secrecy of the previously described former Soviet Union in this novel.

KGB Lt. Colonel Vladimir Putin departed that spy agency when it became apparent that the Cold War was coming to an end and entered politics. Since 1990 he has served three different terms as president of Russia. In just a little over twenty years, in addition to serving alternatively as president, he has skillfully acquired unheard of wealth, even by western standards, and is assessed to be the wealthiest leader in the world at $43 Billion in acquired assets. The sources of this great wealth including ownership of nine villas; one on the Black Sea valued at $20 Million with an accompanying million dollar yacht are not entirely visible. This sudden phenomenon has undoubtedly greatly contributed to a growing revival of arrogance in the once collapsed Cold War Russia.

A few illustrations to ponder: during the month of June 2010, the FBI arrested twelve undocumented Russians living undercover within the United States with assumed American names and false identifications. Their presence and motives were never determined because the State Department quickly loaded them on an aircraft and sent them back to Russia without the benefit of interrogation. This sort of discovery might well have occurred back in the last *Millennia*, during the Cold War era, when similar incidents occurred more frequently than we ever told. But this most recent episode took place *twenty years* after the Cold War was essentially over; or was it? Were we surprised? After all, the President of the United States just a week prior to those arrests, had hosted then *alternating* Russian President Dmitry Medvedev to an Official State Visit in the nations capital.

Again, on April 18, 2012, as the President of the United States was meeting with the newly reelected Russian President, Vladimir Putin, at the E-8 Conference in Mexico, thirty Russian strategic bombers, along with aerial tankers flew up the Aleutian Chain into and over the U.S. sovereign territory of Alaska. When they were intercepted by U.S. Air Defense fighters, they just as casually reversed course and flew back across the Pacific to their home bases.

Six months later, on Oct 10, 2012, the Russian government made a surprise announcement that it would not renew the 20-year old Nunn-Lugar nuclear weapons threat reduction partnership agreement to safeguard and dismantle nuclear and chemical weapons in the former Soviet Union when the program expires in 2013. This was yet another potentially grave provocation in the fraying relationship between former Cold War enemies.

In December 2012, President Putin announced that there would be no further adoptions of Russian orphans by Americans. Adoptions in progress were also cancelled, leaving families which had spent considerable money and time traveling to Russia to meet, choose and bond with an orphan child to become their own.

Finally on February 12, 2013 as this book goes to press, and on the night of President Obama's State of Union Address, two Russian TU-95 strategic nuclear bombers once again casually circled over U.S. sovereign territory and the Island of Guam. Two U.S. Air Force F-15 fighters scrambled and intercepted the bombers as they casually headed back northward. This event was the latest sign of Moscow's growing strategic assertiveness toward the United States.

Provocative relationships with Middle Eastern dissident governments such as Syria and Iran serve further to question the motives of this once onerous now reviving super power.

These factually unsettling events are left in closing as a reminder that while much within this novel is satire in order to carry the story and make for exciting reading; the questions persist and the *elephant in the room* appears to be once again gaining weight.

God Bless America!

GLOSSARY

Common Usage Russian Terms:

Aktivinyye Meropriatia	Active Measures
Aeroflot	Soviet State Owned Airline
Apparatchik	Politician
Besporyadok	Disturbance; Unruly conduct
Centre'	Reference to KGB and GRU Hdqs
Chairman/Premier	Head of the Soviet Government
Dah	*"Yes"*
Da sveedah'neeya	*"Goodbye"*
Do'briy d'en	*"Good Afternoon"*
Do'briy niche	*"Good Night"*
Do'broye oo'tro	*"Good Morning"*
Do'briy ve'cher	*"Good Evening"*
Eenastrah'nets	Foreigner
Gaspazhah	Madame
Khodinka	GRU Headquarters
Kopec	Monetary denomination, e.g. *"penny"*
Krushki	Banned Intellectual Study Group
Lubiyanka	KGB Headquarters in Moscow
Mackorova	Masquerade
MVD	Internal Police
Nyet	*"No"*
Prospekt	Street
Razvedka	Intelligence
Razvedupr	"GRU" (Military Intelligence)
Rezidentura	Residence *("Safe house")*
Sheremetevo II	Moscow Central Airport
Ruble or *R*	Monetary Denomination, e.g. *"dollar"*

Spasee'ba	*"Thank You"*
Spetsnaz	Soviet Elite Special Force
Stood'e'nts	Students
Tavah'reeshch	Comrade
Tooel'et	Toilet
Tooree'sts	Tourists
Vaidee'te	*"Come in"*
Yavka	Secret Agent Meeting Place

Russian Proverbs:

"You needn't be afraid of a barking dog, but you should avoid a silent one." (People who make loud threats seldom carry them out, but beware of those who seethe quietly.) Prologue.

"There is no evil without good." (A misfortune may well turn into a benefit.) Chapter One.

"Any sandpiper is great in his own swamp." (It is easy to brag about your own deeds in your own surroundings, and you are not likely to be put to proof.) Chapter Two.

"All cats are gray at night." (All shapes and colors are obscure in the dark.) Chapter Three.

"As you make your bed, so you will sleep in it." (A person must take responsibility for the results of his own unwise actions.) Chapter Four.

"There will be trouble if the cobbler starts making pies." (A person should concern himself with his own business not engage in the business of others.) Chapter Five.

"Cut down the tree that you are able to." (Do not undertake more than you are able to successfully perform.) Chapter Six.

"Stormy weather cannot stay all the time; the red sun will come out soon." (Things are usually at their worst just before they get better.) Chapter Seven.

"The tallest blade of grass is the first to be cut by the scythe." (He that sticks his head above the rest may lose it first.) Chapter Eight.

"The appetite comes during the meal." (Desire and interest increases as an activity proceeds.) Chapter Nine.

"Any fish is good if it is on the hook." (One should make use of every opportunity that comes along, large or small.) Chapter Ten.

"A Wolf won't eat wolf." (People of the same origin or group should live together in amity.) Chapter Eleven.

"Once burned by milk, you will drink vodka." (After some bitter or painful experience, you will be on your guard against similar troubles or sufferings.) Chapter Twelve.

"A fly will not get into a closed mouth." (It is desirable and even may be effective to remain silent in some circumstances.) Chapter Thirteen.

"Chickens are counted in the autumn." (Do not be sure of success and brag until the reward is actually yours.) Chapter Fourteen.

"The sun will shine into your yard again." (Neither the weather nor people can remain disturbed for long; calm will follow.) Chapter Fifteen.

"Lord, rescue me against friends, against enemies I can rescue myself." (Those we trust the most can often be the most difficult to disengage.) Chapter Sixteen.

"A word is like a sparrow when it flies out; you cannot catch it." (Once you speak, you cannot prevent the consequences of your words.) Chapter Seventeen.

"The end is the crown of any affair." (All you did can be evaluated after it is over.) Chapter Eighteen.

"The legend is still fresh but hard to believe." (Often it is difficult to believe that an event actually happened.) Epilogue.

THE AUTHORS

Chris Adams is a retired US Air Force Major General, former National Laboratory associate director, and industry executive who worked five years in the former Soviet Union. Adams has written nine books—fiction and nonfiction—on the Cold War era.

Mary Ward is a retired bank president and industry consultant who is involved in historical literary research. She is a senior executive, lecturer, and creative writer.